Joseph Horsfall Turner

Biographia Halifaxiensis : or, Halifax Families and Worthies

A biographical and genealogical History of Halifax Parish - Vol. I

Joseph Horsfall Turner

Biographia Halifaxiensis : or, Halifax Families and Worthies
A biographical and genealogical History of Halifax Parish - Vol. I

ISBN/EAN: 9783337075156

Printed in Europe, USA, Canada, Australia, Japan

Cover: Foto ©Raphael Reischuk / pixelio.de

More available books at **www.hansebooks.com**

The Rev. John Watson. A.M. F.S.A.

BIOGRAPHIA HALIFAXIENSIS:

OR,

Halifax Families and Worthies.

A

BIOGRAPHICAL AND GENEALOGICAL HISTORY OF HALIFAX PARISH.

COMPILED BY J. HORSFALL TURNER.

Vol I.

PRINTED FOR THE COMPILER.

BINGLEY:
T. HARRISON, PRINTER, BOOKBINDER, PUBLISHER, ETC., QUEEN STREET.
1883.

Antiquities of Halifax Church.
Plate I.
P. 390
Upon a Plate of Brass fixed to a seat in the Body of the Church
I am the Resurrection &c. &c.
On the same Pew-door in Saxon Characters.
John Waterhowse of Halyfax and Agnes hys wyff,
which John departed from thys worlde the 27 day of
January anno Dñi. MCCCCCXXX.
Upon a Gravestone in the Chancel
P. 383
Lacyes Arms.
P. 382
the Body of
Here lyth Inclosed
Mr John Lacy of Brearles
P. 381
For the Soule of Thomas Savile of Copley Esquyer

Upon a Pillar
on the South Side of the Quire.
P.377
10 FAVOUR

P.390
of Bryan Waterhouse
Here lieth the Body
of Halifax

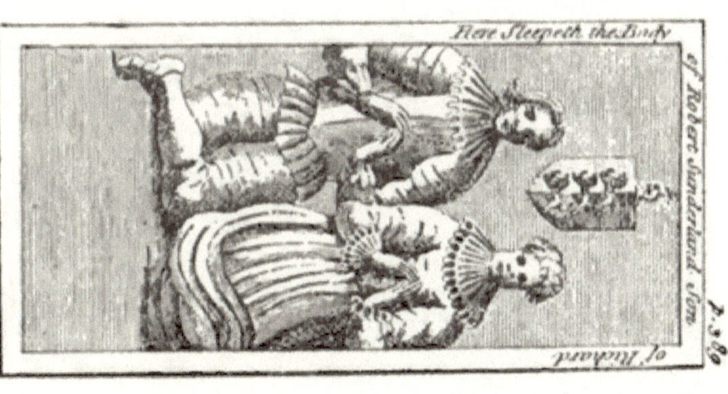
Here Sleepeth the Body
of Robert Sunderland Esm
of Richard
P.389

Antiquities of Eland
Chapel
p.403
The Monument of Waterhouse lately removed from Halifax Church.
ELIZABETH
MARY
IANE
DORITHY
Plate III.

In the Chancel belonging to Savile of Methley & Thornhill of Fixby.

6 p.71.
7 p.70.
8 p.70.
9 p.146.
5. p.460.
Ireland Halfpenny.
Halifax Halfpenny.
3 p.61.
11 p.301.
12 p.314.
10 p.221.
p.223.
13 p.31.

*** *The Pages engraved on the Plates refer to " Watson's Halifax."*

Introduction.

IN this volume, the reader has presented before him one half of Mr. Watson's "Halifax," (that is the Biographical Portion), a book that is seldom found in the market, and fetches over four guineas when one is offered for sale. More than a hundred years have passed since the book was printed, and, as might be expected, many of the pedigrees require amplifying and correcting, and a large number of others, representing the leading families of the parish to-day,—the yeomanry of the past six centuries, demand admittance. Even some of Mr. Watson's "Worthies" require re-writing, as, for example, the Memoir of General Guest; and equally worthy "Worthies" have honoured the parish since his days, not to mention such as Capt. Hodgson, Bishop Horsfall, and others, that escaped the notice of our indefatigable historian. It was deemed just to leave Mr. Watson's collection as far as possible as he printed it, and thus build on his foundation. The Editor has promises of new pedigrees, revised ones, and original biographical sketches for the next volume, and respectfully solicits further assistance.

J. H. T.

IDEL, BRADFORD,
    DEC. 2ND, 1882.

CONTENTS.

𝕭iographia 𝕳alifaxiensis.

[From Watson's "Halifax," 4to, 1775, and Jacob's Reprint (with abridgements) of the same, 8vo.]

We* shall now give some account of such tradesmens tokens as have been coined within this parish, and come to our knowledge.

First.—RICHARD DOLLIFFE. In the center a swan. Rev. round the edge, IN HALLIFAX. 1666. In the center, HIS HALFE PENNY. The Dolliffes were owners of the Swan inn, in Halifax, and if they had any arms this might belong to them.

Second,—EDWARD. NOVBLE. AT. YE. In the center, a Cock. Rev. IN. HALLIFAX. 1668. In the center, HIS HALFE PENY.

Third,— GABRIELL. LEAROYD. In the center, THEIR HALF PENY. Rev. HOLLIFAX. GL. 68. In the center, a full blown rose. These three were in the possession of the Rev. Mr. Watson, late rector of Stockport.†

Fourth,—On one side, JOHN. DEANE. 1667. In the center, IN. HALLIFAX. On the other side, GABRIELL. LEAROYD. In the center, THEIR HALF PENY. This belongs to Mr. Benjamin Bartlet, of London, late of Bradford, in Yorkshire, F. S. A.

---

* Jacob's Edition, page 42. Mr. Watson writes, at page 70,—"I shall conclude this chapter with an account of such tradesmen's tokens as have been coined within this parish, and come to my knowledge." Jacob ungraciously ignores Mr. Watson's labours, omits the Author's name from the title-page, hides himself invariably in the editorial "We," and yet gives almost a literatim copy. He re-arranges some of the chapters, and omits the pedigrees and Latin sentences. He substitutes 'says' for 'sais,' 'uncle' for 'unkle,' 'Eland' for 'Ealand.'

† These are in my possession, Watson.

Fifth,—JOHN. EXLEY. In the center, a crown over a cross patée. Rev. IN HALLIFAX. 1667. In the center, HIS HALFE PENNY.

Sixth,—JOHN. PARKER. 1667. In the center, on a shield, the Drapers arms. These two also belong to Mr. Bartlet.

Seventh,—TIMOTHY OLEAROID. In the center, A PENNY. Rev. OF. HALLIFAX. 1670. In the center, a Dolphin.

Eighth,—HVGH. RAMSDEN IN. In the center, a full blown rose, seeded. Rev. STAINLAND. 1670. In the center, HIS PENNY.—These two last from copies in the hands of John Wilson, Esq; of Broomhead, in Yorkshire.

Ninth,—JOHN RHODES. In the center, a lion rampant. Rev. IN. HALLIFAX. In the center, $^{*R*}_{I,S}$. This, by its size, must have gone for a farthing. The lion rampart was probably part of a coat of arms, for Guillim, in his Heraldry, page 364. edit. 1724. says, "that Rodes of New Halifax, as he calls it, bore Argent on a cross engrailed between four lions rampant, gules five besants."

Tenth,—IOHN. CLAYTON. In the center, a swan. Rev. OF RIBONDIN. 1668. In the center, HIS HALF PENY. N.B. This John Clayton, was buried at Ripponden April 15, 1688, as appears by the register.

Eleventh,—ABRAHAM SLATER. In the center, a fleur de lis. Rev. OF EALAND. . . . In the center, HIS HALF PENY. These three* last were in the possession of the late Rev. Mr. Watson aforesaid.

Snelling, in his View of the copper coin and coinage of England, page 27, in the list of places where he has found these tradesmens tokens to have been made, mentions Lightcliff, near Halifax, and at page 28, Stainland, in Yorkshire, both in this parish. At page 30, is the following coin engraved, ROBERT. WATMOVGH. 1667. In the center, A loaded horse. Rev. CARRIER FOR HALLYFAX. In center, HIS HALFE PENNY.

On the subject of these ["*nummorum famuli*" I] we shall only observe, that private persons, especially those in trade, found themselves under a necessity of assuming this power of coinage, owing to the want of copper money coined by authority; they first made their appearances about 1648,

* These three are in my own possession, Watson.

and kept gradually increasing till 1672, when they were cried down by proclamation. [A few of the above (1, 3, 11,) are engraved by way of specimen in the Miscellaneous Plate. Watson.]

The town of Halifax has the **honour to** give **title** to the **noble family of** MONTAGU, **of Horton,** in the county of **Northampton.—The** first person **on whom the** dignity **was conferred, was** Charles Montagu, **who, on the 4th** of December, 1700, **was made baron** Halifax, **in the** county **of York,** with limitation **of that** honour **to** George Montagu, esq; **eldest** son **and heir of** Edward Montagu, esq; his eldest brother, and the **heirs** male of his body; the reasons **for this** royal act of favour are copied from the preamble to the patent in Collins's Peerage, Vol. III. page 694. and are such as reflect the highest lustre on his character. His merit employed the **pens** of the best writers of the time, amongst **the** rest, **the** author of a poem in the Spectator, Vol. VIII. **No.** 620. **to this** purport,

> Whom shall the muse from **out the** shining throng
> Select, to heighten, and adorn **her** song ?
> Thee, Hallifax. To thy capacious mind,
> O man approv'd, is Britain's wealth consign'd.
> Her coin (while Nassau fought) debas'd and rude,
> By thee in beauty, and in truth renew'd,
> An arduous work ! Again thy charge we **see,**
> And thy own care once more returns to **thee.**
> O ! form'd in ev'ry scene to awe and please,
> Mix wit with pomp, and dignity with ease :
> Tho' call'd to shine aloft, thou wilt not scorn
> To smile on arts thyself did once adorn :
> For this thy name succeeding time shall **praise,**
> And envy less thy garter,* than thy bays.

** He was knight of the garter.*

October 26, 1714, he was advanced to the dignity of earl of Halifax and viscount Sunbury, with limitation of those honours to his nephew above-mentioned, who succeeded to them on the death of his uncle, May 19, 1715. Previous to this, the town had given title to George Savile, who, in the 10th year of the reign of Charles II. was created baron Savile of Eland, and Viscount Halifax; and in 1682, farther advanced to the title of marquis of Halifax, which continued till August 31, 1700, when, at the death of William, son of the above George, without issue male, the title became extinct. [The Savile pedigree here follows in Watson's 4to History.]

—::—

AN ACCOUNT OF THE
CHARITABLE DONATIONS*
WITHIN THE
VICARAGE OF HALIFAX.

BENEFACTIONS IN THE TOWNSHIP OF BARKISLAND.

EXTRACT FROM THE
WILL OF THOMAS GLEDHILL,
OF BARKISLAND,

Dated March 23, 1656.

"I GIVE and bequeath the sum of one hundred and twenty pounds, of lawful money of England, to be bestowed upon lands, to the uses following, that is to say, to and for the only use of a lawful preaching minister of the word of God at Ripponden Chapel, that shall be settled there from time to time; my will and mind is, that the profits of the same lands, from year to year, to succeeding ages, shall come and be paid to the hand of such Minister, or Ministers, for ever; which said sum of one hundred and twenty pounds I have given in my life time into the hands of my uncle, Joshua Horton, of Sowerby, in the said county, Esq; intreating him to bestow, or cause to be bestowed, the said moneys upon lands, in some convenient

* Jacob, p. 98; Watson, p. 549.

place, to the best profit he can, and to put it into feoffees estate, himself being one, the profits whereof to be collected to the use of the abovesaid Minister of Ripponden. And in commemoration whereof, or for which gratuity of augmentation, the said minister or ministers, shall preach one Sermon yearly, upon the first day of May, if it be not of the Lord's day, and if so, then in the week following, at the Minister's choice of the day.

And if there fall out any time of vacancy that there be no preaching Minister of the Gospel at the place aforesaid, my will and mind is, that at the time or times of such vacancy, the profits of the same lands shall go and be paid to the most needful poor people of the township of Barkisland, especially to such as are laborious, and endeavour to keep themselves from being chargeable to the said town.

And also I have given into the hands of my uncle, Joshua Horton, the sum of fifty pounds, by him to be bestowed on lands as aforesaid, at his best discretion; the profits of which lands shall be vested by feoffees as aforesaid, and yearly paid to the most needful poor of the township of Barkisland, from time to time to succeeding ages for ever, especially to such as labour to keep themselves from being chargeable to the said town."

In consequence of the above donation, the said Joshua Horton, of Sowerby, Esq; Thomas Horton, of Barkisland; Richard Firth, of the Height, in Barkisland; and John Ramsden, of Bowers, in Barkisland, as trustees, purchased an estate in Gleadcliff, in Northouram, of one Nathan Hoile, of Halifax, for the sum of 170*l.* the original purchase Deed of which is at the seat of Sir Watts Horton, at Chaderton, in Lancashire, with other papers, &c. respecting the title. The present rent is 8*l.* 10s. per annum, of which 6*l.* yearly is paid to the Minister of Ripponden, and the rest to the poor of Barkisland. There has not, that we* know of, been any conveyance of this trust since the above purchase.

Where the original Will is to be met with we* cannot tell, for there are no wills in the office at York from 1652 to 1660.

* I. [Watson.]

EXTRACT FROM THE

WILL OF SARAH GLEDHILL,

OF LONDON,

LATE OF BARKISLAND,

Dated October 13, 1657.

—"I do give and bequeath the sum of two hundred pounds current English money, unto the use of a Schoolmaster, for teaching such poor children of the township of Barkisland, whose parents are, or shall not be able, to bring them up in learning; and I do will that my Executors, hereafter named, bestow the said sum of two hundred pounds in some convenient place, in the purchase of lands, and put the same in feoffees estate, the profits whereof to be yearly gathered by such feoffees, and their heirs, to succeeding ages for ever, and paid by them, from time to time, to such Schoolmaster, or Schoolmasters, as shall be by them in their discretions placed or appointed in the town or township aforesaid; for which said yearly profit the said Schoolmaster shall teach such a competent number of poor children of the said town and township of Barkisland, to read English, and to write, or cast account, or farther learning, as the said feoffees shall think meet and convenient, and as the said money so raised will extend."

In pursuance of the above, an indenture was executed, July 10, 1658, between John Walker, of the Closes, in Great Gomersal, in the parish of Burstal, yeoman, of the one party, and Joshua Horton, of Sowerby, Esq; Elizabeth Horton, of Barkisland, (Executors of the last will and testament of the above Sarah Gledhill,) and Thomas Horton, of Barkisland, Gent. of the other party, wherein, for the consideration of the sum of 200*l.* paid by the said Joshua and Elizabeth Horton, the said John Walker sold to Joshua and Thomas Horton, aforesaid, and their heirs, a messuage or tenement in Great Gomersal aforesaid, with several closes of land thereto belonging, three of which were known by the name of Brookhouses, near adjoining to the said messuage

or tenement, one whereof lay on the east part of the said
messuage, and the other two on the west and south parts of
a barn belonging to the said messuage; also three other
closes of land, called by the said name of Brookhouses,
described in the said indenture, by the lands on which they
abutted.

In 1763, the heirs of the above named Executors agreed
to have a new trust deed executed, and the Trustees therein
appointed were William Horton, of Chaderton, Esq; (afterwards Sir William Horton, Bart.) Joshua Horton, of
Howroyd, John Lloyd, (then) of Holme, Richard Beaumont,
of Whitley, and Thomas Patten, of Bank, near Warrington,
Esqrs.

The School has lately been repaired, the estate surveyed,
and the yearly rent fixed at sixteen pounds per annum.

—::—

<h1 style="text-align:center">EXTRACT FROM THE
WILL OF ELIZABETH HORTON,</h1>

Of BARKISLAND,

Dated July 13, 1670.

—"I give and devise unto the poor people of Barkisland,
the sum of five pounds per annum for ever, to be paid forth ·
of the rents, issues, and profits of one messuage, and the
lands and tenements therewith used in Barkisland, called
Pearce-hey, to be distributed amongst them at the discretion
of the owners for the time being, for ever, of Barkisland-hall.
Item, I give and devise to the Minister of the Gospel of
Ripponden Chapel, five pounds per annum for ever, he
preaching a Sermon there on every Good Friday yearly for
ever, to be paid forth of the rents, issues, and profits of the
said messuage and lands called Pearce-hey, in Barkisland
aforesaid, provided such Minister for the time being be an
orthodox person, and such as the owner of Barkisland-hall

for time being for ever shall approve of, and in case of non-approbation, and so long as such dislike shall continue, then the said five pounds per annum shall be paid and distributed to the poor people of Barkisland aforesaid."

The above sums are paid agreeable to the intention of the donor by the present owner of Barkisland-hall. This extract was made from an attested copy out of the Office at York. [in my own possession, Watson.]

Thomas Horton, Esq. who died about 1698, left by Deed the one half part of a farm or tenement called the Hill-top, near Steel-lane, in Barkisland, to the Minister of Ripponden Chapel, who, in consideration and commeration thereof, is to preach yearly for ever, a Sermon upon St. Thomas's Day.

This account is taken from the copy of an old terrier without date, in the Register Book belonging to Ripponden Chapel. The whole is regularly fulfilled; and the rent paid yearly to the Minister of Ripponden is four pounds five shillings.

—::—

EXTRACT FROM THE
WILL OF WILLIAM HORTON,
Of HOWROYD, Esq.

Dated October 8, 1718.

—"I give unto my Executors and Trustees aforesaid, the sum of sixty pounds of lawful money, which I order them to put out at interest, until that they, or the survivors of them, or the heirs of the survivors of them, can purchase a small estate or annuity therewith; and I do further will and order, that my said Executors and Trustees, and the owners of Howroyd aforesaid, shall, for ever, pay, imploy, and dispose of the growing interest thereof, until such purchase be made, and of the rents, issues, and profits of such estate or annuity, so to be purchased as aforesaid, from the time of such purchase, to such use and uses as are herein after mentioned, that is to say, one moiety, or half part of such yearly interest as aforesaid, and of the said yearly rents, issues, and profits of the said annuity, or purchase, unto the Curate of Ripponden for the time being, to be paid on every twenty-fourth day of June, for ever, to him, to preach a Sermon in Ripponden Chapel, on every the said twenty-fourth day of June for ever. And the other moiety, or half part of the said interests, and of the said rents, issues, and profits, to be yearly, on every Easter Monday for ever, paid and distributed unto and amongst the poor people of Barkisland, at the discretion of my said Executors, and the owners of Howroyd aforesaid, or the major part of them.—And in default or want of preaching such Sermon as aforesaid, that then, and so often as such default shall happen to be made, I order that such interest, or rents and profits, as should have been paid unto the said Curate of Ripponden, to preach such Sermon or Sermons, shall be paid and distributed unto and amongst the poor people of Barkisland aforesaid, as aforesaid.

A quit-rent of three pounds per annum was purchased with the above money, out of a farm in Blackwood, within Sowerby, called Jackson Ings, and it is regularly paid as directed, the land tax being first deducted by the owner of the farm.

Mrs. Mary Horton, of Howroyd, widow of the above William, did, by an indenture, executed Sept. 27, 1749, make an addition of thirty shillings yearly, for preaching the above Sermon, but not living twelve calendar months after the date thereof, as the last Mortmain Act requires, the money is not paid.

EXTRACT FROM THE

WILL OF JAMES RILEY, Clerk,

Dated May 6, 1723.

AFTER giving to Joseph Riley, of Kirkcliffe, in Soyland, his brother, and to his heirs, a tenement situate on the common, or waste, called High-Moor, in the township of   , in trust, to pay out of the rents thereof, yearly, the sum of five pounds, to the several persons and uses therein mentioned; the last benefaction in the Will runs thus:—"Item, I will that one pound, part of the residue of the said five pounds, payable out of the said yearly rents and profits, be paid by the said Joseph Riley, and his heirs, upon the second day of February yearly, and every year, for ever, to the Overseer or Overseers of the poor for the township of Barkisland, in the said county of York, for the time being, and to their successors, Overseers of the poor of the same township, for the use of, and to be distributed to seven poor widowers, or widows, and for want of such, to the most necessitous persons of the said town of Barkisland, at the discretion of the aforesaid master or owner of Kirkcliffe, and of the said Overseers, and one or more of the chief inhabitants of Barkisland aforesaid, which said several yearly payments of one pound, (alluding to other payments named in the Will, besides this to Barkisland,) to be made by the said Joseph Riley and his heirs, as abovesaid, I will that the same be respectively made and paid at the times above-mentioned, the time and space of full three months intervening betwixt the times that the said yearly rents and profits of the abovesaid tenement or dwelling house shall become due and payable to the said Joseph Riley, and his heirs, and the respective times of payment of the several and respective sums of one pound above-mentioned."

The above James Riley was Curate of Hartshead, and Domestic Chaplain to Sir John Armitage, of Kirklees.

The charity is regularly distributed.

BOUNTY MONEY TO
RIPPONDEN CHAPEL.

THIS Chapel (which is situated in the township of Barkisland) has received Queen Anne's bounty once, as appears by the following account :

On the 9th of June, 1726, an agreement was made and executed between Richard Nayler, of Hepton-bridge, in the parish of Halifax, and William Sunderland, Clerk, Curate of Ripponden, wherein the former sold to the latter, and his successors in the said Curacy, for the sum of three hundred pounds, one messuage in Soyland, called Crosswells, and another messuage also in Soyland, called Blackshaw-clough, with lands, &c. to each of them belonging.

These farms lie together, and have upwards of thirty days work of land belonging to them. The rest of the money was laid out in the purchase of a croft adjoining to the Curate's house at Ripponden, and two cottages by the said croft, in value about six pounds a year.

The clear yearly value of this Chapel, as given by the Governors of Queen Ann's Bounty, in their Return, printed in 1736, pursuant to an order of the House of Lords, of the 16th of April in that year, at page 218, was twenty-two pounds, thirteen shillings and four-pence ; and we beg leave to observe, once for all, that at the same page of this book, which is in folio, is contained the clear yearly value, as it stood in the second and third years of Queen Anne, when the Act was passed for *making more effectual her Majesty's gracious intentions for the augmentation of the maintenance of the poor Clergy, by enabling her Majesty to grant in perpetuity the revenues of the first fruits and tenths, and also for enabling any other persons to make grants for the same purpose.*

It is said in Ecton's Thesaurus, that the above Bounty was obtained by means of Mrs. Mary Horton, and others, in the year 1724.

Since writing the above, we* have met with a Deed bearing date the 23rd day of September, 1730, between Nathan Fielden, of Soyland, of the first part, and the Governors of the Bounty of Queen Anne, Mary Horton, of Howroyd, widow, Charles Radcliffe, Elkana Hoyle, and Samuel Hill,

* I have met with a Deed indented. Watson.

of the second part; wherein, for the sum of 400*l.* the said
Nathan Fielden did sell, for the use of the Curates of
Ripponden, Blackshaw-clough, and the customary or copy-
hold messuage or tenement called Crosswells, both in Soy-
land; also the houses and little croft which he had at
Ripponden. [A Memorial of this Deed was registered at
Wakefield, October 16, 1730, in Lib. 200, p. 126, and No.
173, Watson.]

RIPPONDEN CHAPEL-YARD.

Ann Horton, of Barkisland-hall, spinster, William Horton,
of Coley-hall, Esq; Richard Horton, of Howroyd, brother to
the said William, Thomas Horton, of Chaderton, Esq;
Susanna Beaumont, of Whitley, widow, and Peter Bold, of
Bold, Esq; sold by indenture, dated July 10, 1729, one
hundred and seventy square yards of a close called the
Holme, and ninety square yards of a garden, for enlarging
the Chapel-yard at Ripponden, and removing the old chapel
there, in order to rebuild it on higher ground, at a greater
distance from Ripponden-brook, to prevent such damages as
it had some time before sustained, by the flooding of the
said brook.

The Archbishop's Licence for rebuilding Ripponden
Chapel was dated April the sixth, 1729.

The sum got by Brief was 541*l.* 0s. 4d. besides the sub-
scriptions of the neighbouring Gentlemen.

—::—

COPY OF A CLAUSE IN THE CODICIL

ANNEXED TO THE

WILL OF THOMAS HOLROIDE,

OF HALIFAX,

The Will is dated May 29, 1729, and the Codicil
March 8, 1729-30.

—" I give a rent-charge of five pounds per annum out of
my two farms in Bottomley, in the township of Barkisland,
now or late in the occupation of Susan Whiteley, to the
Curate of Ripponden Chapel, for the time being, for ever,

for reading the Prayers according to the Liturgy of the Church of England, every Wednesday and Friday, in the morning, throughout the year."

These Farms are called by the name of Wormald, and the money is regularly **paid** as directed.

PART OF A DEED CONTAINING
Mrs. MARY HORTON's CHARITY
TO THE POOR
OF BARKISLAND.

" THIS Indenture, made February 16, 1743, **between** Mrs. Mary Horton of Howroyd, in Barkisland, in the county of York, widow of the one part, and Tho. Horton, of Chaderton, in the county of Lancaster, Esq; of **the** other part, witnesseth, that the said Mary Horton, in consideration of five shillings to her **now in** hand paid by the said Tho. Horton, the receipt whereof **is** hereby acknowledged, and for the charitable uses, intents and purposes herein after mentioned, and **for** divers other good causes and considerations her thereunto moving, she, **the** said Mary Horton, hath **given,** granted, bargained, sold, **and** confirmed, and by **these** presents **doth give,** grant, bargain, **sell,** and confirm **unto** the said **Thomas** Horton, his heirs and assigns, **one annuity,** or clear yearly rent of thirty shillings, **of lawful money** of Great Britain, to be yearly issuing and payable, without any manner of deduction whatsoever, at the Feasts of Pentecost, and St. Martin **the** Bishop in winter, by **equal** proportions, for ever, out and **forth of** all that **one** messuage or tenement on Stainland Green, in Stainland, **in the** county of York aforesaid, called or known by the **name of** the New Laith, and three closes of land, arable, meadow, **or** pasture, thereto belonging, or therewith used or enjoyed, called the Lath Croft, the Kiln Croft, and the Town Ing, or by what other name or names soever the same, or any of them are, or have been called or known, containing together, by estimation, three days work and a half, be the same more or less. To have and to hold the annuity or yearly rent of

thirty shillings aforesaid, unto the said Thomas Horton, his
heirs and assigns, to the use and behoof of him the said
Thomas Horton, his heirs and assigns, for ever; In trust,
nevertheless, that he, the said Tho. Horton, his heirs and
assigns, and the owners of the capital messuage of her the
said Mary Horton, at Howroyd aforesaid, shall yearly, for
ever, pay, distribute, and dispose of the said annuity, or clear
yearly rent of thirty shillings, on every Easter Monday, for
ever, unto and amongst such of the poor people of Barkisland aforesaid, as the said Thomas Horton, and his heirs,
and the owners of Howroyd aforesaid, for the time being,
shall judge do best deserve the same, in such proportions as
they shall think fit." [The rest of the Deed gives power to
Thomas Horton, and his heirs, to enter upon the premises
in case of non-payment; and concludes with a covenant
relating to Mary Horton's title to the estate. It was registered at Wakefield, March 9th, 1743, in Book S. S. p. 106,
Number 154, and inrolled in Chancery, April 6th, 1744.
Watson.]

The money is yearly distributed by the present owner of
Howroyd.

The original Deed is at the seat of Sir Watts Horton, at
Chaderton, in Lancashire, from whence the above was
copied.

—::—

EXTRACT FROM THE

WILL OF Mrs. ANN HORTON.

Dated August 2, 1745.

—" I give and devise unto Peter Bold, Esq; and his heirs
for ever, all my messuages, lands, tenements, and hereditaments whatsoever.—But my earnest desire is, and I do
hereby signify it to the said Peter Bold, Esq; that he or his
heirs do, so soon as he or they can, after my decease, grant,
or settle in trust, or otherwise, a rent charge of four pounds
a year, to be for ever issuing out of all that my messuage

situate in Barkisland, and now in the tenure of Timothy Turner, and the lands thereto belonging, by two equal portions, at Michaelmas and Lady-day in every year, and to be by the Overseer or Overseers for the time being, of the poor of Barkisland aforesaid, with the advice and assistance of six of the chief inhabitants thereof, distributed, from time to time, within the space of ten days next after Michaelmas-day and Lady-day, yearly for ever, amongst such of the poor inhabitants, for the time being, of Barkisland, as shall belong to, and not have public relief of or from that town.

And it is also my earnest desire, that the same rent charge may be settled firmly according to law, so as not to be defeated by any of the Mortmain Laws, or otherwise, however, save by the death of the Granter or Grantees within twelve calendar months next after such grant or settlement made, and so as the same may be well recovered by the said Overseers for the afore mentioned use and purpose, from time to time, as the same shall become due, for ever, by distress and sale of goods in like manner as aforesaid.

The messuage from whence the above rent charge arises is called Steel-lane. The premises have not yet been settled in trust, or otherwise, but the money is regularly distributed every year, by order of the owner of Barkisland-hall. The original Will is at Bold, in Lancashire, from whence the above was copied.

RICHARD FIRTH, of Ripponden, gave (but whether by Will or Deed is uncertain) two messuages, or cottages, with appurtenances, at Ripponden, for which the Minister of the Chapel there was to preach five Sermons upon the first Wednesday in the several months of April, May, June, July, and August, in the said Chapel at Ripponden successively, and annually for ever. [This account is taken from the copy of an old terrier, without date, in the Register Book belonging to Ripponden Chapel. Watson.]

The intention of the Donor, as expressed above, is regularly fulfilled. This account is taken from the Register Book at Ripponden Chapel.

EALAND.

EXTRACT FROM THE

WILL OF ROBERT INMAN,
OF EALAND,

Dated April 12, 1638.

—" I give, devise, and bequeath unto my brother George Ramsden, of Greetland, and Joseph Ramsden, of the same, my nephew, their heirs and assigns, one annuity or yearly rent of twenty shillings, of lawful money of England, to be issuing forth of those messuages or tenements, called the Lee, with the appurtenances, in Old Linley, within the township of Stainland, in the county of York, and forth of all the lands, tenements, closes, and hereditaments, to the same belonging, or with the same now or commonly demised, used, or occupied, and forth of all other my lands and tenements in Old Linley aforesaid, which I late bought and purchased of William Holdsworth, payable yearly on the Feasts of Pentecost, and St. Martin the Bishop in winter, by equal portions, to have, hold, levy, and take the said annuity, or yearly rent of twenty shillings, in form aforesaid, to be paid unto them the said George Ramsden and Joseph Ramsden, their heirs and assigns, for ever.

Nevertheless, in trust and confidence, and to the intent and purpose that they, the said George Ramsden and Joseph Ramsden, and their heirs, and the survivor of them and his heirs, shall dispose of the same yearly rent of twenty shillings, and all the profits thereof, from time to time, to and for the use and better maintenance of a Preacher, who shall preach the word of God at the parochial Chapel of Eland aforesaid, from time to time, to succeeding ages for ever, the first payment thereof to be made at the Feast of Pentecost, or St. Martin the Bishop, in winter, which shall next ensue the day of my decease."

Then follows a clause, impowering the said George Ramsden and Joseph Ramsden, their heirs and assigns, to make distress on the premises in case of non payment of the said sum of twenty shillings, or any part thereof, for the space of twenty days next ensuing either of the said Feasts

whereon it became payable, being lawfully demanded.
The above was copied from the Register-book at Eland.

—::—

EXTRACT FROM THE
WILL OF HENRY WILSON,
OF ELAND,

Dated June 28, 1652.

—" I give, devise, and bequeath unto Gilbert **Savile, of** Greetland, Gentleman, and to Abraham Dyson, Jeremy Bentley, and to John Whittel, of Whittel Place, in Eland, Yeoman, and to their heirs for ever, five closes of new land in the Broad Car, which my father purchased of Sir William Savile, Bart. as also one house, or cottage, with the appurtenances in Eland aforesaid, and one backside thereunto belonging, now in the tenure or occupation of Joseph Whiteley, or his assigns; and also one ruinated house, or house-stead, and one backside thereunto adjoining, with the appurtenances, in Eland aforesaid, between the smithy now in the tenure of John Gillot, and the house now in the occupations of Jonas Clay and Brian Rawnsley there; and also all my parts and purports of the said smithy, and the two houses now in the tenures of the said John Gillot, Jonas Clay, and Brian Rawnsley, or their assigns; and also one whole chamber now or late in the tenure of Sarah Hinchliffe, or her assigns, and one whole shop, with the appurtenances, in Eland aforesaid, now in the tenure or occupation of John Hanson, or his assigns, with all other ways, passages, waters, watercourses, easements, and hereditaments whatsoever, to the above granted premises, or any part thereof belonging or appertaining, or to, or with the same now or commonly demised, used, or occupied, with all their rights, members, and appurtenances, in Eland aforesaid, as they are severally mentioned in one deed of sale past to me from Elias Wilson, lying near the Cross, in Eland, which he, the said Elias Wilson, lately purchased of Mr. John Farrar, of Brearly, to have and to hold the said five closes,

c

with one house and appurtenances, and one house or house-stead and backside with appurtenances, and part of the smithy, and **two houses**, and one chamber, and **one** shop, **with** appurtenances, **unto** the said Gilbert Savile, Abraham **Dyson**, Jeremy Bentley, and John Whittel, **and to** their heirs **and** assigns for ever, yielding therefore **unto me**, and **my heirs, the rent of** one red rose, **in** the time of **roses, if it be asked, of intent,** and confidence and trust, that **they the aforesaid Gilbert Savile**, Abraham Dyson, Jeremy Bentley, **and John Whittel, shall** first pay out of the same **all such** rents **as now are** accustomed to be **paid by me the above-**said Henry **Wilson,** and the profits **of the said five closes,** homes, backsides, and part of the **smithy,** and two **houses, and over** chamber, and one shop, **with the** appurtenances above-mentioned, **my** will and mind is, **shall** be used and employed **by my said** Trustees, Demisees, **and** their heirs **for ever, to and** for **him and his use, benefit, and** commodity, **who from time to time, to succeeding generations for** ever, **shall be stipendiary Preacher or Minister of God's word,** at **and in the** parochial Chapel **of Eland** aforesaid, the said **Minister or Preacher having the consent** of the **said Trustees beforenamed, or their heirs or assigns, or** any three **of them.**

Item, I give to the aforesaid Gilbert Savile, Abraham **Dyson, Jeremy Bentley, and John Whittle,** fifty pounds, **to be paid by my Executors to them, or** any two of them, **towards building of an house upon the** ground I lately **bought of Elias Wilson, near the** Cross, in Eland, **to be paid when the foundation of the house** shall **be laid, which house,** my **mind and will is, shall** be used **and** employed by my said Trustees, **and their heirs** for ever, **to** and **for the** use of **the Minister of God's word,** at the parochial Chapel of Eland **aforesaid, and chiefly for** the said Minister to live **in** if he **be married, or otherwise,** if he shall desire it, he **having** the consent of **my said Trustees, or** their heirs or **assigns,** as abovesaid."

"Memorandum. It is Henry Wilson's will and mind, **that** during that time **that there** is not such a Minister at **Eland, as** his aforesaid **Trustees,** their heirs or assigns, shall approve **of,** that then the **said** profits, formerly given to a Minister, shall be disposed **of** by them to such a Minister as the aforesaid Trustees, their heirs, or **any** three of them,

shall think fit, the said Minister officiating and doing **service**
for the same in the parochial Chapel **of** Eland aforesaid."

This Memorandum was added to **the** Will before it was
sealed and signed. The **whole was** transcribed **from the**
Register Book **at** Eland.

Jeremy Bentley, **one of the Trustees,** took upon him the
care of building the house, and laid out, **besides the** fifty
pounds left by the above Will (including the purchase of an
old smithy, &c. **on** which part of the house was built,) of his
own money, forty-five pounds, for which he had **a quit** rent
of three pounds per annum **out** of the house **and land** left
by Henry Wilson, granted **him by the rest of the** trustees,
till he should be satisfied **some other way.** At this time
the interest of money was **eight per cent.**

This yearly quit rent of **three pounds was paid till about**
1676, after which there **were only** forty **shillings per annum**
received till 1689, **when Jeremy Bentley, of Woodhouse,**
grandson and **heir of Jeremy Bentley, one of the Trustees**
above mentioned, **coming to his** age, **did eject the tenants on**
the Minister's house, in order **to recover the arrears due** to
him ; but by **the mediation of** friends, **he agreed to abate** the
14*l.* in arrear, **also** 3*l.* **spent in** law, together **with** 2*l.* **of** the
principal **money, which** was 45*l.* and in consideration of 43*l.*
paid by **John Savile, of** Methley, Esq ; Brian Thornhill, of
Fixby, Esq ; **Thomas Horton,** of Barkisland, Esq ; Thomas
Ramsden, **of Crowstone, and** Robert Whittel, of Eland,
Gent. he did resign **over, and confirm** the said premises
wholly to them and **their heirs, and to** the survivor or
survivors of them, and **his heirs for ever,** to the intent that
they may be fully **possessed of them, in** trust for the Minister
of Eland.

The five closes **above named contain about four acres of**
land.

EXTRACT FROM THE

WILL OF Mrs. FRANCES GRANTHAM,

Who died March 12, 1692.

—" I give and bequeath to the poor of Eland and Fikesby, to be paid on Christmas day yearly for ever, as followeth, to twenty poor men **one** shilling a piece; and to twenty poor women **one** shilling a-piece, and to twelve boys one shilling a piece; and to **secure the** payment **of this** money, my will and mind **is, that fifty-two** pounds be **put into** such hands as my sister Thornhill **shall** think meet, **that the** interest thereof may yearly **pay the same.**"

It is also said that Mrs. Grantham gave ten shillings yearly to the poor of Eland, and the same sum to the poor of Rastrick and Fixby.

JOSEPH BROOKSBANK,

Citizen and Haberdasher of London, did by indenture, executed Oct. 4, 1712, convey to Trustees, a messuage or tenement, with a barn, an orchard, a yard, and a croft, containing one acre, in or near a street in Eland, called the Westgate, **and** also four selions of land in a field at Eland, called Longmanslands, or Lowmost-town-field, one land being in number the thirteenth, another the thirty-fifth, another the thirty-fourth, and another the forty-fifth; and also four lands in the middle or Stainland-steel-field, one land lying in the lower shutt there from the footway, in number the thirty-third land, and two lands lying in the upper shutt from the marshes, in number the sixteenth and seventeenth lands, and from the footway to Stainland the sixty-second land; and also four lands lying in the High-town-field; one land lying from the Lidgate, in number the eleventh land, ranging clear through the field, and commonly accounted for two lands; and two other lands, lying from Oyl Mabb-top, in number the fifteenth and sixteenth land.

Also six messuages or tenements at the west end of the town of Eland, in a street or place there called the Town-end. Also a messuage or tenement called the Little Upper Harper Royd, in the township of Norland, containing by estimation ten days work :

In trust, that the said Trustees, **and** such other person **or** persons on whom the said trust from time to time should devolve, and the survivors and survivor of them, and the heirs and assigns of such survivor, **should** permit a certain messuage or tenement in Ealand, **(mentioned in** the above indenture to have **been late in the occupation of** one Lawrence Manknowles, School-master, **and intended by** the said **Joseph** Brooksbank **to** be settled as **for** a free **school,** for the educating **and teaching** forty poor children, **boys and** girls, belonging to **the town** of Ealand,) **to** be from **time to** time, for ever hereafter, used and enjoyed as and **for the** school-house of **the said free-school.**

And should yearly **out of the clear rents and profits of the above** granted messuages, **lands,** and **premises (after the** necessary charges in repairing **and** supporting **the same should** be from time **to time** deducted) pay, **or** cause to **be** paid, by equal quarterly payments, unto **a** School-master, for teaching the said forty poor children **to** read the English tongue, till **such time as** they **can readily** read **the** Bible, and repeat **without book the Catechism, (commonly** called **the** Assemblies Catechism) the **clear sum of** ten pounds, without **deduction of or** for any **manner of taxes.** And upon farther trust yearly **to** expend the **sum of thirty** shillings in buying **of** ten Bibles and twenty **Catechisms,** (commonly called the Assemblies Catechisms) to **be yearly** distributed and divided amongst the said forty poor **children, in** such manner **as** the major part **of** the Trustees, **for** the **time** being, shall think fit.—And if, after the **above** mentioned trusts should be **fully** satisfied and discharged, **there** should, **out** of the clear yearly rents, issues, and **profits** of the above granted premises, remain **in the** hands **of the** said Trustees, more monies than were sufficient to discharge the said trusts, and **such** necessary charges of **repairs** as aforesaid, and after **incident charges in execution of the said trusts, then** upon **farther trust to** pay **yearly the overplus, if any,** unto such **School-master,** for **the time being, as an** addition to his allowance, **or** salary, for **teaching the** forty **poor** children above-mentioned, and for no **other use,** intent or purpose whatsoever. **And to** the end **the trusts** mentioned in the **said indenture might be the better performed,** it was there-in **declared, that the School-master of the** said free-school **should be, from time to time, chosen** by the said Trustees, or the major part of them; and that upon every vacancy of the School-master's place, or office, by death or otherwise, another School-master should by them be elected, within three calendar months next after such vacancy. Also, that the said Trustees, or the major part of them, for the time being, should have the sole power, of nominating and electing the said forty poor children, to be taught to read as aforesaid, and of removing or displacing the same, or any of them, from time to time, and of putting others in the room of those who die, or are dismissed, or go away from the said School. And also, that in case the said School-master should be negligent or careless in the discharge of his duty, or otherwise misbehave himself in his said office, it should be lawful for the said Trustees, or the major part of them, for the time being, from time to time to remove and displace such School-master, and to elect and place another in his room. The said School-master also, for the time being, was not at any time to receive or take any fee or reward from the parents, relations, or friends of all, or any of the said poor children, for or in respect of their being taught to read as aforesaid, (the wages, or salary thereby allowed him only excepted,) under the pain of forfeiting and losing his place or office of School-master.

When the Trustees were reduced to two, or under, the survivor or survivors, were to convey to others; and if at any time the Trustees for the time being, or any of them, should not be suffered to perform the trusts in them reposed, or the said School-master should in any wise be obstructed in the performance of his office, then, and in either of the said cases, the said Trustees for the time being might, and they were directed and enjoined, to reconvey and assure the above messuages, lands, and premises to the use of the said Joseph Brooksbank, his heirs and assigns for ever."

EXTRACT FROM THE

WILL OF Mrs. FRANCES THORNHILL,

Dated the last Day of July, 1718.

—" I give and bequeath the sum of nine hundred pounds to be laid out to pious and charitable uses in manner following, viz. I devise and give the sum of one hundred and fifty pounds, and the interest thereof, into the hands of the heir and chief of our family of Fickisby, my nephew, Thomas Thornhill, Esq. to be the first Trustee. And my will and mind is, that his heirs, being the principals of our name and family of Fickisby aforesaid, shall successively for ever be Trustees to see the said one hundred and fifty pounds laid out in a purchase, for building or making a proper habitation for teaching and improving ten poor girls in spinning wool, knitting, sewing, reading, and writing, and to be taught the Catechism of the Church of England, and private prayers for them every morning and night.

And for the continuance of this my good intention for ever, I devise four hundred pounds of lawful money of Great Britain, being further part of the said nine hundred pounds, to rest in the heir of Fickisby's hands for the time being, whom I desire to consult with the Minister of Eland aforesaid for the time being, to chuse a proper Master and Dame to teach and instruct the said ten poor girls as is above mentioned, and pursuant to the intent and meaning of this my last will, the interest of which said sum of four hundred pounds, my mind is, shall be annually laid out and paid for the salaries of the said Master and Dame, and maintenance of the said poor girls, in such manner and proportion as the said heir of Fickisby, or Trustee for this my charity for the time being, shall see proper and convenient.

And my desire is, that the said poor girls may, from time to time, be chosen out of the greatest objects of charity which shall then be living in Fickisby, and the town and parish of Eland, so as the said school may be preserved and kept up for ever for the purposes aforesaid,

And my will and mind is, that the heir and owner of Fickisby for the time being, take great care in his choice of a Master and Dame as aforesaid, for the good teaching and looking after these **ten** poor **girls, so** that they may have all necessaries provided for them, and that the said Master may **read unto them the prayers** of the Church of **England,** every **night after the** girls give over work.

And also I **devise** two hundred **pounds more,** part of the said nine hundred pounds, **to rest in** the heir or **owner of Fickisby** land for the time being, for ever, to the **end that the Minister of** Eland, for the time being, may receive the **interest thereof,** as an augmentation for his better subsist-ence.

And my **will and** mind is, in consideration of the said **interest to be paid to the** said Minister, **that** he do and shall **read every** morning, in the Church of Eland, the common **prayers of the** Church of England, at six of the clock in the **morning in summer,** and at eleven **o'clock in** the morning in **winter, and the** charity girls, with their Master and Dame, **may attend** and **be** present **at** the said times **and** hours of **prayer and** devotion.

And my **will and mind is, that if in** case the Minister of **Eland refuse** to **attend and read** prayers, according to this **request and** intent, that **then the** said interest of the **said two hundred** pounds, designed **for the** Minister aforesaid, **I desire, and** my mind is, that the same may go to the said **poor** girls, for their better maintenance and subsistence. **Item,** my will **and mind** is, that that part of my will only **that** relates **to the** charity-school of Eland, and the Minister of the same, **be** read every Christmas-day in the morning, between prayers and sermon, in the Parish-church of Eland."

The above **was** copied from the Register-book at Eland.

THOMAS CHAMBERLAIN,

Of Skipton in Craven, who died October 29, 1721, gave by will twenty shillings per annum, **for ever, to** be distributed amongst four poor widows in Eland, by the Minister and Churchwardens, on the 6th day **of** June yearly; the pay-ment whereof is charged on a house at the south end of Eland, belonging, in 1727, to William Chamberlain, Salter, in Halifax.

The above account was taken from the Register-book at Eland.

EXTRACT FROM THE
WILL OF GRACE RAMSDEN,
OF HAWKSWORTH,
IN YORKSHIRE,

Dated Dec. 13, 1734.

AFTER leaving to the Trustees named in her **Will**, one clear annuity or yearly rent of three pounds ten shillings, and after the decease of several persons mentioned in the said Will, and failure of issue, as there at large is expressed, **one other** annuity or yearly rent of thirteen pounds, issuing out of several tenements in the parish of Bingley, the Will proceeds thus :

—" And whereas my sister (Mrs. Susannah Ramsden) **had it** in intention to found a school in Eland, in this county, for the instruction of poor boys in the English tongue, **but** died without founding the same, now I do hereby give and devise to Sir John Lister Kay, Richard Richardson, the son of William Richardson, Gregory Rhodes, John Wilkinson, the Reverend Thomas Hudson, Samuel Hill, Elkanah Hoyle, Gilbert Brooksbank, John Dyson, and William Wilkinson, (her Trustees), and their heirs, to the use of them, their heirs and assigns, all those my several farms, lands, tenements, and hereditaments, situate, lying, and being in the parish of Bingley, and now or late in the several occupations of William Jennings, and Thomas Laycock, or their assigns, with the appurtenances, and of the yearly value of thirty-two pounds, upon special trust and confidence, that they, my said devisees, and their heirs and assigns, at all times, after my decease, shall and may receive and take the rents, issues, and profits of the same to them demised premises, and order and dispose thereof in manner following :

First, I will, that in case I shall not in my life-time purchase a convenient house or building in Eland aforesaid, and settle the same in trust, to be made use of as a school for the instruction of such poor children as are hereinafter described, **then, that** my said devisees of the said tenements and premises, raise money, not exceeding forty pounds in the whole, and shall apply the same, or so much thereof as to my said Trustees shall seem requisite, to the purchase of one house or building, or of a plot or parcel of ground, situate in Eland aforesaid, and near to the church there, such tenements so to be purchased to be of the nature of freehold, and the estate therein to be purchased to be an absolute fee-simple in possession.

And if an house or building, which I would rather have to be purchased if it conveniently may be, cannot be purchased in convenient time, then that my said Trustees, having purchased such plot of ground as aforesaid, shall apply the residue of the said money, remaining after payments of the consideration of such purchase, to the erecting an house or buildings thereon, convenient for the purpose herein after mentioned.

And I will, that such building, so purchased or erected as aforesaid, all which I would have done within the space of one year next after my decease, shall at all times thenceforth be made use of as a school-house for the teaching of poor boys of the township of Eland with Greetland, the children of such parents lawfully settled there, who in the judgment of my said Trustees shall not be of ability to pay for teaching of their children.

And to that intent I will that my said Trustees, devisees of my said tenements in the occupation of William Jennings and Thomas Laycock, shall, immediately after the purchase or erecting of the said school-house, elect a grave man of good life and conversation, a true member of the Church of England as by law established, a good Grammar Scholar, and an expert Writer, and Arithmetician, and shall appoint the person so elected to be master of the said school; and at all times thenceforth, so long as he shall continue Master of the said school, shall pay to him, out of the rents and profits of the said devised tenements, yearly and every year, the sum of twenty pounds, of lawful British money, without any deduction thereout, on any account whatsoever, at two usual Feasts in the year, that is to say, the Feasts of the Annunciation of the Blessed Virgin, and St. Michael the Archangel, by equal portions, the first payment to be at such of the said Feasts as shall first happen next after his being instituted Master as aforesaid.

And I will, that, upon the death or removal of the said Master, or his ceasing to be Master of the said school, the

Trustees of the said school-house and devised tenements last mentioned, for the time being, assemble at the said school-house, or the greater number of them who shall there assemble, on public notice of the vacancy of such school, or place of Master, to be given in the church or church-yard, on a Sunday, immediately after the Morning Service is ended, and within fourteen days after such vacancy, of the time of meeting at such school-house, for a choice of a new Master, which time of meeting shall not be within less than fourteen days after such notice, shall and may elect and appoint another fit person, so qualified as aforesaid, to be Master of the said school, and so from time to time, and as often as the place of Master of the said school shall be vacant, a new Master so qualified as aforesaid, shall and may be elected and appointed, in the manner, and by the Trustees of the said tenements, for the time being, as is herein before directed touching the election and appointing of a Master, upon the first vacancy of the school or place of Master.

And that my said Trustees and Devisees, and their heirs and assigns, shall, out of the rents and profits of the said to them devised tenements, as aforesaid, pay to the Master of the school, for the time being, such annuity or salary of twenty pounds, as is herein before directed to be paid to the first Master of the said School, and at the same days herein before provided for payment thereof.

And if any Master of the said school shall die, remove, or be displaced by my said Trustees, as is herein after provided, then I will, that my said Devisees and Trustees, their heirs and assigns, shall and may apportion the salary to become payable at such of the said Feasts as shall happen next after such vacancy of the said school or place of Master, between or amongst the said Master so removing, or being displaced, or the Executors or Administrators of such Master by whose death the school shall become vacant, and the person or persons by whom the office or place of Master of the said school shall be supplied, till the appointment of a new Master by my said Trustees as aforesaid, and such succeeding Master as they, my said Trustees for the time being, or the major number of them, in their discretions shall think meet. And forasmuch as I would have the said school duly attended, I will and recommend to the Minister of the

church of Eland, for the time being, that immediately upon
the vacancy of the said school, or place of Master, so often as
such vacancy shall happen, the said Minister shall provide
a fit person to teach and instruct the poor children therein,
until a Master shall be appointed by my said Trustees and
Devisees to supply the vacancy of the said school, or place
of Master. And I will, that the person so provided by the
said Minister shall have a share, or part of the said twenty
pounds yearly salary, proportioned to the time he shall so
serve the said school.

And my will and mind also is, that my said Devisees,
their heirs and assigns, of the said tenements in the
possession of the said Thomas Laycock and William
Jennings as aforesaid, or the major number of them, at all
times after erecting of the said school-house, and electing
and appointing a Master thereof, shall and may, at their
will and pleasure, to be expressed in writing, signed by
them, or the major number of them, and to be notified to
the Master of the said school for the time being, remove or
displace not only such first appointed Master, but any other
person or persons who thereafter shall be appointed Master
or Masters, or to serve as Master or Masters, either by my
said Trustees for the time being, or by the Minister of the
said church of Eland, and in manner herein before directed
for the appointment of a new Master upon a vacancy, elect
and appoint another fit person to supply the place of Master
of the said school, in the place and stead of the Master so
by my Trustees amoved or displaced.

And my will and mind is, that the Master of the said
school, for the time being, shall, on every day of the week
throughout the whole year, (not being the Lord's Day, or
other day appointed by the Church or State to be observed
as a Holy Day, except the last ten days of the Month of
December, and except three days before and three days after
either of the great Festivals of Easter Sunday and Pentecost,
and except also the afternoons of every Saturday in the
year,) both the forenoons and afternoons of such days, (except as before excepted,) diligently apply himself at the said
school to the teaching of poor boys, the children of such
poor persons lawfully settled in Eland with Greetland, as
aforesaid, which boys I would have to be twenty-four in
number, to read the English language, and write a plain,

legible hand or character, and to understand common arithmetic, so as the said children may be thereby better qualified to gain a livelihood than the children of such poor parents usually are.

And I will, that **the** poor boys **to be first admitted after** erecting the said school-house, and so taught **there, shall be** nominated by my **said** Trustees of **the** said school, **or the** greater number of them, and that all other the said boys to be therefore admitted to be taught there, shall be nominated thereunto by the **Trustees** for the time being, or the greater **number of** them, **or in case** of default of such nomination **by** the space of one month next after the said boys there taught shall not **be** in number twenty-four, then by any two **or more** of **such** Trustees.

And **I** will that the Master of the said school, for **the time** being, shall also faithfully instruct the said poor children in the Principles, Doctrines, and Precepts of the Christian Religion, and shall particularly oblige them **to learn** the Catechism of the Church of England, and to repeat the same to him without book, at least once in every week, after they have so learned that they shall be able to repeat the same to him, and that **on** such occasions he shall explain the same, **or** some parts thereof, **to** the said children, in a manner suited to their capacities; and that at all times whilst the said children are under his care, he shall watch their behaviour, and in a proper manner, by gentle means if it may **be**, and if not, by modern punishment, restrain them from **all** immoralities and indecencies.

And my will and mind also is, that the Master of the **said** school, for the time being, on every day of the week in which the Morning Service, according to the Liturgy of the Church of England, shall **be read** in the said church of Eland, shall devoutly attend the same Service there, and oblige his said scholars to attend there with him, and take care that they **behave** themselves there decently, and with due reverence, **as** their respective ages will admit.

And I will that my said Trustees shall **apply** the residue **of the rents** and profits of the said tenements, in the **possession** of the said William Jennings **and** Thomas Laycock, after satisfying thereout the Master's said salary, to the buying of books as shall be requisite for the learning of the said boys, till they can read well the English Bible, and for the buying of paper, quills, and ink, for such of them as shall be taught writing and arithmetic, which writing and arithmetic I would have taught to every of the said boys, after he can read well in the Bible, for the space of six months next after.

And I will also, that there be given to every one of the said boys that shall be taught and instructed at the said school till he can read well in the Bible, besides his Bible, a new Common Prayer Book, and a Whole Duty of Man, at his quitting the said school, which books my Trustees, for the time being, shall also provide out of such residue of the said rents and profits of the said farms so to them devised, after payment of the said salary to the said Master, as aforesaid.

And as for and concerning the said annuity of three pounds ten shillings, herein before devised to my said Trustees, the same is to them devised upon trust, that so much of the sum of fifty shillings, part thereof, as shall be requisite, shall be yearly, and every year, expended in providing and laying in coals for a fire to be kept in the said school-house, during the winter season, for the benefit of the said Master and scholars there ; and that the residue of the said fifty shillings, or so much of such residue as shall be needful, be laid out, as occasion shall require, in the supporting and keeping in repair the said school-house.

And as to the sum of twenty shillings, residue of the said annuity of three pounds ten shillings, I will that the same shall and may be expended by my said Trustees, for the time being, at any meeting or meetings to be had by them, or the greater number of them, in Eland aforesaid, touching the said school, or the trust thereof, which I desire may be at the least once in every year, and as often as my said Trustees in their discretion shall see meet.

And I recommend to them, and every of them, that at such their meetings, or on any other occasion, they, or any one or more of them, do visit the said school, and enquire into the conduct of the Master of the said school, and the proficiency of the poor boys there, in their learning and knowledge.

And for the encouragement of the said poor boys, I will that so much of the said annuity of three pounds ten shillings as shall not be expended in any year, shall be distributed to and amongst such of the said boys, as in the judgment of my said Trustees, or the major number of them, shall appear to have best behaved **themselves.**

And **as for and** concerning the **said annuity of** thirteen pounds, herein **before** devised **to my said Trustees, in case** the same shall become **payable, I will that the same be expended and disbursed for** the **benefit of the** poor **children** thereafter to **be taught** and instructed at the said **school, in** such manner **as to my** Trustees for the time **being shall seem meet, only I will that** from and after **such annuity of thirteen** pounds shall take place, the number of poor boys to be taught **in** the said school-house shall **be increased,** and **that such** additional boys shall be children **of** like poor **parents, and** be in like **manner** nominated, taught, **in-structed,** governed, **and provided** for, as is herein before limited, of and concerning **the** poor boys **to be** admitted to **the** said school, before **the** falling of the said last mentioned annuity.

And for the better continuance of the said **trust,** my will is, that my said Devisees **and** Trustees of the said farm and school-house, **within three months next after the** decease of any two **of** them, **shall elect two other** honest men, of good real or personal estate, **and, if to** my said Trustees shall seem meet, residing in **or near** Eland **aforesaid, to be** with **such** survivors co-trustees of the said school-house, farms, **and** annuities, **and** shall convey the same school-house, **farms,** and annuities, to the use of themselves, and **such like** new elected Trustees, and their **heirs and** assigns on **the** trusts herein thereof before **limited;** and that in the like manner, **from time to time, and at all times, so often as any two** of the Trustees **of the said school-house, farms, and an-**nuities, **for the time** being, **shall** die, **the** survivors **of** them shall, within three months next after, elect **two such** other honest **men** of good estate, (and if **to such** survivors it shall seem meet), residing in or near Eland aforesaid, to be with them co-trustees of the said trust premises, and convey the **same** to the use of such survivors and new elected Trustees, and their heirs and **assigns,** on the said trusts herein before thereof limited.

And I also will that the Trustees for the time being, of the said school-house and premises, or any two or more of

them, shall have power and authority, at their will and
pleasure, to turn out, and remove from the said school, and
from all benefit and advantage thereof, any poor boy there
admitted to be taught and instructed, on complaint to them
made of the misbehaviour of such **poor** boy.

And my will **and** mind **further is,** that the Master and
scholars of the said school **shall at** all times conform themselves to such rules and orders as the Trustees of the said
school-house and premises shall institute and appoint, **so as**
the same rules and orders be not repugnant to what I **have**
here directed.

Provided further, and my will is, that it shall be lawful to
and for all and every the Trustees **of** the said tenements
herein before devised to **be** sold, **and** Trustees of the said
school-house, farms, and annuities, for **the time** being, to
deduct and retain to themselves by and **out of** the rents and
profits of the said tenements devised to be sold, and farms,
or either of them, and by and out of the said annuities, **or
either of them,** so to my said Trustees respectively devised,
all such sum or sums of money, damages, costs and charges,
as they **shall or** may respectively reasonably expend, sustain,
bear, or be put unto in or about the executing of the trusts
hereby in them reposed, or any of such trusts or in defence
thereof, or of the titles **of the** said to them respectively **de-**
vised premises, or any part thereof, and that such Trustees
shall not be answerable one for **another,** or one for the acts,
receipts, deeds, or defaults of the other, but every of them
severally for his proper acts, receipts, deeds, or defaults
only, **and none of them for more money than** they shall
respectively actually receive.

JOSEPH BROOKSBANK,

Of Hackney, in **the** county of Middlesex, Esq ; did, by
Indenture, executed June 5, 1756, convey to the Rev. Joseph
Brooksbank, of London, Joseph Hulme, of Halifax, M.D.
the Rev. John Smith, of Bradford, John Gream, of Heath,
near Halifax, Gent. Richard Taylor, of Norland, Clothier,
and the **Rev.** Joshua Dodson, of Cockey Moor, near Bolton,
in Lancashire, all that messuage, or tenement, and one
cottage, called by the name of Cinder-hills, in the township
of Southouram, and also eight closes of land to the same

belonging, known by the names of the Upper Ing, the Lower Ing, the Long Field, two Coal-pit Brows, the Little Steass Mires, the Sough Mires, and the Small Long Close, in trust that they, and such other person and persons on whom the trust therein mentioned should, from time to time, devolve, and the survivors and survivor of them, and the heirs and assigns of such survivor, shall yearly out of the clear rents and profits of the above granted messuage and cottage, and lands, (after the necessary charges of repairing and supporting the said messuage and cottage, and of the execution of the trusts thereby created were, from time to time, deducted), in the first place pay, or cause to be paid, by two equal half yearly payments, as the said rents shall come in and be received, the clear yearly sum of ten pounds of lawful money of Great Britain, without deduction of or for any manner of taxes, to the Minister, for the time being, of the Congregation of Protestant Dissenters meeting or assembling for the worship of God, in the present Meeting-house made use of for that purpose at Eland, in the county of York, so long as there shall be such a Minister, and the exercise of divine worship by Protestants dissenting from the Church of England shall be permitted therein by the laws of this realm, and no longer.

And on this further trust, that the said Trustees, for the time being, shall yearly out of said rents expend the sum of forty shillings, in the purchase of such books of piety and devotion as they shall think fit, to be by them given and distributed amongst the forty poor children taught at the free-school in Eland, which was formerly founded and endowed by Joseph Brooksbank, deceased, grandfather of the above named Joseph Brooksbank, owner of Cinder-hills aforesaid.

And upon trust, to pay, or cause to be paid, all the remainder of the said clear rents and profits of the said premises yearly unto the School-master, for the time being, of the said school, as an addition to his allowance, or salary, for teaching and instructing the said children in manner directed by the said Joseph Brooksbank, founder of the said school, and to and for no other use, intent, or purpose whatsoever.

D

When the Trustees are, by death, reduced to two, or under, the survivor or survivors are to convey to as many as are necessary to make the number seven.

Provided always, and the whole agreement was on this express condition, that if the Trustees for the time being, or any of them, should not be permitted to perform all or any of the trusts in them reposed, or if the exercise of divine worship by Protestants dissenting from the Church of England, shall not be permitted in the said Meeting-house by the laws of this realm, or if the said School-master, for the time being, shall be in any wise obstructed in the performance of his office, pursuant to the resolution and intention of the said Joseph Brooksbank, founder of the said school, it should be lawful to and for the said Trustees, for the time being, and they were directed and enjoined to reconvey, and assure the above granted premises to the use of the said Joseph Brooksbank, his heirs and assigns for ever.

Ealand Chapel, (which has parochial rights), was, in 1736, returned by the Governors of Queen Ann's Bounty, to have had, 3d of Ann, a clear yearly value of twenty-six pounds ten shillings.

BOUNTY AT EALAND CHAPEL.

The money for this purpose was subscribed about the year 1724, by means of Mr. John Lancaster, and others, but no purchase was made with it till after the year 1733, when a farm was bought by the then Curate, Mr. Thomas Alderson, called Blean Farm, in the parish of Askarth, near Askrig, containing about thirty days work of land, with liberty of thirteen cattle gates, in four different pastures, and a common right for an hundred sheep.

This farm was let, in 1764, for twenty-one years, at the clear yearly rent of seventeen pounds.

A MR. WHITTLE,

Of Marshall-hall, is said to have left twenty shillings yearly out of that estate, to the Curate of Ealand; but this only appears from old Terriers in the Office at York, not from either Will, or Deed, therefore the Curate's title to it is uncertain, for nothing of this sort is recoverable at law, unless the lands out of which it is issuable, can be ascertained.

As for the Terriers, they seem to have been made on the supposition that the money was fixed upon those lands, because paid by the owners of them; but there ought to be a better assurance than this.

For this reason there was an intermission of payment for some years in Mr. Petty's time, till he acknowledged it a bounty, and not a right.

THE REV. MR. STOCKS,

Rector of Kirkheaton, is likewise said to have given to the Curates of Ealand, a close in Stainland, worth ten or twenty shillings a year; but we can give no particular account of this, any more than we can of six pounds a year, said to be bequeathed to the poor of Ealand, by a Mrs. Preston, of Methley.

HALIFAX.

BRIAN OTES,

Of Halifax, surrendered, by copy of court-roll, into the hands of the Lord of the Manor, bearing date 2 Henry VIII. (1511), one cottage, and two closes of land, containing by estimation three acres, with appurtenances, in Halifax, to the use of certain feoffees, and their heirs, in trust, as appears by his Will, dated April 28, 1529, to the use of the said Brian for life, and after his decease, to the Church-wardens of Halifax, and their successors for ever, they paying six shillings and eight-pence yearly, for ever, to the amending of an highway between Halifax and Shipden Brook, six shillings and eight-pence for a dirge or mass, in the Parish Church of Halifax, to be sung or said, and the rest of the profits to the Morning priest there.

Mr. John Brearcliffe says in a manuscript, writ in 1651, that these closes were called Lister Lands, and belonged to one John Exley, of Halifax.*

The above land lay below Goldsmith's grave, in the way from thence towards the Bull Close; the cottage is taken away, and the charity was detained by the said John Exley, who had the land at that time. None of the above charity is now paid, except that for repairing the Highway. [Mr. Wright, page 105, says, none of the charity was paid in 1738, except that for repairing the highway.]

* From a manuscript, wrote by Mr. John Brearcliffe, an Apothecary in Halifax, called by him, " Halifax Inquiries for the finding out of several gifts, given to pious uses, by divers persons, deceased Dec. 22, 1651.

By an inquisition taken at Guisley, April 10, 1667, it was found, that at the court of John Waterhouse, late of Shibden, Gentleman, deceased, and Robert Waterhouse, son and heir of the said John Waterhouse, holden of the Manor of Halifax, October 12, in the 4th and 5th year of the reign of Philip and Mary, that Brian Bates, of Wakefield, and Elizabeth his wife, surrendered into the hands of the Lord, the reversion, after the decease of the said Elizabeth, of one messuage, four closes of land, and a yearly rent of twelve shillings, issuing out of certain lands in Halifax, to the use of Thomas Lister, William Lister, and James Lister, and their heirs for ever; and that after the decease of the said Brian and Elizabeth, the said Thomas Lister, William Lister, and James Lister, did surrender into the hands of the Lord of the said Manor, one annuity, or yearly rent of twenty shillings, issuing out of the said messuage and four closes of land, unto certain other Trustees, to the use of the poor people within the town of Halifax, yearly, to be distributed for ever upon Good Friday, by the discretion of the Lord of the said Town of Halifax, and his heirs, and of the Churchwardens of the church there, with liberty to the said Lord and Churchwardens to make distress upon the premisses, in case of non-payment of the said yearly rent.

And it was farther found, by the said inquisition, that the said messuage and closes of land, after the death of the said Elizabeth Bates, came to the possession of Elizabeth Blythman, of the city of York, widow, who had received the whole rents and profits thereof for several years, and converted the same to her own use, without paying the said sum of twenty shillings yearly to the poor of Halifax, as directed; whereupon the Commissioners, after a due hearing, did decree, that the said Elizabeth Blythman should, within twenty days after notice of the said decree, pay to the Churchwardens and Overseers of the Town of Halifax, for the time being, and others named in the said decree, the sum of thirty-three pounds, being the arrears then due; and that the said Elizabeth Blythman, and the heirs, owners, and occupiers of the said messuage and closes, chargeable with the said charitable use, should for ever after yearly pay the said twenty shillings, according to the direction of the Donor. And to the end the said charity might the better be secured and kept up, Samuel Mitchel, John Brearcliffe,

Joshua Dunn, Samuel Greenwood, Thomas Rigg, Joseph Fourness, and Thomas Hinde, were by the said Commissioners appointed Trustees thereof, with power, in case of death, to the survivors, to make new election.

To which decree the said Elizabeth Blythman and Jasper Blythman, Esq. did exhibit their exceptions in the Court of Chancery, Nov. 28, 1667, to which an Answer was filed, on behalf of the poor of Halifax, Nov. 28, 1668; and Nov. 27, 1669, the cause being heard before the Right Honourable Sir Orlando Bridgman, Lord keeper of the Great Seal of England, the exceptions were over-ruled, and the Decree of the Commissioners confirmed by a Decree of that Court, the Exceptants to pay the Respondent costs of suit.

The above messuage and lands are said in Brearcliffe's Manuscript, to go by the name of Yeathouse, and to lie at Blackledge Steel; they are also called by the same name in the Register-book at Halifax.

This charity both Mr. Brearcliffe and Mr. Wright have attributed to one widow Pymond, who was no other than Elizabeth Bates above-named.—She married to her first husband Richard Pymond, Citizen and Merchant Taylor of London, who lived in Wakefield, and left by his Will, dated May 20, 1547, many legacies, but none to Halifax.*

In the above manuscript of Mr. Brearcliffe, are the informations of two evidences, to prove that the sum payable out of Yeathouse, to the poor of Halifax, was forty shillings yearly; and one of them, the wife of one Robert Dean, of Priestley, said she had gone with her sister-in-law, Mrs. Blythman, who was buried at Eland, March 7, 1633, to help her to distribute the same. This is a difficulty not easily to be solved; it is, however, we think, safer to follow the words of the above Inquisition, and particularly the surrender therein quoted, which makes it only twenty shillings.

The premises belong, at present, to Sir Watts Horton, of Chaderton, Baronet, who pays the money as directed. The original Decree relating to the above, was in the hands of the late Mr. Valentine Stead, of Nottingham, who permitted us to take a copy of it, and whose sudden death deprived us of the benefit of many valuable papers, relating to the charities in this parish.

* Nov 7, 1547, she married Brian Bates, and was buried Jan. 20, 1552.

RICHARD CLARKE,

Of Halifax, gave to the poor of that town, six shillings and
eight-pence, yearly for ever, to be paid out of his house near
Loveledge-lane, in Halifax, as appears from the copy of a
court-roll, in the time of Robert Waterhouse, Esq. dated
April 15, 1597.

In Mr. Brearcliffe's Manuscript, from whence this account
is taken; it is said, that Richard Clarke gave this house to
one Robert Cunliffe, who either sold or mortgaged it to
Humphry Drake, and that in 1651 it was in the hands of
John Drake, Minister, son of Humphry, who paid the six
shillings and eight-pence yearly, since which we have seen
no account of it. This John Drake was Sub-dean of Rippon,
Prebendary of York, and Rector of Dunnington.

SIR   RICHARD   SALTONSTALL,

Knight, Alderman of London, (who was Sheriff there in
1588, and Lord Mayor in 1597,) left by will, about the year
1600, one hundred pounds to buy rents with; which rents
were yearly to be distributed in the Parish Church of
Halifax, to the poor of the said town and parish, in money
or bread, at the discretion of the Church-wardens for the
time being.

All this (as Mr. Brearcliffe observes) was confirmed by an
Award, made July 8, 43 Eliz. also by the consent of Dame
Susan Saltonstall, Samuel Saltonstall, and others, her
children; and the said Dame Saltonstall and Samuel being
Executors to the said Sir Richard, were to bestow the said
hundred pounds to the most profit, before the 25th day of
March next after the said Award.

It could not, however, be found, by the Inquisition taken
at Halifax, in 1651, in whose hands the money arising from
this charity remained, nor whether the same had been disposed of or not; and Mr. Wright thought it was long since
lost, or converted to private uses.

HUGH   ATWELL,

Parson of St. Tewe, in Cornwall, gave, March 10, 1605,
one pound thirteen shillings and four-pence, to the use of
the poor of Halifax town, to be lent to some poor man for

year, to be disposed of by the Magistrates and Officers of Halifax, which money was for a time lent accordingly.

In 1608, it was lent by Symon Binns and Thomas Taylor, Constables, to one Allan Pennington ; and Jane Crowther, the Benefactress, gave her word for it. This is Mr. Brearcliffe's account ; but in Halifax Register, under the year 1605, it is said to have been given to keep the poor in work, the stock to remain for ever, the gain to be the poor's ; to be at the disposition of the Magistrates and Officers of the town of Halifax, or else such as they shall think fit, for the true disposition thereof. I have seen no farther account of this.

—::—

EXTRACT FROM THE

WILL OF BRIAN CROWTHER,

OF HALIFAX.

Dated September 9th, 1606.

—" I do will, give, devise and bequeath to John Favour, Doctor of Laws, and Vicar of Halifax, Robert Law, of the same, &c. and their heirs for ever, to the use of the poor of the town of Halifax, one annuity, or yearly rent of ten pounds of lawful English money, yearly issuing, and to be received in the Feasts of St. Martin and Pentecost, by even portions, of, in, and forth of all and singular the said messuages, lands, tenements, reversions, possessions and hereditaments in Armin aforesaid, and the first payment thereof to begin in whether of the said Feasts shall first and immediately happen next after the decease of me, the said Brian Crowther.

And I will and grant, that for want of payment of the said yearly rent of ten pounds in the Feasts aforesaid, and by the space of twenty days then next following, that it shall be lawful for the persons aforenamed, and their heirs, to distrain in and upon the said tenements and premises in Armyn aforesaid, till they be of the said yearly rent of ten pounds fully satisfied and paid.

And I will, and my mind is, that the said yearly rent of ten pounds shall be distributed to and amongst the said poor of the said town of Halifax, by and at the discretion of six honest and sufficient persons of the said town of Halifax, whereof I will that the said Vicar there, and the Church-wardens of the said town for the time being, shall be three."

This Benefaction, Mr. Brearcliffe observes, was dealt all the days of Dr. Favour, who died March 10, 1623, after this it remained unpaid till his successor, Dr. Clay, gave it to the poor at Christmas in 1627; it was then converted to the Workhouse.—So far the manuscript.

On the 16th of August, in the 9th year of the reign of Charles the first, an indenture was executed (a copy of which is in our possession) between Sir Arthur Ingram, the elder, of the city of York, knight, and Sir Arthur Ingram, the younger, Henry Ramsden, Vicar of Halifax, Samuel Crowther, Nathaniel Waterhouse, and others, reciting, that whereas the said Samuel Crowther pretended to have a title to a rent-charge of ten pounds a year, issuing out of certain lands, &c. in Armine, in the county of York, supposed to have been granted to him, John Favour, Doctor of Laws, Vicar of Halifax, and others, by the last will and testament of Brian Crowther, deceased, in trust for the poor of Halifax aforesaid; the said Samuel Crowther, with the consent of divers of the best inhabitants in Halifax, and for the considerations afterwards in the said indenture mentioned, released, and for ever quit claimed the same to the said Sir Arthur Ingram, the elder, and Sir Arthur Ingram, the younger, their heirs and assigns for ever.

And in lieu thereof, the said Sir Arthur Ingram, the elder, and Sir Arthur Ingram, the younger, did for them, and their heirs, grant and assign to the said Henry Ramsden, &c., their Executors and Administrators, the yearly sum of twenty pounds, to arise and be payable out of an annual rent of three hundred and forty-six pounds ten shillings, which was made payable to the said Sir Arthur Ingram, the elder, and Sir Arthur Ingram, the younger, from one John Smithson, who held under them certain lands and tenements in Halifax, Skircoat, Northouram, and Southouram, by lease to him, his Executors, Administrators, and Assigns, for the term of one hundred years: To have and to hold the said yearly rent of twenty pounds to the said Henry Ramsden, &c., their Executors, Administrators and Assigns, for and during the term of eleven years, from thence next

following the date of this indenture; and after the expiration
of the said term of eleven years, the yearly sum of ten
pounds during the residue of the said term of one hundred
years in the indenture to the said John Smithson mentioned,
which indenture was dated August 31, 2 Cha. I.   This
latter sum of ten pounds yearly was made payable out of
two messuages and two water-cornmills in Siddal, Southouram, and Skircoat, or some of them, and out of all houses,
buildings, lands and tenements to the same belonging, to be
paid to the said Henry Ramsden, &c. their heirs and assigns,
in the south porch of the Church of Halifax, at the Feasts
of St. Michael, and the Annunciation of the Virgin Mary, by
equal portions, the first payment thereof to begin at the
Feast of St. Michael, which shall be next after the determination of the said term of one hundred years, with power of
distress in case of non-payment after twenty days, and a
forfeit of ten shillings for every such default.

At an inquisition taken at Halifax, February 16, 1651, it
was found, that the above yearly rent of twenty pounds was
paid for eight years and a half next after the date of the
above indenture; after which it was received and with-held
by one Anthony Foxcroft, so that there remained in arrear,
at the time of taking the said inquisition, the sum of one
hundred and twenty-five pounds; the Commissioners, therefore, decreed, that the said Anthony Foxcroft should pay the
said sum of one hundred and twenty-five pounds to Thomas
Binns, the surviving Trustee; twenty-five pounds whereof
was to be distributed to the poor of Halifax, and the remaining hundred pounds bestowed upon lands, rents, or hereditaments of inheritance, in fee simple, and the profits thereof
distributed to the poor of Halifax, in such manner as the
said yearly rent, or sum of ten pounds, was by the above
Indenture directed to be disposed of.

Also Anthony Foxcroft, the younger, of Halifax, Joseph
Fourness, of Booth's Town, Richard Blackett, of Halifax,
John Brearcliffe, Robert Allenson, and Daniel Greenwood,
of the same, were appointed co-trustees with Thomas Binns;
and to these, Anthony Foxcroft, in obedience to the above
Decree, did by Indenture, bearing date Jan. 4, 1652, grant
an annuity of six pounds fifteen shillings, out of four closes
of land, at Goldsmith's Grave, near Halifax, payable to the
said Trustees, their heirs and assigns, for ever, at Lady-day

and Michaelmas, to be distributed according to the will of
Brian Crowther, with a clause of distress in case of non-
payment for twenty days.

This annuity is the same which Mr. Wright, page 131,
says he could procure no particular account of.

September 17, 1698, seven Trustees were added to the
above, but how, or by what authority, is uncertain.*

Under an account of the above charity were formerly the
following lines, on a tablet hanging at the quire door, in
Halifax Church :

> "Some labour hard to leave their children store,
>   Some stir and strive t' advance their stock in blood!
> Some work for Commonwealth, which are bless'd more,
>   And happy they that care for Church's good,
>   And leave for poor, for widows, orphans, food.
> Thus he that had no children of his own,
>   Hath left for many children to be taught ;
> Who father is to caitifes of this town,
>   And hence to Heav'n is gone, with works full fraught,
>   Whose gracious deeds shall never come to naught.
> His body now here lies at quiet rest,
> His soul with God shall evermore be blest.
>   In hope poor Saints do crave,
>   In faith so do, so have.   B.C.

ELLEN HOPKINSON, AND JANE,

Formerly wife of Brian Crowther, built in their life-times
the alms-houses in Halifax, containing eighteen rooms for
as many poor widows, and two rooms for a School-master ;
the former was buried January 15, 1610, [and is said in
Halifax Register to have been, "*Fœmina pia, quæ medictatem
Xenodochii ædificavit ut viduarum domicilium esset in perpetuum,*"]
and the latter died about three years after.

Mr. Wright says, "Over the Alms-houses door, on a stone
in the wall is the following inscription" :

"In favour of Church and Commonwealth, to the glory of
the Blessed Trinity, these Alms-houses were built by the
Christian Charity of Ellen Hopkinson, and Jane Crowther,
of the family of Hemingway, of the Overbrea, sisters,
widows, for eighteen widows of the town of Halifax, and
one Master, to teach poor Children the Catechism, whose

---

* Mr. Crowther's burial is thus entered in Halifax Register:—*Sepultus
est Januarii 12, 1607, Brian Crowther, de Halifax, qui legavit Scholæ
Grammat. Vicar. de Halifax viginti libras, et pauperibus ejusdem villæ
decem libras annui redditus ex dominis sive manerio de Armyn, in comitatu
Eboru. in perpetuum.*

memory be blessed for ever.—Blessed is he that judgeth wisely of the poor; the Lord shall deliver him in the time of trouble, Psalm 41.   1610."

These Alms-houses being rebuilt, were made to contain twenty-four rooms, twenty for twenty widows, three for the Master, **and one at** the time of this information not used.

EXTRACT FROM THE
WILL OF RICHARD SOMERSCALES,
OF HALIFAX.

Dated March 17, 1612.

AFTER leaving certain estates in Ovenden and Halifax (no otherwise described than by the names of the tenants and occupants) to his sister, then wife of John **Holdsworth,** for life, and vesting the **same** in Trustees, it follows :

"My will, mind, and meaning is, that **the said Robert** Law, Richard Nichol, Humphry Drake, John **Hayley,** Thomas Pighles, and John Crowther, (his Trustees), and their heirs, **and** the survivors of them, and **their** heirs, shall, from and after **the** decease of the said Alice, my sister, yearly, and from **year to** year, for ever, dispose, distribute, and take all the whole rents, **issues,** and profits of all **the** said messuages or tenements, closes, hereditaments, and premises, with the appurtenances, in **Ovenden and** Halifax, **to** and amongst the poor and needy of **the said** towns of Ovenden and Halifax, at the discretion of my said feoffees and their heirs, with the assistance and help of the Churchwardens of the said two towns, for the time being, **save that I will twenty shillings** shall be given out of the first **year's** profits of the premises, after my said sister's decease, towards the repairing of Illingworth Chapel, situate in Ovenden aforesaid ; and I do appoint the Vicar of the Parish **Church** of **Halifax,** and his successors, **for the time being, to take an** account yearly of my said feoffees and their heirs, **of the distributing** and disposing of the **rents,** issues, and **profits** aforesaid, to the use of the poor aforesaid ; and **I do** hereby charge my said feoffees, and every of them, and their heirs, to deal faithfully and uprightly in the **disposing of the** said rents, issues, and profits of my said lands and tenements, according to the true meaning of this my last Will and Testament, as they will answer me at the dreadful Day of Judgment.

And, nevertheless, my will and meaning is, that the said feoffees, and their heirs, shall, **from** time to time, have to them allowed out of the said **rents**, issues, and profits, all **costs** and charges **by them to be paid or** disbursed, **in or about the repairing of the houses and** buildings of the premises, **or in the defence of the title of** the aforesaid lands, tenements, **and premises, and also all** other their **reasonable** costs and charges **in or about the performance of this my** present Will and Testament."

The abovesaid Richard Somerscales, got his estate by labour, being first a poor Shepherd, and towards his latter end a Waller. [Lord Oxford's collection of MSS., British Museum, No. 797.] He died April 8, 1618.

In 1651, one Daniel Greenwood, who was then a feoffee in trust, made oath, that the proportion for **Halifax** town, being four pounds thirteen shillings and **four-pence** yearly, had been truly paid to that time, and that the lands, from whence the said monies came, lay at the Espes, near **Mount Pellan, in Halifax.** The other estate, according to **Mr. Wright, is at Bradshaw-Lane-Ends, in** Ovenden.

Dec. 26, 1664, the feoffees then in trust, being for **Halifax, Daniel Greenwood, John Bretcliffe,** and Thomas Rigg; and for **Ovenden, John Illingworth, James Bates,** and Abraham Brigg, **executed to each other reciprocally, articles of** agreement, **that it might be certainly known, how** much of Richard **Somerscales' charity ought to be** distributed to the poor of **Halifax, and how much to the poor of** Ovenden; in which **it was agreed, that so much of the** premises as lay within the **township of Ovenden, should belong to the** poor of Ovenden, **and so much as lay within the township of** Halifax, should **belong to the poor of** Halifax.

This **agreement, it ought to be** observed, divides the body, which, according **to the donor's Will,** should consist of six feoffees, seized jointly of **all** the premises, both in Ovenden and Halifax, into two distinct bodies, each acting separately from the other; it remains, therefore, to be considered, how far these agreements are valid, and whether they do not affect later conveyances, &c., relating to this charity.

In 1710, Abraham Brigg conveyed to Messrs. Skelton and

Stott, as Trustees for Ovenden ; and by deed, dated January 19, John Batley, Thomas Rigg, John Holroyd, Samuel Steed, William Chamberlain, Jonathan Steed, Thomas Holden, and Robert Butterfield, were put in trust; but **why** so many were appointed, **or** whether it was for Halifax **only, we can-** not say.

The estate in Ovenden, belonging to this charity, was, in 1788, and had **been** for eighty **years** before, let **for** three pounds a year ; **that in** Halifax for six pounds.

The following **is on a stone on the** west wall **of Halifax** Church.

"Mr. Richard **Somerscales,** of Halyfax, who died **April** the 8th, **A.D. 1618, and** who, **by his** last will, gave **all his lands** in Halyfax and Ovenden (after the decease of his sister) **to the poor** of the said towns **for** ever, amongst whom **he gave** forty shillings **to** his sister's husband for the term of his life."

—::—

EXTRACT FROM THE

WILL OF JANE CROWTHER,

OF HALIFAX.

Dated Jan. 18, 1613.

—"I give, **devise, and** bequeath **unto** John Favour, Doctor of Laws, **and Vicar** of Halifax, Samuel Lister, of Southouram, William **Slater, George** Bentley, William Whitaker, and Humphry Drake all of Halifax aforesaid, Yeomen, and their heirs, for ever, one annuity or yearly rent of eight pounds, of lawful money of England, yearly, issuing **and to** be levied of, in, and forth of **all that the manor,** lordship, or grange of Arnforth, or by what other name or names soever the same is called, with the appurtenances, in the town, township, and parish **of** Long Preston, and all the lands, houses, tenements and hereditaments thereunto belonging, **which rent** I late had and purchased, to me, my heirs and assigns for ever, of John Pudsey, of Arnforth, Gent. with my whole power and authority to distrain of and for the same, and all sums of money and penalties to be forfeited nomine pœnæ for non-payment of the same, or any part thereof, of intent and purpose that they and their heirs shall for ever dispose, bestow, and employ the aforesaid annuity, or yearly rent of eight pounds, and every part thereof for and towards the maintenance of one School and School-master, who shall teach the children of the poorest people of Halifax to read and learn their Catechisms, thereby to know their duties towards God, and enable them the better unto several services in the Church or Common-wealth.

Item, I do give and devise the sum of ten pounds, to be lent from time to time, for ever, to the godliest and poor people of Halifax, the securing whereof so to remain for ever to the disposition and discretion of my Executors and Overseers."

Jane Crowther was buried Jan. 24, 1613. In 1651, fifty-two pounds of these rents were behind, and a great deal of money spent in suing for the same.

The Trustees were constrained to release the said annuity, and to take an 100 pounds in lieu thereof, which sum of one hundred pounds was, by Samuel Lister and Humphrey Drake, put to interest to John Greenwood, of Elfabrough-hall, in Sowerby, who repaid it, and it was, by the consent of Thomas Lister, of Shibden-hall, Executor to the said Samuel Lister his father, put out for eight pounds yearly to Joseph Lister, his late brother, and one Jonas Peverson, the said Thomas taking bond for the same in his own name.

Joseph, during the life, paid the said eight pounds yearly to the School-master, and Thomas paid it also for one year after the death of the said Joseph, which happened Dec. 27, 1644; but at the Inquisition taken at Halifax, Feb. 16, 1651, it was found that the said Thomas Lister had not paid the yearly interest of eight pounds to the then School-master for five years last past, but that he had paid the said School-master, Thomas Marshal, five pounds yearly, which he said was of his own free will, and not any part of the interest of the said hundred pounds; this caused a bill to be filed in Chancery against the said Thomas Lister, complaining, that the Devisee of the Will of Jane Crowther had sold or conveyed away, the yearly rent of eight pounds, by her left to the use already mentioned, or had otherwise granted and released the same to the tenant of the land charged with the payment thereof, and had accepted of the sum of one hundred pounds for the same, which sum had been let out to interest for some time, and the profits thereof imployed as directed; but afterwards the said Devisees severally dying, and Samuel Lister, the survivor of them, before his death, receiving in the said hundred pounds, Tho. Lister, his **heir and execu**tor, had put out the same to interest, and taken security in **his own** name, refusing to re-pay the said hundred pounds, **or any** interest for it, or to secure the same for the charitable **use for** which it was left, and praying for relief.

To these complaints we have **seen** no other reply than **what** is contained in **an** Indenture, dated May 16, **1657,** **between** the **said** Thomas Lister of the one part, and **Henry** Power of Halifax, Doctor in Physic, Samuel Lister, **of Shib**den-hall, son and heir apparent **of** the said Thomas **Lister,** **Robert** Hall, of Booth-town, and Samuel Mitchel, of **Halifax,** **of the** other part, wherein it is said that the Trustees of **the** **Will of** Sarah Crowther, or some of them, did grant away **their** estate, interest, and right in and to an annuity of eight pounds a year, by her left for the sum of one hundred pounds; and that Samuel Lister, father of the said Thomas, did put out the said sum of one hundred pounds at interest, in the name of the said Thomas Lister, as **heir to** the surviving Trustee, and **that** the said Thomas, endeavoring **to** have put to interest **the said** sum, for the advantage of the school to which it was **left,** the creditors in whose hands it was, died, and their heirs and executors became insolvent, whereby the legacy was lost; in regard, however, that the said sum was so let out as aforesaid, and in full satisfaction for the **same,** the said Thomas Lister did, by this Indenture, for and from him, his heirs and assigns, grant and confirm to the said Henry Power, &c. one annuity, or yearly rent charge of five pounds, out of a messuage, or tenement, in Southouram, with lands, &c. thereto belonging, called the Haines, to hold **to them, their** heirs and assigns, in trust for **the purposes** **mentioned in the** Will of the said Sarah Crowther, **and** to be for ever payable, at, or in, the south porch of Halifax, at the Feasts of Pentecost, and St. Martin the Bishop, in winter, by equal portions, with power of distress in case of non-payment for twenty days; and in case no distress could be found and the said annuity was unpaid for forty days, to enter and take the profits of **the** said tenements, till the arrear was paid.

At an Inquisition executed at Halifax, May 14, 1719, it was **found** that the above rent had been duly paid and applied to the charitable use ; that all the Grantees of the said rent were dead, and that Samuel Lister survived his said Grantees his cousin and heir being James Lister, of Shibden-hall, Gentleman, whereupon the Commissioners decreed, that the said James Lister, should convey the said yearly sum of five pounds to Samuel Stead, John Ramsden, Thomas Butterfield, Daniel Whitaker, Thomas Drake, Joseph Ellis, John Hillhouse the elder, Abraham Milner, and James Edwards all of Halifax, and to their heirs and assigns, for the use of the said school, according to the Will of Jane Crowther. In obedience to which Decree, the said James Lister did, by Indenture, dated October 21, 1721, convey the same to the Trustees last named, except John Hillhouse and James Edwards, who were then dead, with a clause, that when any five of them should die, the survivor or survivors should, within three months after, at the request of Jonathan Stead and John Caygill, of Halifax, (made parties in the Deed,) their Heirs, Executors, and Administrators, and the major part of the Governors of the late Nathaniel Waterhouse's workhouse in Halifax aforesaid, for the time being, for ever, grant and assign over the said yearly rent to such other nine persons of Halifax, their heirs and assigns, as the said Jonathan Stead and John Caygill, their Heirs, Executors, or Administrators, and the major part of the said Governors should nominate and appoint, in trust, for the purposes mentioned in the Will of Jane Crowther.

In the year 1761, we were particularly informed, that after no application for near thirty years, Jane Crowther's charity was then well managed by the acting Trustees ; that the School was kept in part of the Alms-houses given by Jane Crowther and Ellen Hopkinson, and the Master duly paid ten pounds a year, for teaching twenty poor children to read, write, and say their Catechism.

ISABEL MAUD,

Of Halifax, Widow, gave by Will, dated June 12, 1614, to the School in the Alms-houses in Halifax, ten pounds, for the buying of some annuity towards the maintenance thereof, to be disposed by the Overseers of her last Will, who were Dr. Favour, Samuel Lister, Samuel Mitchel, and John Clough.

Also to the poor of the town of Halifax eight pounds to be lent, from year to year, to four Tradesmen for ever ; and that her Overseers, or the most **part of** them, should **take** such order that the continuance thereof might remain.

The above is entered in Halifax Register. She also **gave** twenty pounds to Coley Chapel, but for what purpose **we** have not seen. *Halifax Inquiries, wrote by Mr. Brearcliffe.* **Query**: if she was not widow of **John Maud, of Halifax,** who gave in 1608, **one** hundred **and twenty one pounds** four shillings **to pious** uses, but in **what particular** manner is **now** unknown.

RICHARD NICALL,

Of Halifax, **gave by** Will, dated March 20, 1617, **to Robert Law and Thomas Houlden,** and their heirs, as feoffees in **trust,** a yearly rent of thirteen shillings and four-pence **for ever,** out of an house and certain lands in Halifax, **to be, by** and with the consent of the Church-wardens **for the time** being, paid to the most needful poor of Halifax town.

Mr. Wright, p. 114, says this house and lands lie at Mount-Pellon, quoting Mr. Brearcliffe for **his** assertion, but I can find nothing of this in his manuscript, which only says farther that the money was detained by Richard Nicall, the son, **who was** Executor to his father.

JOHN BOYES,

Clerk, Minister of Halifax Church, gave by Will, dated July 14, 1619, **the** sum of eight pounds, **to** be lent to the **poor** of Halifax, **at the** discretion of his Overseers, or the **greater** part of **them,** viz. **Dr.** Favour, William Boyes, his **brother,** John Boyes, of Halifax, Humphry Drake, Samuel **Lister,** John Whiteley, and William Whitaker. Halifax **Register,** An. 1620.

ALICE HAWARTH,

Widow, (as appears from an **inquisition taken** at Halifax, February 16, 1651,) gave by **her last Will,** dated February 6, 1622, **the sum** of twenty pounds **to be** paid by her Executors to Anthony Foxcroft, and **others,** to purchase lands or rents, and with the assistance **of the** Church-wardens of Halifax, to distribute the profits thereof, amongst the poor, impotent, and **aged** people **of the** said town.

And by the said Inquisition it was found, that Abraham Parkinson, and Ellen his wife, were Executors of the said Will, which Abraham acknowledged the said twenty pounds to be in his hands, also that neither principal nor consideration had been paid, though the said Alice had been dead twenty-eight years; alledging for himself, that he was never required by the said Anthony Foxcroft, or others in the Will named, to pay in the same; in respect, however, that the same had continued so long in his hands, he was willing to pay, in lieu thereof, the sum of twenty-five pounds, or else, by good and sufficient assurance, to convey to the said Anthony Foxcroft, and such other persons as the Commissioners should think meet, and their heirs, one annuity or rent charge of twenty-five shillings to be issuing out of his lands and tenements in Halifax for ever.

The Commissioners therefore did decree, that the said Abraham Parkinson should pay to the said Anthony Foxcroft, Richard Blacket, John Brearcliffe, and Robert Allenson, of Halifax, or some of them, the sum of twenty-five pounds, before the twenty-fourth day of June next following, and that they, as Trustees, should purchase with the same, to them and heirs, for the use of the poor of Halifax, and according to the intent of the last Will and Testament of the said Alice Hawarth, one annuity or rent charge of twenty-five shillings, or else some lands or tenements of the same annual value; or else the said Abraham Parkinson was to make to them the like conveyance and assurance.

In obedience to which Decree, Abraham Parkinson did, by his Indenture, executed August 25th, in the year 1652, give and confirm to the said Anthony Foxcroft, Richard Blacket, John Brearcliffe, and Robert Allenson, their heirs and assigns, for ever, as Trustees of Alice Hawarth's charity, one annuity or yearly rent of twenty-five shillings, issuing forth of all that one messuage, or tenement, and of all houses, barns, buildings, and gardens thereto belonging, lying on the south side of a lane leading from Goldsmith's grave to Brainthwaites on the moor; and also four closes of land, all adjoining to the south side of the said lane, some of them adjoining on the said house, payable yearly at the Feasts of St. Martin and Pentecost.

This farm is called Parkinson Houses, and was the property of Mr. Samuel Stead, of Rochdale. I have heard of no new deed since that of Parkinson's. **The** minutes of the above Inquisition, wrote by Mr. Brearcliffe, were in the hands **of** the late Mr. Valentine Stead, of Nottingham.

GODFREY WALKER

Gave forty shillings a-year, for ever, **to the Vicar** of Halifax, for a sermon **to** be preached in Commemoration of him, **in** the parish church of Halifax, in **the** month **of** April, for ever. He was buried April 4, 1633. This account is taken **from** Mr. Wright, p. 114.

A paper **which** I met with **in the** box belonging **to the** Trustees of Crowther and Hopkinson's charity says, **that** Henry **Riley,** of London, Esq; by Will, (confirmed by **Gill's** bargain **and** sale), gave forty shillings per annum, for **ever,** to the Vicar of Halifax, for a sermon to be preached in **com-**memoration of Godfrey Walker, **and** Catharine his **wife, in** **the** parish church of Halifax, in the month of April, **for** ever, to be paid **on** the third Wednesday **in** April, yearly, out of a tenement called Netherhouse, in Hipperholme-cum-Brighouse.

ANN SNYDALL,

Of Halifax, gave by Will, dated June 23, 1638, twenty shillings yearly, for ever, to have a sermon preached in Halifax church, every **St.** Peter's Day, **by** the Vicar or his substitute.

A manuscript, however, **in our** possession, on what authority we know not, says, this sermon was to be preached on that day, wherein, in the revolution of the year, it should fall **out** that she should be buried, if it be not on the Lord's Day, and if it be, then the day after. She was buried June 29, 1638.

The word Substitute, in this Will, seems to mean the Vicar's Curate, or any Clergyman whom the Vicar may think proper to substitute in his place, to preach the said sermon; but Mr. Brearcliffe says, this substitute, we (the Enquirers into Halifax Charities in 1651,) conceive **to** be none other than whatsoever Minister is substituted in the room of the Vicar for the Ministry of Halifax, which John Ryall, the Executor of the said Testatrix, well knowing, did, in the years 1643 and 1644, pay **unto** Mr. Roote, then Minister of the same place, the said sum of twenty shillings, according to the true meaning of the said Will and Testament.

Afterwards, the said John Ryall refused to pay the same, **because there was no** Vicar or Substitute at Halifax resident **there, but a Stipendiary Minister.**

This explains the **passage in Mr.** Brearcliffe's manuscript, **where** he says, **that** the money **in** 1651, rested in John **Ryall's** hands. **Mr.** Wright, p. 87, says that with **Mrs.** Ann Snydall's legacy **of** twenty pounds, and some addition of Vicar Hooke's (which was eleven pounds), the close behind **the** Vicarage-house **was purchased.**

The inhabitants **of Sowerby** gave towards this **seven** pounds ten shillings, for Dr. Hooke's consent to their having **a** licence from the Archbishop of York **to bury** and baptize at Sowerby Chapel.

The close was purchased in 1668, of one Nicholas Elberke, of Halifax, as appears by a Deed made **by him** to Feoffees in trust for the Vicars of Halifax.

NATHANIEL WATERHOUSE,

Of Halifax, is the next benefactor in order of time, but to **give a proper account of** his charities, we must go back **to what is** called the Corporation Charter of Halifax, or the **Letters** Patent which he obtained of King Charles the First, **in** these words:

" Charles, by the grace **of God** King of England, Scotland, France, and Ireland, Defender of the Faith, &c., to all to whom these presents shall come greeting.

Whereas by the humble petition of our well-beloved and faithful Subjects, the inhabitants of the town and parish of Halifax, in the county **of** York, we are given to understand that the said **town of** Halifax being anciently and yet a place of great clothing, **most** of the inhabitants within the same town and parish being Clothiers, is now of late much impoverished, and like to be ruined, by reason of the great multitude of poor people there daily increasing, which hath occasioned many able men within the said town and parish to remove from thence to other places, being oppressed with the heavy burden of the assessments towards the maintenance of the poor within the said parish, there being above forty pounds paid monthly to the poor there, and most years eighteen or nineteen months assessments collected for one year.

And for that Nathaniel Waterhouse, Gentleman, one of the Petitioners, hath given a large house within the said town, to the end the same might be employed for a work-house, to set the poor within the said town and parish on work, yet in regard there are no Justices of the Peace within or near the said town, to govern and well order the said house, (the poor people in the said town and parish being most of them idle and disorderly people, imbezzling or spoil-ing the work brought to them,) the said house is become of no use, but is like to return to the donor, it being not employed according to his intent; wherefore the inhabitants of the said town and parish have humbly besought us, that we would be graciously pleased to take the premises into our royal and gracious consideration, and to grant unto the Petitioners, that the said house may by our Letters Patent under the Great Seal of England, be made and established a workhouse for ever, for the setting of the poor within the said town and parish on work, by the name of a workhouse for the said poor within the said town and parish of Halifax; and likewise to grant unto the Petitioners, that thirteen of the most able and discreet persons within the said town and parish may be nominated and elected Governors of the said house, by the name of the Master and Governors of the workhouse for the poor within the said town and parish of Halifax, and that the said Master and Governors may be a Body Politic for ever, and may have a perpetual succession; and that any of our Subjects may have power to give to the said Master and Governors, and their successors, any lands or tenements whatsoever, to the yearly value of one hundred pounds, towards the maintenance of the said workhouse, and that the said Master and Governors, and their successors, may have power to take, receive, and purchase any such lands, tenements, or possessions, so to be given by any of our said subjects, without licence of Mortmain, and that they, or the greater number of them, may have power to make bye-laws and constitutions for the well ordering and govern-ing of the said workhouse, and may have power to search any suspected houses within the said town and parish, for idle vagabonds, ruffians, and sturdy beggars, and to take such idle vagrant persons, and sturdy beggars and ruffians, as shall be found within any such suspected houses, and to place them in the said workhouse, there to be set on work, and to be corrected and punished according to the good and wholesome laws of this our realm of England.

And that we would be further graciously pleased to give unto the Petitioners such further powers, for the well ordering and governing the said workhouse, and the poor people therein to be placed and employed, according to a like Grant made by our late predecessor King Edward the Sixth, for the government of Bridewell, in the city of London.

Know ye therefore, that we, for the considerations aforesaid, graciously inclining and condescending to the humble suit of the said Petitioners, and being of our own princely inclination willing and desirous to cherish and promote all pious and charitable works of that nature, and to establish the said house according to the good intent and meaning of the said donor, of our especial grace, certain knowledge, and mere motion, have made, constituted, ordained, and established, and by these presents, for us, our heirs, and successors, do make, constitute, ordain, and establish, that the said workhouse heretofore given by the said Nathaniel Waterhouse as aforesaid, situate within the said town of Halifax, shall forever hereafter be, and be called by the name of a workhouse for the poor within the town and parish of Halifax, in the county of York, and to that use shall be for ever hereafter employed.

And for the better government, ordering, and guiding of the said poor in their employment, and punishing of those that shall be found obstinate and refractory, we further will, constitute, ordain, and appoint, that thirteen of the ablest and most discreet persons in the said town and parish shall be for ever hereafter A BODY CORPORATE AND POLITIC, by the name of Master and Governors of the workhouse for the poor within the town and parish of Halifax, in the county of York.

And to the end that this charitable and pious work may take the better effect, we will, and by these presents, for us, our heirs, and successors, of our like especial grace, certain knowledge and mere motion, do grant, ordain, and constitute, that the said Master and Governors of the said workhouse, and their successors, for ever hereafter shall be one body corporate and politic of themselves, in matter, deed, and name, by the name of Master and Governors of the workhouse for the poor within the town and parish of Halifax, in the county of York.

We do for us, **our** heirs, and successors, incorporate them into one body corporate and politic, by the same name for ever to continue really and fully, we do, for us, our heirs and successors, erect, make, ordain, create, constitute, and establish, by these presents, and that by the same name **they** may have perpetual succession; and that they and their successors, by the name of Master and Governors of the workhouse for **the** poor within the town and parish of Halifax, in the county of York, shall and may, for **ever** hereafter, be able and capable in law to have, purchase, **receive**, and possess, lands, tenements, rectories, tythes, liberties, priveleges, franchises, jurisdictions, and hereditaments whatsoever, to them and their successors, in fee **and** perpetuity, or for term of life or lives, or years, or otherwise howsoever, and also goods and chattels, and all other things whatsoever, of what kind or quality soever they be; and also to give, grant, lease, assign, and otherwise to dispose the same lands, tenements, and hereditaments, goods, and chattels, as they please, and to do, perform, fulfil, and execute all and other things and matters whatsoever to them belonging and appertaining; and that by the name of Master and Governors of the workhouse for the poor within the town and parish of Halifax, in the county of York, they **shall** and may, for ever hereafter, implead and be impleaded, answer and be answered unto, defend and be defended, in whatsoever Courts and places, and before whatsoever Judges and Justices, or other Officers or Ministers of us, our heirs or successors, or other persons whatsoever, in all and singular actions, pleas, suits, complaints, causes, matters, and demands whatsoever, of what kind, nature, **or** form soever they be, in as ample manner and form **as** any our liege people within this our realm of England, **or** as any other body corporate or politic within the same.

And that the said Master and Governors of the said workhouse for the poor, within the town and parish of Halifax in the county of York, and their successors, for ever hereafter, shall have a common Seal, to serve for the causes and business of them and their successors, to be done and executed; and that it shall and may be lawful, to and for the said Master and Governors of the said workhouse, and their successors, for the time being, the same Seal, from time to time, to break, change, alter, and make anew, as to them shall be thought expedient.

And further, of our own especial grace, and of our royal authority, certain knowledge, and mere motion, we do, for us, our heirs and successors, as much as in us lieth, give and grant unto the said Master and Governors of the said workhouse for the poor, within the said town and parish of Halifax, and their successors, for ever, that it shall and may be lawful to and for the said Master and Governors, for the time being, or the major part of them, at all times, and from time to time hereafter, when and so often as they please to assemble themselves and meet together at the said workhouse in the said town, or in any other convenient place within the said town, and in those assemblies and meetings (when and so often as to them shall be thought expedient, and as necessity shall so require) to ordain, constitute, and make such fit, wholesome, and honest laws, ordinances, statutes, rules, and constitutions, as shall be expedient for the right government and well ordering of the workhouse, and the poor therein to be maintained and employed; and also full power and authority to examine all and singular persons idly wandering within the town and parish of Halifax aforesaid, and to compel them to labour and work in the said workhouse for their living.

And we do also, by these presents, give and grant, for us, our heirs and successors, unto the said Master and Governors of the said workhouse for the poor, within the said town and parish of Halifax, and their successors for ever, full power and authority for them, or the major part of them, from time to time, to nominate, appoint, make, and ordain such and so many Officers, Ministers, and Governors under them in the said workhouse, as they, or the greater part of them, shall think fit and meet, who shall, from time to time, oversee and provide, that the poor therein may be well and honestly ordered and provided for, and also to order and govern them in such manner, as to them shall seem meet and convenient, without the impeachment of us, our heirs or successors, Justices, Escheators, Sheriffs, Ministers, Servants, or other the subjects of us, our heirs or successors whatsoever, any statute, law, or ordinance heretofore made or done, or hereafter to be made or done, to the contrary notwithstanding, so as the said ordinances, laws, rules, and statutes be not contrary or repugnant to the laws and statutes of our realm of England or prerogative royal.

And moreover, we will and grant, for us, our heirs and successors, to the said Master and Governors of the said workhouse, for the poor within the said town and parish of Halifax, and to their successors, for ever, that it shall and may be lawful, as well to and for the said Master and Governors of the said workhouse for the time being, and every or any of them, as to and for such Officers, Ministers, and Governors, as the aforesaid Master and Governors, or the major part of them, shall appoint under their common seal, from time to time, to be Officers, Governors, or Ministers under them, as aforesaid, or any two or more of them, so to be appointed as aforesaid, from time to time, and at all times hereafter, diligently to find out and search (by all the lawful ways and means they can use, whereby they may best come to the light thereof, according to their wisdoms and discretion) all and all manner of taverns, inns, victualling-houses, alehouses, diceing and gaming-houses, within the said town and parish of Halifax, as well within liberties as without, and also all and singular suspicious houses or places whatsoever, within the said town and parish, for the discovering and finding out of all and all manner of ruffians, vagabonds, sturdy beggars, idle, vagrant, and suspicious persons, and to apprehend not only such ruffians, vagabonds, sturdy beggars, idle, vagrant, and suspicious persons, but also the tenants, masters, keepers or occupiers of such houses or places where such persons shall be found, and upon examination, to be taken by the said Master and Governors for the time being, or any one or more of them, and every of them, into the said workhouse to commit, and there to detain and compel them to labour and work as aforesaid, or by any other lawful ways or means to punish, as to them shall seem meet and expedient, unless the said tenants, keepers, or occupiers of such houses and places can honestly and justly excuse and discharge themselves before the Master and Governors of the said workhouse for the time being, wherefore such ruffians, vagabonds, sturdy beggars, idle, vagrant, and suspicious persons, be so upheld and cherished by them, or permitted to lie, be conversant, or to frequent their houses, or unless such men and women so suspected, and being vagabond persons as aforesaid, shall sufficiently make it appear, that he, she, or they be of honest and good conversation, and by what means they do maintain themselves, and for what cause they do so wander and daily frequent such suspicious houses, and such secret and prohibited places, and also shall find such sufficient security, that they, **and every** of them, shall afterwards honestly demean themselves.

And furthermore, **we do** by these presents, for us, our **heirs** and successors, give and grant to the said Master and Governors of the said workhouse, and their successors, for **ever**, that it shall and may be lawful, to and for the said **Master** and Governors for the time being, or the major part **of them**, from time to time to appoint such correction and **order in the** premises, as unto them, or the major part of **them as aforesaid**, shall be thought convenient and most **commodious**; **and** that it shall and may be lawful, to and for **every and any** of the said Officers, Governors, and Ministers **under them**, from time to time, to execute and **perform** the same accordingly, without the impeachment of **us, our** heirs, and successors, Justices, Escheators, Sheriffs, Ministers, Servants, or other the subjects of us, our heirs **and** successors whatsoever, **any** statute, law or ordinance **heretofore** made or done, or hereafter to be made or done to **the** contrary notwithstanding.

And for the better execution of our will and pleasure in this behalf, **we** have assigned, nominated, constituted, and made, **and by** these presents do, for us, our heirs and successors, assign, name, constitute, and make the said Nathaniel Waterhouse to be the first and modern Master of the said workhouse, willing that **the** said Nathaniel Waterhouse, in the **said** office or place **of** Master of the said workhouse, shall remain and continue from the time of the taking of his oath of Master, as hereafter in these presents is expressed, until the Feast of St. Michael the Archangel, which shall be in the year of our Lord God, one thousand six hundred thirty and six, and from thence until a new election shall be made of another Master, in form hereafter mentioned, and he be sworn in form hereafter mentioned in these presents; and that after the said Feast of St. Michael, which shall be in the same year **of our Lord God** one thousand six hundred thirty and six, a new election of another Master shall be made, and oath by him taken, as is expressed; the said Nathaniel Waterhouse shall be prime Governor of the said workhouse, next in order to the Master thereof for the time being, during his natural life, unless for **ill** aberring, or other just cause, he shall be removed from **that** place or office of Prime Governor of the said workhouse **as aforesaid**; and if the said Nathaniel Waterhouse shall happen to die before the said Feast of St. Michael the Archangel, which shall be **anno** Dom. 1636, then our will and **pleasure** is, and we do hereby ordain, that the said twelve Governors **for** the time being, or the major part of them, shall **elect** and swear one other of the said Governors to be Master **of** the said workhouse until the said Feast of St. Michael, which shall be in the year of **our Lord** God 1636, and **from** thence until another Master shall be **chosen** and **sworn, as** in these presents is hereafter mentioned.

And we do further, by these **presents, for us, our** heirs and successors, give and grant **unto the** said Master and Governors of the said workhouse, and their successors for ever, that it shall and may be lawful to and for the said Master and twelve Governors, or the major part of them for the time being, once in every year for ever, that is to say, **on** the Feast of St. Michael the Archangel yearly, (if it be not on Sunday, and if Sunday then the next day after,) to elect and choose one of the ablest and discreetest persons of the said twelve Governors of the said workhouse, to be Master **of** the same for one year then next following, and until another shall be elected and sworn, as hereafter **is** mentioned; and after every such election made, and before the person so elected be admitted to the execution of his office, the person so elected, within seven days **after**, shall take his corporal oath before the Master, and the rest of the Governors for the time being, (or so many of them as will be present), for the due execution of his office of Master of the said Workhouse.

And as often as any Master of the said workhouse shall happen to die within and before the expiration of his year wherein he shall be Master, we do by these presents, for us, our heirs and successors, give and grant unto the twelve Governors, or the Major part of them, for the time being, full power and lawful authority, from time to time, to elect and choose out of themselves another Master, who being so duly elected and sworn, as hereafter is expressed, shall continue Master of the said workhouse until the next ensuing Feast of St. Michael the Archangel next after his election, and from thenceforth until another of the said Governors shall be duly elected and sworn Master of the said workhouse as aforesaid; and as often also as it shall happen any Master of the said workhouse, in form aforesaid elected, after his election made, and before his oath taken, to die, or refuse to take the said place upon him, that then, and so often we will, for us, our heirs and successors, that there be the like election forthwith made, and that the person so to be newly elected, taking his oath as is hereafter mentioned, shall execute the place of Master of the said workhouse, in form aforesaid.

And we have also assigned, named, constituted, and appointed, and by these presents, for us, our heirs and successors, do assign, name, constitute, and make, our well beloved Anthony Foxcroft, Gentleman, Robert Exley, Thomas Binns, John Power, Thomas Radcliffe, Richard Barraclough, Thomas Lister, Simeon Binns, Hugh Currer, Samuel Clough, Samuel Mitchel, and John Wade, to be the first twelve present and modern Governors of the said workhouse, to continue in the said place of Governor during their several and respective lives, saving when and for such time only as they shall be Masters, unless they shall be removed as hereafter is mentioned.

And we do hereby for us, our heirs and successors, give and grant unto the said Master and Governors, and their successors for ever, full power and lawful authority, that they, or the major part of them, immediately from and after the decease or removal, as hereafter is mentioned, of any of the said twelve Governors by these presents constituted, or of any other Governor or Governors hereafter to be elected and made, may from time to time elect and choose one or more Governor or Governors in his or their place or stead, which shall so happen to die or be removed, out of the ablest and discreetest inhabitants within the said town and parish; who, within convenient time after his or their election, and before his or their admission into the place of Governor or Governors of the said workhouse, shall take his and their corporal oath before the said Master and surviving Governors for the time being, or the major part of them, for the due execution and performance of the said place, and after such oath taken, shall continue Governor, or Governors, of the said workhouse during his and their natural lives respectively, saving for such time only as he and they shall supply the place of Master of the said workhouse, unless for misbehaviour in his or their place, or places, or other just or reasonable cause he or they should be removed from the same; and every of them, after the time of his being Master ended, shall return again unto his place of Governor, in the same rank, order and antiquity as he was before; and if it shall happen that any of the said twelve Governors, by these presents constituted, or hereafter to be elected and sworn, as aforesaid, shall misbehave, or misdemean him or themselves, in his or their said place, or places, of Governor, or Governors, or if there shall be any other just or reasonable cause to remove him, or them, then it shall and may be lawful to and for the said Master, and the rest of the said Governors, or the major of them, for the time being, upon or for such misdemeanors, or other reasonable and just cause, to remove, displace, and put out, any such Governor or Governors, and thereupon in the place and stead of him or them so removed, to elect and swear one or more of the ablest and discreetest of the inhabitants within the said town and parish, as the case shall require, to be Governor or Governors of the said workhouse, to continue during his or their natural life or lives respectively, unless for misbehaviour, or other just cause as aforesaid, he or they shall be removed from the same.

And so the like course to be held from time to time, when as often as occasion shall be, and also when and as often as it shall happen any Governor or Governors of the said workhouse, after his or their election, and before his or their oath taken, shall die, or refuse to take the said place upon him or them, that then and so often there be a like election forthwith made; and that the person or persons so to be newly elected taking his or their oath as aforesaid, shall execute the place of Governor or Governors of the said workhouse in form aforesaid.

And to the end that justice may be the better done and executed within the said town, and the extents, limits and precincts thereof, and that the said workhouse and persons therein to be placed and employed may be the better ordered and governed, our will and pleasure is, and we do hereby, for us, our heirs and successors, constitute and appoint, that the said Nathaniel Waterhouse, named for the present Master, and the said Anthony Foxcroft, being the first named of those appointed to be present Governors, shall be justices of peace, within the said town of Halifax, that is to say, the said Nathaniel Waterhouse for the time that he shall be and continue Master of the said workhouse, and the said Anthony Foxcroft, as Prime Governor, for so long as the said Nathaniel Waterhouse shall continue Master, and after a new Master chosen and sworn as aforesaid, then the said Master for the time being, during his time of being Master, and the said Nathaniel Waterhouse, as Prime Governor, during his life, unless he shall be removed as aforesaid, shall be Justices of the Peace within the said town and liberties thereof; and so from time to time for ever, after the Master for the time being, during the time of his being Master, and the Governor for the time being next in order to the Master, according as they are in and by these presents named and ranked, and as hereafter they shall be in antiquity by election, during the time of being Prime or next Governor, to be from henceforth for ever Justices of the Peace within the said town of Halifax, and the extents, limits, and precincts of the same, to do and faithfully to execute all things whatsoever to the place and office of Justice of the Peace belonging, in as ample a manner as any Justice of the Peace within the West-Riding of our said county of York, may or ought to do within the said Riding, according to the laws and statutes of this our realm of England made and provided, and according to the true intent and meaning of these presents, and to send or commit, when there shall be cause, to the common Gaol or Gaols appointed, or to be appointed for the said Riding, as other Justices of the Peace there.

And our will and pleasure is, and we do hereby, for us, our heirs and successors, will and command the Sheriffs of the said county of York, and their Under Sheriffs, Gaolers, and others, whom in that behalf it shall or may concern, to receive and take all prisoners to be committed by them the said Master and Governor, or either of them, for the time being, into their charge and custody, and them to detain and keep in prison until they shall be discharged by due course of law, which said Justices of Peace for the said Town of Halifax, and every of them, for the time being, before he or they be admitted to execute the office of Justice of Peace, shall also for ever hereafter respectively, according to the laws and statutes in such cases made and provided, each, and every of them take his corporal oath upon the Holy Evangelist, (that is to say) the Master for the time being before the last Master, and the rest of the Governors for the time being or so many of them as will be present, and the Prime Governors next in order to the said Master for the time as aforesaid, before the then Master, and the rest of the Governors for the time being, or so many of them as will be personally present, for the due execution of the said office of Justices of the Peace within the said town, during the several and respective times of their being Master and Prime or next Governor respectively, as aforesaid.

And we do hereby give and grant full power and authority unto our well-beloved Sir William Savile, Baronet, John Farrer, Esq; and Henry Ramsden, Clerk, or to any two of them, to administer an oath upon the Holy Evangelist unto the said Nathaniel Waterhouse, for the due execution of the place and office of the Master of the said workhouse, according to the true intent and meaning of these presents, during the time he shall continue Master of the same, and also for the executing the office or place of Justice of the Peace within the said town of Halifax, during the time of his being Master there, according to the laws and statutes in that behalf made and provided.

And we do also, by these presents, give like power and authority unto the said Nathaniel Waterhouse, to administer an oath upon the Holy Evangelist unto every of the said twelve modern Governors before particularly named, for the due execution of their places respectively, during the time they shall continue in the same, according to the true intent and meaning of these presents; and also to administer an oath upon the Holy Evangelist unto the said Anthony Foxcroft, for the due execution of the office of Justice of the Peace within the said town of Halifax, during the time he shall continue prime or next Governor, as aforesaid, according to the laws and statutes in that behalf made and provided.

And these our Letters Patents, or the enrollment thereof, shall be unto the said Sir William Savile, John Farrer, and Henry Ramsden, and unto every of them, and unto the said Nathaniel Waterhouse, and unto the succeeding Masters and Governors of the said workhouse, for the time being, and unto every of them, a sufficient warrant and discharge in that behalf.

And further we will, and by these presents, for us, our heirs and successors, do grant unto the Master and Governors of the said workhouse, or to their successors, for ever, that if any person or persons inhabiting within the same town or parish of Halifax, and being unto the offices or places of Master or Governor of the said workhouse, in due and lawful manner elected and chosen, according to the true intent of these presents, and having thereof notice to him or them respectively given, shall deny or refuse to have, hold, or take upon him, or them, the execution of the said offices or places of Master, Governor, or Governors of the said workhouse respectively, that then, and so often, and in every such case, it shall and may be lawful to and for the Master and Governors of the said workhouse for the time being, or the major part of them, from time to time, and at all times hereafter, to tax, assess, and impose upon all and every such person and persons so as aforesaid refusing to have, hold, and take upon him or them the execution of such office or place as aforesaid respectively, such reasonable fines, for the contempt and offence in that behalf, as to them the Master and Governors of the said workhouse, for the time being, or the major part of them, shall be thought meet and convenient.

And further, that it shall and may be lawful to and for the Master and Governors of the said workhouse, for the time being, the same fines so taken and imposed, to levy, have, and receive, from time to time, by distraining of the goods and chattels, and cattle of such persons so refusing, to the use of the Master and Governors of the said workhouse, for the time being, or otherwise to sue for the same by action of debt, information, bill, or plaint, in any of our Courts of Record, or other Courts, in the name and to the only use and behoof of the said Master and Governors of the said workhouse for the time being, and their successors for ever.

And further we will, and for us, our heirs and successors, do give and grant, by these presents, unto the said Master and Governors of the said workhouse for the poor within the town and parish of Halifax, in the county of York, and to their successors for ever, special license and free and lawful power and authority to have, purchase, and possess to them and their successors for ever, in fee and perpetuity, or for time of life, lives, or years, or otherwise howsoever, messuages, lands, tenements, rectories, tythes, rents, reversions, liberties, privileges, franchises, jurisdictions, and other hereditaments, as well of us, our heirs and successors, as of any other person or persons whatsoever, which are not holden of us, our heirs or successors, in capite, or by Knight's service, or of any other person or persons by Knight's service whatsoever, so that the said manors, lands, tenements, rectories, tythes, rents, reversions, or other hereditaments, do not exceed in the whole the clear yearly value of one hundred marks, over and above all charges and reprizes, and over and above the said workhouse, with the appurtenances.

And also we will, and for us, our heirs and successors, do give and grant by these presents, unto all and every person and persons whatsoever, like licence, and free and lawful power and authority to give, alien, sell, dispose, and convey unto the said Master and Governors of the said workhouse, and to their successors for ever, in fee, or perpetuity, or for term of life, lives, or years, or otherwise howsoever, messuages, lands, tenements, rectories, tythes, rents, reversions, liberties, privileges, franchises, jurisdictions, and other hereditaments, and also all goods and chattels, of what kind or quality soever they be, according to the true intent and meaning of these presents, the statute of lands and tenements not to be put in Mortmain, or any other statute, act, ordinance, or provision heretofore had, done, obtained, or provided, or any other matter, cause, or thing to the contrary thereof, in any wise notwithstanding.

And we will and grant, by these presents, for us, our heirs and successors, to the said Master and Governors, and their successors for ever, that these our Letters Patents, or the Enrollment thereof, shall be unto all and every the said Master and Governors of the said workhouse, for the time being, and their successors for ever, a sufficient warrant and discharge for the doing, executing and performing of all and singular the premises, according to the true intent and meaning of these presents, although express mention of the

F

true yearly value or certainty of the premises, or any of them, or of any other gifts or grants by us, or by any of our progenitors or predecessors, to the said Master and Governors of the workhouse for the poor within the town and parish of Halifax, in the county of York, heretofore made in these presents, is not made, or any statute, act, ordinance, provision, proclamation, or restraint to the contrary thereof heretofore had, made, ordained, or provided, or any other thing, cause, or matter whatsoever in any wise notwithstanding.

In witness whereof we have caused these our Letters to be made Patents.

Witness ourself at Canterbury, the fourteenth day of September, in the eleventh year of our reign.

WOLSELEY."

N.B.—As the original of the above is supposed to be lost, this is printed from a careful comparison of several copies. It may be worth remarking that the original was produced at Halifax to the Commissioners of Pious Uses in the year 1719, as appears from an Inquisition by them signed relating to the workhouse there.

The Letters Patents thus obtained, the Master, Prime Governor, and modern Governors therein named, did qualify themselves for their respective offices, October 9, 1635.

The form of the Master's oath, used on this occasion, was, "You shall duly execute the office and place of the Master of the workhouse for the poor, within the town and parish of Halifax, in the county of York, according to the true intent and meaning of his Majesty's Letters Patents, during the time you shall continue Master of the said workhouse."

And changing the term Master for Governor, the Governor's oath the same.

October 12, 1635, a warrant was granted by Sir William Savile, Baronet, and Henry Ramsden, Clerk, requiring the Churchwardens and Overseers within the town and parish of Halifax, to assess and gather of the inhabitants within the said town and parish, six months assessments for the poor, according to the monthly assessment then assessed upon the said inhabitants, over and above the assessments already then assessed, and to pay the same to the Master and Governors of the workhouse, because there wanted a convenient stock for the setting on work and maintaining of the poor within the said town and parish.

At the meeting held Oct. 14, 1635, Treasurers were appointed; and at the Court held October 21, 1635, a Clerk, Overseer, and Beadle were chosen, the workhouse ordered to be repaired, and a room to be enlarged and made ready therein, for the meeting of the Master and Governors; the wheels, &c. to be viewed, and the seal of the Castle declared to be the Common Seal for all their business about the said workhouse, till farther order should be taken for changing or altering thereof.

At other Courts, orders were made for such as were likely to become chargeable to the town and parish, to be removed; such as kept them in their families contrary to order, were fined; security was taken from all who received any stranger to dwell in their houses, that such stranger should not be chargeable to the town and parish; such as were convicted of swearing, keeping or using gaming-houses, and tippling at unseasonable hours, were fined; such as embezzled, spouted, or spoiled their work, or were idle, or unruly, or made a practice of begging, were whipped, set to work, or sent to the place of their settlement, and sometimes allowed only bread and water for several days: And, in short, such strict regulations were made, and put in execution for keeping the poor in order, that near seventy different persons from December 9, 1635, when this punishment was first inflicted, to the 10th of October, 1638, when it seems, for a time, to have ceased, were whipped at the whipping-stock within this workhouse, and some of them repeatedly.

December 21, 1635, Sir William Savile, of Thornhill, Baronet, composed a difference between the Master and Governors of the workhouse, and the inhabitants of Halifax, by awarding, first, that every man within the parish, for giving of four-pence, should have bond given him by the Master and Governors, that neither they, nor any of their issue, should be chosen Governors without their own consent, provided they came in before Candlemas following.

Secondly, That whereas there was an intention to have six months assessment within the parish, they should be contented with three months assessment within the whole Vicarage; and, thirdly, that if any thing there promised could not lawfully be done, the Patent should be mended at the charge of the town.

This caused a petition at the next General Quarter Sessions of the Peace, that the three months assessment appointed by warrant from Sir William Savile, Baronet, John Farrer, Esq., and Henry Ramsden, Clerk, three of his Majesty's Justices, to be paid throughout the whole Vicarage of Halifax, to the Master and Governors, for a stock for the poor, might be released to Heptonstall and Ealand ; but the Court, January 13, 1635, confirmed the warrant, and ordered that such as refused to pay, should be apprehended and carried before a Justice of the Peace, to be bound to appear at the next Sessions.

At the Court within the workhouse, January 19, 1635, an acquittance was given to Mr. Ramsden, for seventy-two pounds nine shillings and eight-pence, by him paid towards procuring the above Letters Patent.

This money Mr. Ramsden had received on account of the workhouse, after it was agreed by the Overseers, Church-wardens, and several inhabitants of the town and parish, to procure a government to be established for the setting the poor on work within the said town and parish, by Letters Patent, and consisting of different benefactions, not left for this particular purpose, but to be employed to good uses in general.

Several parishioners excepted against such application thereof, but the matter being referred, by joint consent, to Sir William Savile, on hearing the allegations on both sides, he approved of what had been done.

At the Court held January 27, 1635, the Master and Governors agreed to divide the town into five precincts, in which particular members were to make view every month, and give in at the next meeting a particular account thereof, and also to keep privy watch therein once every fortnight at least.

The poor in the workhouse, as ordered at the Court held March 23, 1635, were to work every year, between Michael-mas and Lady-day, from six in the morning till nine at night, having fire and candles at the house charge ; and from Lady-day to Michaelmas, from five till eight o'clock, save only in September, when they were to work from morning to night, being allowed half an hour at breakfast time, and an hour at dinner.

Thus was this workhouse regulated and managed, under the inspection of him who gave it, as appears from the original Book of Rules, &c. kept therein, a copy of which was in the possession of the late Mr. Watson, taken from the original, lent by the late Mr. Stead of Nottingham.

In this manuscript is a remarkable chasm, from December, 1638, to October 1682, excepting which, it is a continued register of what was done in and about the workhouse, from its first institution, to September 29, 1704, at which time the last entry was made in it.

Besides this, there was also a book of accounts, both which were produced at the dispute in 1721, this latter marked A, and the former B.

A copy of the will of Mr. Waterhouse next follows.

—::—

BIOGRAPHICAL HISTORY

OF

HALIFAX PARISH.

THE design of the following chapter is to give some account, in alphabetical order, of such authors, and persons of note, as have been born, or have lived, in the parish of Halifax.

AINSWORTH, WILLIAM,

Curate of Lightcliffe, in this parish, published "Triplex memoriale, or the substance of three commemoration sermons, whereof the titles are these, viz. 1. The memory of the Just. 2. A pattern for pious uses. 3. The fifth beatitude, or the merciful man's blessing. Preached at Halifax in remembrance of Mr. Nathaniel Waterhouse, deceased. Whereunto is added, an extract out of the last Will and Testament of the said Mr. Nathaniel Waterhouse, containing his several gifts and donations for pious and charitable uses. By William Ainsworth,* late Lecturer at St. Peter's, Chester. York, Printed by Thomas Broad, 1650."

This book, which contains ninety-six pages in octavo, begins with an epistle dedicatory to the Right worshipful Sir John Savile, Knight, High Sheriff of the county of York.

* His "Marrow of the Bible" is not mentioned here. I have searched for a copy of the "Triplex" for many years, but have never seen one.

Next follows the Author's Apology to the reverend Dodecasty of Ministers within the vicarage of Halifax, especially to Mr. Robert Booth, then Minister there. In this he mentions his being related to Mr. Waterhouse. The first of these sermons was preached December 1, 1647, from Psalm cxii. **6.** The second, December 6, **1648**, from Nehemiah, **xiii. 14**; and the third, December 5, 1649. The two last dedicated to the Right worshipful Langdale Sunderland, and William Rookes, junior, Esqrs. to whom the Author says " **he was bound in those days** of his under-hand fortune, wherein (as **every bird will have a** peck at an owl) he had suffered very **foul things from** all sorts of hands." **This** work contains **several strong complaints of the poverty of the** Clergy in **those days; particularly at page 78, where he says,** " The **Ministry in this Church of England is, for the most** part, **the** poorest trade **that any man drives, the inferior sort** of Ministers **having neither a** competency **while they live,** nor **provision made for their** families **after** their **death, contrary to the practice of** other reformed churches.

Every man thinks he is at liberty to pay **to the** Minister or forbeare, though **he be** content to be bound in every thing else.

Men would **have Ministers to burn** like lamps, **but** will **afford them no oyle to keep in the light;** like Pharaoh's hard **task-masters,** they think we **should** make brick **without straw."** And a little farther, **" The** poorest Ballad-singer **and Piper in** the country live better of their trades than Ministers do."

We shall only observe, that if this **was** the case in the succeeding **reign,** it is not to be wondered at that so many Curates suffered themselves to be ejected from the Chapels in this neighbourhood.—**It** is said, that **Mr.** Ainsworth taught school, notwithstanding **which he** declares, that by reason of the late civil storms he was as poorly provided of accommodations for study, as Cleanthes was for writing his philosophical notes, when having wrought all day long in the **vineyards,** he wrote at night on bare stones instead of paper.

BREARCLIFFE, JOHN,

An Apothecary in Halifax, where he was born, and where he died of a fever, December 4, 1682, aged 63. He wrote collections relating to the antiquities of Halifax in Yorkshire, a manuscript which the late Mr. Wilson, of Leeds, (Author of the manuscript collections of the lives and writings of English, Scotch, and Irish Historians, their several editions, and where their manuscripts are deposited, now lodged at the Free-school in Leeds) says Mr. Thoresby, the Antiquary, saw in the library at Halifax Church, but to our own knowledge, there has been no such thing there for more than twenty years.

The title of one of these papers was, " A particular survey of all the houseinge and lands within the townshippe of Halifax, accordinge to the best information that could be had, taken the 22nd day of November, 1648."

This Mr. Brearcliffe seems to have been fond of collecting together every thing which fell in his way, relating to the affairs of his native town and parish. Amongst the rest, we have twenty pages in folio, in his own hand writing, intitled " Halifax inquieryes for the findeinge out of severall gifts given to pious uses by divers persons deceased. Written December 22, 1651."

BENTLEY, WILLIAM,

Born in Halifax, and the reputed Author of a book, called " Halifax and its Gibbet Law placed in a true light. Together with a description of the town, the nature of the soil, the temper and disposition of the people; the antiquity of its customary law, and the reasonableness thereof; with an account of the Gentry, and other eminent persons, born and inhabiting within the said town, and the liberties thereof."

" To which are added, the unparalled tragedies committed by Sir John Eland, of Eland, and his grand antagonists. London, printed by J. How, for William Bentley, at Halifax, 1708." It contains 174 pages in 8vo.

The son of the above William Bentley caused another to be printed at Halifax, by P. Darby, in 1761.

The first edition is that which Wright, in his History of Halifax, quotes by the name of the Old Gibbet-law Book.

It leads off with a short dedication to the Duke of Leeds, signed by William Bentley, from whence many have concluded, that he was the author of it; but there is reason to believe that it was wrote by one Dr. Samuel Midgley, of Halifax. Next follows a preface.

Chapter I. contains a short description of Halifax, and the origin of its name; encomiums on its air, and the church, and how, and when the rectory became impropriate, with the number of chapels under the said church, and an account of the Free Grammar-school near the town, and some observations on the trade of Halifax.

Chapter II. treats of the Gibbet-law.

Chapter III. contains a narrative of the manner of trying felons at Halifax, and executing of them at the Gibbet.

Chapter IV. gives an account of eminent persons within the precincts of Halifax, concluding with a catalogue of the Vicars of Halifax church. To all which is added a piece, called, "Revenge upon Revenge, or an historical narrative of the tragical practices of Sir John Eland of Eland, High Sheriff of the county of York, committed upon the persons of Sir Robert Beamont, and his alliances, in the reign of King Edward III, together with an account of the revenge which Adam the son of Sir Robert Beamont, and his accomplices, took upon the persons of Sir John Eland, and his posterity."

This William Bentley was Clerk of the parish church of Halifax.

BENTLEY, ELI,

Was born in the township of Sowerby, in this parish, at an house called Bentley Hollins. Calamy, vol. ii. page 804, says, that he was Fellow of Trinity College, in Cambridge; that in August, 1652, he became assistant to Mr. Booth, at Halifax, and after his death continued alone till August, 1662. He fled before the Five Mile Act, but in 1672 returned to Halifax, and preached in his own house. He died July 31, 1675, aged 49.

The character which this Author gives of Mr. Bentley, is, that he was a man of good parts, a solid, serious Preacher, of a very humble behaviour, and very useful in his place; that he lived desired, and died lamented.

On his death bed he thus expressed himself to a particular friend: "God will take a course with these unreasonable men, that require such terms of communion, as a man cannot with a safe conscience subscribe to."

He was Author of an explanation of one of St. Paul's Epistles, which was printed, but is now very scarce. It is so scarce, that we have some suspicion he has mistaken this name for that of J. Booth, [? Boyse,] mentioned below.

For the inscription over Mr. Bentley's remains, see the epitaphs belonging to Halifax Church.

BENTLEY, BRIAN,

Was buried at Halifax, June 9, 1679, where he had lived with the character of being a good Poet; but for our own part, we can say little to this, having never seen any composition of his, either in print or manuscript.

BRERETON, ROBERT,

Published a Sermon from Ecclesiastes xii. 13. entitled, " The great duty of fearing God, and keeping his commandments, with their advantage (if duly observed) to mankind, while on earth, preached in the Chapel of Luddenden, May 24, 1741.—Leeds, printed by James Lister."

Mr. Brereton (who was, in 1773, one of the joint Rectors in Liverpool) was at that time Curate of Luddenden, and Chaplain to Colonel Houghton's Regiment. Before the Sermon, is a short Address to the inhabitants of Midgley, Luddenden and Warley, in which he tells them that his sincere desire to promote virtue and holiness, was the reason of its being sent amongst them.

BRIGG, HENRY,

Was born at an house called Daisy Bank, adjoining to Warley Wood, (not as a Wood has expressed it, in an obscure hamlet, called Warley Wood.) His life has been wrote in Latin by the Reverend Dr. Thomas Smith. Also by the late Dr. Ward, in his lives of the Gresham Professors, page 120, who sets off with saying, that the time of his birth is uncertain.

In Halifax Register is the following entry, which we think will determine the dispute: " Henricus, filius Thome Bridge de Warley, bapt. 23, Feb. 1560." The different spelling of the name will make no alteration, if it be considered how little care was used to be taken in this respect, and also that

Bridge is generally here pronounced Brigg, or Briggs. As for other particulars relating to this very learned, and useful man, we refer the Reader to the Author above-mentioned, and to the Biographia Britannica, where he will receive ample satisfaction.

BROWN, SIR THOMAS,

Is said, in Bentley's History, page **89,** to have fixed himself in this parish, in his juvenile years, as a Physician, and to **have** wrote here, his Religio Medici.

Wright, page **152,** asserts the same, adding, that he composed this Piece at Shipden-hall, near Halifax, where he lived about the year 1630. **Whence** these Anecdotes were **obtained we** cannot say, for **little or** no tradition of this sort **remains there** now. Mr. Watson, late Rector of Stockport, **had an** edition of **his** Works in folio, printed at London, in **1686,** and Wright quotes another at London, in 1736. The **first** of these has an engraved head prefixed to it, done by Robert White, and underneath these arms:—Argent, **two** bendlets sable, between as many ogresses. For crest, on **a** Knight's helmet, with open **beaver,** a wreath, above all, **a lion** sedant.

BOSCO, JOHANNES DE SACRO.

Bentley, page 49, and **Wright, page** 137, have both mentioned this great Mathematician, **&c.** as a native of this parish. The first of these, we believe, depended upon report, **and** the second on what he read in Leland's Commentary de Scriptoribus **Britannicis,** page **353.** But **the** conjecture there is **certainly built on** a wrong foundation, that Sacroboscus is the same as Halifax ; for this may signify holy face, or holy hair, but cannot mean holy wood, nor did **we** ever see this name in any deed relating to Halifax parish.

We should be glad to shew, that Halifax was really the birthplace of this valuable **man, for, as ten** cities are said to have **laid** claim to Homer, the writers even of three kingdoms have **contended** for this extraordinary genius. Leland, as above, **that** he was an Englishman, and Thoresby, in his Topography, page 194, affirming that he lay on his back on the hill at Halifax, to observe the motion of the stars, when he wrote his celebrated book, De Sphæra. Dempster asserting that he was a Scotchman ; and Stanihurst, and others, that he was born at Dublin.

If Halifax parish has any right to him, the most likely place for him to be born at, is, we think, in Southouram, where is now the Chapel in the Groves, for we take that to have been used as a place for the exercise of Religion in very early times, perhaps as far back as that of the Druids.—If Ireland gave him birth, he came from Holy-wood, in the county of Dublin ; and if he had his name from any part of Scotland, it was from the Monastery called Sacer Boscus, or Halywood, mentioned in the Monasticon, vol. ii. page, 1057.

The Corporation Seal at Halifax, had a virgin hung in a tree by her hair, and a man holding up a globe in his hand, the first alluding to the common story of the young woman being put to death by the Monk ; and the second, to the above John's treatise on the Sphere ; it was a little unfortunate that the first of these is a disputed fact, and that the latter lays claim to a man who probably was never in Halifax parish in his life.

BOYSE, JOHN,

Was Preacher at Halifax Church in the time of Dr. Favour, the Vicar there. He was born in or near Halifax, and left a legacy to the poor there. It does not appear that any thing he wrote was printed, but in Thoresby's Museum (see Topography, page 539.) was a Manuscript Catechism of his, wherein he catechized the congregation at Halifax ; and his principles for the poor people there.

BOIS, WILLIAM,

Born in Halifax, and, according to the custom of the time and place, instructed in music and singing, wherein he afterward attained to great proficiency.

His education was at Cambridge, and having a dislike to Popery, he was obliged to retire to some place of safety in the reign of Queen Mary, and he seems to have pitched upon Nettlestead, near Hadley, in Suffolk, where, though he was in Orders, he took a farm, and lived as a Layman, marrying there Mirable Poolye, a Gentlewoman of good family, who survived him about ten years.

In the reign of Queen Elizabeth, Mrs. Bois urged her husband to act in the Ministry; on which account he took upon him to serve the Cure of Elmesett, near Hadley; and, after the death of the Incumbent, was presented by the Lord Keeper, to the Rectory; and not long after to the Rectory of West Stow, at the presentation of his brother-in-law, Mr. Poolye.

He died in the 68th year of his age. He had several children by his wife, but none lived any considerable time but one, who proved an ornament to his country, viz. Dr. John Bois, born Jan. 3, 1560, who had a considerable hand in the present translation of the Bible, and the sketch of whose life may be seen in Peck's Desiderata Curiosa, lib. viii. page 38.

In this sketch we are further told, page 40, that the Doctor's father was a great scholar, being excellently well learned in the Hebrew and Greek, which, considering the time he lived in, was almost a miracle.

BOOTH, ROBERT,

First Curate of Sowerby Bridge, afterwards Minister of Halifax, where he was buried July 28, 1657.

In Bentley's History of Halifax, page 81, we are told, " that this Mr. Booth, was a man of that worth and excellency in learning and divinity, that he deserved the title of another Apollos, and seemed, like Jeremiah, and the Baptist, to be separated from the womb to the ministerial office; so temperate and healthful, so industrious and indefatigable in the labours of his study, and so divinely contemplative in the exercise of his mind, that he appeared to be made up of virtue, being a stranger to all things but the service of heaven, for when he spoke to his congregation from the pulpit, it was with that power of truth, and elegance of style, that he charmed his hearers into love and admiration."

BROOKBANK, JOSEPH,

Son of George Brookbank, of Halifax, was entered a Batler in Brazen Nose College, in Michaelmas Term, 1632, aged 20, took a Degree in Arts, went into Orders, and had a Curacy. At length retiring to London he taught a school in Fleet street, and exercised the Ministry there.

He published, 1. Breviate of King's whole Latin Grammar, vulgarly called Lilly's ; or a brief grammatical table thereof, &c. London, 1660, 8vo. 2. The well tuned Organ ; or an exercitation, wherein this question is fully and largely discussed. Whether or no instrumental and organical music be lawfully in holy public assemblies. Affirmatur, London, 1660, 4to. in nine sheets and a half. 3. Rebels tried and cast, in three sermons, on Romans xiii. 2, &c. London, 1661, 12º.

BURTON, THOMAS,

Was M.A. and Vicar of Halifax. He published a Sermon preached in the parish church of Halifax, from Psalm xlvi. 10. on Tuesday July 7th, 1713, being the day appointed by her Majesty for a public thanksgiving for the peace. London, 1713, containing 16 pages in 8vo.

The principles advanced in this discourse are something extraordinary. At page 7, he says, " Kings receive no authority and power from their subjects, and therefore it is neither reasonable nor just that they should be accountable to them.—Some men are for storming Heaven, and snatching God's authority out of His hands, who has declared that by Him Princes reign, and yet they will tell you it is by them they reign, and the plainest Scriptures in the world cannot drive them out of this wicked and blasphemous opinion."

Speaking of the peace, he says, " It is such as our allies could reasonably desire ; 'tis a just, and therefore an honourable peace ; a peace that answers all the ends proposed when we engaged in a most bloody, and expensive war."

" We ought thankfully to own, that God overthrew our enemies, and reduced a powerful Prince to sue for peace ; and it would have been hard measure not to have granted it to him on such terms as we, among our little selves, should think it hard to be denied it.

To take from him what was his own, would be nothing less than robbery, and to reduce him to such circumstances that he shall not be capable of doing us, and his neighbours mischief, is as much as any honest and good man ought to desire ; and that he is reduced to such circumstances—no man can doubt, but such to whom it is natural to find fault with every thing, and who are of such a querulous temper as to complain when they are **not** hurt, and who, rather **than** to quarrel, will quarrel, even with peace itself, and who endeavour to disturb the nation with noise and clamour, without either sense or reason."

CRABTREE, HENRY,

Sometimes **wrote Krabtree, was** born, as some have thought, in Norland, **as others, in the** village of Sowerby, where he **was initiated in school learning** with Archbishop Tillotson.

He has left behind him **the** character of being **a good Mathematician** and Astronomer.

He published " Merlinus Rusticus, **or a** Country Almanack, yet treating of courtly matters, and the most sublime affairs now in agitation throughout the whole world.

1. Shewing the beginning, encrease, and continuance of the Turkish or Ottoman Empire.

2. Predicting the fate, and state **of the Roman and Turk-**ish Empires.

3. Foretelling what success **the** Grand Seignior shall have in this his war, in which he is now engaged against the German Emperor.

All these are endeavoured to be proved from the most probable, and indubitable arguments of history, theology, **astro**logy, together with the ordinary furniture of other Almanacks, by Henry Krabtree, Curate of Todmurden, in Lancashire.—London, printed for the Company of Stationers, 1685,"

COCKCROFT, WILLIAM,

Born, **as we take** it, at Souterhouse, in Wadsworth, where his father, and elder brother Thomas lived. He was of the family of the Cockcrofts, of Mayroyd, in Wadsworth.

He was an apprentice **in** Halifax, and afterwards a Cadet **in Mark** Ker's dragoons ; went to America, and married an **Indian** Lady, and was made Colonel **of** one of the provincial **regiments** in the province of New York, which regiment he commanded under Sir William Johnson, against the French, under M. Deskau, when, in the year 1755, the English arms were crowned with victory.

CROWTHER, [JOSHUA,]

Was born at Ealand, and was first a Dissenting Minister, afterwards he conformed, and being recommended by Lord Irwin to Archbishop Herrin, he was, by his interest with the Crown, made Vicar of Otley, in Yorkshire. He published a Sermon, but we can give the Reader no account of it.

DRAKE, FRANCIS,

Lived part of his time in Halifax, and died there. He took the degree of M.A. and published, " The nature of lying and of moral truth, set forth in two sermons, from Ephes. iv. 25, preached in the church of Halifax. Halifax, printed by P. Darby, 1760," forty pages in 4to. preceded by a short address to the Reader. The Author has also wrote a practical exposition on the church catechism, which is still in manuscript.

DEANE, RICHARD.

This Richard was son of Gilbert Deane, of Saltonstall, in this parish, by Elizabeth his wife, daughter of Edmund Jennings, of Silsden, in Craven ; that he was born at Saltonstall, and having been educated in Grammaticals in his own country, became, at seventeen years old, a Student in Merton College, in 1587, where continuing about five years as a Portionist he retired to Alban-hall, where he took the Degree of Bachelor of Arts, in October, 1592, and that of Master three years after, which was the highest Degree he took in this University.

A note, which came from Caermarthen, in Wales, asserted that he had taught School there, but we doubt the truth of it.

He was made Dean of Kilkenny, in Ireland, and, in the year 1609, succeeded Dr. Horsfall in the Bishopric of Ossory. He died on the 20th of February, 1612, and lies buried in the Cathedral at Kilkenny, under a marble monument near the Bishop's throne.

DEANE, EDMUND,

Brother to the above Richard, entered a Student in Merton College, in Lent Term, 1591, aged nineteen, where he took

one Degree in Arts, and then retired to Alban-hall, where
he became Bachelor and Doctor of Physic. He settled in
the city of York, and practised there till about the beginning
of the Civil Wars.

We have before us a small quarto pamphlet of his, intitled, "Spadacrene Anglica, or the English Spaw-Fountaine;
being a brief Treatise of the acide or tart Fountaine, in the
Forest of Knaresborow, in the West-Riding of Yorkshire.
As also a relation of other medicinall waters in the said
forest. By Edmund Deane, Doctor in Physicke, Oxon,
dwelling in the city of York." London, 1626.

The medicinal water at Haregate (commonly called
Harrowgate) is here described, and recommended, and it
appears that the first person who discovered it to have any
quality of this sort, was one Mr. William Slingsby, a Gentleman of a family in this neighbourhood, who, about 1571,
having drank of this water, found it to have the same virtues
as those at Spaw, in Germany.

FAVOUR, JOHN,

Born at Southampton, where he was educated in grammatical
learning, but finished for the University at Archbishop
Wykeham's school at Winchester. He was elected Probationer Fellow of New College, in 1576, and two years after
was made complete Fellow. June 5, 1592, he proceeded
Doctor of the Civil Law, and, according to Wood's Athenæ,
page 487, was made Vicar of Halifax, January 4, 1593.
August 1, 1608, he was made Warden or Master of St. Mary
Magdalen's Hospital at Ripon. March 23, 1616, he was
collated to the Prebendship of Driffield, and to the Cantor-
ship of the Church of York. He was also Chaplain to the
Archbishop, and Residentiary.

In the late Mr. Thoresby's Museum (Topography, page
539) were the heads of some Manuscript Sermons, preached
at the exercise at Halifax by this Vicar. In the same place
were also Manuscript marginal notes upon a very scarce
book, called, Fasciculus Temporum, published about 1485,
in the infancy of the art of printing. But his most considerable composition was a book printed in London in 1619,
containing 602 pages in quarto, and intitled, "Antiquitie
triumphing over Noveltie; whereby it is proved, that Antiquitie is a true and certaine note of the christian catholicke

church and verity, against all new and late upstart heresies, advancing themselves against the religious honour of **old** Rome, whose ancient faith was so much commended by St. Paul's pen, and after sealed with **the** bloud of many martyrs **and** worthy Bishops of that See. With other necessarie and important questions, incident and **proper** to the same subject."

It begins with a dedication to Tobie Matthews, Archbishop **of York,** wherein it appears, that the work was **begun** when **the** author was sixty years old, at the desire, and carried **on** under the encouragement of the said Archbishop. Next follows an epistle to the readers, wherein, amongst the impediments to this work, he reckons up preaching every Sabbath-day, lecturing every day in the week, exercising justice in the commonwealth, practising of physic and chirurgery.

This serves to confirm what **is said** of him in Halifax **to** this day, that he was **a** good Divine, **a** good Physician, and a good Lawyer. The Doctor, as an instance of the ignorance of the common people, when the Bible was kept from them, tells **us, at page** 334, a story **of** a woman, who, when she heard **the passion** of Christ read in her own tongue, wept bitterly, **and** tenderly compassioned so great outrage done to the Son **of God;** but after some pause, and recollection of her spirits, she asked, where this was done? and when it was answered, many thousand miles **hence,** at Jerusalem, and about fifteen hundred years ago; "then (says she) if it **was so far** off, and **so** long ago, by the grace of God it might **prove a lie,"** and therein she comforted herself.

This learned, useful man died March 10, 1623, and was **buried** in Halifax church. Thoresby, p. 260, says that he **married** at Leedes, **Nov.** 12, 1595, Ann, daughter of William **Power, Rector** of Berwick, [in Elmete.]

See the epitaphs belonging to this church.

FARRER, ROBERT,

Born in Halifax parish, perhaps at Ewood, for Thoresby, page 196, **seems** to think that he belonged to the family settled at Ewood, and Wright, page 140, says positively that he was born there. Dr. Johnson, in his Manuscript Collections for Yorkshire, says he left lands to his friends, called Threaphead, within four miles of Halifax, but I know not the situation of it.

He became, when a young man, a Canon regular of the Order of St. Austin, but in what priory or abbey is uncertain. Having partly received his academical education in Cambridge, he retired to a nursery for the Canons of St. Austin, in Oxford, called St. Marie's College, situated in the Bayley, where he was in 1526, as also October 14, 1533, when, as a Member of the said College, he was admitted to the reading of the Sentences, having a little before opposed in Divinity.

About the same time be became Chaplain to Archbishop Cranmer, after whose example he married, a practice at that time disallowed amongst the Popish Clergy. Willis, in his Survey of the Cathedrals, vol. I, p. 125, says he was the last Prior of Nostel in Yorkshire, to which was annexed the Prebend of Bramham, in York Cathedral, and that he surrendered his Convent in 1540, and had a pension of £100 per annum allowed him, which he received till his promotion in 1547, or 1548, to the Bishopric of St. David's, where, as Willis, p. 121, tells us, he became a most miserable dilapidator, yielding up everything to craving Courtiers. But this writer, I think, treats his character too severely; as likewise does A. Wood.

In the reign of Edward VI. fifty-six articles and informations were laid against him, by George Constantine, David Walter, his servant, Thomas Young, (after Archbishop of York,) Rowland Merick, LL.D. (afterwards Bishop of Bangor,) Tho. Lee, Hugh Rawlins, and others.

He was, partly on the importunate suit of his adversaries, partly on the fall of the Duke of Somerset, by whom he had been promoted and maintained, detained in prison till the death of King Edward, and the coming in of Queen Máry, when he was involved in fresh trouble; for he was now accused, and examined for his faith and doctrine, as he had before been for abuse of the authority committed to him, for wilful negligence, superstition, covetousness, and folly.

February 4, 1555, he was examined before the Bishop of Winchester (who was Lord Chancellor) and others, and being kept in prison uncondemned till the fourteenth day of the same month, he was sent down into Wales, there to receive sentence of condemnation; and being several times brought before Doctor Henry Morgan, the Popish Bishop of St.

David's, and refusing to renounce his heresies, schisms, and errors, as the said Morgan called them, he was degraded, condemned, and burned at Caermarthen, on the south side of the Market-cross there, March 30, 1555.

It was remarkable that one Jones coming to the Bishop a little before his execution, lamented the painfulness of the death he had to suffer; but was answered, that if he once saw him stir in the pains of his burning, he should then give no credit to his doctrine,

And what he said he fully performed, for he stood patiently, and never moved, till he was beat down with a staff.

The character of this man, is very differently related, Bishop Godwin asserting, that his ruin was owing to his own rigid, rough behaviour: A. Wood, that his doings were unworthy, and that he was not able to answer the first set of articles exhibited against him.

On the other hand, Fox, in his Book of Martyrs, seems clearly of opinion, that the first prosecution against him was unnecessary, and malicious; and that the second was commenced because he was a Protestant.

It is certain that some of the articles which he was put to answer in the reign of Edward VI. were to the last degree frivolous, and shewed themselves to be the offspring of a revengeful mind, such as riding a Scottish pad, with a bridle with white studs and snaffle, white Scottish stirrups, and white spurs—wearing a hat instead of a cap—whistling to his child—laying the blame of the scarcity of herrings to the covetousness of fishers, who, in time of plenty, took so many that they destroyed the breeders; and lastly wishing, that at the alteration of the coin, whatever metal it was made of, the penny should be in weight worth a penny of the same metal.

It is no great wonder, indeed, that malice should shew itself on this occasion, for it seems that two of the chief managers of this persecution, Dr. Young and Dr. Merick, had been removed from their offices by this Bishop, as he writes to the Lord Chancellor, "for their covetous respect to their own glory, and lucre, not regarding the reformation of sin, and especially of shameless whoredom."

The fall of the Duke of Somerset, then Lord Protector, to whom he was Chaplain, seems, in fact, to have been his greatest guilt; it certainly exposed him to the resentment of those who wished him ill; and who, we think, got very little credit to themselves as Reformers of religion, by their conduct towards him. Amongst the Harleian MSS., (see No. 420, of the Catalogue,) are several papers relating to the trial of Bishop Farrer, not printed in Fox. The book is called the 5th vol. of Mr. John Fox's Papers, bought of Mr. Strype.

FLETCHER, NATHANIEL,

A Schoolmaster, in Ovenden, in this parish, wrote 1. A Methodist dissected, or a description of their errors.

2. The tradesman's Arithmetic, in which is shewn the rules of common Arithmetic so plain and easy, that a boy of any tolerable capacity may learn them in a week's time, without the help of a Master. Halifax, printed by P. Darby. No date, but it was published in 1761.

FOE, DANIEL DE,

Being forced to abscond on account of his political writings, resided at Halifax, in the Back-lane, at the sign of the Rose and Crown, being known to Dr. Nettleton, the Physician, and the Revd. Mr. Priestley, Minister of the Dissenting Congregation there.

Here he employed himself in writing his piece, "De Jure divino," amongst other things; but in particular he is here said to have composed "The Adventures of Robinson Crusoe," the subject of which was taken from the papers of Alexander Selkirk, who had been left some time on the uninhabited island of Juan de Fernandas, and had given his memoirs to this Daniel, to methodise, who, instead of doing as his friend desired, struck out this entertaining Novel, and by the publication of it prevented Alexander's design of making some advantage from a recital of his adventures.

To this, the Author seems to allude in the Preface to the 3d. vol. called, "Serious Reflections," when he says, "That there is a man alive, and well known too, the actions of whose life are the just subject of these volumes, and to whom all or most part of the story most directly alludes, which may be depended upon for truth."

GRAHAM, WILLIAM,

A Dissenting Minister, living in Halifax, and late Preacher at Warley chapel, in that neighbourhood, took in Scotland a Degree in Arts.

He published a Sermon from Matthew x. 34, which he preached in Kingston upon Hull, June 21, 1758, at the Ordination of the Rev. Mr. John Beverley. London, 1759. The design of it is to vindicate Christianity from the charge of promoting disorders in society, whether civil or sacred; and to enquire whence such arose, and to what causes we must ascribe them.

GRÆME, WILLIAM,

A Gentleman of fortune, who lived at Heath, in Skircoat, near Halifax, was the Author of "A short Speech addressed to the antient and honourable Society of Free and Accepted Masons in a Lodge held at the Rose and Crown, in Halifax, upon Friday, the 24th of June, 1763."

Halifax, printed by Brother P. Darby, 1763.—And in the year of Masonry, 5763.

GREENWOOD, DANIEL, D.D.

Born in the township of Sowerby; was first Fellow, and afterwards made Principal of Brasen Nose College, in Oxford, by the Parliament Visitors in 1648, and was Vice Chancellor of that University in 1650 and 1651; in this latter year he was at the head of an association for the Parliament, raising, at the charge of the Heads of Houses, &c. 120 horse, and allowing the Governor of Oxford to acquaint the Council, that they had engaged to raise a regiment of foot out of the University and city.

This place he held no longer than the Restoration, when he was ejected from it.

We find him afterwards called Rector of Studley, in Oxfordshire, though Wood, in his "Fasti," says only, that on this event, he and his wife retired to Studley, and continued there in a private condition till her death.

This Author, under the year 1649, tells us, that this Daniel then took his Degree of D.D. and that he was a severe and good Governor, as well in his Vice Chancellorship as Principality.

After his wife's death, he lived in the house of his nephew, Mr. Daniel Greenwood, Rector of Steeple-Aston, near Dedington, in Oxfordshire, where dying Jan. 29, 1673, he was buried in the chancel of the church there, and soon after had a monument put over his grave with the following inscription, printed in Le Neve's Monumenta Anglicana, vol. I, p. 157, "Memorial Reverendi, pii, doctiq; Viri Danielis Greenwood, S.T. Professoris, Sowerbiæ in Com. Ebor. nati, Coll. Æn. Na. apud Oxoniense, primo Socii, dein Principalis, et eiusdem Academiæ per duos annos Vice Cancellarii; qui obiit 29 Jan., Anno Dni, 1673, æt. suæ 71."

GREENWOOD, DANIEL,

Son of John, was born in Sowerby abovesaid, became Scholar of Christ's College, Camb. and in 1648 was made Fellow of Brazen Nose College, in Oxford, by the endeavours of his uncle, Dr. Daniel Greenwood, the Principal of the said College, several Fellows being that year ejected on account of their attachment to the King.

In 1653, he was presented by the College to the Rectory of Steeple Aston, in Oxfordshire. He died of an apoplexy at Woodstock, in 1679, and was buried near the grave of his uncle above-named. Over his remains was a table of marble, fixed to the North wall of the chancel above named, with this inscription: "Heic etiam deponuntur reliquiæ rev. viri Danielis Greenwood, hujus ecclesiæ per annos xxv Rectoris, qui singulari erga Deum pietate, pauperes munificente, et omnibus quibus innotuit humanitate feliciter decurso huius vitæ stadio in cælest. patriam festinans, triste sui desiderium moriens reliquit, Oct. xiv. Au. Dom. 1679, æt. suæ 51." He published, 1. A Sermon at Steeple Aston, at the funeral of Mr. Franc. Croke, of that place, Aug. 2, 1672, on Isaiah lvii. 1-2. Oxford, 1680, 4to. 2. A Sermon at the funeral of Alexander Croke, of Studley, in Oxfordshire, Esq., buried at Chilton in Bucks, Oct. 24, 1672, on 2 Cor. vi, 7-8, Oxford, 1680, 4to.

GUEST, [JOSHUA.]

It is said that General Guest, (who bravely defended Edenburgh Castle against the Rebels in 1745,) was once a

servant at the Angel Inn at Halifax, which greatly redounds
to his honour, as probably he was promoted for his merit.

His parents lived at Lidgate, in Lightcliffe.—See the
epitaphs there. [A fuller account will be given in vol. 2.]

HARTLEY, DAVID, M.A.

Was born at Illingworth, in this parish. His father was
Curate there, and married, May 25, 1707, a daughter of the
Reverend Mr. Edward Wilkinson, his predecessor. This
Curacy Mr. Hartley afterwards resigned for the Chapel of
Armley, in the parish of Leeds, where he died, and left be-
hind him eight children.

This son David was brought up by one Mrs. Brooksbank,
near Halifax, and received his academical education at Jesus
College, Cambridge, of which he was a Fellow. He first
began to practice physic at Newark, in Nottinghamshire,
from whence he removed to St. Edmund's Bury, in Suffolk.
After this, he settled for some time in London, and lastly
went to live at Bath, where he died September 30, 1757,
aged 53. He left two sons and a daughter.

His elder son got a travelling Fellowship, and his younger
was entered at Oxford in Michaelmas Term, 1757. He published, "A View of the present evidence for and against
Mrs. Stephen's Medicines as a Solvent for the Stone, containing 155 Cases, with some Experiments and Observations."
London, 1739.

This book, which contains 204 pages in octavo, is dedicated
to the President and Fellows of the Royal College of Phy-
sicians, London, wherein the Author informs that body, that
about a year before, he published some cases and experiments, which seemed to him sufficient evidences of a dissolving power in the urine of such persons as take Mrs.
Stephen's medicines, tho' he did not then enter into the
discussion of that point, but left the facts to speak for themselves; finding, however, that a quite contrary conclusion
had been drawn from those instances, and others of a like
nature, as if the medicines did not dissolve, but generate
stones; he therefore republishes the same cases and experiments, with all cases favourable or unfavourable, perfect or
imperfect, which he had been able to procure, hoping that
he had obviated all objections, and even proved a dissolving
power in the medicated urine.

At page 175, of this book, are proposals for making Mrs. Stephen's medicines public, and a list is annexed of the contributions for this purpose, from April 11, 1738, to February 24 following, the amount of which was £1387 13s. He was the chief instrument in procuring for Mrs. Stephens the £5000 granted by Parliament. His own case is the 123rd in the above book. He is said to have died of the stone, after having taken above two hundred pounds weight of soap.

Mrs. Stephen's medicine was made public in the Gazette, from Saturday June 16th, to Tuesday, June 19th, 1739.

James Parsons, M.D., Fellow of the Royal Society, published an octavo, printed in London, 1742, containing "Animadversions on Lithontriptic medicines, particularly those of Mrs. Stephens, and an account of the dissections of some bodies of persons who died after the use of them." In this book are several cases laid down in Dr. Hartley's own words, and afterwards critically examined, in order to shew (particularly from those in whose bladders stones were found after death) that that celebrated medicine had no power of dissolving stones in the kidneys or bladder. And it must be owned, though with regret, that this Writer has succeeded in his proofs.

Dr. Hartley is said to have wrote against Dr. Warren, of St. Edmund's Bury, in defence of Inoculation; and some letters of his are to be met with in the "Philosophical Transactions." He was certainly a man of learning, and a reputed good Physician, but too fond of nostrums.

The Doctor's most considerable literary production, is a work intitled "Observations on man, his frame, his duty, and his expectations, in two parts." London, 1749, 2 vols. octavo.

The first part contains "Observations on the frame of the human body and mind, and on their mutual connections, and influences."

The work, it seems, took its rise from the Revd. Mr. Gay's asserting the possibility of deducing all our intellectual pleasures and pains from association, in a dissertation on the fundamental principle of virtue, prefixed to Law's translation of King's origin of evil.

The sentiments in this piece, led our Author to enquire into the power of association, and to examine its consequences in respect of morality and religion, and also its physicial cause, when by degrees many disquisitions foreign to the doctrine of association, or at least not immediately connected with it, intermixed themselves; for this reason, he has added thereto vibrations, and endeavoured to establish a connection between these; and has taken a great deal of pains to shew the general use of these two in explaining the nature of our sensations.

The second part contains "Observations on the duty and expectations of mankind," before which is an introduction, in which he says, that the contemplation of our frame and constitution appeared to him to have a peculiar tendency to lessen the difficulties attending natural and revealed religion, and to improve their evidences, as well as to concur with them in their determination of man's duty and expectations; with which view he drew up the foregoing "Observations on the frame and connection of the body and mind"; and in prosecution of the same design, he goes on in this part, from this foundation, and upon the other phænomena of nature, to deduce the evidences for the being and attributes of God, and the general truths of natural religion.

Secondly, Laying down all these as a new foundation whereon to build the evidences for revealed religion.

Thirdly, To enquire into the rule of life, and the particular applications of it, which result from the frame of our natures, the dictates of natural religion, and the precepts of the Scripture taken together, compared with, and casting light upon each other.

Fourthly, To enquire into the genuine doctrines of natural and revealed religion, thus illustrated, concerning the expectations of mankind here and hereafter, in consequence of their observance, or violation of the rule of life.

HEYWOOD, OLIVER,

Son of Richard, was born at Little Lever, in Bolton parish, in Lancashire, March 1629, and baptized in Bolton church the 15th of the same month.

He was designed by his parents for the Ministry from his birth, and he was also himself inclined that way.

In 1647, he was admitted Pensioner in Trinity College, Cambridge, under the tuition of Mr. Akhurst. Here he took the degree of B.A. but was afterwards called home from thence, his father not being able to support him there. Here for some time he lived retiredly, but at length became a Preacher, by the advice and solicitation of the neighbouring Ministers; and having preached some time about the country occasionally, he was invited to Coley Chapel, in this parish; soon after which, viz. Aug. 4, 1652, he was ordained in Bury Church, in Lancashire, by the Ministers of the second classes there.

He married to his first wife Elizabeth, daughter of the Rev. Mr. Angier, of Denton, in Lancashire, in 1655, by whom he had several children.

He had several disputes with part of his congregation; some were displeased with him because he would not admit all comers promiscuously to the Lord's Table without distinction; others, because he would not thank God for killing the Scots.

Once he was carried before Cornet Denham, by some of Colonel Lilburne's soldiers, and the Cornet told him that he was one of the Cheshire rebels; but by the mediation of friends he was dismist.

His annual income from Coley did not exceed £36 per annum; but he held a Lecture every Thursday, for several years, at the house of one Samuel Hopkinson, at the Stubbing, in Sowerby, for which he had a consideration: He had also a small paternal estate in Lancashire, exclusive of what he might receive from Mr. Angier's effects.

He had a presentation to the vicarage of Preston, in Lancashire, worth at that time an hundred pounds per annum, sent him by Sir Richard Hoghton, of Hoghton Tower, but on some account or other he declined it.

After the Restoration of King Charles II. he was prosecuted in the Consistory Court at York for not reading the Common Prayer a year before the Act of Uniformity commenced, and suspended ab officio; the suspension was published at Halifax, June 29, 1662.

On this he forbore preaching at Coley, but did not attempt to get off his suspension, because of the Act of Uniformity, which was to take place in Aug. following, and to which he could not conform.

Before it took place, however, he ventured to take leave of his flock, by two or three days preaching among them.

November 2, the same year, an excommunication was published against him in Halifax Church; on which he went to York, but found that nothing could be done for him, unless he would take the oath " de parendo juri, et stando mandatis ecclesiæ," which his conscience would not permit him to do.

In 1664 came out the " Writ de excommunicato capiendo," but he was not taken, though he ventured to preach to a few in his own house, and now and then even officiating in public churches, where there was a vacancy, with the leave of the Churchwardens.

On the coming out of the Five-mile Act, he left his family, and went into Lancashire and Cheshire, returning home but seldom.

After the edge of that Act was a little worn off, he took more liberty, and preached often publickly in the chapels of Idle, Bramhup, Bramley, Farnley, Morley, Pudsey, and Hunslet.

In 1669, preaching occasionally in a private house near Leeds, he was carried before the Mayor, who sent him to prison, but released him the next day at the intercession of some friends.

July, the same year, he preached in Coley Chapel, in the absence of Mr. Hoole, the Minister, at the desire of several of the people, for which a warrant was issued out to distrain upon ten pound's worth of his goods, but Calamy tells us that nobody would buy them.

At last he was restored, by the King's declaration, March 15, 1672, to ministerial employment in his own house, by Licence, as appears from a private register kept by himself. He ventured, however, to preach at Alverthorp, Lassel-Hall, Sowerby, Warley, &c. on the week-days.

On the calling in of those Licences he met with fresh troubles; for August 15, 1680, he was again cited into the Consistory Court at York, with his wife and others, for not going to the Sacrament at the Parish-church at Halifax; and for contempt in not appearing, they were all excommunicated, the sentences being read in Halifax Church, Oct. following, but keeping private, the storm soon blew over.

After this, he was indicted at Wakefield Sessions for a riotous assembly in his own house, and fined fifty pounds, for non-payment of which, and not finding sureties for his good behaviour in forbearing to preach, he was committed to York Castle, where he had both an expensive and troublesome confinement, and from which he was not freed without much difficulty. After a fatiguing, troublesome life, he died March 4, 1702, in the 73rd year of his age.

In a manuscript of his, sent **to one** Mrs. Hannah Stansfeld, in Sowerby, he says, "I have now been above fifty years labouring in the Lord's vineyard, studying, praying, and preaching, **at home and abroad,** travelling where Providence hath called, **and** have arrived well towards two years beyond the age **of a** man; now at last I am incapacitated for travel, not only with age, but a very sore shortness **of** breathing, called the asthma, so that I am confined much to **mine** own house, only can study, **preach in** my chapel, and exercise myself in writing **books, and** sermons, for those that desire them."

Thoresby, page 542, **says he** had a Diary **of this** Oliver Heywood's, whereby it appeared, that **in one year he** preached **one hundred and** five times, besides the Lord's days, kept **fifty** days of fasting and prayer, nine of thanksgiving, **and** travelled fourteen hundred miles in his Master's service.

In another part of his **Diary are** the following entries: "**This** year, 1677, I preached, besides Lord's days, sixty times, kept . . . . . **fasts, eight** days of thanksgiving, and travelled eleven hundred and ninety-eight miles.

"**This** year, 1678, **I preached** sixty-four times on week-days, **have** kept fifty **fast-days,** four days **of** thanksgiving, and travelled one thousand and thirty-four miles.

"**This** year, 1679, **I** preached seventy-seven times on week-days, **kept** fifty-two fast days, seven days of thanksgiving, and travelled thirteen hundred and eighty-six miles."

Under June 2, 1678, **is** the following remarkable passage: "Lord's day. **Preached too** long, being under a mistake a whole hour. I was employed six hours. **Not** weary."

His printed **works are** these: 1, "Heart Treasure," 1667. 2, "Closet Prayer," 1671. 3, "Sure Mercies of David," 1672. 4, "Life in God's Favour, 1679. 5, "Israel's Lamentations," 1681. 6, "Mr. Angier's Life." 7, "Baptismal **Bonds,**" 1687. 8, "Meetness for Heaven," 1690. 9, "Family Altar," 1693. 10, "Best Entail," 1693. 11, "A New Creature," 1693. 12, "Job's Appeal," 1695. 13, "Heavenly Converse," 1697. 14, "The Two Worlds," 1701.

15, "A Treatise of Christ's Intercession," 1701. Besides which he printed and prefaced several books of others. In the above Diary, which I saw in the hands of Mr. Dickenson, of Northouram, are these entries: [Jan. 18, 1677—Aug. 1679. See Vol. 2, Heywood's Diaries, just printed.—J.H.T.] Thoresby had a MS. copy of this [Angier's] Life, with notes and additions by Mr. Newcome, of Manchester.

The following is in Halifax Register: "Mr. Oliver Heywood, of Northouram, Clerke, aged twenty-five years, and Mrs. Elizabeth **Angier, of** Denton, Gentlewoman, aged twenty-one years, were published at the public meeting place, called Halifax Church, **at the** close of the morning exercise upon three Lord's Days, viz. April the 1st, the 8th, **the 15th, 1655."** Their marriage is not inserted in that Register.

I have seen, in the possession of the late Mr. David Stansfield, of Halifax, an original three quarters painting of this Oliver Heywood.

HEYWOOD, NATHANIEL,

Brother **to Oliver, was born at** Little Lever aforesaid, in September, 1638, educated in Trinity College, in Cambridge, and afterwards **with** Mr. Edward Gee, of Eccleston.

His first preferment was Illingworth Chapel, in this parish; from thence he removed in 1657, to Ormskirk, in Lancashire, where he continued till he was silenced in 1662.

This account is from Calamy, page 394; but if Mr. Heywood did not remove from Illingworth till 1657, he had ceased to be Curate there in 1656, for a Mr. Bradshaw signed a receipt in that year, **as** Curate of Illingworth, in the Book of Accounts belonging to Mr. Waterhouse's Trustees, at Halifax. On the liberty, in 1672, he licenced Bickerstaff and Scaresbrick, both in Ormskirk parish, preaching there each week alternately.

He died December **16, 1677.** After his death some Sermons of his were printed, entitled, "Christ displayed, as the choicest Gift, and the best Master," 8vo. 1679. They were published by his brother Oliver, who wrote the Epistle Dedicatory thereto.

Calamy tells us that one of his hearers, when he was going to quit his Living, expressing a desire for him still to preach in the Church, Mr. Heywood said he would as gladly preach, as they could desire it, if he could conform with a safe conscience; to which the man replied, "Oh, Sir! many a man, now-a-days, makes a great gash in his conscience, cannot you make a little nick in yours?"

HOOKE, RICHARD,

Probably the same who is mentioned in Wood's "Fasti," page 261, as having taken his degree of B.A. from New Inn Hall, in Oxford, in 1635, and supposed to be a Northampton-shire man; if so, he took the rest of his Degrees at Cambridge, being D.D.

When he was M.A. he was Minister of Lowdham, in Nottinghamshire, and wrote, "The Laver of Regeneration, and the Cup of salvation, in two treatises concerning Baptism, and the Lord's Supper." London, 1653.

This is Wood's account, and if true, shews that this per-formance had a second impression, for we have seen a work under his name, entitled, "The Laver of Regeneration, and the Cup of Salvation; two plain and profitable discourses upon the two Sacraments, the first laying open the nature of Baptism, and earnestly pressing the serious consideration, and religious observation of the sacred vow made by all Christians in their baptism.

The other, pressing as earnestly the frequent renewing of our baptismal vow at the Lord's holy table; demonstrating the indispensable necessity of receiving, and the great sin and danger of neglecting the Lord's Supper, with answers to the chief pretences, whereby the absenters would excuse themselves." 8vo. London, Printed, 1684, with a dedication to the inhabitants of the town and parish of Halifax.

The first discourse is from John i. 26, the second from 1 Cor. xi. 28. Wood says, that he also published one or more Sermons.

He was likewise Author of "The Nonconformist Champion his challenge accepted, or an answer to Mr. Baxter's "Petition for Peace," written long since, but now first published, upon his repeated provocations, and importunate clamors, that it was never answered.

"Whereunto is prefixed, an Epistle to Mr. Baxter, with some remarks upon his Holy Common-wealth; upon his

Sermon to the then House of Commons; upon his Non-conformist's plea for peace, and upon his answer to Dr. Stillingfleet." London, 1682, 157 pages in 8vo. Thoresby, in his Museum, (Topog. p. 542) had an 8vo. MS. in answer to this, entitled "The Duelling Doctor defeated," by T.J.M.A. (The just man's advocate, alias Mr. Thomas Sharp, whose mark this was,) being given by his widow [to Thoresby.]

Dr. Hooke died January 1, 1688-9, having languished for some time under great pain of a fistula. See the epitaphs at Halifax Church.

HOYLE, JOSHUA,

Born at Sowerby, received his first academical education in Magdalene-hall, in Oxford, and being afterwards invited to Ireland, was made Fellow of Trinity College, Dublin; there he took the Degree of D.D. and was elected Divinity Professor in that University. In this office he expounded the whole Bible through in daily lectures, and in the chiefest books ordinarily a verse each day, which work held him almost fifteen years.

Some time before he ended that work, he began the second exposition of the whole Bible in the Church of Trinity College, and within ten years ended all the New Testament (excepting one book and a piece) all the Prophets, all Solomon, and Job. He preached also and expounded thrice every Sabbath for the far greater part of the year, once every holy-day, and sometimes twice.

To these may be added, his weekly lectures (as Professor) in the controversies, and his answers to all Bellarmine's writings. On the breaking out of the Irish Rebellion, in 1641, he came into England, and was made Vicar of Stepney, near London, but being too scholastical, he did not please the parishioners.

He was constituted about this time, one of the Assembly of Divines, and furnished evidence against Archbishop Laud, on his trial, as to matter relating to the University of Dublin, whilst he was Chancellor thereof. At length, by the favour of the Committee of Parliament for the reformation of the University of Oxford, he became Master of University College, and the King's Professor of Divinity.

He was respected by Dr. Usher, the learned Primate of Ireland, in whose vindication he wrote, "A Rejoinder to

William Malone, Jesuit, his reply concerning the real presence." Dublin, 1641, in a thick quarto.

Dr. Hoyle died December 6, 1654, and was buried in that little old Chapel of University College, which was pulled down in 1668, and which stood in that place which is now the middle part of the present quadrangle, in that College.

HULME, NATHANIEL, M.D.

Lived for some time in Halifax with his uncle, . . . Hulme, M.D. He wrote, "Libellus de natura, causa, curationeque Scorbuti. To this is annexed a proposal for preventing the Scurvy in the British Navy, octavo." London, 1768.

KNIGHT, TITUS,

A Collier in this parish, who turned Preacher, published a Discourse, printed at Leeds, entitled, "The Faith of the Saints, being the substance of a Sermon preached at the opening of the New Meeting House, belonging to the Independents, in Blanket-row, Hull, on Sunday, April 9, 1769." By Titus Knight, Minister of the Gospel at Halifax, in Yorkshire. [A clever Collier too, Mr. Watson, and father of a Vicar of Halifax.]

LAKE, JOHN,

Was born, as I have been several times credibly informed, in that part of Halifax called Petticoat-lane ; his father's name was Thomas, and he was baptised at Halifax, December 5, 1624, as appears from the Register there.—His first education was at the Grammar-school near Halifax, from whence he was sent to St. John's College, Cambridge, before he was complete thirteen years of age, and put under the care of the famous Mr. Cleveland, whose Poems, Orations, Epistles, &c., he and his friend Dr. Drake, Vicar of Pontefract, collected into one volume, to which they prefixed his Life and Parentalia, and dedicated them to Bishop Turner, then Master of the College, octavo. London, 1687.

When he was B.A. he was made prisoner in College with the royal party, but escaping from thence, he fled to Oxford, and continued four years in the King's army. He was at Basing-house when it was taken, as also at Wallingford.—

When the royal cause was at the lowest, he refused the Engagement, as he had done the Covenant before, and entered into Episcopal Orders.—July 26, 1647, he preached his first Sermon, as Lecturer, at Halifax, but continued not long in that employment on account of his principles. In 1652, he went, as I take it, to Oldham, in Lancashire.

May 21, 1660, he was made Vicar of Leeds, but met with so much opposition from those who were for introducing Mr. Bowles, of York, that the Church doors were barred against him, and they were under a necessity of sending for a party of soldiers to secure his induction.

Being appointed to preach the first Synod Sermon at York, he performed it with so much applause, that Dr. Hitch, then Rector of Guiseley, and his great friend, desired a copy of it, which, without his knowledge, he shewed to Dr. Sheldon, Bishop of London, who soon after gave Mr. Lake the Rectory of St. Botolph's without Bishopsgate, London.

Here began (what he esteemed the principal honour and felicity of his life) his friendship with Dr. Sancroft, then Dean of St. Paul's, afterwards Archbishop of Canterbury, who had a particular esteem for him.

He returned, for some reason or other, to his native soil, and having, October 17, 1668, been instituted to the Rectory of Prestwich, in Lancashire, he was collated, July 16, 1670, to the Prebend of Fridaythorp at York, and on the same day to the Prebend of Halloughton, in Southwell, and to the Rectory of Carlton, in Lindrick, both in Nottinghamshire.

He was now Residentiary at York, and endeavouring to break the bad custom of walking in the body of the Cathedral during the time of divine service, he was insulted by the rabble, who, after breaking open the south door of the Minster, followed him home, assaulted him in his own house, and even took off a great part of the tiling, so that he was obliged to be rescued from them by Capt. Honeywood, the Deputy Governor.

May 7, 1671, he was collated to the Mastership and custody of the Hospital of St. Mary Magdalene, near Bautry; and October 9, 1680, installed Archdeacon of Cleveland.

Being nominated by William Earl of Derby to the Bishopric of Sodor in Man, he was consecrated December, 1682. And thence, by King Charles II, he was translated to Bristol

H

August 12, 1684, with liberty to hold his Prebend in commendam.

In the time of Monmouth's Rebellion, he went down to reside at Bristol, by order of King James II. though he was at that time much afflicted with the gout, and narrowly escaped being taken by the Duke's forces.

His conduct on that occasion was so pleasing to the King, that, before his return, he nominated him to the Bishopric of Chichester, in which he was confirmed October 19, 1685.

April 27, 1688, King James II. having renewed the Declaration he had set out the year before, for liberty of conscience, to favour the cause of Popery, was resolved to oblige the Clergy to read it in all their Churches; but Dr. Lake having first prevented the sending down the Declarations into his Diocese, went up to London, and after consultation with Archbishop Sancroft, and five other Bishops, at Lambeth, they agreed to petition the King, and therein to lay before him their reasons which inclined them to disobey the Order of Council which had been sent to them.

This Petition was delivered accordingly on the 18th day of May; and for this, such as had signed it were cited to appear before the Council; where refusing, on account of their Peerage, to give bonds to appear in the Court of King's Bench, the Archbishop, and six other Bishops, (amongst whom was Lake) were committed to the Tower by a warrant signed June 8th, and on the 15th were brought to the King's Bench Bar, arraigned, tried, and acquitted on the 29th, to the great joy of the generality of the people.

At the Revolution he refused to take the Oaths of Allegiance and Supremacy to King William and Queen Mary, for which he was suspended ab officio, and would have been deprived had he lived a little longer.

August 27, 1689, he made the following Declaration (which, no doubt, was meant as a vindication of this last act of his conduct) before Dr. Green, the Parish Minister, Dr. Hicks, Dean of Worcester, Mr. Jenkins, his Chaplain, Mr. Powell, his Secretary, and Mr. Wilson, his Amanuensis.

" Being called by a sick, and I think a dying bed, and the good hand of God upon me in it, to take the last, and best viaticum, the Sacrament of my dear Lord's body and blood, I take myself obliged to make this short recognition and profession.

"That whereas I was baptised into the Religion of the Church of England, and sucked it in with my milk, I have constantly adhered to it through the whole course of my life, and now if it so be the will of God, shall die in it, and I had resolved, through God's grace assisting me, **to have** died so, though at a stake.

"And **whereas** that Religion **of the Church of** England **taught me the** doctrine of non-resistance and **passive** obedience, **which I have** accordingly inculcated **into others**, and **which I took to** be the distinguishing character of the Church **of England, I** adhere no less firmly, and steadfastly **to** that, **and in** consequence of it, have incurred a suspension from **the exercise** of my office, and expected a deprivation. I find **in** so doing much inward satisfaction, and if the oath had **been** tendered at the peril **of my** life, I could only **have** obeyed by suffering.

"I desire you, my worthy **friends** and brethren, to bear witness of this upon occasion, and **to** believe it **as** the last words of a dying man ; and who is **now** engaged in the most sacred **and** solemn act of conversing **with** God **in** this world, and may, **for ought** he knows **to** the contrary, appear **with** these **very words in** his mouth at the dreadful tribunal.

Signed,   **Johan.** Cicestrensis."

This declaration caused many pamphlets **to be** published pro and con ; and may be considered as the beginning of the disputes **on** this subject, which, though but imperfectly at that time understood, is **now** too clear to need a comment.

Sir John Dalrymple, in his Memoirs, page 396, says, "the **above** was a weak declaration from a weak man, yet as the **last** words of a martyr, **it** was spread through the **nation, and** at that period of **civil** and religious ferment, **added** the **impulses** of religion to those of party in enthusiastic minds."

On the 21st of August, before the making **of** the above declaration, **he had** been seized with **a** trembling fit, which was the forerunner **of a** malignant **fever, and** convulsions, which carried **him off.**

On the application of **painful** remedies, he said, "And is life worth all **this,** at threescore years and five ? "

He died August 30th, 1689, and was buried in St. Botolph's Church, September 3rd.

We cannot find that he published anything except two Sermons, viz. 1, "A Sermon preached at Whitehall, May 29th, 1670, published by his Majesty's command," London, 1671. 2, "The true Christian's Character and Crown, preached in St. Botolph's Church, July 15, 1669, at the Funeral of Mr. William Cade, Deputy of that Ward." London, 1671, 4to.

MARSH, RICHARD,

Was born at Finhamsted, in Hertfordshire, in 1585, and educated at Cambridge, (though some have said that he was Fellow of All Souls College, Oxford.) He took the Degree of D.D. at Oxford, in 1636. In 1614, he was made Vicar of Birstall, in the West-riding of Yorkshire; in 1625, Prebendary of Southwell; and in 1634, he succeeded Archbishop Bramhall in the Prebend of Husthwaite, in the Church of York.

April 17, 1638, he was inducted into the Vicarage of Halifax, as appears by an entry wrote with his own hand.

In 1641, the King presented him to the Archdeaconry of York, or of the West-riding of Yorkshire; and in November, 1644, nominated him to the Deanry, on the death of Dr. Scott, the King being then at Oxford; but the confusions of those times would not permit him to be elected, much less installed, till the Restoration, when the former of these was performed August 17, and the other the 20th, 1660.

Dr. Peter Heylin made great interest, by his friends, to obtain this dignity, but was denied, to make way for Dr. Marsh, whom King Charles had so great a value for, that he desired him to be one of the Chaplains to attend him, when the Parliament had got him into their hands in 1648.

He was also Prebendary of Rippon, and as Walker, in his Sufferings of the Clergy, page 82, says, Vicar of Bourson, in Yorkshire, but we know not any such place.

And as the Doctor had these good preferments, so he was a great and very early sufferer for his attachment to the King his patron; for in 1642, he had his living of Halifax sequestered, for delinquency, to the use of the forces under Lord Fairfax, himself narrowly escaping from the town, but taken prisoner at Blackstone-edge, and carried to Manchester, where he was confined for some time, till he made his escape from thence, and got to the King at Oxford.

Thus he lost the benefit of his living for eighteen years together, and saw Halifax no more till the Restoration, when he returned, Sept. 16, 1660, and took possession of his Church again.

An old man, who was present, told **Mr. Beckwith**, of York, "that the Doctor went into the Church, with his Prayer-book under his arm, and finding Eli Bentley officiating there, he turned him out of the Desk, and read Prayers himself."

The loss which the Doctor sustained at Halifax (besides other places) amounted to more than four thousand pounds.

He did not live long to enjoy his Deanry, for he died October 13, aged 78, and was buried the 15th, 1663, in York Minster, near the Grave of Matthew Hutton, Archbishop of York, in the south aisle of the choir, and over him was an atchievement with his arms, impailing Grice, of Wakefield, but that atchievement is destroyed, and there only remained, in 1766, an escutcheon hung up near his grave, with his arms, viz. Gules, an horse's head couped argent. (That in Halifax Church is erased.)

He had resigned the Vicarage of Halifax some time before his death. He had been Chaplain to King Charles I., to Archbishop Laud, and to Dr. Matthews, Archbishop of York.

He was three times married. His first wife was the daughter of Mr. Stephens, by whom he had, 1, Tobias, born in 1633, (so called, we presume, after his patron the Archbishop); 2, Henry, baptized at Birstal, November 16, 1637; 3, Frances, married to Lewis West, father of Captain Richard West, of Underbank, whose only daughter married Mr. Fenton, of Underbank; 4, A daughter, married to Mr. Driffield, of Rippon; 5, Another daughter, married to Mr. Wymberley, of Post-Witham.

The Doctor's second wife was Elisabeth, daughter of Robert Batt, of Okewell-hall, near Birstal, and Fellow and Vice Master of the University College, Oxford, by whom one daughter, Catharine, born in trouble; for when her mother was big with child of her, the soldiers coming into the house in search of Dr. Marsh, and not finding him, supposed he might be hid in bed, and therefore stabbed their swords into the bed where his wife was laid, and so frightened and wounded her, that it immediately threw her into labour, and she expired almost as soon as she was delivered.

The Doctor fled to save himself, and a trusty servant-maid made her escape with the child in the night, with nothing but her shift on, carrying it in that condition in the dark, for fourteen miles, to a relation of the Doctor's, where it remained till the Restoration, when her father was at liberty to return.

This daughter, Catharine, married Mr. John Kay, of Gomersal, near Birstal, and died at Howley-hall, about 1730, leaving, by said Mr. Kay, 1, Robert Kay, of Howley-hall, whose daughter married Mr. Thomas Beckwith, of York; 2, Martha, wife to Dr. Robert Tomlinson, Rector of Wickham; which Martha was, in 1766 in her 104th or 105th year, and gave part of this account.

The Doctor's third wife was Frances, daughter of Mr. Grice, of Wakefield. She was buried in York Minster, July 25, 1665.

Mr. Beckwith, above-named, had, in 1766, an original painting of Dr. Marsh in his robes, which seemed to have been done when he was about sixty years of age.

The wives and children of delinquents being, by public ordinances, allowed the fifth part of the estate and goods which had been seized upon, the following Petition was sent in against Dr. Marsh, which we took from a paper, dated in 1650, containing a set of reasons against their receiving the said fifth part; but what was the effect of it we cannot tell.

" 1, Dr. Marsh was long since cast out of the Vicarage of Halifax for misdemeanors.

" 2, As wee conceive the said Dr. Marsh was never actually sequestered, or if hee was, never yet made his composition.

" 3, There was never any yett settled by authoritty in the room of the said Viccor to receive the profitts, except Mr. Wayte, who was appointed Viccor by the late Lord Fairfax.

" 4, The wholle profitts of the Vicarage doe in a manere wholy consist in Easter dewes, and Comunicant two penses, which wee conceive in equitty cannot be demanded, seeing thatt Easter comunicants have soe longe seased.

" 5, The people in that Viccarage have beene att greate charge in mayntayneing the Ministers, there beeing 12 chappelreyes in the said Viccarage att which they have had for the most part preaching Ministers, and very little or noe mayntayneance to most of them.

"6, The said Dr. Marsh had, when hee was expelled the Viccarage, several other Liveinges, as att Birstall, Yorke, Rippon, Sussex, hee was the latte Kinges Chaplayen, and one of the hie Comishon att Yorke, besides he hath a good estate of his owne in land, to the valeu of £30. per ann. and upwards.

"And whereas itt is declared, thatt this now demanded is for his children, being a fifth part, wee make bold humly to certiefie, thatt if itt should bee expected, and the people forst to pay itt, the greattest part of itt must come from those that are in far greater nesesitie then any of his children is likely yett to come too, and from those who have hazerded their lives, and laid out their estates in the Parliament's servise, and whose sufferings and loses have been very greate.

"The Peticioners unanimously, as well the inhabittants within the mother-church whom the said small tithes did chiefely concerne, and all the rest of the Vicarage, make it theire humble request, that the said Dr. Marshe's order for his fifth part may bee called in, and that the same, and all the rest of the said tithes or Easter oblacions may either wholy bee taken of, or otherwayes that the said tithes may be devided amongst the several Chapells and Mother-church, as the same was certified by the Com'. for the West Rideing of the county of Yorke upon an Act or Order of Parliment."

It must be observed, that the estate of one John Marsh, D.D. who was said to have been late of Halifax, in the county of York, was declared forfeited for treason, by an Act of November 18, 1652, but this we have reason to think was a misnomer.

Walker, in his Sufferings, &c., page 83, says, that the Doctor had one or more Sermons extant, but I have not seen any account of them.

MARSDEN, GAMALIEL,

A Student in Trinity College, Dublin, where he continued ten years, and part of the time was Fellow there.

He was turned out with Dr. Winter, on King Charles' Restoration, and came to England.

He had but five pounds when he landed at Liverpool, and knew no relations or friends he could repair to ; but resolved to go to Coley, in this parish, where his father had been minister. There he found friends, and was fixed in St. Ann's Chapel, in Southouram, from whence he was ejected by the Act of Uniformity.

He afterwards went into Holland, and, at his return, taught Philosophy, &c., to some young Students at Hague-hall. He was also Pastor of the Congregational Church at Woodkirk. He died May 25, 1681, aged forty seven.

MIDGLEY, SAMUEL,

The real Author of the History of Halifax, which goes under the name of William Bentley.—This man was a prisoner for debt in York Castle, in 1685, where he was acquainted with Oliver Heywood. He was also three times in Halifax jayl, for debt. Here it was he wrote the above History; and here he died, July 18, 1695.

His poverty prevented him from printing the Book, which he wrote for his own support; and he not only lost the benefit of his labours in his life-time, but had another man's name put to his Work when he was dead. " Sic vos non vobis, &c."

He practised Physic, and was the son of William Midgley, who was buried at Luddenden, August 21, 1695, aged eighty-one.

MILNER, JOHN,

The second son of John Milner, of Skircoat, near Halifax, by Mary, daughter of Mr. Gilbert Ramsden, was baptized February 10, 1627-8. The foundation of his great learning was laid in the Grammar school there, from whence he was sent, at fourteen years of age, to Christ's College, Cambridge, where he took the Degrees of B.A., M.A. and B.D. He was first Curate of Middleton, in Lancashire, but was forced thence, on Sir George Booth's unsuccessful attempt to restore King Charles II. a little before the fight at Worcester. After this he retired to the place of his nativity, where he lived till 1661, when Dr. Lake, then Vicar of Leeds, and his brother-in-law, gave him the Curacy of Beeston, in his parish. In 1662, he took the Degree of B.D. and the same year was made Minister of St. John's, in Leeds. He was elected Vicar of Leeds, and was inducted thereto August 4,

1673, and March 29, 1681, was chosen Prebendary of Ripon. In 1688, not being satisfied about the **Revolution**, he retired from his Vicarage, and was deprived **of all his** Preferments; on **which** he retired **to** St. John's, in **Cambridge**, where he spent **the remainder of his** days, **continuing a** Nonjuror till his death, which **happened** in the **said College**, February 16, 1702. **He was buried in the Chapel there, on the** 19th, **aged** seventy-five, **leaving an only son, Thomas Milner,** M.A. **Vicar** of Bexhill, **in Sussex.**

It is remarkable, **that both Bishop Lake** and he were born in Halifax **parish**, both **educated** in Cambridge, were both **Vicars of Leeds**, and both **lost their** preferments **for Non-jurancy, in 1688.** His Works are **these:** 1.—Conjectanea **in Isaiam ix. 1, 2.** London, 4to., **1673."** This he published **whilst he was Minister** of St. John's, in Leedes. It **was** dedicated to his learned friend, **Dr.** Duport, Master **of Magdalene** College, Cambridge. Dr. Castel, Professor of Arabic at Cambridge, called this " a most excellent Essay, wherein the Author shewed incredible reading and diligence, in perusing so many copies, versions, and various lections, with the best **interpreters** of Sacred Writ. " See Vicaria Leodiensis, p. 114.

2.—A **collection of the Church** History of Palestine, **from** the Birth of Christ, to the beginning of **the** Empire of Diocletian, **London,** 1688, **4to.**

3.—A short Dissertation concerning **the four last Kings of** Judah. London, 1689, 4to.

4.—De Nethenim **sive** Nethinæis, &c. Cantab. 1690, 4to.

5.—An Answer to the Vindication of a Letter from a Person of Quality in the North, concerning the Profession of John, **late** Bishop of Chichester, London, 4to. 1690.

6.—A Defence of the Profession of John, Lord Bishop of **Chichester,** made upon his death bed, concerning Passive Obedience, and the New **Oaths; with** some passages of his Lordship's Life. London, **4to,** 1690. These two last are omitted by Thoresby, in his Vicaria Leodiensis, p. 116.

7.—A Defence of Archbishop Usher against Dr. Cary and Dr. Is. Vossius, &c., Camb. 1694, 8vo.

8.—A Discourse of Conscience, &c., with Reflections upon the Author of Christianity not Mysterious, &c., London, 1697, 8vo.

9.—A **View** of the Dissertation upon the Epistles **of** Phalaris, &c., lately published by the Rev. Dr. Bentley, also, of the Examination of that Dissertation, by the Hon. Mr. Boyle. London, 1698, **8vo.**

10.—**A brief** Examination **of some Passages in the Chron-ological Part** of a Letter written to **Dr.** Sherlock.

11.—**A further** Examination of ditto.

12.—**An Account of Mr.** Locke's Religion, London, **1700,** 8vo.

13.—Animadversions upon **Mons.** Le Clerc's Reflections upon our Saviour, &c., Camb. 1702, 8vo.

He also left the following manuscripts behind him, which came to the hands of his son :

1.—A Translation of the Targum.

2.—A Chronological History from **the Flood** to our Saviour's Birth.

3.—Ditto of the five first Centuries, A.D.

4.—Animadversions on the Historical Account of the Jewish High Priests.

5.—An **Answer unto, or** Animadversions upon **R.H. on** Controversies.

6.—Ditto upon T.C's. Labyrinthus Cantuariensis. This he lived **not to finish.**

7.—Animadversions upon Irenicum.

8.—A Vindication of the Church of England in reference to Antiphones, Responds, &c.

9.—A Latin Comment on part of Genesis.

10.—Ditto upon Psalms 1, 42.

11.—Diatriba de igne Purgatorio.

12.—Fax nova Linguæ Sanctæ.

I will only add the **character** which Dr. Gower, Lady Margaret's Professor at Cambridge, gave of this Mr. Milner, to Mr. Thoresby.——" Great learning and piety made him **really a** great man ; he was eminent in both, and nothing but his humility and modesty kept him from being more noted for being so. He was a blessing to the whole Society, by the example he gave in every good thing. He died beloved, and much lamented here, and his memory is hon-ourable and precious amongst us, and will long continue so."

MITTON, JOHN,

Son of Thomas, was born at Geslingroid, in the township of Barkisland, in this parish, and died at London about the latter end of the year 1736. He turned his thoughts, it seems, to natural philosophy, for in Thoresby's Museum (Topog. page 548) was a manuscript diary, giving an account of the rising and falling of the Barometer, the point of the compass the wind was upon, and some account of the temperature of the air, as rain, snow, frost, mist, &c., from Octo. 1710, till December, 1713, by Mr. John Mitton, of Barkisland, near Halifax.

NABB, ...

Wrote a Poem in 4to, called, "Calista, or, The injured Beauty, a Poem founded on fact." London, 1759. It is anonymous, and only said to be written by a Clergyman; but the Author, who resided some time at Halifax, being dead, I have ventured to give the public as much as I knew of his name.

NALSON, ROBERT,

The Collector of a folio manuscript, intitled, "Miscellanea sive Observationes collectaniæ," and signed Robert Nalson, 1665. This volume (which is in my own collection,) consists of a vast variety of subjects, chiefly transcripts, but interspersed with original papers, and others so scarce that they are nearly as valuable as if they were known originals. Wright, at page 80 of his history says, this manuscript unfortunately fell into ill hands, and had several pages, all of them relating to the Gibbet Executions, torn out, before the book was returned to the proper owner. Where he received that information I cannot tell, but it appears not from the book itself.

The late Mr. Wilson, of Leeds, in his manuscript account of the English Historians, in two volumes folio, now at the Free Grammar School at Leeds, says, that Mr. Nalson left manuscripts to Halifax Library, but nothing of that sort appears now, and I judge it to be a mistake.—The Author tells us, that he received confirmation from Archbishop Frewin in 1664, in his own chapel at Bishopthorpe, and that he was then about thirty-nine years of age.

NETTLETON, THOMAS,

Son of John, born at Dewsbury, settled at Halifax, and practised Physic there for several years with great success, having taken degree of M.D. at Leyden. He and Mr. West, of Under-bank, near Penniston, in Yorkshire, were the first who instructed Professor Sanderson in the principles of mathematics, and the Doctor used to say, that the Scholar soon became more knowing than his Masters. In the Philosophical Transactions appear several pieces of the Doctor's, which were communicated by Dr. Jurin, who was his friend and acquaintance, viz. "An account of the height of the Barometer at different elevations above the surface of the earth."

We have here the altitude of Halifax Bank determined at five hundred and seven feet; and after some observations on the air, follows a table, shewing the number of feet ascending, required to make the mercury fall to any given height in the tube from thirty to twenty-six inches; as also the number of feet descending, required to make the mercury rise from thirty to thirty-one inches; and also a table shewing the number of feet required to make the mercury fall one tenth of an inch from any given height in the tube from thirty-one to twenty-six inches, In Vol. vi. page 121 of the "Transactions" abridged by Reid and Gray, is an account of inoculation of the small-pox, by the Doctor; and at page 129, another treatise by him on the same subject.

In a paper of Dr. Jurin's, page 131, it appears, that Dr. Nettleton had inoculated sixty-one persons, when all others in England (as far as could be gathered) had only inoculated one hundred and twenty-one. At page 161, is a discourse by the Doctor, shewing that the refractions of the air are different at different times. From his observations it likewise appears that Halifax is in the latitude of 53. 47. that the height of Blackstone-edge, at Robin-hood's-bed, is two hundred and thirty-nine yards and a quarter; that Halifax Bank bears from this 60° from north to east; Manchester 40. 30. from south to west; Rochdale 70. 20. from south to west.

The Doctor was Author of a pamphlet, intitled, "Some Thoughts concerning Virtue and Happiness, in a Letter to a Clergyman." London, 1729, 8vo., which he afterwards much enlarged. It was reprinted in **1736, and 1751,** at London, both in **8vo.** but the former of these is the more valuable, because it had the Author's finishing hand. The design of this valuable work is to shew that happiness is the end of all our actions; how we deviate from our true happiness; and how these deviations may be prevented. He has also given us some excellent rules for the management of our several passions, and has undeniably proved, that virtue is the best and chiefest good; that it is not only the support and ornament of society, and beneficial to mankind in general, but the truest, and most substantial happiness to every particular person, as it yields the greatest pleasure, both in its immediate exercise, and in its consequences and effects; that it gives a relish to all other pleasures, and where it is wanting, there can be no true nor lasting pleasure, but all will be bitterness, horror, and remorse, without the least mixture of any thing gentle and agreeable.

The following story is told of the Doctor: That being in company with several Gentlemen, one of them was laying great stress on Dean Echard's account of Cromwell's selling himself to the Devil before the Battle of Worcester; affirming, that the bargain was intended to be for twenty-one years, but that the Devil had put a trick upon Oliver, by changing the twenty-one into twelve, and then turning hastily to the Doctor, asked him, "What could be the Devil's motive for so doing?" The Doctor, without hesitation, answered, "That he could not tell what was his motive, unless he was in a hurry about the Restoration."

The Doctor married, March **30, 1708,** Elizabeth Cotton, of Haigh-hall, by whom he had several children. He died January **9, 1741-2,** at Halifax, and was buried on the 12th, at Dewsbury, with the following epitaph on the south wall of the Church.

H.S.E.

THOMAS NETTLETON, M.D.

Artis suæ Facultate
Prope singulari **insignis;**
Aliarumque Artium
Quæ ad Humanitatem excolendam
Et Virtutem promovendam pertinent,
Laude cumulatus.

> Modesta Ingenii Sagacitas vere amabilem,
> Pietas autem non simulata,
> Comitate condita Gravitas,
> Ac simplex Morum Candor
> Amabiliorem præstiterunt.
> Nec Famæ celebritati,
> Nec Divitiarum incremento studuit ;
> Eum ratus uberrimum solertiæ quæstum,
> Quamplurimus prodesse.
> Indolem hanc adprime liberalem
> Natura ingenuit,
> **Vitæ** institutum aluit.
> Studium denique humanioris Philosophiæ,
> Ac diuturna cum **Viris** maximis
> Sandersono, Halleio, **Newtono,**
> Consuetudo abunde **confirmavit.**
> Scriptis Auctor limatissimus,
> Atque hoc Monumento perennioribus,
> Elegantem Virtutis, et Felicitatis imaginem
> Mirus Artifex adumbravit :
> Illustrissimum antem Exemplar
> Nativo colore Vitæ expressit.
> Tot, tantisque Dotibus ornatus
> Vixit annos LVIII.
> **IV.** Id. Jan. MDCCXLI.

OGDEN, SAMUEL,

Born, as I take it, in **or near** Manchester, was Curate of Coley, **in** this parish, afterward **Master** of the Free Grammar-school near Halifax, and Curate of Eland. He was Fellow of **St.** John's College, in Cambridge, where he took the Degree **of D.D.** and was made **Vicar** of Damerham, in Wiltshire. **He published two Sermons,** preached before **the** University **of Cambridge, in 1758,** one from 1 Thess. v. **13.** upon May 29, **being the Anniversary of the Restoration of** King Charles II. **the** other from Deut. iv. 6. on June 22, **being** the Anniversary of the Accession of his Majesty King **George II.** Both dedicated to his Patron the Duke of Newcastle, Chancellor of the University of Cambridge. He has also published some Sermons on the Efficacy of Prayer and Intercession, printed at Cambridge. The Doctor was chosen Woodwardian **Professor** of the University of Cambridge.

PATCHIT, BENJAMIN,

An inhabitant of Upper Saltonstall, in the higher part of Warley, in this parish, published a pamphlet, intitled, "A short Inquiry into the proper Qualifications of Gospel Ministers, considered as the Servants, not of Men, but of Jesus Christ; with some Directions, how we, who are Hearers, may know whether the Doctrines our Ministers deliver from the Pulpit, are according to God's Will and Mind, or not. And also how we are to attend on the Word preached in a profitable manner." Halifax, 1759, 8vo.

POWER, HENRY,

Took the Degree of M.D. and practised Physic in Halifax, from whence Wright, in his History, page 171, says, he removed to New Hall, near Eland, and died there; but Wilson, in his manuscript account of the English Historians, already mentioned, tells us, that he removed from Halifax to Wakefield, where he died December 23, 1668. He wrote a Treatise, intitled, "Experimental Philosophy, in three books, containing new Experiments, microscopical, mercurial, and magnetical," 4to. London, 1664.——The Doctor was buried at Wakefield, for on a brass plate on the chancel floor in the Church there is the following inscription :

"M.S.
Desideratissimi Capitis
HENRICI POWERI,
Medicinæ Professoris,
Ingenio, judicio, Moribus excultissimi,
Qui si vixisset diutius
Non in Arte solum, verum etiam in Humanitate
Bene multa Coum ipsum, Pergamenmq; docuisset.
Si quid dubites, Hospes, si repugnes, Ecce !
Non in re microscopica, et hydrargyrica,
Sed in reliqua philosophica, medicaque
Poweri singularis eruditio,
Perennitatis in Larario,
(Justa cum Doctorum admiratione)
Tum ex peremptis hic illic morborum seminibus
Cum ex editis in lucem Doctrinæ pignoribus
Jamdudum inclaruit.
Annos natus XXXV. non major obiit.
Vir cognitione quam ætate grandior.
Obiit XXIII Decembris, MDCLXVIII."

RAMSDEN, HENRY,

Was son of Geoffry Ramsden, of Greetland, in this parish, and was admitted a Commoner of Magdalene Hall, in Oxford, in 1610.

He took the Degrees in Arts, and was elected Fellow of Lincoln College, in 1621, and five years afterwards, leaving that place, became a Preacher in London, and was much resorted to for his edifying and puritanical sermons.

At length, on the death of Hugh Ramsden, his elder brother, he was made Vicar of Halifax, where he continued till his death, in 1637, and was buried in the Chancel of Halifax Church, with an inscription to his memory, which see amongst the Halifax Epitaphs.

After his death were published, under his name, by John Goodwin, with his Epistle before them, four Sermons, viz.

1.—The Gate to Happiness, on Romans vi. 8.   2.—The wounded Saviour, on Isaiah liii. 5.   3.—Epicure's Caution, on Luke xxi. 34.   4.—Generation of Seekers, on Coloss. iii. 1.   The book was intitled, " A Gleaning of God's Harvest." London, 1639, 4to.

The Register at Halifax has this entry : "Henricus Ramsden, filius Galfridi Ramsden, de Greetland, infra Vicariam de Hallifax, frater natu minor, M.A., Socius Collegii Lincolniensis, Oxon. inductus est Vicarius de Hallifax decimo calend. Septembris, Anno 1629.'' His widow died at Eland, May 11, 1682.

RICHIE, JAMES,

Is said to have been M.D.   He was a Dissenting Minister at Mixenden Chapel, in this parish, and practised Physic in that neighbourhood.   His publications were :

A Criticism upon modern Notions of Sacrifices, being an Examination of Dr. Taylor's Scripture Doctrine of Atonement examined, in relation, 1.—To Jewish Sacrifices.   2.— To the Sacrifice of our Lord Jesus Christ.   To which is added an Appendix, containing an Examination of another Notion of Jewish Sacrifices, which is exhibited in an anonymous piece published at London in 1746, and intitled, " An Essay on the Nature, Design, and Origin of Sacrifices." London, 1761.

This was intended as a prelude to a larger work afterwards printed, and intitled, "The peculiar Doctrines of Revelation, relating to piacular Sacrifices, Redemption by Christ, Faith in him, the Treatment of different moral Characters by the Deity, under the several Dispensations of **Revealed** Religion, &c., exhibited as they are taught in Holy **Scripture,** and the Rationale **of them** illustrated, in **two** Essays, **viz.**

1.—On the Rectitude of divine moral Government, in the Treatment of Rational Creatures.

2.—On the Rectitude of divine moral Government, in the Treatment of different moral Characters, under the several Dispensations of Revealed Religion, viz. the Adamical, Patriarchal, Hebrew, and Christian.

To which are subjoined two Dissertations, viz.

1.—On the Office of Jesus Christ as Mediator, and Surety of the New Covenant.

2.—On the Person of Jesus Christ." With a Preface to the whole. Warrington, **1766,** 2 vols. 4to.

This Work was posthumous, though the Author had put the finishing hand to it, and had even sent the manuscript to the press. It was published by subscription, and subscribers' names were printed.

ROOKEBY, WILLIAM,

Born, as Wilson asserts, in his manuscript account of English Historians, at Kirk Sandal, in Yorkshire, though Tanner says that he was born in Halifax.

He was educated, says Wood, in his Athenæ, vol. i. page 659, partly in an ancient Hostle for the reception of Canonists in St. Aldate's parish in Oxford; he himself being afterwards Doctor of the Canon Law.

He was made Rector of Sandal, where he was born, and Vicar of Halifax. In **1498,** according to Sir James Ware, vol. i. page 153, he was made Lord Chancellor of Ireland by King Henry VII., but Wood fixes this to the year 1515, not knowing that this was his second election into that high office, which he is supposed after this to have held for life.

In 1507 he was advanced to the Bishopric of Meath, by Pope Julius II. and the same year called into the Privy Council by King Henry VII. And was afterwards, by the same Pope, translated to the See of Dublin, January 28,

I

1511-12, and on the 22nd of June following had restitution of the Temporalties.

In 1518, he convened a Provincial Synod, the Canons of which are yet extant in the Red Book of the Church of Ossory; and were from thence published by Sir Henry Spelman, tom. ii. page 726. See also Wilkins, vol. ii. page 660.

He died November 29, 1521, and his body was buried (says Sir James Ware) in his own Cathedral of St. Patrick's, Dublin, only his heart was conveyed into England, and deposited in the monument of his ancestors.

This may be true, but it is directly contrary to the words of his Will, which ordered that he should be embowelled, and his bowels and heart buried in the Church of Halifax, within the choir, and his body to be buried in the new Chapel at Sandal, and thereon a tomb of stone to be made, and about the same to be written:

"Ego Willielmus, Dublin, Archiepiscopus, quondam Rector istius Ecclesiæ, credo quod Redemptor meus vivit—Qui obiit —cujus animæ propitietur Deus, Amen."

There is no proof, it must be owned, that his body was conveyed to Sandal. That his heart and bowels were buried at Halifax seems certain, for Wright, page 43, says, they were buried in the Chancel of Halifax Church, and over them was laid a stone, with the figure of an heart engraved thereon; and that when the Chapel, which he had ordered to be built on the north side of Halifax Church, was finished, they were removed into it, with the stone which lay over them, which yet remains, though his heart and bowels may not be there, for the earth has been suffered to be opened, and once, if not oftener, the little lead box which contained them has been dug up.

The Archbishop beautified and repaired the Vicarage-house at Halifax.

ROOTE, HENRY.

This was the person whom Mr. Tillotson (afterwards Archbishop) consulted, in 1649, about taking the Engagement at Clare-hall, Cambridge. He published a pamphlet, intitled, "A just Apologie for the Church of Duckenfield," 4to. This was a defence of one Eaton, who was at the head of a congregational Assembly there, **against** the reflections **of one** Edwards, and is dated from Sowerby, March 2, 1646.

SAVILE, Sir JOHN,

Eldest son of Henry Savile, Esq ; **of** Bradley, **in the town- ship** of Stainland, **in** this parish, by Ellen, daughter **of Mr.** Robert Ramsden, was born **at** Bradley, in 1545, **and entered a** Commoner **of** Brasen-Nose College about the **year 1561 ; from** whence, before **he** took **any** Degree, he **was removed to the** Middle Temple, where, being called **to** the Bar, **he became** Autumn Reader of that House in **1586, Steward of the** Seigniory or Lordship **of** Wakefield, and was **called to the** Degree and Honor of **the** Coif in 1594, made **one of the** Barons of the Exchequer 1598 ; **and** about the **same time, one of** the Justices of **Assize. When** King James came to the Crown, he not only continued him in his Baron's place, but conferred on him, **July 23, 1603, a** little before his Coronation, the honour **of Knighthood, being one of the** Judges who were to attend **that** solemnity.

He died **at** London, Feb. **2, 1606,** aged sixty-one, and **was buried in St.** Dunstan's Church **in the** West, in Fleet-street ; his heart **being** carried **to Methley Church, in** Yorkshire, and buried **in the** south aisle there, **and** a monument erected over it, with **the** figure of the deceased, cut in **stone,** in his Judge's robes, and the following inscription :

"M.S. Viri clarissimi et Judicis integerrimi Johannis **Savile,** Equitis **Aurati,** Scaccarii Regii Baronum unius, ac ex speciali gratia Regis in proprio Comitatu suo Justiciarii Assiz. Filii et Hæredis Henrici Savile, de Overbradley, in Stainland, juxta Eland, **in isto** agro Eboracen. Armig. ex antiqua Savillorum prosapia oriundi. Que sedo die Februarii, **Anno** Dom. 1606, ætatis **61.** Londini (ubi corpus ejus in Ecclesia Sancti Dunstani **in** Occidente inhumatur, Cor vero **secundo** hic inter Antecessores) placidissime **in** Domino obdormivit.

"Vir fuit pietatis zelo, ingenii perspicatia, morum suavit- ate, rerum Principis et Patriæ agendarum dexteritate, variis et exquisitis animi dotibus undique conspicuus.

"Ex uxore prima, Jana. filia Richardi Garth, de Morden, in Com. Surr. Armigeri, habuit Henricum Savile, postea Militem et Baronettum, ia hoc tumulis repositum; Elizabeth- am, **uxorem** Henrici Gooderick, Militis, modo viventem.

Ex uxore secunda, Elisabetha, **filia** Thomas Wentworth, de Elmshall, **in** Co. Ebor. Armig. habuit Johannem Savile, **superstitem,** prefati Fratris **sui successorem et** hæredem propinquum, **et** Helenam, quæ **in minovie ætate** obiit.

"Patri pientissimo filius obsequntissimus superstes **sup-**radictus hoc amoris memoraculo parentavit."

Camden, **vol.** ii., **page 857, sais, that his** work was much indebted **to the learning of this Sir John** Savile, and himself **to** his civility.

He left behind him at his **death several** pieces fit for **the press,** of which only the following **is made** public, "**Reports of divers** special **Cases, as** well **in the** Court of Common **Pleas** as of the Exchequer, **in the time of Queen** Elizabeth." London, 1675, **in a** thin folio, **printed in old French,** in a **black character, and** published **by John Richardson,** of the **Inner Temple.**

SAVILE, Sir HENRY,

Brother to Sir John, last named, **was** born at Bradley afore**said, November 30, 1549. In the** beginning **of** the year **1561,** he was admitted **into Merton** College, Oxford, and **January 14, 1565,** took the **degree of B.A.,** soon after which he was elected Fellow of **Merton.** April 30, 1570, he proceeded M.A. reading **for that** degree on the Almagest of **Ptolemy,** which procured **him** the reputation **of** a man **wonderfully** skilled in the Greek language, and the Mathematics. **In this** last he voluntarily read **a** public Lecture in the University for some **time.** Having now great interest, he was elected Proctor for two years together, viz. 1575 and 1576, **an** honour **not** very common, for **as the** Proctors were then chosen **out of the** whole body of the University, by the Doctors and **Masters, and the** election **was not,** as now, confined to particular **Colleges,** none but men of learning, and **such** as had considerable **interest, durst aspire** to that honor. **In 1578, he** travelled **into France, and other countries, where** improving himself in several branches of useful learning, and the knowledge **of the** world, he returned a very accomplished gentleman; and was made Tutor for the Greek tongue **to Queen** Elizabeth, who very much approved of him. In 1585, **he** was chosen Warden of Merton College, through the Queen's favor; and in 1596, she made him Provost of Eaton College. King James I. expressed a particular regard

for him, and would have advanced him either in State **or**
Church, but he declined it, and only accepted of the honor
of Knighthood from him at Windsor, September 21, **1604.**
About that time, losing his only son, he thenceforth devoted
his time and **fortune** to the interests **of** learning. In **1619,**
he founded two Lectures, or Professorships, in the **University**
of Oxford, one for Geometry, and the other **for** Astronomy,
which **he** endowed with a salary of £160 **a year each,** besides
a legacy of **£600 for** purchasing more lands for **the same use.**
He also **furnished a** library with mathematical **books, near**
the Mathematical School, for the use of his Professors. **He**
gave £100 to the mathematical chest of his own appointing ;
adding afterwards a legacy of £40 a year to the same chest,
and to the University and his Professors jointly. **He gave**
likewise £120 towards the new building of the **Schools ;**
several rare manuscripts, and printed books **to the Bodleian**
Library, and a good quantity of matrices, **and** Greek types,
to the Printing-press at Oxford. Part of **the** endowment of
the above Professorships **was the manor of** Little Hays, **in**
Essex, as appears from Morant, **vol. i, page 41.** Sir Henry
died **February 19,** 1621-2, at Eaton College, and was buried
in the **Chapel there,** on the south side **of** the communion
table, near **the** body of his son Henry, **with** this inscription
over him, on a black marble stone :

" Hic jacent ossa et cineres Henrici Savill, **sub** spe certa
resurrectionis ; natus apud Bradley, juxta Hallifax, in Com-
itatio Ebor. **Anno** Dom. 1549, ultimo die mensis Novembris ;
obiit **in** Collegio Etonensi, Anno Dom. 1621, 19 die mensis,
Februarii.

A sumptuous monument was also erected to his memory
on the south wall, at the upper end of the choir of the
Church, adjoining **to Merton** College, with the following
inscription :

M.S.

HENRICUS SAVILE, MILES,

Collegii { Mertonensis Custos,
Etonensis Præpositus.

Svi

Exvvias corporis frustra sit qui hic quæra.
Servat prænobile depositum Etona,
Perennem virtvtvm ac benefactorvm memoriam

Quibus collegium utrumq; Q. Academiam imprimis
Oxoniensem complexus est, Ipsumq; adeo
        Mvndvm habet sibi debendi revm,
        Affectvs insvper pientissimæ Uxoris,
                Possidet iste lapis.
        B.M.P. Margareta, Conjvx obseqventissima,
        In hoc vno qvod posvit pie immorigera.
Obiit Ao Dni M,DCXXI, Febrvar. xix.

The works of this learned man, are,

1. An English translation of part of Tacitus. London,
1581, fol. He added some notes, which Isaac Gruter translated into Latin, and published at Amsterdam, in 1649, 12mo.

2. A view of certain military Matters, or Commentaries
concerning Roman warfare. Folio, London, 1598. Translated into Latin by Freherus, Heidelberg, 1601, but having
become exceeding scarce, was re-printed by Gruter, who
subjoined it to the notes above-mentioned.

3. Rerum Anglicarum Scriptores post Bedam præcipui.
Fol. London, 1596, 1599, and at Frankfort 1601. This
collection contains Malmesbury's History, Hoveden's Annals,
Ethelwerd's Chronicles, &c. Wharton (Pref. Anglia Sacra,)
sais that Sir Henry printed Malmesbury's History from an
incorrect manuscript. It seems as if the above Historians
were expected by Sir Henry to have come from a more
noble hand than his own, as may be collected from the
following Letter of his amongst the Harleian MSS. Brit.
Museum, No. 374, folio 24, directed to his most speciall good
frend Ma^r. John Stowe, in Cornewall, in London.

" After my most hartie commendacions, being verie glad
and desirous to heare from you, trustinge in our Lord that
you be in good health, or els I might be hertelye sorie, for
that I have founde at all tymes good favoure of youe since
our first acquaintance, and other acquaintance in London I
have none but that I have by your means, as good Master
Hare, unto whom I pray youe commende me, and desire
him to let me understande in what towordsnes his good
workes for the priveleges of Oxforth is; and forther I besech
you to certifye me, if Wigornensis is printed, and wheare I
may sende to buye it, and the price; and gladlye of all other
I woulde understande that your last booke weare forthe,
that I might sende unto you for one or twoe for my money.

Forther I woulde understande if my Lord's Grace be aboute to print Roger Howden, Maulbesburie, and Huntingtone, and in what forwardnes they be. Good owlde Frend lett me have your letter in the premisses, and, God willinge, it shall be recompensed or it be longe; and I must forther desire you to have answere by this bearer at this time.

From Halifaxe, this first of May,

By your lovinge Frende,

HENRY SAVILL.

The following Letter, taken from the said manuscript, No. 530, folio 1, will shew, I think, in what year the above was written.

"Mr. Stowe.

"After my hartie commendacions, your letter, dated the tenthe of May, I receaved at Halyfax with thanks, and synce I am come to Oxford, wheare I made enquirie to knowe weare the **booke** showlde bee that Master Hare showlde sende hyther, as your letter dyd ymporte, and as yet I cannot heere of the same, thearfore I desyer you to goo unto the good Gentleman, Master Hare, in my name, and reqweste hym to let me understande by whome, and abowte what tyme, hee sente the booke, and to what place hee made his direction, and whoo showlde have the custodie thearof, for greate pitie yt weare that so worthie worke showlde be embeazeled; and I pray you with speede to certefy me in **writynge** and delyver your letter at the signe of the Owle, that yt maye be delivered unto the Carryer, Richard Barker, who commethe homeward on Wensdaye nexte.

"Further I praye you let me knowe whoo is the Prenter of Wygornensis, and wheare he dwellethe, and who is the Prenter of your booke. I have heere sente you a mild sixpence **to** dryncke a qwarte of wyne in your travell. Thus wisshinge you healthe, I byd you farewell. Oxon, this Sonedaye Trinite, 21 Maii, 1592, your lovinge Friend,

Henry Savill.

"Directe your letters, I praye, to Master Henrie Shirbourne, over agaynste Merton Colledge, to be delyvered to me."

4. Sir Henry next published a fine edition of St. Chrysostom's Works, with this title in the middle of a well-engraved copper-plate " S. Johannis Chrysostomi Opera, Græce, octo voluminibus, Etonæ, in Collegio Regali, 1613." In the preface he tells the Reader, "that he had visited himself, about twelve years before, all the public and private libraries in Britain, and copied out from thence whatever he thought useful for his design ; and had then sent learned men into France, Germany, Italy, and the East, to transcribe such parts as he had not already, and to collate others with the best manuscripts, acknowledging that he had received considerable assistance from several learned foreigners there mentioned." In the 8th volume are inserted Sir Henry's own Notes, with those of the learned John Bois, Thomas Allen, Andrew Downes, &c.

The whole charge of this impression cost Sir Henry eight thousand pounds. As soon as it was finished, the Bishops and Clergy of France employed Fronto Ducæus, a learned Jesuit, to reprint it at Paris, with a Latin translation, which lessened the price of Sir Henry's edition ; yet we are told, that the thousand copies which he printed were all sold.

This work required such long and close application, that Sir Henry's Lady thought herself neglected, and coming to him one day into his study, she said " Sir Henry, I would I were a Book too, and then you would a little more respect me !" To which one standing by, replied, " You must then be an Almanack, Madam, that he might change every year." Which answer displeased her.

The same Lady, a little before Chrysostome was finished, when Sir Henry lay sick, said, " If Sir Harry died, she would burn Chrysostome for killing her husband." Which Mr. Bois hearing, told her, " that would be a great pity, for he was one of the sweetest Preachers since the Apostles' times ; with which she was so well satisfied, that she said, " She would not do it for all the world."

5. Thomæ Bradwardini, Archiepiscopi olim Cantuariensis, de Causa Dei contra Pelagium. Londini, 1618, fol. This book was printed from six MS. copies, carefully collated with each other. He has prefixed thereto Bradwardine's Life, compiled by himself. It is dedicated to K. James, and concludes with what Sir Henry calls, " Ad suos Mertonenses Epistola posterior."

6. Nazianzen's Steliteutics, 1610. Towards this, he was favoured with the MS. Epistles of Nazianzen out of the Bodleian Library, which was a singular courtesy, and done because of his affection to the storing, **and** preserving of the Library. Oldys' Brit. Libr. 247.

7. Xenophon's Institution **of Cyrus**, Gr. 1613, 4to.

8. Prælectiones tresdecim in principium Elementorum Euclidis, Oxoniæ habitæ. Oxon, 1621, 4to. These were his own Lectures; **some** of them when he was Junior Master.

9. Oratio **coram** Regina Elizabetha, Oxoniæ habita An. 1592, published **by** Mr. (afterwards Bishop) Barlow, in 1658, from the original in the Bodleian Library, and also by Dr. John Lamphire, in the second edition of Monarchia Britannica, Oxford, 1681, 8vo.

10. Latin Translations of **K. James** the **First's Apology** for the Oath of Allegiance.

11. Six Letters of his, wrote to Hugo Blotius, **and** Sebastian Tengnagelius. Lambecius, vol. 3.

12. Four Letters **of his to** Mr. Camden. Camdeni Epistolæ, &c.

13. One Letter **of his**, 4th **vol. of Strype's Annals.** Besides these, it should be remembered, that he was concerned in the new Translation of the Bible, now in use, done by the command of King James I. being **one of the** eight persons at Oxford who undertook **to translate** the four Gospels, Acts, and Revelations.

He also left behind him several manuscripts, some of which are now in the Bodleian Library, **such** as, 1. Orations, 2. Tract of the Original of Monasteries. 3. Tract concerning the Union of England and Scotland, written at the command of King James I. **He also made** several notes with **his** pen in many of his books, **particularly** in Eusebius's Ecclesiastical History, made **use of by Henry** Valesius in his edition of that History, in 1659. Likewise in those **books** which he gave to the Mathematical Library in the School Tower, in Oxford, and in many others.

Sir Henry is mentioned **as a** Member of the Society of Antiquaries, in the Introduction to the Miscellaneous Tracts, relating to Antiquity, published by the Society of Antiquaries of London, in 1770, page 21. So well did he deserve the character given of him, **that he** was Musarum Patronus et Literarum Mæcenas, **being an** encourager of all sorts of useful learning, and universally well spoken of by all disinterested Scholars. There is a painting of him in the Picture Gallery at Oxford.

SAVILE, THOMAS,

Younger brother to Sir John and Sir Henry just mentioned, born likewise at Over Bradley, in Stainland, was admitted Probationer Fellow of Merton College, in 1580, and afterwards proceeding in Arts, he went abroad, and travelling through various countries, improved himself in several parts of learning. After his return, he became, through the interest of his brother, one of the Fellows of Eaton College, where he did credit to his brother's choice, being reckoned amongst the first rate Scholars. He was made Proctor of Oxford, April 5, 1592, and died the 12th of January following, at London; from whence his body was removed to Oxford, and interred with great solemnity in the choir of Merton College Church, the following eulogium to his memory, being entered in the Register of that House: "Fuit Sidus lucidissimum, qui apud suos, et exteros, literarum et virtutis fama ac morum urbanitate percelebris, &c."

He wrote, "Epistolæ variæ ad illustres viros." Fifteen of these were wrote to Camden, and are published by Dr. Thomas Smith, of Magdalen College, Oxford, in a book intitled, "V. Cl. Gulielmi Cambdeni, et illustrium Virorum ad G. Cambdenum Epistolæ, etc." London, 1691, 4to. This was the reason why Camden, in his Preliminary Discourse to the Brigantes, calls this Thomas his learned friend in 1582; and it is something strange that Wood, in his Fasti, page 127, should have any doubt of this being the same person, when, in his Athenæ, he had mentioned the above fifteen Letters.

SAVILE, HENRY,

Of Shaw-hill, in Skircoat, in this parish, commonly called Long Harry Savile, was of the Saviles of Bank, near Halifax, entered a student of Merton College in 1587, (his kinsman, Mr. Henry Savile, being then Warden,) and was soon after made one of the Portionists, commonly called Postmasters.

After he had taken the Degree of B.A. he left Merton College, and retired to St. Alban-hall, where, in 1595, he took the Degree of **M.A.** **Being all this** time **under the** inspection of his kinsman, he became an eminent Scholar, especially in the Mathematics, Physic, (in which faculty he was admitted by the University to **practise,**) Chemistry, Painting, Heraldry, **and** Antiquities.

Afterwards **for** the completing **of his knowledge,** he travelled **into Italy,** France, and Germany, **where he** greatly **improved himself.** He wrote several **things, but, I** think, committed **nothing to the press.**

He gave **Camden the "Antient exemplar of Asser Menevensis,"** which he published in 1602, **and** which contains **the story** of the discord **between the new** Scholars which Grim-**bald** brought with him **to Oxford, at the** restoration **of the University** by King Alfred **with the old Clerks which Grim-**bald found there. This Henry **Savile** lived **for** some **years after** his return from foreign **countries,** in the parish **of** St. Martin in the Fields, near **London,** and died there April 29th, 1617, aged forty-nine **years,** and was buried in the Chancel belonging to the **parish Church** there, a monument being **set over** his grave on **the north** wall, **with his bust to the middle,** carved in stone, and painted, **the right hand** resting **on a** book, and the left **on a death's head.** The inscription **worn** out.

One HENRY SAVILE, **Esq; was** Captain of **the** Adventure under Sir Francis Drake and Sir John Hawkins, **against** the Spaniards in the West Indies, and wrote **a** book called, " A Libel **of Spanish Lies** found **at the** Sack **of** Cales, discoursing the Fight in the West Indies between the English and the Spaniards, and of the death of Sir Francis Drake; with an Answer, confuting the said Spanish Lies, &c." London, 1596. This was an answer **to** a letter wrote by the Spanish General, asserting that **Sir** Francis Drake died of Grief, because he had lost so many barks and men, and that the English Fleet fled from the Spaniards **in** 1695. This Captain Savile is supposed **to** have been a relation **of** the above.

In Queen Elizabeth's time, **three** Henry Saviles of York-shire, were matriculated as Members of Merton College, Oxford, viz. **one, son** of Plebeian, in 1588, another, son of an Esquire, in 1593, and a third, son of an Esquire, in 1595.

STANSFIELD, ELY,

Of Sowerby, published a book called "Psalmody epitomised; being a brief collection of plain and useful Psalm tunes, both old and new, in four parts, with a plain and familiar introduction, by way of question and answer." A second edition of this was printed in London in 1731. These tunes are most of them the old Church tenors, in use above an hundred years ago. The contra, medius, and bassus, the Author has added. He has likewise intermixed several tunes wholly of his own composition. The introduction seems to be a good one. Amongst several local tunes, he has given us "Warley" new tune to Psalm c; and "Sowerby" tune to Psalm xcviii.

SLADDIN, JOHN,

Of Ovenden, in this parish, printed a pamphlet intitled, " A brief Description of the Methodists, and a Confutation of their dangerous Principles." York, 1749. 8vo. It has a short Address to the Archbishop of York, and a Preface to the Reader.

SMITH, MATTHEW,

Was born in the city of York, in 1650, and was sent, after he had made a sufficient progress in classical learning, to the University of Edinburgh, where he took the degree of M.A. Soon after his return from thence he began his Ministry amongst the Dissenters, preaching alternately at Warley and Mixenden, in this parish. At the last of these places, he had only, at the beginning, one person (whose name was John Hanson) to encourage his preaching, the Dissenters from the establishment in that neighbourhood being then chiefly Antimonians. The Civil Magistrates being at that time severe with such Nonconformists as held any public assemblies, he was obliged to preach privately, often in the night, and to hide himself from their resentment; and though parties of soldiers were frequently detached to secure him, he was always fortunate enough to elude their vigilance, and at last when times were more settled, he had a flourishing congregation.

One part of his life he was settled at York, but was forced to fly from thence into the parish of Halifax, to avoid the opposition which he met with. He was offered a living in the Church of £200 per annum, but having some scruples about conformity, he declined it.

Towards the latter part of his life he was afflicted with the palsy, and died April 29, 1736, aged 85, and was buried at Mixenden. He wrote a book with this title, " The true notion of imputed Righteousness, and our Justification thereby, &c., by the **Rev. M. S.**, a Country Minister, **London,** 1700, 8vo., to which is added, "A Defence of the foregoing Doctrine, against **some** glowing Opposition among **Neighbors,** Ministers, **and** others." Printed in the same year. He also **wrote a** Treatise concerning the Decrees of God, **the manu-** script **of** which **was in the** late Mr. Thoresby's **Museum.** See Topog. p. 543.

There are likewise printed **of his,** five Sermons: **to which the** Editor, the Rev. Mr. John **Smith,** first a Dissenting Minister at Mixenden, afterwards **at** Bradford, in Yorkshire, and son of the above Matthew, has prefixed his father's life, and added three discourses of his own. London, 1737. The above John Smith died at Bradford, April 7, 1768, after a severe stroke **of the** palsy, or, as some thought, a disorder of the convulsive kind, which carried him off in about **four** days.

TAYLOR, JOHN,

Concerning whose birth **Dr. Plot, in his** History **of** Stafford-shire, page 277, says, " that it seldom falls **out** that three children are born together, either perfect **or** living, and yet this happened at Barton, in Staffordshire; one Taylor, who **lived in a** little **cottage there,** having three sons at a birth, **which being** presented **as a** rarity **to** King Henry VII. **as he** came **that** way (perhaps to hunt **in** Needwood), he **ordered** them **to** be put to school; **and** they all lived to be men, **and to be** Doctors, coming to good preferment."

At page 296, the same Author tells us, "**that this** John Taylor, who **was** then Dr. of **Laws,** Archdeacon **of** Derby and Buckingham, and was Master **of** the Rolls **in** the time of King Hen. VIII. and the oldest of the three above-mentioned, built, **in** 1517, the Chapel **of** Barton, on or near the place where **the** cottage stood wherein he was born, as appeared from **the** inscriptions **in** Saxon characters, in re-lieve work, over every other pillar of the north and south **sides of the** Nave of the said Chapel:

Over the first pillar, "**J. T. horum trium*** Gemellorum **natu** maximus,"

Over the third, "**Decretorum Doctor, et Sacrorum Canonum Professor;**"

Over the fifth, "**Archidiaconus Derbiæ et** Bukkynham, **nec non et**"

Over the seventh, "**Magister** Rotulorum, illustrissimi Regis **H.VIII. An.** Reg. **sui 20.**"

On the **second,** fourth, **sixth, and** eighth pillars **were** placed interchangeably his **coat of arms.**

Wood, in his Fasti, vol. i. **page 34,** informs **us, that this** John Taylor, **Dr.** of **Decrees, and** of the Sacred Canons beyond the **Seas, having been lately** incorporated **at Cambridge, desired the same favour at Oxford, which was** granted; adding, that **he had been Rector of** Sutton Colefield, in Warwickshire, **Clerk of the** Parliaments which sat in 1515, (in the **seventh year of the reign of** Henry VIII.) and Prolocutor **of the** Convocation of the Clergy, which was dissolved December **21, the same** year; that he **was** made Master of **the** Rolls in 1528, **having** before been employed in **several** embassies beyond **the** seas, and discharged in 1534; **that he succeeded** Rokesby, Archbishop of Dublin, **in the Vicarage of Halifax, and** died in 1534.

Willis, in his **Survey of** Cathedrals, vol. i , p. 440, sais, that **this** Dr. Taylor was made Prebendary of Litchfield, being admitted to the Prebend of Eccleshall there, Jan. 3, 1508, which he quitted in 1532. His Archdeaconry of Derby he resigned in 1528, but his other Archdeaconry he seems to have held till **his** death.

TILLOTSON, JOHN,

Born at **Haugh-end, in** the township **of** Sowerby, in this parish. **There is the** less reason to be particular about the actions of his life, **on account of** the following publications, viz.

"**1.** The Life **of the** most revd. Father in God John **Tillotson,** Archbishop of Canterbury, compiled from the minutes **of the** revd. Mr. Young, late Dean of Salisbury. By **F. H. M.** A. with many curious memoirs, communicated by **the late** right revd. Gilbert, Lord Bishop of Sarum." London, **1717,** 8vo.

* This should have been Trimellorum.

"2 The Life of the most revd. **Dr.** John Tillotson, Lord Archbishop of Canterbury, compiled chiefly from his original Papers, and Letters.—By Thomas Birch, D.D." London, 8vo. 1753, second edition.

3. His Life inserted in the Biographia Britannica, page 3944. We shall, therefore, only take notice of what these, and others have omitted.

It is very remarkable, that Wright, in his Hist' of Halifax, page 154, speaking of the dispute relating to the Archbishop's being baptized in the Church, says, " I myself have twenty times looked at his name in the register, and to the best of my remembrance, there were four others christened the same day with him, whose names were all wrote down in the same hand, and same ink, without the least interlineation."

Such an information as this, one would think, might be depended upon as exact; and yet when we searched the same Register, we found his name to be the last of seven, who were baptised together, and entered in these words, "Bapt. Octr. 3, 1630, John Robert Tilletson, Sourb."

The following original Letter, which is in my possession, seems not to have been known to any of the Compilers of the Archbishop's Life.

" For his much respecd. frend Mr. Roote, att Sorbey, are these.

in Yorkeshire.

" Sir,

" To excuse the slownes and infrequency of writeing, is growne a thing soe complementall and common in the frontispeece of every letter, that I have made choice rather to put myselfe upon your candor to frame an excuse for mee, then goe about my selfe to doe it.

" I cannot but thankefully acknowledge my engagements to you for your kindnes showne to mee, both when I was in the country, and at other times; I shall not here let my pen run out into complementall lines, gratitude (and that as much as may bee) being all that I desire to expresse.

" As for our University affayres, things are as they was [so in original] before I came into the country, only wee have lesse hopes of procuring Mr. Thomas Goodwin for our Master then we then had. Wee are in expectation of the

Visitors every day, but what will be done at their comming wee cannot guesse.

"The Engagement is either comming downe hither, or (as I heare) already **come, to** which how soone wee shall bee called upon to subscribe, wee knowe not; as for my selfe I do not (for present) at all scruple the taking of it, yet because I dare not confinde too much **to my** owne judgement, or apprehension **of** things, and because matters **of** such serious consequence require no little caution and consideration, therefore I shall desire you (as soone as with convenience you can) to returne mee your **opinion** of it in too or three lines.

"Mr. Rich. Holbrooke desired me to present his respects to you and your wife, to whome alsoe I desire you to present my best respects, as alsoe to your son, Joh. Hopkinson, and his wife.   Noe more, but your prayers for him who remains,

Yours whilst

JOH.   TILLOTSON."

Clare-Hall, Dec. 6,
  1649.

What sort of answer was **given** to the above, **does** not appear, but as Mr. Roote, **who at that** time was Preacher at Sowerby Chapel, was one of the Puritans, it **is** probable that he would not dissuade Mr. Tillotson from complying with that Engagement here mentioned, which **was an** Act substituted in **the** room of **the Oaths of Allegiance** and Supremacy, **and was** ordered to be taken by every one who held either **Office, or** Benefice, "that they would be true and faithful **to the** Government established, without King or House **of Peers.**

Add to **this, that Mr.** Tillotson, who **at that** time was an Under-graduate of Clare-hall, and very young, was under the care of Mr. Clarkson, a Tutor there, who also **was a** Puritan, and attached to the Government then in being.

It **does** not appear however, that Mr. Tillotson long **adhered to** the principles, especially the religious ones, which he may have been supposed to have received **either from** his Father, **or** College Tutor, for his writings **breathe a** quite different spirit from the stiff rigid sentiments of **those** times; in particular, when Dean of Canterbury, he preached before his father at Sowerby Chapel, against the doctrine of Calvin, probably with an intent to rectify his father's notions ; and one Dr. Maud, who had frequent disputes with the Archbishop's father about predestination, asking him, how he liked his son's discourse ? the old man replied, in his usual way when he asserted any thing with earnestness, "I profess he has done more harm than good."

The following anecdote was told by the late Rev'd. Mr. Tillotson, Sur-master of St. Paul's School. who had it from Dr. Secker, when Bishop of Oxford.—When the famous Duke of Buckingham presented Dr. Tillotson to King Charles II. after saying that he introduced to his Majesty the gravest Divine of the Church of England, he stepped forward, and in a lower tone said to the King, "And of so much wit, that if he chose it, he could make a better comedy than ever your Majesty laughed at."

But on what grounds the Duke said this we cannot conceive, for the Doctor has left no specimen of this kind of wit behind him. Perhaps he had an inclination to serve the Doctor, and knew that this was one effectual way to recommend him to the King.

It is commonly said about Sowerby, that Robert Tillotson went to London to see his son, then Dean of Canterbury, and being in the dress of a plain countryman, was insulted by one of the Dean's servants, for enquiring if John Tillotson was at home ; his person, however, being described to the Dean, he immediately went to the door, and in the sight of his servants fell down upon his knees to ask a blessing of the stranger.

TILSON, HENRY,

Born, as it is said, in the parish of Halifax, but in what particular part is uncertain. The name has been common in several townships there, especially in Sowerby and Ovenden. He was entered a Student at Baliol College, Oxford, in 1593, was made B.A. in 1596, soon after which he got a Fellowship in University College, and there took his degree of M.A.

In October 1615, he succeeded R. Kenion in the Vicarage of Rochdale, in Lancashire, where, after he had resided some years, he went Chaplain to Thomas Earl of Strafford, Lord Lieutenant of Ireland, who made him Dean of Christ

Church, in Dublin, Pro Vice-Chancellor of the University of Dublin, and Bishop of Elphin, to which he was consecrated September 23, 1639; but this he did not long enjoy, on account of the rebellion which soon after broke out.

Sir James Ware, in his History of the Irish Bishops, page 635, says, that on the 16th of August, 1645, he delivered the castle of Elphin into the hands of the Lord President of Connaught; his son, Captain Henry Tilson, who was Governor of Elphin, having just before joined with Sir Charles Coot in opposition to the King's interest.

And about the same time, his library and goods were pillaged by Boetius Egan, the titular Bishop of Elphin, his damages amounting to the sum of four hundred pounds. He himself fled for safety into England, and settled at Soothill-hall, in the parish of Dewsbury, where some of his relations lived, and where he resided three years, intending to have returned, but never did.

Having thirteen persons, however, in his family, and being stript of his income, he was obliged to have recourse to such means for subsistence as his station in the Church put in his power; for this purpose he consecrated a room in the said Hall, called to this day the Bishop's Parlour, where he privately ordained, and did weekly the offices of a Clergyman, some of his neighbours being both hearers and benefactors to him; till Sir William Wentworth, of Breton, out of compassion to his distressed circumstances, employed him to preach at Comberworth, allowing him a salary to support him.

Thus was this Prelate obliged to stoop to become a country Curate! The following extract from the Register belonging to Dewsbury Church, shews when and where he was interred.

"Henry Lord Bishop of Elphin, buried the 2d day of April, 1655." In the south-east corner of the said Church, in a Chapel which belonged to the Soothills, of Soothill, is a monument on the wall, with this inscription:

"P.M.

Reverendi in Christo Patris

HENRICI TILSON,

Hen. F.

Episcopi Elphinensis

In Hibernia,

Nati A° 1576, juxta Halifax,
In Agro Eboracenci,
Denati 31 Die Martii, A° 1655,
in eodem Agro.
Viri **ob** Eruditionem et **Pietatem**
Insignis.
Parentis charissimi
P.
Nathan **Tilson.**
Hen. F. Hen. N."

The Arms on this monument are, Or, a bend cotised between two garbs azure, charged with a mitre of the field, which are so like the Arms of Tillotson, that one would almost imagine that their names, if not their families, were originally the same.

I have credibly been informed, that the late James Tilson, Esq., who died at Cadiz, said this Bishop's family came originally from Tilston, in Cheshire; if so, they were absolutely the same.

For a nephew of the Bishop's, see Walpole's Anecdotes of Paintings, vol. iii., p. 103, edit. 1763.

The Tilsons long farmed Soothill-hall; they were there in 1748.

TOPHAM, EDWARD,

Was Schoolmaster at the Free Grammar-school, near Halifax, and published a Sermon, preached at Selby, in Yorkshire. Wright, page 25, calls him Matthew.

WATKINSON, EDWARD,

Was M.D. Rector of Little Chart, in Kent, and some time Curate of Luddenden Chapel, in this parish. Having had his house at Little Chart broke open and plundered, he was so terrified with what was done, that he durst not live any longer in that neighbourhood, but removed to Ackworth, near Pontefract, in Yorkshire, where he died, Oct. 19, 1767.

He published, " An Essay on Œconomy," (of which he printed four editions, chiefly to give away.) " An Essay upon Gratitude." " An Admonition to the younger Clergy;" a recommendation of which may be seen in the Christian's Magazine for January, 1765, page 29.

WATSON, JOHN,

The Author of this* book, was the eldest son of Legh Watson, by Hesther, daughter, and at last heiress, of Mr. John Yates, of Swinton, in Lancashire.

He was born in the township of Lyme-cum-Hanley, in the parish of Prestbury, in Cheshire, March 26, 1724, O.S. and having been brought up at the Grammar-schools of Eccles, Wigan, and Manchester, all in Lancashire, he was admitted a Commoner in Brazen-nose College, Oxford, April 7, 1742.

In Michaelmas Term, 1745, he took the Degree of B.A. June 27, 1746, he was elected a Fellow of Brazen-nose College, being chosen into a Cheshire Fellowship, as being a Prestbury parish man. On the title of his Fellowship, he was ordained a Deacon at Chester, by Dr. Samuel Peploe, Bishop of Chester, December 21, 1746.

After his year of Probation, as Fellow, was ended and his residence at Oxford no longer required, he left the College; and his first employment in the Church, was the Curacy of Runcorn, in Cheshire; here he staid only three months, and removed from thence to Ardwick, near Manchester, where he was an Assistant Curate at the Chapel there, and private Tutor to the three sons of Samuel Birch, of Ardwick, Esq.

During his residence here, he was privately ordained a Priest at Chester, by the above Dr. Peploe, May 1, 1748, and took the Degree of M.A. at Oxford, in Act Term, the same year. From Ardwick he removed to Halifax, and was licensed to the Curacy there Oct. 17, 1750, by Dr. Matthew Hutton, Archbishop of York.

June 1, 1752, he married Susanna, daughter and heiress of the late Revd. Mr. Allon, Vicar of Sandbach, in Cheshire, vacating thereby his Fellowship at Oxford.

September 3, 1754, he was licensed by the above Dr. Hutton, on the presentation of George Legh, LL.D. Vicar of Halifax, to the Perpetual Curacy of Ripponden, in the parish of Halifax. Here he rebuilt the Curate's house, at his own expence, laying out above four hundred pounds upon the same, which was more than a fourth part of the whole sum he there received, notwithstanding which, his worthy successor threatened him with a prosecution in the Spiritual Court, if he did not allow him ten pounds for dilapidations, which, for the sake of peace, he complied with.

* Watson's " Halifax," 4to., London, 1775.

February 17, **1759,** he was elected a Fellow of the Society of Antiquaries in London, being invited to accept of that honour by the Right Hon. the Lord Willoughby, of Parham, President of that Society.

July 11, **1761,** he was married **at Ealand, in Halifax** parish, to **Ann, daughter** of Mr. James Jaques, of Leeds, Merchant.

August 17, **1766,** he was inducted to the Rectory of Meningsby, in **Lincolnshire, being** presented **thereto** by the Right Hon. Lord Strange, **then** Chancellor of the Dutchy of Lancaster, which he resigned in the year 1769, on being **promoted** to the valuable Rectory **of** Stockport in Cheshire. **His** presentation to this, by Sir George Warren, bore date July 30, **1769, and he was** inducted thereto **August the 2d** following.

April 11, **1770,** he was appointed one of the Domestic Chaplains to the Right **Hon. the Earl** of Dysart.

April 24, 1770, having received **his** Dedimus for acting **as** a Justice of **the** Peace **in** the **county of** Chester, he was sworn into **that** office **on that** day.

He has published, **1. a** Discourse **from** Philipp. iv. 5. preached **in** Halifax Church, July **28, 1751,** intitled, Moderation; or, a candid Disposition towards those that differ from us, recommended and enforced : **with a** Preface, containing the reason of its publication. The first impression of this being quickly sold, it passed through a second edition.

2. An Apolygy for his Conduct yearly, on the 30th of **January,** printed at Manchester, in 8vo. and annexed to this, is a Sermon preached in Ripponden-chapel, on the 30th of January, 1755, **from** Romans xiii. 4. intitled, "Kings should obey the **Laws."**

3. A Letter to the Clergy of **the** Church, known by the name of Unitas Fratrum, or Moravians, **concerning a** remarkable Book of Hymns used **in** their Congregations, pointing **out** several Inconsistencies and Absurdities in the said Book.—This also was printed at Manchester, in 1756, 8vo.

4. Some account of a Roman Station lately discovered on the borders of Yorkshire, read before the Society of Antiquaries, Feb. **20, 1786,** and printed in the Archæologia, vol. **i., p. 215.**

5. A mistaken passage in Bede's Eccles. Hist. explained; read Feb. 27, 1766, *Arch.* i., p. 221.

6. Druidical Remains in or near the parish of Halifax, discovered and explained; read Nov. 21, 1771. *Arch.* ii., p. 353. This last is reprinted in the History of Halifax, with alterations.

Also several other fugitive pieces of his have been published in different periodical Papers without his name; and he has in manuscript, ready for the press,* An History of the Antient Earls of Warren and Surry, proving the Warrens of Poynton, in Cheshire, to be lineally and legally descended from them. He is also preparing to publish the Antiquities of a part of the County of Chester; likewise those of a part of the County of Lancaster.

WILKINSON, HENRY,

Born (sais Wood, *Athenæ*, ii., p. 112,) in the Vicarage of Halifax, October 9, 1566; entered at Oxford in Lent Term, 1581; elected Probationer Fellow of Merton College, by favour of his kinsman, Mr. Henry Savile, the Warden, in 1586; proceeded in Arts; took the Degree of B.D. and in 1601 had the Living of Waddesdon, in Bucks.

In 1643 he was elected one of the Assembly of Divines; and dying March 19, 1647, was buried at Waddesdon. He wrote, 1. A Catechism for the Use of the Congregation of Waddesdon, which has been several times printed in octavo; and the fourth impression came out at London in 1637. 2. The Debt Book, or a Treatise on Romans xiii. 8., wherein is handled the civil debt of money or goods. London, 1625. octavo; and some other things. He had a son Henry, for whom see Wood's *Athenæ* ii., p. 543.

WILKINSON, JOHN.

In Bentley's History of Halifax, page 81, it is said, that "Doctor Wilkinson was born in Halifax parish, and brought up in Oxford, where he attained to that eminency in learning, as to become Divinity Professor in that University."

This we take to have been the same who is said in Wood's Fasti, vol. i. page 173. to have had the honour, when he was B.D. and Fellow of Magdalen College, to be appointed

------

* Afterwards printed.

Tutor to Henry Prince of Wales, eldest son of King James I. He was afterwards President of Magdalen Hall, and finally, President of Magdalen College. It seems that the Doctor fled from Oxford to the Parliament, and was deprived of his Presidentship.

WRIGHT, THOMAS,

Born at Blackburn, in Lancashire, August 12, 1707, was educated in the Grammar School there founded by Q. Eliz. about 1567; took the Degree of B.A. at St. John's College, Cambridge; was several years Curate of Halifax, which he left in the year 1750, being then presented to the Curacy of Ripponden.

He died in June 1754, having wrote "The Antiquities of the Town of Halifax, in Yorkshire; wherein is given an account of the Town, Church, and twelve Chapels, the Free Grammar School, a List of the Vicars and School-masters; the ancient and customary Law, called Halifax Gibbet Law, with the names of the Persons that suffered thereby, and the Times when; the public Charities to Church and Poor; the Men of Learning, whether Natives or Inhabitants; together with the most remarkable Epitaphs and Inscriptions in the Church and Church Yard. The whole faithfully collected from printed Authors, Rolls of Courts, Registers, Old Wills, and other authentic Writings." Leeds, 1738. With a Preface.

It is remarkable that Mr. Wright was my immediate predecessor in both the Curacies of Halifax and Ripponden, and that we have both wrote the Antiquites of Halifax.

—::—

COATS OF ARMS.

There is in this [Halifax] church an antient and very curious wooden cover to the font, which font the register tells us was re-erected in 1660. Also the royal arms, placed between the body of the church and the chancel, and facing both. On account of these, there is the following entry in an old church book: "1704, paid to John Aked, for Queen's arms, in part, ten pounds fifteen shillings."

This JOHN AKED was an inhabitant of Halifax, and has put his name thereon; it is said, however, that they were finished in London; be this as it will, both the arms and supporters are done in a very masterly manner.

On the roof of this church are painted, in different compartments, the following arms, (1.) Wilkinson; (2.) Archbishop Tillotson; (3.) Savile, impaled with four others, viz. 1st, Gules, three lions passant guardant; 2dly, Howard; 3dly, Warren; 4thly, Gules, a lion rampant argent. (4.) Archbishop Sharp; (5.) Lister; (6.) Farrer, a martlet for difference; (7.) Farrer, no distinction. (8.) Sable, a chevron between three escallops argent.—(9.) Cockcroft, of Mayroid, but the colours, as I apprehend, mistaken; a martlet for difference; (10.) Same arms, crescent for difference; (11.) Greenwood, impaled with another coat, forgot.—(12.) Prescot; (13.) Argent, a chevron gules between three elephants passant sable. (14.) Argent, a fess between three crescents gules. (15.) Savile. (16.) Argent, a lion rampant gules. (17.) Argent, on a pale gules between two......three towers of the first, and in chief, gules, a crescent betwen two escallops......(18.) Naylor; (19.) Argent, on a fess sable, between three crescents, as many mullets, gules, or something like it; for this, and two others quartered with it, I could not distinctly make out, owing to their great distance from the eye, (20.) Midgley, of Midgley. (21.) Argent, a plain cross azure. (22.) Argent, two bars gemells gules, and in chief three torteauxes. (23.) Argent, three pales sable. (24.) Same as the last. (25.) Lister, but wants the canton. (26.) Waterhouse. (27 and 28.) The Clothworkers' arms. (29.) Lindley. (30.) Drake, impaled with ......(31.) Or, a chevron gules between three towers argent. (32.) Argent, in chief gules, three escallops......(33.) Azure, on a chevron argent, between three griffins passant or, three escallops gules. (34.) Naylor. (35.) Murgatroyd, as I take it. (36.) Sable, a fess lozengy, and in base an escallop argent, on a chief indented of the second, three escallops of the first. (37.) Same as No. 35. (38.) Sable, a chevron between three roses argent. (39.) Midgley of Midgley. (40.) Livesey. (41.) Argent, two bars nebule, over all a bend gules, quartered with, Argent, a chief indented sable.— (42.) Ramsden, of Crawstone. (43.) Argent, three crosses forme, five times pierced of the field. (44.) Gules, a griffin passant or. [Some of these are now left out, and the arrangement is totally different.—J.H.T.]

After these follow the arms of the Vicars, which I shall insert in the list of the Vicars, each under his respective name.

—::—

LIST OF THE VICARS

OF HALIFAX CHURCH.

1. INGOLARD TURBARD, or TURBERD, or, **as I have** seen it wrote, TURBAT, was probably one of the Monks of St. Pancrace, at Lewis. He was the first Vicar of this church, being presented thereto by the Prior and **Convent** of Lewis, who, by themselves, or assigns, presented every Vicar to this Church till the time of Dr. William Rokeby, inclusive.

This Vicar's **presentation** bears date January 25, 1273, and he was inducted into the living May 3, 1274, and died May 28, 1315.—Arms, Azure, a fess ermine between three turbats naiant, proper.

2. JOHN, called AARON DE GRYDINTON, instituted 11 calend. July (June 21,) 1315. His institution dated at Burton, near Beverley, as by Will. **de** Greenhill's register at York, vol. II. folio. 87.—Arms, Gules, a fess or between two frets, argent.

3. THOMAS DE GAYTINGTON, or Getingdon, instituted on the **nones (or** 5th) of June, 1321, who died September 10, 1349. —Arms, Argent, on a bend **sable** three goats passant of the first.

4. JOHN DE STANDFORD, or Stamford, wrote **also Stainforth,** and Stamforth, was instituted, according to **Mr. Wright,** February 7, but as by other authorities, February 4, 1349, and died either on the 20th or 29th of October, 1362.

Arms, Barry of six argent and azure, a canton, or.

It must here be observed, that a RICHARD DE OVENDEN is put down **in one** of the manuscripts which I saw at York, marked Af 39, as Vicar of Halifax, and said to be instituted October 8, 1349, but no notice is taken of him either by Mr. Wright, or **on** the roof of Halifax church, which might be owing to his having enjoyed this benefice so very short a time.   If he was Vicar, I take him to have been the first parish man who was presented thereto.

5. RICHARD (son of Henry) DE HETON, instituted, according to Mr. Wright, November 3, but by a manuscript at York, November 10, 1362.—Died March 9, 1389.

He was of the Hetons of Over Shibden, in Northouram, as is evident from the copy of a deed in my possession; whereby he, by the express name of Ric. de Heton, Vicar of the church of Halifax, conveys in trust all his lands, tenements, &c., in Northouram, in a certain hamlet in the said vill, called Overshypden, in the 4th year of the reign of Richard II. 1380.   And in 1389, a grant was made, by consent of sir Ric. de Heton, Vicar of Halifax, to Will. Heton, Esq., of Schipden, son of said Richard, by certain trustees, of all the lands, tenements, &c., in Over Schipden, in the vill of Northouram, called Schipden-hall, and Hyngandrode, which they had of the feoffment of the said Richard.

Arms of this Vicar, Argent, on a bend sable, three bulls heads cabossed of the first, half faced looking to the left.— This coat is borne by a family in Devonshire, of this name.

6. JOHN KYNGE, inducted March 13, 1389, who died March 13th, or 14th, 1437.—Arms, sable, three escallops on a chevron argent.

N. B.   Here in my manuscript list, occurs Dominus THOMAS ELAND, as Vicar of Halifax, said to be instituted May 20, 1438, but he is not noticed either in Wright, or on the roof of the church.   If he really was Vicar, it is probable that he was of the Eland family in this parish, as I take his predecessor John Kynge to have been of the family of that name in Skircoat, for he gave lands, &c., in Skircoat, to Henry Savile, and Elen his wife, in the 4th year of the reign of Henry IVth or Vth.

7. THOMAS WILKYNSON, born, as tradition informs us, at Brackenbed, in Ovenden, within this parish, and instituted, says Mr. Wright, page 40, May 16, 1439.

His will bore date in 1477, as we are told by Dr. Favour, in his book intitled "Antiquity triumphing over Novelty," page 330; and he died, says Mr. Wright, January 25, 1480.

I cannot but take notice here that I have the copy of a deed dated August 5, in the 16th year of the reign of Henry VI. which was in the year 1437, wherein express mention is made of Thomas Wilkinson, Vicar of the church of Halifax ; what Mr. Wright says therefore of the time of his institution must be false, as must also the account of the time of the institution of Thomas **Eland**.

It is also remarkable, that amongst the testamentary burials at Halifax, inserted in Torr's manuscript, at York, it is said that Thomas Wilkinson, Vicar of Halifax, made his will June **1, 1481,** and left his **soul to** God Almighty, Saint Mary, **and all** Saints, and ordered his body to be buried in the **parish church** of St. John Baptist, Halifax. Arms of **this Vicar, Gules, a** fess varie, in chief **an unicorn** currant, **argent, armed . . .** between two roses **or, in a** bordure . . . . . He made, **at** his own expence, **the great** window **in the chancel.**

8. Richard **Simmys,** or **Simms,** distinguished **in my** manuscript list, by the title **of** Magister, as all the **Vicars** before him had been by that of Dominus.

He was instituted, says Wright, February 11, 1480, (i. e. 1480-1,) and died November 10, **1496.** He seems to have been an Halifax parish man, from **the** institution deed of Willeby's Chauntry.

Arms, Ermine, three increscents gules, which **coat** was **also** granted **(as** we are told by Guillim, p. 91,) to Edward Syms, (or **Symmes,) of** Daventry, **in** Northamptonshire, in 1592, by **Robert Cook.**

9. Magister Thomas **Brent, L.D. instituted** November 27, **1496.** He resigned **this Vicarage, and it was** the first **instance** of its having **become vacant** any other way than by **death.**

Arms, Azure, a **Fer de** Moline argent, pierced of the field.

10. Magister William Rokeby, instituted 14th of **June, 1502.—Died** November 29, 1521. **Arms,** impaled with the Archiepiscopal arms **of** Dublin, argent, on a chevron sable, between three rooks closed proper, three mullets of the field.

An account of him was given in the list of the Halifax parish Worthies, **as also of Dr.** Taylor.

11. John Taylor, LL.D., instituted some time in the year 1521.—Mr. Wright thinks he resigned the vicarage before his death, which happened in 1534, **but of** this there is no proof.—Arms, Gules, on a chevron between three dolphins naiant argent, **a fleur** de lis, and **on** each side of it, a grey-hound counter current, sable.

These arms do certainly belong to the name of Taylor; but Plot, in his History of Staffordshire, page 296, has given us the following, from the chapel of Barton, in the said county, built by the Doctor himself, viz. Sable, on a chevron argent, three violets slipt, the flowers of the second (Q.?) the stalks and leaves or, between three children's heads couped at the shoulders, also of the second haired, and vested of the third, in a chief of the same a 𝔗 azure, between two roses gules, seeded of the chief.

Now if these were really the Doctor's arms, by what authority are the others put up here? This gives one a suspicion about some of the rest. **The reader,** however, has them as I found them.

12. Dominus ROBERT HOLDESWORTH, L.D., the time of whose institution is uncertain. He **was** of the family of the Holdsworths, of Astey, (or Ashdale) in Southouram, and was possessed of an estate in that township.

He was murdered in the night time by thieves, in the Vicarage-house, which stood on different ground from the present one.—An old manuscript says, this event happened in the great chamber of the north, and the lower part of **the** house, in a part thereof turning towards the east.

He was buried at Halifax, May 10, 1556, without any inscription, under **the** great tombstone in the south chapel, which he built in his life time **at his** own expence.—Arms, Argent, on the stump of a tree raguled **in** bend, a crow perched near the top, proper.

It is to be noted, that the inscription relating to Dr. Holdesworth, already mentioned in the description of this south chapel, makes him to be the twelfth Vicar, thereby excluding from the **list,** both Ric. de Ovenden, and Tho. de Eland.

13. Dominus JOHN HARRISON, instituted July 13, 1556, (not May 3, as in Wright, for that was before the death of **his** predecessor,) being presented thereto by the Lady Ann Cleve, as my manuscript list informs me, but other accounts say that the benefice of Halifax was not granted to the Lady Ann when the manor there was settled upon her for life, but that the same was kept in the King's hands; besides, **we** are told that the Lady Ann Cleve died in 1555, which was before **the** date of this presentation.

He was buried at Halifax, 17th February, 1558, as by the Register there; but Mr. Wright says, 15th February, 1559.

Arms, Argent, three lions (or bears) paws erased and erected, gules.

14.—Christopher Ashburn, instituted in the beginning of Lent, 1559.—He was the first Protestant Vicar here.—In his time the Vicarage of Halifax is said to have offered to Queen Elizabeth by address, to raise three or four thousand men against the northern insurgents, but she found she had no need of them.

This has been quoted as evidence of the good effects of the diligent preaching of the Gospel; particularly by Archbishop Gryndall, in his letter to the Queen, to dissuade her from abridging the number of Preachers; the words are these:

"What bred the rebellion in the North? Was it not "Papistry, and the ignorance of God's holy word, through "want of preaching?—And in the time of that rebellion, "were not all men of all estates that made profession of the "Gospel, most ready to offer their lives for your defence?— "Insomuch that one poor parish in Yorkshire, which, by "continual preaching, had been better instructed than the "rest, Halifax I mean, was ready to bring three or four "thousand able men into the field, to serve you against the "said rebels."——

As this Gentleman was so remarkable for doing good by his preaching, it is a pity that he should have been guilty of letting the Vicarage-house run strangely out of repair, as Mr. Wright has expressed it, page 49, or, as I have seen it in a manuscript "of defacing and selling off much of the "housing of the Vicarage."

In Halifax Register is the following note.

"Memorandum, That the yere of our Lorde, 1565, John "Ramsden, of Langley, Gentleman, dyd recover of Xpofer "Ashburn, Clerk, Vicar of Halyfax, by the lawe, certayn "sumes of money for the dett of Sir John Herrison, prede- "cessor to the sayd Xpofer, by means of certayn offring days, "spent and endyd befor the death of the sayd Herrison, "which the sayd Xpofer, at his entrye, recevyd for them for "longe tyme after; the four offring daies were only at "Ester payable, and neverthelesse provyd by the lawe to be

"dewe every several day, and therfore so many of the offryng
"days as were expyrd before the deathe of the sayd Herrison,
"were provyd to be hys goods."

"Wytnes herof, the whole multitude of people then
"lyvynge within the sayd vicarage of Halifax, per me, Xpo.
"Ashburn, tunc ibm Vicar."

Mr. Wright, page 49, says, he takes this to be the same
person mentioned in Willis's Survey of Cathedrals, page
170, as Rector of one of the medieties of Bishop's-hill, York,
and admitted Prebendary of Tockerington, in the Cathedral
there, August 27, 1570, which prebend he resigned, as it
seems he did also the Vicarage of Halifax, in 1573.

Afterwards, as Willis again informs us, page 155, he was
made Prebendary of North Newbald, in the said Cathedral,
which place he held till his death. He was buried at Halifax, December 7, 1584, as by the register there.

15.—Francis Ashburn, son of the above Christopher, was
M.A., and educated at Trinity College, Cambridge; he was
instituted June 3d. according to Mr. Wright, but my manuscript says the last day of June, 1573, having been presented
by Queen Elizabeth, his father, no doubt, having resigned
in his favour, whilst he had a friend at Court.

But this resignation was not of so much benefit to the
family as was hoped for, because he died soon after his
father, July 18, 1585.

Arms of Ashburne, Gules, a fess between six martlets
argent, born by a family of the name in Worcestershire.
These arms are repeated on Halifax church roof, on account
of the father and son.

16.—Henry Ledsam, or Ledsham, D.D., Fellow of Merton
College, in Oxford, presented by Queen Elizabeth, and instituted September 12, 1585.—He resigned the vicarage
November 29, 1593, and was murdered in London, in 1598,
by one who afterwards was hanged at Tyburn, and confessed
the fact just before his execution.

Arms, Quarterly, sable and argent, four leopards heads
counter-changed.

17.—John Favour, L.D., who, according to my manuscript, was instituted December 3, 1593, having been presented by Queen Elizabeth. Mr. Wright sais he was
inducted January 4, 1593, which should be, as we reckon
now, 1594. He died March 10, 1623.

Arms, Parted per pale, argent, three eagles with two heads displayed sable and vert, three dolphins naiant proper, two and one, each coat dimidiated.—For an account of this Vicar, see my list of the most considerable persons belonging to this parish.

18.—Robert Clay, D.D. of the family of Clay, of Clay-house, in Greetland, in this parish, where he was born, was educated in Merton College, Oxford, where he took his Doctor's degree, July 19, 1609.

He was instituted, according to my manuscript, to the vicarage of Halifax, March 18, but as Mr. Wright sais, March 20, 1623, having been presented thereto by Sir Henry Savile, Knight and Baronet.

He died April 9, 1628, leaving by will to Merton College one hundred pounds, for two sermons yearly to be preached to the University, by a Yorkshireman, if any such was Fellow or Chaplain of that College; who, in his prayer, was to mention Dr. Clay, sometime Vicar of Halifax, as the founder of those sermons. See Wood's Fasti, vol. i., p. 184.

He was buried in the library (which he is said to have built) in Halifax church, April 14, 1628, with the following inscription on his grave-stone:

"Robertus Clay, S.T.P. Vicarius de Halifax, obiit Aprilis nono die, Anno Domini 1628."

The Register contains the following entry:

"Robertus Clay, D.D. Oxoniensis Merton, post quadrinum apud Halifax multa cum diligentia et pastorali cura in zodiaco animarum cursum attigisset, dulciter et quiete placida [this should be placidam] vitam transmisit in celestia. Obiit Aprilis nono, et sepultus decimo quarto ejusdem mensis, Anno Dom. 1628."

This character agrees not with the articles exhibited against him by one Smith, and to be found in Godolphin's Repertorium Canonicum, page 189.

"1.—That he read the holy Bible in an irreverent and undecent manner, to the scandal of the whole congregation.

2.—That he did not do his duty in preaching; but, against his oath and the ecclesiastical canon, had neglected for sundry mornings to preach.

3.—That he took the cups, and sundry vessels of the church, consecrated to holy use, and employed them in his own house, and put barm in the cups, that they were so polluted, that the communicants of the parish were loth to drink out of them.

4.—That he did not observe the last fast (proclaimed upon the Wednesday) but on the Thursday, because it was an holiday.

5.—That he retained one Stepheson in one of the chapels of ease, who was a man of ill-life and conversation, viz. an adulterer and a drunkard.

6.—That he did not catechize according to the parish canon, but only bought many of Dr. Wilkinson's catechisms, for every of which he paid two-pence, and sold them to the parishioners for three-pence, without any examination or instruction for their benefit.

And that he, when any commissions were directed to him to compel any person in his parish to do penance, exacted money of them, and so they were dismissed, without inflicting any penalty upon them, as their censure was.

And that he and his servants used divers menaces to his parishioners, and that he abused himself, and disgraced his function, by divers base labours, viz. "he made mortar, "having a leathern apron before him, and he himself took a "tythe pig out of the pigsty, and afterwards he himself gelded it."

And when he had divers presents sent him, as by some flesh, by some fish, and by others ale, he did not spend it in the invitation of his friends and neighbours, or give it to the poor; but sold the flesh to butchers, and the ale to ale-wives.

And that he commanded his curate to marry a couple in a private house without any licence; and that he suffered divers to preach, which peradventure had not any licence, and which were suspected persons and of evil life.

But how far these charges were true does not appear, a prohibition having been granted in the case.

Arms, Gules, on a chevron ingrailed between three trefoils slipt argent, a mullet sable.

19.—HUGH RAMSDEN, B.D. educated likewise at Merton College, of which he was Fellow.

He was baptized at Ealand, March 17, 1594; was inducted into the Vicarage of Halifax, Oct. 7, 1628, on the presentation of King Charles I. having been before made Rector of Methley, in Yorkshire. He died of fever at York, July 16, and was buried in Halifax chancel, July 19, 1629. See the inscription to his memory in the epitaphs belonging to Halifax church. The Register there has this: "Hugo Ramsden, filius Galfridi Ramsden, de Greetland, infra Vicariam de Hallifax, B.D., inductus est Vicarius de Hallifax, 7° Oct., 1628, primoque anno Vicariatus nondum expleto, febri perperacuta correptus mortuus est 17° calend. Augusti, 1629. tristi sui apud omnes bonos, pacisq; Ecclesiæ cultores, relicto desiderio."

Arms, Argent, between three fleurs de lis on a chevron sable, as many rams' heads of the first.

20.—Henry Ramsden, brother to Hugh, was instituted to this Vicarage at the presentation of King Charles I. according to my manuscript August 15, but after Mr. Wright, August 19, and inducted the 23d.

He died March 23, and was buried March 28, 1638. Arms, same as last.

21.—Richard Marsh, D.D., instituted at the presentation of King Charles I. April 12, 1638, and inducted April 17, following.

He was obliged to fly from his living in 1642, to which he did not return till after the King's restoration.—Arms, Gules, a nag's head erased, argent.

After the Doctor's departure, I find that one Wayte was appointed Vicar by the Lord Fairfax, but how long he officiated there I cannot tell.

Mr. Wright, page 61, sais, that Mr. Root was Minister here in 1643 and 1644; John Lake, in 1647 and 1649, (which is true, see a mem. of his at the end of vol. iii. of the Register.)

Then Robert Booth, in 1650, who was buried at Halifax, July 28, 1657.

Lastly, Eli Bentley, born in Sowerby, who was Assistant to Booth, and after his death continued in the place till he was turned out for refusing to comply with the Act of Uniformity, as we are told by Mr. Wright, who has taken his description from Calamy's Account of ejected Ministers, vol. ii., page 804, 2d. edit.

This writer says, that Bentley was bred at Cambridge, and was Fellow of Trinity College there; that he became assistant to Booth in August, 1652—that he fled before the five-mile act, but in 1672 returned to Halifax, and preached in his own house: and that he died July 31, 1675, aged 49.

K

The character he gives of him is, that he was a man of **good parts, a** solid serious Preacher, of a very humble be-**haviour,** and very useful in his place; that he lived desired, **and died** lamented.

I **have** somewhere **seen that after** the removal of Mr. **Root,** Halifax was served, **till the** return of Dr. Marsh, by **stipendiary** Priests, which **from** several circumstances, I believe to be true.

22.—Richard Hooke, D.D., instituted June 10, 1662, at the presentation of King Charles II. and inducted the 29th or 30th following.

He died **January 1, 1688-9.** Being an Author, the farther account of him is inserted in the list of Authors. Arms, **Gules, a fess between six fleurs de lis, argent.**

23.—Edmund Hough, M.A., inducted June 26, 1689, on the presentation of King James II.

From the first edition of Calamy's **Account of** ejected Ministers **it** appears, that this Mr. Hough **was turned** out of his Fellowship in Jesus College, Cambridge, by **the** Act of Uniformity; after this, however, he thought fit to conform, and was made Rector of Thornton, in Craven, and Vicar of Halifax.

He died April 1, 1691, and **was** buried in the **chancel** at Halifax, with an inscription over him, which **see** amongst the Epitaphs. Arms, Argent, **a** bend sable.

Mr. Thoresby had **some** manuscript sermons **of this Vicar** in his museum.

In Halifax register **is this entry:** "Edmundus Hough, A.M. **inductus erat in Vicar. de** Halifax per Jacobum Roberts, **Vicar. de Bingley, 26° die Junii, 1689.** Sepultus 3° Aprilis, **1691.—Vir de tota** ecclesia tam pietatis quam doctrinæ ergo optime **meritus,** industrius Pastor, **et efficax** Evangelii Concionator quondam dignus, Coll. Jesu Cant. Socius, et. Ecclesiæ Thorntonensis doctus et diligens Rector, **tandem** hujus Ecclesiæ sedulus **per** biennium Vicarius."

24.—Joseph Wilkinson, M.A. **instituted** Sept. 7th, or 17th **and** inducted October **26, 1691, having** been presented by King William III.

He was first Vicar of Chapel-izod, near Dublin, and Pre-bendary of Casterknock, in the Cathedral of St. Patrick's, Dublin, afterwards rector of Wigginton, in Yorkshire.

He died December 28, 1711, and was buried in the chancel at Halifax, the 31st following.

For the inscription over him see the Epitaphs.—Arms, Gules, a fess vaire, in chief an unicorn passant or, in a bordure. . . .

25.—Thomas Burton, M.A., Rector of **Lofthouse**, and **curate** of **Yarum**, in Yorkshire, was instituted March 28, **and inducted April 3d. or 4th, 1712, on** the presentation of **Queen Anne.**

March **1, 1715, he** was made Prebendary of the Prebend of Gevendale, in the Cathedral of York. He died July 22, 1731, **and was** buried in **the** Chancel at Halifax, without **any** memorial of him, **July 25, 1731.**

Arms, Quarterly, first, a **fess** between three talbots' heads, couped or.—2dly, Azure, a **spread eagle** and a chief **or, first as** fourth, second as third.

26.—George Legh, LL.D. inducted, as **Mr.** Wright **sais,** October 2, 1731, **but** another **account sais,** August 2. **Presented by King George II.**

He has **since been** made Prebendary of York, in the Bottevant-**hall there.** He was **a** Cheshire man, and the arms **of his** family **are,** argent, **a** lion **rampant,** gules, langued and armed azure, a crescent for difference.

He died the 6th of December, 1775, in **the 82d year** of his age, and **was buried in** the Vestry **at Halifax,** where an elegant monument **is erected, with** the following inscription:

"Near this place, in the same **vault,** are deposited the **remains** of the Rev. George Legh, LL.D. and his two beloved **Wives,** Frances and Elisabeth; **to whose** joint memory this **Monument is erected.**

He was Vicar of this Church and Vicarage **of** Halifax above forty four years; during which time he interested himself, with laudable zeal, in the cause of religious liberty and sincerity; being the last survivor of those worthy men, who **distinguished** themselves by their opposition to ecclesiastical tyranny. **He** defended the rights of mankind in that memorable **Hoadlian** controversy.

The Bible **he considered** as the only standard of faith and practice.—To **the** poor and distressed, and public charities, he was a generous benefactor. By his Will he ordered Bibles **to be given for the benefit of** the Poor.

He did honour to his profession as a Clergyman and Christian.—He was esteemed when living, and in death lamented.—He died composed on the 6th of December, 1775, in the 82d. Year of his age. His Wife Frances died Dec. 9th, 1749.—Elisabeth, Feb. 8th, 1765.

27.—The Revd. HENRY WOOD, D.D. the present Vicar of Halifax, was inducted February 14, 1776.

—::—

LIST OF LECTURERS

AT HALIFAX CHURCH.

J. Booth. — Eli Bentley. — . . . Mitchel. — . . . Lambert, came in 1676. — . . . Hanson. — Francis Parrot, above fifty years. — John Holdsworth, in 1740. — Samuel Sandford, made Vicar of Huddersfield, and afterwards Rector of Thornhill. — . . . . Charlesworth. — . . . . Meyrick.

Mr. Wright, p. 165, sais, that John Lake, (afterwards Bishop of Chichester) was Lecturer in 1647; but at p. 61, he had told us, that he was at that time in possession of the living.

It may not be amiss to insert here the form of a declaration enjoined in the Act of Uniformity of public prayer, 14 Cha. II. made by one of these Lecturers, and transcribed from the original.

"I Thomas Hanson, Clerk, and M^r of Arts, now to be "admitted Lecturer of the Parish Church of Halifax, in the "county and diocese of York, do declare that it is not law-"full, upon any pretence whatsoever, to take armes against "the King: And that I do abhorr that trayterous position "of taking arms, by his authority, against his person, or "against those that are commissionated by him. And that "I will conform to the Liturgy of the Church of England, "as it is now by law established. Tho. Hanson." Then "follows the certificate.

"This declaration and acknowledgement was subscribed "by the above named Thomas Hanson, Lecturer of Halifax, "in the diocese of York, before me. Witness my hand and "seal, this second day of October, in the year of our Lord, "1683." In the margin, the small Archiepiscopal seal, and "under it, "Joh. Ebor."

A Mr. Mitchel was hired in 1669, by the consent of the town and parish, either as Lecturer, or Curate, but probably the former; however the Vicar at present chuses both, by custom.

EPITAPHS IN THE

CHURCH AND CHURCH-YARD

AT HALIFAX.

THE method I shall observe herein will be to give those belonging to each respective family apart, in an alphabetical manner, that they may be sooner found by inspection.

ALLENSON.

On a stone of blue marble* in the South Chapel: "Under this marble is interred the body of the reverend and learned JAMES ALLENSON, A.M. Rector of Thornton, in Craven, who died the 26th and was buried the 29th day of November, 1730.

ALDERSON.

On a tomb-stone over ANN ALDERSON, of Bull-close, in the Church-yard: "She was of an admirable, sweet, obliging temper, free from censure, passion, and pride, generous, charitable, and respectful, a person worthy of imitation."

BROADLEY.

In the wall of the south-side, over a door, on a brass plate: "Mr. Jo. BROADLEY, late Minister at Sowerby Chapp. died Feb. 14, 1625, and Mary, his wife, also died March the 2d, 1625, and here lie buried.

> Here lies interr'd a zealous grave Divine,
>   Meek, loving, lov'd, only with sin at strife;
> Who heard him, saw life in his doctrine shine,
>   Who saw him, heard sound doctrine in his life;
>   And in the same cold bed here rests his Wife.
> Nor are they dead, but sleep; for he ne'er dies
> That waits for his sweet Saviour's word, *Arise*."

* I was more than displeased to find that during the 1880 renovations this blue stone was deliberately cut in two, and a stone covering Vicar Knight had part of the inscription cut off, when half-a-yard at the bottom might have been taken instead, without detriment. This was even worse than boiling the oak pews!

BATLEY.

Near the font, on a marble monument in the north wall: "Near this place is interred, the body of John Batley, late of this town, Salter. A man just in his dealings, exemplary in his life and conversation, a kind and affectionate husband, a tender and indulgent parent, a pious and sincere Christian; he finished this life, hoping for a happy immortality. To his memory, Susannah, his widow, caused this monument to be erected. He departed the 28th day of July, 1717, aged 66 years, and one day.—In the same place lieth the body of Thomas, eldest son of the said John Batley, who departed this life the 28th day of March, 1702, aged 19 years, 7 weeks and 2 days."

BREARCLIFFE.

On a pillar on the south side of the font: An epitaph on Ester, late wife of Edmond Brearcliffe, of Halifax, who died June 16th, 1629, and on Favour, their son, who died March 5th, 1628.

> "Here rest three Saints; the one a little Brother,
> The Favour of his scarce surviving Mother:
> Then she expired, and bore unto her tomb,
> An unborn infant coffin'd in her womb."

This Mr. Brearcliffe, as we are told by Mr. Wright, was, October 1, 1623, made Parish Clerk by Dr. Favour, then Vicar, and having a son christened the 14th of March following, out of gratitude, called him Favour.

BENTLEY.

On a gravestone in the South Chapel: "Eli Bentley, son of Richard Bentley, of Sowerby Dene, M.A. some time Fellow of Trinity College, in Cambridge, and late Minister of the Gospel at Halifax, departed this life July 30th 1675, in the 45th year of his age."

On a stone in the Church-yard: "Here were buried three children of the Rev. Mr. Daniel Bentley, Curate of Illingworth, and of Elizabeth, his wife, daughter of John Wadsworth, late of Holdsworth. Also the Rev. Mr. Daniel Bentley, who was Curate of Illingworth above 30 years, died the 15th of November, 1748."

CAYGILL.

In the north-east corner of the Quire, is erected a neat monument, with the following inscription :

Sacred to the **Memory of**
JOHN CAYGILL, Esq.,
Who departed this life the 22d **of May, 1787,**
Aged 79 Years.

CROWTHER.

On a tomb in the Church-yard : "Here lieth the **body of** HENRY CROWTHER, who was born in Norland, died at Ball-Green, in Sowerby, December 21, Anno Dom. 1635." Round the border these lines :

"Eighty-four years I liv'd ; wouldst thou **so do,**
Be thou, as I, quiet, chaste, **and** temp'rate too,
Norland me gave, and Sowerby took my breath ;
Man knows the place of birth, but not of death."

DEAN.

Round the border of a stone near the font : "Here lieth the body of ROBERT DEAN, eldest son of Robert Dean, of Exley, who died January 7, 1619." Within the border : "Here resteth **the** body of Ann, the wife of Mr. Robt. Dean of Exley, who departed this life the 19th day of September, 1661.

There is a God with whom I trust
My soul shall triumph, when my body is dust."

DOLLIFE.

On a brass plate behind the Governor's pew ; "Here resteth the body of Mary, the wife of RICHARD DOLLIFE, of Halifax, who was buried the 12th of August, Anno Dom. 1659.

Reader, **here** lies intomb'd a virtuous wife,
Whose **sweet** deportment whilst she had a life
Procur'd her husband's love, her friends' delight,
But th' **grief** of both since she hath bid good night.

Also RICHARD DOLLIFE, her husband, who departed this life the 14th of September, 1681, in the 64th year of his age."

Tradition says, that the above four lines were composed
by Archbishop Sharp, when a scholar at Bradford school,
which is probable enough, as they seem to be the composition
of a school-boy.

DUN.

On a marble monument upon the wall of the south side
of the Chancel.

M. S.
Hic juxta conditur
Quod reliquum est JOSHUÆ DUN,
Filii Joshuæ et Mariæ Dun, de Halifax,
Collegii Christi dum apud Cantabrigienses floruit Alumni
Quin et Collegii et Academiæ decoris et ornamenti,
Nunc proh dolor! tristis iisdem desiderii;
Juvenis erat, si ætatem; si spectas dotes, vir eximius;
Si quem eximium reddere valeant
Probitas, summum ingenii acumen, acre judicium,
Artium scientia, morum suavitas, urbanitas.
Sese quantumvis ad omne literarum genus aptum natum,
In Medicina persertim excolenda, seu potius ornanda,
Exercuit;
In qua tam mirificos fecit progressus,
Ut brevi istius Facultatis peritus admodum prodierit:
Summatim,
Nisi quodtantum mortalibus fata invidissent virum,
Ad morbos propulsandos,
Et ad redintegrandas labefactatas hominum vires
Plane natus videbatur:
Ast heu! buam aliis potuit sibi-metipsi non concessum est
Opem afferre;
Variolis enim correptus, post duodecim dies,
Cum spes jam eum revaliturum effulserat,
Inter seros nepotes vix æquiparandus,
Haud certe unquam superandus, occubuit,
Die 13 Sept. MDCCIX, annos natus XXV.
Nec procul ab illo recumbit
Pater ejus Joshua Dun,
Qui obiit 7o Aug. A. D. 1715.   Ætatis suæ 80.
Et mater ejus Maria Dun,
Quæ obiit Apr. 5o A. D. 1729.
Ætatis 87.

The above, Mr. Wright, page **180**, says, he was told **was** drawn **up** by the ingenious Mr. Nicholas Sanderson, Professor of Mathematics in the University of Cambridge.

In English.*

Near this **place** lie the remains **of** Joshua Dun, **son** of Joshua and **Mary Dun**, of Halifax, student of Christ College, shedding a lustre **on it** and the University while he lived at Cambridge, **and at his** death deservedly lamented :—**In the** flower of his **age, he** was endowed with those qualities which render a character truly respectable. Though born with a **propensity for** universal literature, **he** excelled chiefly in the **healing art ;** in which he made **so** amazing a progress **as to become** very skilful in that faculty. To sum **up all, he** seemed born to relieve the distresses of his fellow creatures, **had not** divine wisdom thought fit to release so great **a man from** the ties of mortality at so early a period.

Being taken with the small-pox, after an illness of 12 days, he finished life on the 13th of September, 1709, aged 25, with a character hardly to be equalled by posterity. Near his grave rests his Father, Joshua Dun, who died August 17, 1715, aged 80 ; as also his Mother, Mary Dun, who died April 5, 1729, aged 87.

FAVOUR.

On a gravestone in the chancel : " Hic Dormit JOHANNES FAVOUR, Doctor sanctissmus hujus Ecclesiæ......

> Occubuit **scris, heu !** quod non **serius, annis ;**
>> Nec longæva magis quam bona vita fuit.
> Quam sacre velavit speciosum pectore corpus,
>> Dignum equidem tumulo nobiliore tegi.
> Qui quidem extremam fidus permansit ad horam,
>> Non illi tumulus, sed diadema decus.
> Theologus, Medicusq ; obiit, Jurisq ; peritus :
>> I, sequere in cœlos, qui **modo** salvus **eris.**"

In English. *

Here **sleeps** John Favour, **a** pious Doctor of this Church.

> Loaded with honours, **as** with years,
>> He mounts above the starry spheres ;
>> Releas'd from earth by pitying fate,
>> Tho' worthy of a longer date :

* These translations do not appear in Watson. They were probably supplied **to Jacob by the Rev.** E. Nelson.

How weak the monument we raise,
To equal his deserved praise !
Whose soul **was** undismayed by death,
And faithful to his latest breath.
Reader, pursue him to the skies,
Who shalt, like him, in glory rise.

On a pillar on the south side of the quire is a monument, erected to the memory of the above Dr. Favour, who is placed as in a pulpit, drest in his robes, and in an attitude of preaching, with one hand on his breast, and the other on a skull, which rests on the cushion before him.

Jo. Favour, LL. Doct. Medici peritiss.   et hujus
Ecclesiæ Pastoris vigilantissimi.
" Corpora et ægrotant animæ; fremit undiq ; rixa,
Scilicet orba suo turba Favore jacet.
En Pastor, Medicusq ; obiit, Jurisq ; peritus :
I sequere in cœlos, qui modo salvus eris."

In English.*

Jo. Favour, LL.D., practitioner in physic, and a most vigilant Pastor of this Church.
" With sick'ning heart and fainting breath,
We hear the sound of Favour's death ;
The pastor, friend, physician is no more,
Pursue him, Reader, and with him adore."

FAUCIT.

On a brass plate near the font : " Here lieth the body of Hugh Faucit, of Halifax, buried the 8th day of April, A.D. 1641 ; and also Hugh Faucit, his son, was buried the 19th day of August, 1668. Ut enim per Adamum omnes moriuntur, sic per Christum omnes reviviscent."

FOURNIS.

On a monument, upon the north wall of the chancel : " Near this place is interred the body of Captain John Fournis, who died the 10th, and was buried the 12th of November, 1717, aged 35 years." Several more of this family are mentioned here, and on a tablet on one of the pillars on the north side of the chancel, for which see Mr.

* This translation does not appear in Watson. It was probably supplied to Jacob by the Rev. E. Nelson.

Wright, p. 180, 181.   [After "35 years," read "and at a small distance are interred the bodies of two of his children; JANE, his daughter, died the 25th, and was buried the 28th of July, 1720, aged 5 years 11 months; SUSANNAH, his daughter, died the 20th, and was buried the 22d of July, 1722, aged 5 years and 2 months."   On a tablet on the north side of the chancel, on one of the pillars: "Mr. JOSEPH FOURNES departed this life the 3d day of March, 1676, aged 73 years.   HANNAH FOURNES, his daughter, born Aug. 7, 1666, departed this life Apr. 27, 1680.   JOHN FOURNES, his son, was born Jan. 8, 1664, departed this life Oct. 29, 1683. SAMUEL FOURNES, his son, born Dec. 7, 1662, departed this life Feb. 20, 1687.   PHÆBE, daughter of Mr. S. Fournes, was born Oct. 14th, 1687, and died the 21st of March, 1699.] Capt. Fournis lived in Halifax.

GAUKROGER.

On a stone in the church-yard: "Here lieth the body of JOHN GAUKROGER, who faithfully discharged the office of Parish Clerk of Halifax for the space of 22 years.   He departed this life the 6th day of May, 1707, in the 62d year of his age.   He lived beloved, and died lamented of all that knew him."

GREAME.

On a grave-stone in the chancel: "Here lieth the body of HANNAH, the wife of HENRY GREAME, of Shaw-Hill, in Skircoate, who departed this life the 13th day of Sept., 1727, in the 67th year of her age.

> She, that does take her rest within this tomb,
> Had Rachael's face, and Leah's fruitful womb,
> Abigail's wisdom, Lydia's faithful heart,
> Martha's care, and Mary's better part."

On a neat monument in the Quire, is the following inscription:

WILLIAM GREAME,
of Heath, near this Town,
died in April, 1739, aged 44.
He married
Mrs. Frances Kirke, of Alverthorpe,
who died in October 1752, aged 57.

Their Children were
John, William, James, Elizabeth, and Ann,
who, with their Parents,
are all buried in this Quire:
where also is interred
Mrs. Elizabeth Kirke,
twin-sister of Mrs. Frances Kirke:
She died in January, 1756.

This monument was erected with every sentiment of gratitude and respect, by the executors of William Greame last mentioned, who was a Captain in Sir George Savile's Batalion of Militia. An amiable and benevolent temper, joined to an uncommon penetration, and a clear knowledge of men and things, rendered this gentleman a truly valuable member of the community, and of course universally beloved and honoured.

In December 1764, he married Elizabeth Dorothea Zouch, youngest daughter of Charles Zouch, late Vicar of Sandal-magna, and died on May the 27th, 1776, aged 36.

Frances, his only child, who was born about three months after her Father's death, is now (1769) living.

GIBSON.

On a monument in the north west corner of the church: "Near this place is interred ELIZABETH GIBSON, of Slead-Hall, who died A. Æ. S. 23. A.D. 1690. And ROBERT GIBSON, of Slead-Hall, who died A. Æ. S. 63. A. D. 1691. And MICHAEL GIBSON, the son of Michael Gibson, of Slead-Hall, who died A. Æ. S. 1°. A. D. 1711. And RHENETTA, the wife of Robert Gibson, who died A. Æ. S. 84. A.D. 1715. And ELIZABETH, the wife of Michael Gibson, who died A. Æ. S. 52. A. D. 1722. And MICHAEL GIBSON, of Slead-Hall, son of Robert, who died A. Æ. S. 72. A. D. 1738. And ROBERT GIBSON, of Slead-Hall, son of Michael, who died A. Æ. S. 43. A. D. 1746. Also WILLIAM GIBSON, M. D. Anat. Prof. Cantabrigiæ, who died Feb. 16, 1753, aged 39."

HEALD.

On a grave-stone in the chancel: "Hic tecti jacent cineres JEREMIÆ, filii M^{ri} GULIELMI HEALD, nuper Vicarii de Donaghadee, in Hibernia, qui 22do Ætatis anno animam Deo inspiranti retribuit, 5° die Augusti, 1685. Quem tuetur ac diligit Deus, Juvenis supremum mortis intrat limitem."

On another stone in the chancel: "Quæris advena, quid hac abdita incarceratur urna, reliquiæ mortales immortalis animæ terrigenas mortalitatis suæ exuvias ad Dei judicis usq; adventum hic deponentis, cœlo jam triumphantis, si modo virtus pietatis patientiæ virtus cœlum animis æternitati maturis aperit. Nomen humati Lector ambis, GRATIA est, Filia M^ri GULIELMI HEALD, Uxor FRANCISCI PRIESTLEY, quæ geminam prolem fæcunditatis suæ partem hic præmittens, ipsa post plusculum dierum expiravit 16 die Novembris, Anno Dom. 1685. Ætatis 30.

In English.

Here lie the ashes of JEREMY, son of Mr. William Heald, late Vicar of Donaghadee, in Ireland, who yielded his soul up to God who gave it, August 5, 1685, aged 22.

> The youth whom God protects and loves,
> From earth, with pleasing hope removes.

You ask, O stranger, what this hidden Urn contains.

Answer.—The frail remains of an immortal soul, putting off its earthly tabernacle till its Judge appear,—and now triumphing in glory, if piety and patience can open heaven to minds matured for eternity.

Ask you the name of the interred? It is GRACE, the daughter of Mr. William Heald, wife of Francis Priestley, who died a few days after the birth of her two children, viz. November 16, 1685, aged 30.

HILL.

On a tomb in the church-yard is an inscription to the memory of Mr. EDWARD HILL, late Rector of Crofton, aged 79 years, and of ANN, his wife, who having been married 53 years, died both on the same day, and were buried in that tomb, Jan. 29, 1668.

The account which Calamy, in his list of the ejected Ministers, p. 793, gives of this Clergyman, is this: "That he was M.A. of Christ's College, Cambridge; that he had been formerly a Nonconformist, but could not fall in with the new settlement in 1662; that he was a pious, grave, ancient Divine, of an excellent temper; that on the coming forth of the Five-mile Act he removed to Shibden, near Halifax; and that he and his wife had lived together forty years, and died within two hours of one another in Jan. 1668-9." Mr. Wright adds, that he had likewise been Vicar of Huddersfield, and died at Shipden-Hall.

HOOKE.

On a marble monument in the chancel: "P. M. RICHARDI HOOKE, S. T. P. Regimini tam ecclesiastico quam sæculari Anglicano fidelissimi, qui per viginti sex annos huic Ecelesiæ præfuit Vicarius, tribus Archiepiscopis Ebor[bus] a sacris, Hospitiorum sancti Johannis beatæq. Mariæ Magdelenensis sub agro RIPPONENSI Magister, Ecclesiæ Ebor[sis] SOUTHWELL[sis] RIPPONENSISQ. Canonicus. Obiit 1mo Jan. Ætatis suæ 66. Anno Domini 1688-9.

On a gravestone in the chancel: "MATILDA, filia RICHARDI HOOKE, D. D. Vicar. de Halifax, obiit 9 Sept. A. D. 1667. Ætatis suæ 18." And below: "SAMUEL HOOKE, filius Richardi Hooke, M.A. Socius Coll. Jesu Cantabr. vir egregie doctus, et insigniter pius, a societate Jesu in terris exaltatus est ad societatem Jesu in cœlis, Aug. 12, 1687. Ætat. suæ 24."

On a stone near the above: "ANNA HOOKE, Matildæ soror, obiit Dec. 15. An. 20. A. D. 1667. In cœlum tendentibus non est ætatis ratio, non gradus: Majorem natu præcessit minor, quam (sancte invidens) sequuta est, ah cito nimis! Innuptæ in terra Virgines in cœlo nuptæ: At semper Virgines æternum cum Sponso gaudent. ELIZ. HOOKE, filia Ri. Hooke, Virgo pia et casta terrestre tabernaculum pro domo cælesti commutavit, Aug. 30. A. D. 1687. Ætat. suæ 26."

In English.

Erected to the memory of RICHARD HOOKE, S.T.P., equally faithful in his ecclesiastical and civil departments, who was Vicar of this church 26 years; Master of the Seminaries of St. John and Mary Magdalen's, in the county of Rippon, Canon of Southwell, &c. He died January 1, 1688-9. On a gravestone: "MATILDA, the daughter of Richard Hooke, D.D., Vicar of Halifax, died Sept. 9, 1667, aged 18. And below, "SAMUEL HOOKE, son of Richard Hooke, M.A., Fellow of Jesus' College, Cambridge, a man remarkable for his learning and piety, being raised from the society of Jesus'

College on earth to that of Jesus in Heaven, Aug. 12, 1687, aged 24." Near the above.—"ANN HOOKE, sister to Matilda, died Dec. 15, 1667, An. 20. The younger died before the older, who (impelled by a sacred emulation) too quickly followed. Unmarried on earth they are united above. In a state of lasting virginity they rejoice for ever with their God. ELIZABETH HOOKE, daughter of Ri. Hooke, a chaste and pious virgin, changed an earthly habitation for a heavenly mansion, Aug. 30, 1687, aged 26.

HOUGH.

The following inscription was put over Vicar Hough, who was buried in the Chancel: " Sacrum memoriæ EDMUNDI HOUGH, A M. e Coll. Jesu Cant. quondam Socii, Parochiæ de THORNTON postea Rectoris, tandemq; hujus Ecclesiæ Præsidis; qui concionandi perspicuus, disserendo facundus, pietate catholicus, post exiguum autem Olicanæ temporis impensum morienti hanc desideratam requiem sibi dedit Deus. Obiit 1mo die Aprilis, 1691. Anno ætatis 59."

There is an English one to the memory of the same, on a stone in the Chancel, taken from part of the above.

It was a great mistake in the writer of the above epitaph to call Halifax by the name of Olicana, for that was undoubtedly the Roman station at Ilkley.

In English.

Sacred to the memory of EDMUND HOUGH, M. A., Fellow of Jesus' College, Cambridge, afterwards Rector of the parish of Thornton, and lastly Vicar of this Church, a perspicuous preacher, an able rhetorician, and of catholic piety. After a short residence at Halifax, he obtained his desired rest, April 1, 1691, aged 59.

HOLDSWORTH.

On the wall in the South Chapel : " Near this place lieth the body of THO. HOLDSWORTH, of Ashday, in Southouram, Gentleman, who departed this life the 23d of June, 1709 ; and also the body of Mrs. PHEBE HOLDSWORTH, his wife, the daughter of James Oats, of Landshead, in Northouram, who departed this life the 12th of October, 1709 : And also the body of MARY HOLDSWORTH, the daughter of William Midgley, of Halifax, Gentleman, and wife of Tho. Holdsworth, son of

the above mentioned Tho. Holdsworth, **who departed this
life the 25th of October, 1710."**

HOLDEN.

On a stone in the Church-yard, near the sun door, round
the border: "Hic jacent ANNA, ARTHUR, JOHANNES, LIONEL,
TOBIAS HOLDEN, universa Gowaini et Annæ Holden de Halifax, Anno Domini **1642."** Within the border:

> " Ne doleas Genetrix, toties ad funera pregnans
>   Horrida ne timeas mater ad arma ferax.
> Ante togam minor impietas, cita sanctior urna ;
>   Plurimus ille parens solus ad astra parens."

In English.

" **Here rest ANN, &c.,** the entire issue of Gowen and Ann
Holden.

> Lament not, mother, oft the fruitful womb,
> Is but an ante-chamber to the tomb ;
> In tender love th' inspirer of our breath,
> Prevents our sorrows by a speedy **death."**

HOLLINGS.

On the south wall in the Chancel: "Near this place lye
the remains of JEREMIAH HOLLINGS, late of Shipley, in this
county, Esq; and also of MARY, his mother, widow and
relict of Mr. Isaac Hollings, late of Shipley aforesaid. She
was one of the daughters and coheirs of Mr. Jeremiah Rossendale, formerly of Shaw-hill, in Skircoat.

> He ⎫ dyed ⎰August 23d, 1738, aged **26.**
> She ⎭ ⎱May 9th, 1744, aged 53."

The above is cut on a very neat monument, at the foot of
which are the heads of three cherubims, above the writing a
Sarcophagus, the marble rises in the form of a pyramid, on
which are the arms of Hollings impaled with those of
Rossendale.

KITCHINGHAM.

In the Wall in the North Chapel: William, son of WM.
KITCHINGHAM, of Skircoat, buried the 26th of July, 1670.
Martha, his daughter, was buried the 19th of June, 1695,
and Sarah, his wife, was buried the 30th day of July, 1704.
Wright, p. 187, omitted by Watson.

LACY.

Dr. Johnson in his MS. Collections for Yorkshire, sais, that in Halifax Church was the following, in antient characters: "Here lieth enclosed the body of JOHN LACYE, of Brerely, Esq; who was buried the 19th day of August, in the year of our Lord God . . . ." (This date should be 1585.) Part of this stone I saw in 1764; it had cut upon it the figure of a man in armor laid on his back, a cushion under his head, and a lion at his feet; on one side hung a large sword, and a small one on the other; his hands were joined on his breast in a praying posture; on his left arm a shield, with the following coats of arms: 1. Argent, six ogresses, three, two, one, for Lacy. 2. Gules, three crescents argent, on a chief of the second three garbs or. 3. Gules an eagle displayed argent, for Soothill, of Soothill. 4. Argent, three bendlets sable; all these quarterly impaled with Argent, a chevron between three crosses formée, fitchée gules, for Woodrove, of Woolley. The above Dr. Johnson sais farther, that under the arms of Lacy were in old characters, "Orate pro anima Magistri Joannis Lacye." It is not improper to mention here, that on a grave-stone in the Chancel is a large cross, on one side of which is a sword of lead laid in the stone, and on the other, in a shield, the ogresses as above.

LISTER.

In the south west corner of the Church, on a neat monument: "H. S. E. JACOBUS LISTER, de Shibden-hall, Gens. qui Nov. 14, A.D. 1729, Æt. 56, triste sui desiderium viduæ liberisq; decem reliquit.

> Prosiliunt lacrimæ—sed adest spes certa salutis,
> Christus, qui mortis vincula rupta dedit.
> Hic jubet ut memores recolamus gaudia vitæ
> Venturæ, et cæli quæ bona civis habet.

In English.

JAMES LISTER, GENT., who left a disconsolate widow and ten children.

> Nature will weep—but O repress the tear,
> Since Christ and his salvation are so near.

L

> The gospel loud invites us to rejoice,
> Who wou'd not hearken to a Saviour's voice?
> His dear requests with pleasure we obey,
> And wait the morning of a happier day.

In the same grave is interred the body of MARY, widow of the said James Lister. She died Jan. 5, 1756, aged 79.

> Bless'd are the dead proclaims the voice above
> Who die in Christ, abiding in his love.
> They rest from labor in the peacefull tomb,
> Shall rise to glory in the life to come.
>   J. L. F. N. M. P. C.

These last letters stand for Johannes Lister filius natu maximus poni curavit. He was a Clergyman, lived at Shibden-hall, and composed the above.

MADDOCKS.

Near the Font, in a neat gilted frame, is the following inscription :

> Near
> this place, lie the remains of
> JOSEPH MADDOCKS,
> of Cold-Blow, near
> Dublin, in Ireland,
> Who died the 22d and was buried
> the 24th of March, 1769,
> aged 74 Years.

"Those who sleep in Christ, will he bring with him."

MAUD.

On a grave-stone in the Chancel: "Hic situm est corpus THOMÆ, filii JONATH. MAUD, de Halyfax, M. A. qui obiit Decemb. 22, A. D. 1682.

> Si mea cum matris valuissent vota, dedisses
>   Funus idem nobis, quod tibi, nate, damus.
> Sed quoniam votis nostris Deus obstitit æquus,
>   Ante mea et matris funera, funus habe.

In English.

Here is deposited the remains of THOMAS, son of Jonathan Maud.

Had Heav'n vouchsaf'd to hear thy parents' pray'r,
Their sad sepulchral rites had been thy care ;
Impartial wisdom did the wish deny,
And took thee earlier to a world on high.

MIDGLEY.

On the wall in the north chapel : " Near this place resteth the body of MARY, daughter of WILLIAM MIDGLEY, Master of Arts, late of Headley, now of Sowerby, who was born March 3, 1696, and departed this life November 7, 1704.

Mortal by birth, short my stay, here sleeps my dust,
My better part joins consort with the just."

Above this : " Exuviæ GULIELMI MIDGLEY, A. M. Curat. de Sowerby, juxta depositæ Maii 10°, 1706. Anno Ætatis 34."

MITCHELL.

On a brass plate near the font. " Here resteth the body of JAMES MITCHELL, late of Crow-nest, in Hipperholm. He was buried the 1st day of October, A. D. 1679 ; and also three of his children. ANN was buried the 3d of April, 1668. ELISABETH was buried the 29th of May, 1676. SAMUEL, he was buried January the 30th, 1676.

Non abiit, sed obiit, modo rediturus."

NETTLETON.

On a stone in the chancel : " Hic requiescit ANNA filia THOMAS NETTLETON, M. D. nata 23 Octob. 1709. Obiit 23 Jan. 1710-11.—In eodem tumulo conditur frater ejus JOHANNES NETTLETON, nat. 25 Dec. 1715. Obiit 6 Apr. 1717. —Et eorum Amita SUSANNA NETTLETON, quæ obiit 12° Apr. A. D. 1718. Ætatis 23."

In English.

Here rests ANN . . . NETTLETON, born Oct. 23, 1709. Died Jan. 23, 1710. In the same grave is interred her brother, and their aunt.

PARRAT.

On a stone in the chancel : " Here is interred the body of the Rev. Mr. FRANCIS PARRAT, who was Lecturer of Halifax above fifty years, and died the 22d of December, in the 82d year of his age, 1741.

PRESCOT.

On a grave-stone in the north chapel: "Hic jacet PHEBE, Uxor GULIELMI PRESCOT, Chirurgo-Medici. Obiit 10° die Martii, 1704-5, Ætatis suæ 36. Et cum illa dormiunt una Nepotes duo, NATHANAEL, et GULIELMUS FARRER. [In the same grave are interred two grand-children, NATHANIEL and WILLIAM FARRER.]

In the south chapel, on a monument on the wall: "MARY, the daughter of Mr. JOHN PRESCOT, of Halifax, was buried near this place the 18th day of May, 1708. And in the same grave is interred the body of the above-named Mr. JOHN PRESCOT, Practitioner in Physic and Chirurgery, who died the 11th day of November, 1728, in the 53d year of his age. Also SARAH, his wife, who died June 10, 1739, in the 56th year of her age.

RAMSDEN.

On a pillar in the chancel: "Hic jacet HUGO RAMSDEN, filius Galfridi Ramsden, de Greetland, infra Vicariam de Halifax, Bacc. in S.S. Theol. olim Socius Collegii de Merton in Ac. Ox. postea Rector de Methley, in Comit. Ebor. demum Vicarius de Halifax. Vir dubium sanctior, an doctior, ingenii acris, judicii subacti, eruditionis multiplicis, qui omne tempus deperire existimabat quod non aut musæo impertiabatur; qui dum vixit toti circumjacenti Regioni doctrina sua prælucebat, et magis exemplo; atq; moriens triste sui apud omnes bonos, pacisq; Ecclesiæ cultores reliquit Desiderium. Inductus est Vicarius de Halifax Non. Octob. An. Salutis 1628, et decimo septimo Calend. Augusti sequentis vitam cum immortalitate commutavit. Hoc mœrens monumentum posuit Frater ejus natu minor, ejusq; in Vicaria de Halifax impar successor, Henricus Ramsden."

To the word "commutavit," there is the same on a tablet in Methley church, put there in 1680 by one Robert Nalson.

On a pillar opposite to the above: "Hic jacet HENRICUS RAMSDEN, filius natu secundus Galfridi Ramsden, de Greetland, infra Vicariam de Halifax, Artium Magister, necnon Collegii Lincoln. in inclyt. Oxon Academ. quondam Socius, tandemq; Vicarius de Halifax, ibidemq; fratris sui Hugonis permagni. Licet multiq; nominis decessoris haud impar successor, vir equidem multijugis eruditionis, et quod familiam ducit, spectatæ admodum probitatis, quo sane egregie viguit, quicquid est, quod in aliis aut suspicimus eruditi, aut quod veneramur sancti, literarum perinde decus pietatisq; exemplum per duo præter propter annorum lustra memor stationis munerisq; sui huic summopere invigilabat Ecclesiæ, ardens vita, verboq; lucens, quo temporis decursu fidelis erat populi pastor, causæ pauperum propugnator acerrimus, pacis Ecclesiæ strenuus assertor, Justiciæ publicæ, uti pro officio tenebatur, promptus licet cautus tamen et æquus dispensator, hujusce loci ordinis regiminisq; politici cum primis author, tandem lethali correptus victusq; febri triste sui apud omnes relinquens desiderium, gratamque memoriam non sine justitio luctuque publico spiritum in manus Domini reddidit, placideq; spe resurrectionis fultus obdormivit anno Salutis 1637. septim. calend. Martii. Hoc mœrens monumentum posuit frater ejus GULIELMUS RAMSDEN natur minor, Rectorque Ecclesiæ de Edgmund, in agro Salop.

In English.

Here lie the remains of HUGH RAMSDEN, son of G. R., of Greetland, B.A.; formerly Fellow of Merton College, Oxford, afterwards Rector of Methley, and lastly Vicar of Halifax; a pious learned man, of a penetrating judgment, who thought that time was lost which was not employed in the church or study. His example cast a lustre on this place and its environs, and at his death he was deservedly regretted by his parishioners. He was collated to this Vicarage, October, 1628, and put on immortality the 17th of August following. His younger brother and successor, HENRY RAMSDEN, erected this testimony of affection to his memory.

In memory of HENRY RAMSDEN, second son of G. R., M.A., and Fellow of Lincoln College, Oxford, afterwards Vicar of Halifax, which office his brother Hugh Ramsden had enjoyed before him; a person well known for his learning and probity, (the ornament of letters) and an exemplar of piety, faithful in the discharge of his function, and particularly attentive to the Church's interest for near eight years, exemplary in his life and conversation, a zealous defender of the poor, a strenuous asserter of peace, a ready yet impartial dispenser of public justice, and a principal promoter of the political order and good government of this place; being arrested by a violent fever, to the unspeakable regret of all, he rendered his soul into the hand of God, and calmly slept in Jesus, March 7, 1637. **His** brother WILLIAM RAMSDEN, Rector of Edgmund, Shropshire, erected this monument to his memory.

RICHARDSON.

On a gravestone near **the font :** "P. M.* JOHANNIS RICH-ARDSON, obiit anno **Salutis** 1702do, Ætatis suæ 89no. SARAH, daughter of the above John Richardson, and wife of the Rev. **Mr.** Stephen Carr, of Honley, died Easter Eve, 1755, **aged** 90."

ROSSENDALE.

"Here lieth the body of JEREMIAH ROSSENDALE, of Shaw-hill, in Skircoat, who departed this life the 18th day of January, in the second year of his **age,** Anno Dom. 1694. And also the body of Mr. JEREMIAH ROSSENDALE, his father, who departed this life May 17th, and was interred May 27th, 1696."

ROBERTS.

On a stone in the Church-**yard,** opposite the great **door ;** "Here lieth the body of JOHN ROBERTS, of Hipperholme, **who** departed this life the 10th of November, in the **year** of our Lord 1721, and in the hundred and fourteenth year of his age." [Also the body of ANN, wife to the abovesaid John Roberts, who departed this life the 16th day of June, 1728. *Wright*, **p.** 196.] Tradition sais, that he wanted a month. He was a carrier by trade, and used **to** say, that he had never drank above half a pint of liquor of any kind, at one draught.

ROKEBY.

On a monument formerly in the **Chapel on** the north side of the Church, but now removed : " Orate pro anima WILL-IELMI ROKEBY, Jur. Can. Profess. ac etiam Episcopi Medensis et deinde Archiepisc. Dublin. Capellæ fundatoris istius, qui obiit 29 Novembris, An. Dom. **1521."**

In English.

Pray for the soul of WILLIAM ROKEBY, Professor of Law at Cambridge, also Archbishop of Dublin and Founder of that College, who died Nov. 29, 1521.

* To the memory of John.

SAYER.

Facing the North-Isle in Halifax Church, on a very elegant monument, **is** the following **inscription** :

Near this Place
are deposited **the** remains
of Mary, the Wife of Thomas Sayer,
of **Halifax,** Gentleman, and Coheiress
of William **Cockcroft,** of Mayroyd, Esquire.
She died the 12th **of May,** 1779, aged 36 years.

This monument is erected to her memory,
by an affectionate and afflicted husband,
as a respectful token of his esteem for those virtues
which adorned her heart, **and** endeared her to
him,
and to all who had **the** happiness **of** an acquaint-
ance with her.
Ask not, pensive Reader, **a** recital of **those virtues,**
which **her** humility wished her to conceal ;
This silent **marble** refers thee for information,
to the **tears and** cries of the sick and needy,
who lost in her a sympathetic attendant on their
distress,
and a generous **reliever of their** wants :
And **to the** regret of that concourse **of** every **age**
and rank,
who paid an honourable and **voluntary tribute to**
her merit,
by accompanying **her remains to** their interment.
If her amiable example **excite** thy imitation,
forget not to adopt her noblest praise,
by fulfilling every duty of nature and society,
from a principle **of** affection and gratitude
to God, the Friend, the Parent,
the Redeemer of Mankind.

SHARP.

On a tablet in the Chancel, an angel in clouds, blowing a trumpet, and on a cloth hanging from it, these words: " Jo-annes, Dominus Archiepiscopus Eborum, 1704." Arms of Sharp painted near the inscription, impaled with those of the See of York.

This was put up in honour to his memory, as he was born in the neighboring parish of Bradford.

SAVILE.

In the Chancel, round the border of a stone, in antient characters: "(Pray) for the (Sa)wl of THOMAS SAVILE, of Coplay, Esquyer, the . . . . of July, (and) in the yeire of ower Lord God MCCCCCXXXI."

Dr. Johnson sais, the following was round a gravestone in the Chancel, in old characters: "(Pray) for the Sawl of THOMAS SAVILE, of Copley, Esquyre . . . (d)ay of July, the year of our Lord God MCCCCCXXXI," which must, I think, be an imperfect copy of the above. He has given a drawing of this Thomas Savile, in armour, in a praying posture, with the Savile's arms on one side of his head, and those of Beaumont on the other. See Plate 1.

SCARBROUGH.

On a stone near the font: "Here lieth the body of SUSAN late wife of RICHARD SCARBROUGH, of Halifax, who was buried November 17, A. D. 1678.

Spes prolis, Sponsi fulcrum, Matrisq; SUSANNA
Solamen, tumulo hoc, hei! moribunda jacet.
Non tollitur relatio, cui est Mariti melioratio.
Tempus celerrime aufugit.

In English.
Approach and drop the tribute of a tear,
A faithful wife sleeps unmolested here,
Prop of her sinking spouse while life remain'd,
Who all a mother's tender cares sustained;
Such virtue dies not with the mould'ring tomb;
Heir to the glories of a life to come.

STEAD.

"Near this place is interred the body of Mr. VALENTINE STEAD, Merchant, who died May the 16th, 1758, aged 70. Also NAOMI, his wife, who died October the 9th, 1740, aged 47. And seven of their children. Also two children of Valentine Stead the younger, who erected this monument."

Near the font, on a grave-stone: "Here lieth the body of MARY, the wife of SAMUEL STEAD, of Halifax, who was buried the 29th of May, 1734, aged 82 years and 6 months. She was wife of the abovesaid Samuel Stead, Salter, 58 years and 6 months."

Also SAMUEL STEAD, husband to the abovesaid MARY, who departed this life the 4th day of December, 1736, aged 80 years, 10 months, and seven days.

Mr. Wright, p. 195, remarks, that this Gentleman lived to see of his children, grand children, and great grand children sixty-one in number.

SMITH.

On a stone in the Church-yard: " Here lieth the body of DANIEL SMITH, the son of Matthew Smith, of Halifax, who departed this life the 28th day of February, Anno Domini 1729, in the 18th year of his age.

> Under this stone here lies, as you may see,
> A lovely child, who once was dear to me,
> Dearer to God, who took him hence away,
> With whom I leave, until the final day.
> Methinks I hear my lovely child say here,
> Weep not for me, but for your children dear;
> Make haste to follow me, and then you'll see,
> What is provided in eternity."

SOMERSCALES.

On a stone on the west wall of the Church: "Mr. RICHARD SOMERSCALES, of Halyfax, who died April the 8th, A.D. 1613, and who, by his last will, gave all his lands in Halyfax and Ovenden, (after the decease of his sister,) to the poor of the said towns for ever, amongst whom he gave 40s. to his sister's husband, for the term of his life."

SUNDERLAND.

Dr. Johnson sais, that the following was in the south isle of the Chancel: " Here lieth the bodies of ROBERT, son of RICHARD SUNDERLAND, of Coley, Esq: and JUDITH, his daughter, who died January 19th, 1623. February 8th, 1623." This was round a stone, on which were cut, in bad proportion, the figures of a man and woman kneeling down together; over their heads, On a shield, three lions passant; and for crest, On an helmet a goat's head. See Plate 2.

TILLOTSON.

In the Chancel, in letters of gold, on a tablet, with the arms of the Archiepiscopal See of Canterbury impaled with his own :

JOHANES TILLOTSON, Archiepus Cantuar. natus Sowerbiæ, renatus Halyfaxie, 3^{tio} 8^{bris}, 1630. Denatus Lambethæ, 22° Novebris, A. D. 1694. Ætatis suæ 65."

In English.

Archbishop of Canterbury, born at Sowerby, baptized at Halifax, Oct. 3, 1630, died at Lambeth, Nov. 22d, 1694. Aged 65.

THURSTON.

On a stone in the Chancel: " JOHN, the son of JOHN THURSTON, Gentleman, died the 6th of December, 1663. Orimur, morimur, oriemur.[*]

> Blest babe, who art so soon become
> A man in Christ, with him at home."

WATERHOUSE.

In the North Chapel, on a stone with a man in armor upon it, in old characters : " Here lyeth the body of ROBERT WATERHOUSE, of Halyfax, Esquyer, which departed this life the . . . . of June . . . . (hav)ying lyved, as one that should dye."

Mr. Wright has called the above John, instead of Robert, and has put Gregory instead of Bryan, in the next epitaph. The wife of the above Robert was buried in St. Michael Belfray's Church in York. See Drake's Ebor. p. 339. She died may 1st, 1592. See Plate 2.

Near the above, but now destroyed (as supposed) was another figure of a man in armor, with this inscription round, in old characters : " Here lyeth the body of BRYAN WATERHOUSE, of Halyfax, Gentleman, which departed this life the IV day of October, in the year of our Lord God, 1589. Humanius est deridere vitam quam deplorare."

In Dr. Johnson's MS. Collections is the drawing of a tomb said to be removed out of the North Chapel when the stairs were made which lead to the north gallery there, at the head of which was a shield of arms, viz. Waterhouse,

* We rise, we fall, we shall arise.

Or, a pile ingrailed sable, quartered with Savile, parted per pale quarterly, 1. Bosseville, of Gunthwaite. 2. Bendy of thirteen pieces, or and argent. 3 .... A lion rampant ... over all a bend gules; fourth as first. Under these a scroll and motto, "Virtus vincint omnia." On the top of the tomb lay the figure of a man in armor, holding on his breast a shield with the same arms as above. On one side of his head were, on a shield, the arms of Waterhouse, on the other the coats of Waterhouse and Savile, quartered; on one side of his feet, Waterhouse impaled with Bosseville, and on the other, Waterhouse impaled with the same quarterings as are impaled in the shield on his breast. The above stairs were made in 1700. See Plate 3.

In the middle isle of the Church, on brass plates, fixed to a seat near the pulpit, which are all torn off except the heads, a man kneeling, with a book in his hand, and opposite to him a woman kneeling, and a string of beads hanging down from her waist. On a label over the man, in old characters: "Miserere mei Deus, et salva me." On another label near the woman, in like characters: "Miserere mei Deus, secundum magnam misericordiam." On a brass plate over their heads: "I am the resurrection and the life, saith the Lord. He that believeth in me, though he were dead yet shall he live, and he that liveth and believeth in me shall never die." Underneath, in the above characters: "JOHN WATERHOWS, of Halyfax, and AGNES, hys wyff, which John dep'ted from thys worlde the xxvii day of January, anno Dm. MCCCCCXXX.— Something wanting both at beginning and end. See Plate 1.

On the north side of the Church, where the deceased particularly desired to be buried, is a tomb, on which is wrote: "Here lieth the body of Mr. JOHN WATERHOUSE, of Lower Ranns, in Northowram, who died April 4th, 1759, aged 60." On the west end of the tomb:

> "Oh Christian Reader! often think
> Christ will appear,
> How shall I then in judgment stand!"

WATKINSON.

On a pillar on the south side of the Chancel: "H. M. Memoriæ sacrum MARIE, filiæ unicæ Rev^{di} Dnⁱ EDWARDI WATKINSON, Capellæ de Luddenden in hac Vicaria Curat.

Quæ nata vesperi præcedente Pascha, Anno 1723, febre perquam maligna correpta occidit (heu nimium fugax et multum flebilis) Augusti 24to, 1726."

In English.

This monument was erected to the memory of MARY, only daughter of the Rev. Edward Watkinson, Curate of Luddenden, in this Vicarage. She was born on Easter-Eve, 1723, and being taken ill of a violent fever, quitted this life August 24, 1726.

WAINHOUSE.

On a brass plate near the font: "Here lieth the body of MICHAEL WAINHOUSE, late of Binroyd, in Norland, buried the 21st day of October, A. D. 1684. Ut moriens viveret, vixit ut moriturus." [That in dying he might live, he lived as one ready to die.]

WILKINSON.

On a grave-stone in the Chancel: "JOSEPH WILKINSON, A. M. quondam Vicarius de Chapel-Izod, juxta Dublin, in Hibernia, et Prebendarius de Castroknock, Ecclesiæ Cathedralis Sancti Patricii Dublin, postea Rector de Wigginton comitatu Ebor. et tandem huic Ecclesiæ par viginti annos præfuit Vicarius. Obiit 28 die Decembris, Anno Dom. 1711. Ætatis suæ 60."

JOSEPH WILKINSON, M.A., formerly Vicar of Chapel-Izod, near Dublin, Prebend of Castroknock, the Cathedral Church of St. Patrick, Dublin; afterwards Rector of Wigginton, in the County of York, and lastly, Vicar of this Church for near 20 years.

WILSON.

At the bottom of the middle isle: "ANN, the daughter of Mr. JOHN WILSON, Curate of Honly, was buried the 4th day of November, 1725."

At the south end of the West Walk, in the Church, on a stone fixed to the wall: "Here lyeth the body of JOHN WILSON, formerly Clark of the Parish Church of Halyfax, who was buried the 7th day of November, 1701."

This man, who was Clark of Eland, was made Clark of Halifax by Dr. Hooke; and Wilson, in the course of a dispute which happened between them, having arrested the

Doctor, the latter persuaded the other to shew him his licence, and when he had got it in possession would never suffer him to officiate any more.

—::—

TESTAMENTARY BURIALS at HALIFAX.

FROM MR. TORR'S MS.

July 12, 1402, John del Burgh, of Halifax, made his will, and left his soul to God Almighty, St. Mary, and All Saints, and ordered his body to be buried in the parish church of Halifax.

Nov. 21, 1437, Henry Savyle, of Halifax, Esq; Soul and body as above.

March 3, 1439, Richard Pek, of Southouram. Soul as above, body in the quire of the parish church of Halifax.

April 20, 1459, John Sayvell, of Copley, Esq; Soul as above, body in the church, or church-yard of Halifax.

June 1, 1481, Tho. Wilkinson, Vicar of Halifax, already mentioned.

April 4, 1482, William Marshall, Rector of Kirk-Sandal. Soul as above, body in Halifax church.

Feb. 3, 1484, Richard Waterhouse, of Warley. Soul as above, body in the church or church-yard of St. John Baptist, Halifax.

April 29, 1510, Henry Savile, of Copley. Soul as above, body in the New Warke of Halifax.

Feb. 15, 1530, Tho. Savile, of Bladeroyd, in Southouram.—Jan. 5, 1533, Thomas Savile, of Copley, Esq;—1533, John Waterhouse, of Skircoat.—1535, Edward Waterhouse, buried in the church-yard at Halifax.—1538, Richard Waterhouse, of Shipden, body to be buried in the church of the holy prophet St. John Baptist, of Halifax.—1541, John Illingworth, of Illingworth.— 1543, Edward Waterhouse, of Skircoat.—1543, William Illingworth.—1545, Humphry Waterhouse, of Shelf. Soul to God Almighty, hoping through Jesus Christ to be saved. "Here Protestantism "began to shew itself, and mankind began to act more from "principles of reason, and common sense, than to bequeath "their souls to the Virgin Mary, and all the Saints, who are

" only in the same condition that all living Saints will
" shortly be placed in, and who cannot help if they are
" applied to."

1545, John Waterhouse, of Skircoat.—1554, Henry Savile,
of Copley.—1556, John Waterhouse, of Thollinges, in Warley.—1556, Richard Midgley, of Midgley.—1569, Thomas
Savile, of Copley.—1570, Hugh Lacey, of Brearley, in Midgley, Esq;—1570, Thomas Savile, of Southouram, Gent.—
1578, Anthony Waterhouse, of Warley, Gent.—1586, Abraham Sunderland, of High Sunderland, Gent.—1620, John
Holdsworth, of Astey, Gent.

THE PRINCIPAL
EPITAPHS AT EALAND,
ARE THESE:
ASHETON.

On a grave-stone in the Chancel: " Hic in spe christiana
requiescit PETRUS ASHETON, A.M. Ecclesiæ Anglicanæ Presbyter, et Parochiæ de Ealand in sacris Administer : Orthodoxæ
Fidei et Doctrinæ sanæ Theologus : Pietatis Exemplar :
Pacis Cultor ! Qui per decursum annorum triginta et unius
fideliter pastorali functus munere, et reciproco omnium
amore remuneratus, placide gregem simul cum anima Deo
vocanti resignavit 3 ^{Omo} Octobris, A. D. 1691. Ætatis 55to.

Fil.		Die	Mensis	A.D.	
Thomas,		22do	Dec^{bris}	1684	13^{tio}
Johannaes,	obiit	9no	Maii	1675	1mo
Petrus,		9no	Junii	1674	1mo

" Hic etiam (cum Infante) jacet Samuel filius Rich. Petty,
Curati de Ealand, qui unicam P. Asheton filiam uxorem sibi
adjunxit. Obiit Aug. 22, A.D. 1709. Ætatis suæ 2do.

" Hic etiam jacet Susanna ejusdem R^{di}. Petty filia.
Sepulta fuit 11mo Aprilis, A. D. 1711.—Ætatis suæ 8vo."

On a grave-stone in the Chancel: " Reliquiæ hic repositæ
Petri Asheton, Curati de Milnraw, in com. Lancastri, (filii
Petri Asheton propiq ; tumulati) qui animam Deo resignavit
5to die Aug. 1718. Ætatis 42."

" Atque Rich^{di} Petty, Curati de Ealand, qui animam
efflavit vivacem 7mo die Martii, 1723.—Ætatis suæ 49."

In English.

"Here rests in christian hope, PETER ASHTON, A.M. presbyter of the English church, and curate of Ealand; a divine of (an) orthodox faith, and sound doctrine; an example of primeval piety, and a lover of peace: After having faithfully discharged the pastoral office 31 years; being universally beloved, he calmly resigned his flock, together with his soul, at the call of God, October 30, 1691, aged 55.

In this place (with an infant) sleeps Samuel, son of Richard Petty curate of Elland, who married the only daughter of P. Ashton. He died August 22d, A. D. 1709, aged 2 years. Also, Susanna, the daughter of Richard Petty, was interred here, April 11, A. D. 1711, aged 8 years.

In this place are deposited the remains of Peter Ashton, curate of Milnraw, in the county of Lancaster, son of P. Ashton, deceased, who resigned his soul to God. August 5, 1718, aged 42. Richard Petty died March 7, 1723, aged 49."

BOSWELL.

In the North Quire, the figure of the greatest part of a woman, in a praying posture, and four children below, also praying, over the children's heads the names Elizabeth, Mary, Jane, Dorithy. On the right side of the woman's head the arms of Savile; on the left, those of Boswell impaled with .... a saltire ingrailed .... in a chief three roses ....—Inscription round the stone: "Here sleepeth the body of FRANCIS, daughter of Godfrey Boswell, Esq; wife of John Savile, of Newhall, Esquire, whose soul returned to God that gave it, February 26, 1609, aged 60 years."

BAIRSTOW.

In the Chapel yard: "Reliquiæ hic reponuntur JEREMIÆ BAIRSTOW, Viri, si quid venerationis sibi vendicant, Literarum scientia, rerum sacrarum peritia, morum probitas, vitæ sanctitas, reverá reverendi. Qui postquam per annos triginta et amplius, gregi quodam christiano Pastor fidelis invigilasset, officii rationem, animamq; Deo reddidit 27 Julii, 1731." This was composed by the Rev. Mr. Elston. See below.

In English.

"Here is deposited the remains of JEREMY BAIRSTOW, a a truly venerable man, if the science of letters, probity of manners, and sanctity of life have any claim to that character, during a term of more than 30 years. He was a faithful and vigilant Pastor over a christian congregation, and commended his soul to God July 27, 1731."

CLAY.

From Dr. Johnson's manuscript: "Hic jacet sepultus JOHANNES CLAY, de Clayhouse, qui obiit decimo octavo die Junii, 1616." On the same stone: "Here lieth Captain John Clay, deceased, September 13, 1643."

In English.

"Near this place lies interred JOHN CLAY, of Clayhouse, who died June 18, 1616."

ELSTON.

In the Chapel-yard: "M. S. HANANLÆ ELSTON, A. M. qui ingenio acri, limato, subacto, morum probitate, et aperto illo animi recte sibi conscii candore, veram pietatem, fidem, humanitatem, cælitusq; demissam Christianis libertatem, excolebat, tuebatur, promovebat: Qui magnas opes, famamve mortaleis inter neque quæritans, neque assecutus, suorum tamen amorem bonorum omnium, quotquot illum norant, benevolentiam conciliaret, sib summi certe Judicis savorem adeptus est. Quis enim Viator meliore jure beatam speret immortalitem? Obiit 22 Junii, 1738."

This was composed by the Rev. Mr. Crowther, late Vicar of Otley.

In English.

"Sacred to the memory of ANANIAS ELSTON, M. A. who, with a penetrating, correct, yet well-go-verned judgment, by (a) probity of manners, and an open undisguised candour of mind, conscious of its integrity, cherished, defended, and promoted true piety, faith, humanity, and christian liberty; who, without either seeking or acquiring opulence and fame, conciliated the affections of his friends, and the kind regards of all good men who knew him. We trust he has obtained the favour of his Judge——for what mortal traveller had better grounds to hope for a happy immortality? He died 22d June, 1738.

ELLISTONES.

In the Chapel-yard, over HENRY ELLISTONES, who died at Howroyde, 1697: "Ullamne in rebus humanis, Lector, certitudinem esse reris, cum ipsum hominen una dissolvat hora?"

In English.

"Can you suppose, reader, there is any stability in human things, when a single hour can dissolve the man himself?"

GRANTHAM.

On a marble monument: "Heare lyes the body of THOMAS GRANTHAM, of Muxe, in the county of Yorke, Esq; sonne of Thomas Grantham, late of Goltho, in the county of Lincolne, Esquire. He married Frances, the second daughter of Sir George Wentworth, of Wooley, and departed this life the first day of April, at Fixby, in the 35th year of his age, Anno Dom. 1668."

"John Grantham, the youngest sonne of the saide Thomas Grantham, of Goltho, departed this life the seventh day of March, at Fixby, in the 17th year of his age, Anno Dom. 1667, and lyes in this Queare."

"Heer lyes the body of Frances Grantham, wife to Thomas Grantham, Esquire, who died March 12, 1692, and lyes interred in her husband's grave.

Beside them lyes Vincent Grantham, their only son, who died when he was 12 years of age, whose bodyes now rest in peace, waiting the resurrection of the just."

HORTON.

On a marble monument near the communion table: "Near this place below lies interred the body of WILLIAM HORTON, of Howroyde, Esq. who died in the 64th year of his age, 1715-16.

He married Mary, the youngest daughter of Sir Richard Musgrave, of Heaton-Castle, in the county of Cumberland, Baronet, by whom he left two sons, William and Richard; the eldest, William Horton, of Coley, Esq. died in the 38th year of his age, in 1739, and Richard Horton, the younger son, of Howroyde, Esq. who died a bachelor, in the 35th year of his age, in the year 1742. In memory of whom this monument was erected by the relict and mother of the

M

deceased, and present possessor of Howroyde, Mrs. Mary Horton, who designedly omitted many deserved praises, lest some honour should thereby redound to herself," Arms, Horton impaling Musgrave.

On a white marble monument near the Communion Table: "In memory of Thomas Horton, of Barkisland-hall, and Everilde, his wife, daughter of John Thornhill, Esq. of Fekisby, by whom he had six sons and five daughters, of which the only survivors were, Elizabeth, married to Richard Bold, Esq. of Bold, in Lancashire. Susanna, married to Richard Beaumont, Esq. of Whitley-hall, and Anne Horton, here interred, April the 22d, 1750. By whose order this monument was erected."

Arms, Horton quartered with Gledhill, Barkisland, and Thornhill.

There is a mistake made on the above monument, by misplacing the names of Elisabeth, and Susanna, but it is here corrected.

HOILE.

In the Chapel-yard over one JOHN HOILE: Deo, ac conjugi pius, justus ac propositi tenax, amicis certus, omnibus affabilis, ac si quid ultra est, sit tota vita pro epitaphio. Vade, et tu fac similiter."

In English.

Devout towards God, affectionate to his Wife, just and steady to his purpose, sincere to his friends, affable to all, and if aught remains, let his whole life be his Epitaph.— Go and do thou likewise.

HANSON.

From Dr. Johnson's Manuscripts: "Here sleepeth the body of Nicholas Hanson, one of the Attornies of the Common Pleas, Servant to Sir John Savile, Baron of the Ch^r. a favourer of religion, whose soul returned to his Saviour November 7, 1613."

The oldest date upon the grave-stones at Ealand is this "John Hanson de Woodhouse, 1599. Æt. 82."

There are also above twenty pieces of poetry in this Chapel-yard, but the composition is not worth recording; we shall, therefore, only take notice of a singularity on one of

the grave-stones, which is an anagram upon one Maria
Tailour, which it seems will make A mari alto rui, and then
follows this observation, by way of allusion :

" From seas of woes, which were due to my crimes
Death snatcht me hence, to go to rest betimes."

There is also a couplet over one Elizabeth Brooke, which
has been a little admired :

" She was—but room forbids to tell you what ;
Think what a wife should be, for she was that.

—::—

CURATES OF EALAND.

It is impossible to give a perfect list of these ; the following
is the best which I can make out :

THOMAS STRENGER, Chaplain of the Parochial Chapel of
Elande, 1459.

JAMES BUTTERFIELD, 1544 married to Elizabeth Gill. See
Halifax Register.

MICHAEL SAVILE, July, 1561.

ROBERT MILNER, Curat. de Eland, sepult. December 22,
1565.

RICHARD WORRAL, entered to the Curacy, 1588.

CONSTANUS MAUD, was buried November 17, 1600.

EDWARD SUNDERLAND, A.M. of Clare-hall, Camb. entered
to the Curacy in 1601, was buried February 1, 1632.

JOHN THOMPSON, entered in 1633.

ROBERT HOULDSWORTH, 1651.

. . . . ABBOT, in 1650, and 1652.

ROBERT TOWNE, 1652, for whom see Calamy's account of
ejected Ministers, page 809.

R. WALKER, 1656, and to March, 1661.

JOSIAH BRODEHEADE, March 2, 1663 and 1664.

PETER ASHETON, A.M. March 4, 1667. Buried at Ealand,
November 3, 1698.

RICHARD PETTY, March 5, 1699, and 1703.

JEREMIAH BAIRSTOW, 1721, died July 28, 1731.

GEORGE SMITH, died December 4, 1733.

THOMAS ALDERSON, March 1734.

SAMUEL OGDEN, D. D. March, 1747.

GEORGE BURNET.

There was also one HUGH GLEDHILL, Curate here, but at
what time uncertain.

TESTAMENTARY BURIALS AT ELAND.

FROM TORR'S MS.

1399, JOHN SAYVILL, of Eland Chevalier.

1529, JOHN THORNHILL, of Fixby, to be buried within the chapel of our blessed Lady St. Mary, of Eland, in St. Nicholas Quire, or in the Chancel thereto adjoining.

1545, JOHN SAYVILL, of Newhall, Gen. 1566, Henry Sayvil, of Bradley.

1567, JOHN THORNHILL, of Fixby.

1580, THOMAS SAVILE, of Eland.

1583, ELIZABETH, widow of John Thornhill, of Fixby, esq.

1598, BRYAN THORNHILL, of Fixby.

1607, JOHN THORNHILL, of Fixby, esq.

1669, JOHN THORNHILL, of Fixby, esq.

—::—

LIST OF CURATES

AT HEPTONSTALL,

FROM DIFFERENT AUTHORITIES.

21 HENRY VI, Thomas Marshall, of Heptonstall, Capellanus.—1572, William Mitchell.—1579, William Ireland.— 1586, John Hanley.— 1647, Richard Coore.—1652, James Crouchley.—1655, Daniel Towne.—1656, ... Eagland.— 1660, ... Diglin.— July, 1662, ... Ferret.—July, 1663, and to 1665, Jeremy Hay.—1668, and to 1703, Daniel Towne.—1713, Thomas Greenwood.

The list from Heptonstall Register is this: 1609, ... Booth.—1615, ... Scholfeilde.— 1630 and 1631, William Smith.—1632 and 1633, Leonard Burton.—1636 and 1641, Robt. Gilbodie.—1644, Ma. Boothe.—1645 and 1649, Richard Coore.—1654, James Chrichley.—1661, Will. Aiglin.—1662, Joseph Ferret.   He was buried at Halifax.—1663 and 1667, Jeremy Hey.—1669 and 1712, Daniel Towne, who died May 3, 1712.—1712 and 1744, Thomas Greenwood, who had in this last year for his successor, Toby Sutcliffe, the present Curate.

All the above I have found to be Curates in the years specified.

TESTAMENTARY BURIALS
AT HEPTONSTALL.

ROBERT SHAGH, buried in the church-yard of the chapel of St. Thomas the Martyr, of Heptonstall, 1467, in the 7th year of the reign of Edward IV.

This from a manuscript in the British Museum, Harleian Collection. No 797; and from hence may be seen, among numberless other instances which might be produced, what little distinction was formerly made in this parish, between the words church and chapel; they sometimes were certainly meant to convey the same idea, as where Richard Waterhouse, of Shelf, ordered by will, in 1617, some legacies to be paid in the chapel church of Coley.

Laurence Stansfeld, of Stansfeld's, Will, proved March 10, 1534, his body to be buried in the church or chapel of Heptonstall.

George Wheatley, of Heptonstall's, Will, proved August 25, 1586, his body to be buried in the chancei at Heptonstall, amongst the bodies of other faithful people. Registers at York.

In the chancel, near the communion table, is the following epitaph in capitals : "1712. The Revd. Mr. Daniel Towne, who supplied the cure of souls in this church of Heptonstall 44 years, died May 3, and was here buried the 8th, aged 81. His last Text was, *Buye the truth and sell it not*. Prov. xxiii. 23."

In one of the isles is an antient grave-stone, the inscription round which is worn out, but a Calvary Cross is still visible thereon.

On one of the windows are the arms of Stansfield, of Stansfield; date in old numerals, 1508.

—::—

CURATES OF RASTRICK.

1411, Dom. Johannes Pip'. as by deed.—1630, or thereabouts, Roger Attey.— 1650, ... Waterhouse.— Feb. 26, 1652, and to 1655, John Kaye, Pastor of Rastrick.—1655 ...... Mitchel.— 1656 to 1658, ... Jones.— Feb. 1661, ... Robinson.—Feb. 1664, Matthew Shirt.—Feb. 1666, John Baskervile.— Feb. 1674, Peter Bell.— Feb. 1676, Dennis

Hayford.—June, 1688, ... Hanson.—March 5, 1689, ...
Walker.—1694 and 1703, Robert Laycock.—Feb. 1713,
Edward Waring.—Feb. 1719, John Metcalf.—Feb. 1748,
George Braithwaite.

N. B.   Mr. Robinson abovementioned was one of the
ejected Ministers. See Calamy, vol. ii. page 818, where also
a Mr. Ashley is said to have been a Preacher at Rastrick,
though not a fixed one.—For him see Calamy, vol. ii. page
183, 184, 818.

—::—

EPITAPHS AT RIPPONDEN.

AINSWORTH.

The oldest stone in this Chapel-yard is over one HENRY
AINSWORTH, and is dated March 29th, 1657.

HILL.

On a handsome well cut tomb-stone erected over a vault:
"Here lies interred the body of SARAH, daughter of Samuel
and Elisabeth Hill, of Soyland, who departed this life the
23d of July, 1729, aged 15 years.

"Also the body of ANN, their daughter, who died the 3d
of April, 1730, aged 5.

"Also of JOSEPH, their son, who died the 14th of January,
aged 3.

"Also of SAMUEL, their son, who died the 11th of June,
1732, aged 12.

"Also the body of DEBORAH, the wife of James Hill, of
Soyland, who died the 9th of October, 1741, aged 84.

"Also of JAMES, son of the aforesaid Samuel and Eliz.
Hill, who died the 16th of January, 1753, aged 30.

"Also of BETTY, wife of Richard Hill, (daughter of Roger
Kay, near Bury, in Lancashire), who lived unblameable
thro' life, and died lamented, the 25th of October, 1747,
aged 19.

"Also the body of ELIZABETH, wife of Samuel Hill, of
Soyland. She died the 1st of July, 1756, aged 65 years.

"Also of SAMUEL, son of Richard (and grandson of Samuel Hill,) who died 22d of October, 1756, aged 10 years and
8 months.

LIVESAY.

"Here was interred the body of JOHN LIVESAY, A. B. of Brazen Nose College, Oxford, who died the 5th day of April, Anno Dom. 1730, in the 31st year of his age. Also the body of HANNAH, his wife, relict of Mr. John Hoyle, late of Royde, in Soyland, who died the 13th day of March, 1729, aged 40 years."

SUNDERLAND.

"Here was interred the body of JOHN SUNDERLAND, senr Curate of Ripponden, who departed this life the 21st day of April, Anno Dom. 1720."

N. B. The stone on which this is cut, was laid down since the old Chapel was destroyed. There was a stone fixed in the wall of the old Chapel, with this inscription: "Juxta, Johannis Sunderland, hujus Sacelli nuper Pastoris, depositæ sunt exuviæ, die Junii 23, Anno Dom. 1720."

On another stone: "Here was interred the body of JOHN SUNDERLAND, jun. Curate of Sowerby Bridge, Sep. 15th, 1715." And on the same: "Here was interred the body of the Rev. Mr. WILLIAM SUNDERLAND, A. B. Curate of Ripponden above 29 years, who died the 1st day of March, 1749, aged 73 years."

WRIGHT.

"Here lieth interred the body of the Rev. Mr. THO. WRIGHT, A. B. who was Curate of Halifax near 18 years, and of Ripponden 4. He died the 8th day of June, 1754, in the 47th year of his age."

—::—

CURATES OF RIPPONDEN.

1588 and 1593, Henry Sharrock—April 6, 1650 and 1655, Isaac Allen.—1656, and to August 1663, Roger Kenion—April 6, 1664, Ralph Wood, who was buried at Ripponden, Feb. 16, 1696-7.—1699, John Sunderland.—August 1720, William Sunderland, who died March 1, 1749-50.—May 17, 1750, Thomas Wright took possession.—At Martinmass, 1754, John Watson took possession, and after fifteen years resident there, removed to the Rectory of Stockport.

The above Roger Kenion was turned out, (as Calamy, page 837, informs us), by the Bartholomew Act, but afterwards conformed.

We have copies of his two last sermons preached at Ripponden, August 17, 1663, wherein he advises his hearers "not to neglect the first opportunity of closing with another, for he was persuaded that true spiritual bread would be more scarce and precious than it had been."

In all probability they would not easily find one so curious at a simile as he; for in the latter sermon he says, "We are like unto a man that is in a pinakle of a church, and seeth out at a hoale, where he can see nothing but what is before the hoale, but God is like unto a man on the top of the pinakle, that seeth round about."

—::—

CURATES AT LUDDENDEN.

1526, John Robinson.—1606, Marmaduke Farrar, buried in that year; see Halifax Register.—1634, Nathaniel Welch. —1652 and 1662, Jonathan Fairbank.—June 1664 and 1665, Edward Doughty.—June 1666, Robert Dewhirst.—June 7, 1671, ... Gregson.—June 1672, ... Hall.—March 3, 1674, Robert Sutcliffe.—January 1676, Edward Dean.— June 1678, James Roberts.—June 1682, ... Sunderland.— June 1698 and 1702, David Hartley.—June 1706, Thomas Greenwood.—1710 and 1713, Robert Laycock.—June 1720, John Earnshaw.—June 1722, George Smith.—June 6, 1724, came to be Curate Edward Watkinson, M. D. who staid there three years and seven months.—June 1728 Joshua Brooksbank, buried May 9, 1740.—June 1740, Robert Brereton. — June 1743, John Grimshaw. — June 1749, John Welsh.—1750, Benjamin Travis.—1761, Thomas West.

—::—

EPITAPHS AT COLEY.

BRAMFIT.

IN the Chapel-yard: "Here lieth interred the body of JOSEPH BRAMFIT, who departed this life July 10, 1733, in the 33d year of his age; and also SUSANNA, his daughter,

who died the same day, in the 7th year of her age; also
PHEBE, his daughter, who died the same day, in the 5th year
of her age:

> Behold a loving husband, and his two daughters lay;
> They smother'd were by smoke all on **one** day."

HUDSON.

Between **the body of** the Chapel and the Chancel, on a
plain stone **monument**: " Near the door of this seat lie the
remains **of** JOHN HUDSON, **son of** the Revd. Mr. Thomas
Hudson, **and** of MARTHA his **wife, late of** Hipperholm, **who
died July 21,** 1789, aged 4 **years.**

SHARP.

Within the Chapel, **at** the west **end, on** a stone monument: " Near this place lie interred **the body** of ANN, late
wife of Nathan Sharp, of Hipperholm, Clerk, who departed
this life the 20th, and **was** buried **here the** 22d of March,
1727, aged 52 years **and 7** months.

" **As** also the body of her husband, NATHAN SHARP, who
departed this life the 9th, **and was** buried **the 12th of May,**
1733, **aged 58 years and 10 months.**"

Arms below, Sharpe, which, to the best of my remem-
brance, were, Azure a pheon argent, within **a** bordure of the
second, charged with eight torteauxes; impaling, Priestley,
viz. **Gules on** a chevron argent, three grappling irons sable,
between three towers of the second, issuant out of each a
demi **lion rampant, or.**

This **Mr.** Sharpe **was School-master** at Hipperholme **near**
thirty years.

There are some other epitaphs, and a few of them **in the
poetic** strain, but the composition is too low for the press.

—::—

CURATES OF COLEY.

1530, Richard Northend, Capellanus **in** capella de Coolay.
—1613, ... Gibson.—1681, Richard Denton.—August,
1649, Nicholas Cudworth.—1652, Oliver Heywood, ejected
from thence in 1662, (See Calamy, **vol. ii.** page 804, **&c.**)

He was succeeded by John Hool, who was also **Curate** here in 1670.—Nov. 1671, ... Moore.—Nov. 1672, Ichabod Fournes.— Nov. 4, 1674, Andrew Louthian.—Dec. 1676, George Hovie.—1682, and 1689, Timothy Ellison.—1703, Nathan Sharpe.—November 1733, John Holdsworth.—Nov. 1741, Samuel Ogden.—Nov. 1747, Henry Whitworth, who died July 15, 1768.

A Mr. Marsden was Curate here before Oliver Heywood. See Calamy, vol. ii. page 810.

—::—

CURATES OF ILLINGWORTH.

1578, John Best, buried at Halifax, February 22, 1578.— 1650, Richard Clarkson.—1652 to 1655, Nathaniel Heywood. (See Calamy, vol. ii. page 394).—1656, ... Bradshaw.— 1658 and 1664, Paul Greenwood.— Oct. 1668, Edward Wilkinson, who died Jan 4, 1704.—Oct. 1706, David Hartley.—Oct. 1717, Daniel Bentley.—Jan. 1748-9, J. Grimshaw.

—::—

CURATES OF SOWERBY BRIDGE CHAPEL.

1635 and 1646, Robert Booth.—1651 and 1652, ... Ainsworth.—1652 and 1653, ... Thompson.—1655 and 1658, Daniel Bentley.—Sept. 4, 1661, and Sept. 3, 1662, Timothy Root. He was turned out by the Bartholomew Act, (says Calamy, vol. ii. page 837), and afterwards conformed.— September 1663, and 1664, Elnathan Bains.— 1665, John Brotherton.—September 1670 and 1701, ... Berron.—1703, John Sunderland, who died September 15, 1717.—1717, Thomas Dunn.—September 1718, John Lupton, buried March 25, 1730.—September, 1730, Abraham Sharpe, who died April 17, 1732.—September, 1732, William Stackhouse.—Richard Fisher, who entered, July 1746.

EPITAPHS AT LIGHTCLIFFE CHAPEL.

In the Chapel-yard: "Here is interred the body of MARY, the mother of Colonel Guest, of Lidgate, in Lightcliffe, who departed this life Sept. 10, 1729, aged 88."

At the **east-end** within the Chapel: "Here lies interred the Revd. Mr. Joshua Hill, Curate of this chapel near **thirty-two years,** who was buried June the 11th, in the 79th year of his age, A. D. 1739, of whom it has often been said, that he was neither poor, proud, nor covetous."

With some others, not worth publishing.

—::—

CURATES OF LIGHTCLIFFE.

1680, John Peebles, Preacher at Lightclive, (Halifax Register.)—1634, John Burtomood.—1647, 1649, and 1650, William Ainsworth.—1650, ... Heald.—December 1, 1652, John Bell.—1655, ... Hopkins.—1656, and 1661, ... Seddon.—December 1668, and 1673, Alexander Bate.—1673, Paul Bairstow.—December, 1677, ... Walker, late Minister of Lightcliffe.—1678, and 1700, William Clifford.—1703, Thomas Greenwood.—December, 1706, Joshua Hill. (He was blind for some time.)—Jonathan Wright,* Lightcliffe, died June 25, 1727.—October, 1739, Richard Fisher took possession.—December, 1746, Geo. Braithwaite.—December, 1746, Benjamin Travis.—March, 1752, Richard Sutcliffe.

In Mr. Dickenson's manuscript register at Northouram, it is said that the above William Clifford died in Northouram, April eighteen, 1732-3, and was buried at Halifax; that he was many years Curate at Lightcliffe, afterwards at Haworth, and was very old, having not preached of many years.

—::—

CURATES OF ST. ANN'S.

1650, Richd. Core.—February, 1652, Christopher Taylor, Quaker.—1653, ... Waterhouse.—1656, ... Smethurst.—

* A Dissenting Minister; *never* Curate.

January, 1661, Gamaliel Marsden, ejected by the Act of Uniformity. See Calamy, vol. ii. page 810.—1663, Richard Boy.—January, 1665, Christopher Fisher.—1666, Richard Boyes again.—January, 1668, ... Brooke.—January, 1670, ... Clegg.—January, 1675 and 1689, Thomas Walker.— But 1676, in January, Nehemiah Ferne occurs as Curate.

N.B. There is no certainty who was the licensed Minister about this time, for the above Mr. Clegg received part of Mr. Waterhouse's annual legacy to the Curate of St. Ann's, in 1679 and 1680, and afterwards when Thomas Walker is mentioned as Curate there.

January, 1698 and 1703, Joshua Hill.—1708, Stephen Carr.—January, 1714, John Sheffield.—January, 1716, John Godley, who signed " no graduate."—1718, Thomas Lister. —January, 1731, Thomas Haldsworth.—September, 1746, entered Richard Sutcliffe.—Martinmas, 1756, entered Thomas Meyrick.

—::—

CURATES OF SOWERBY.

1572 and 1583, Adam Morris, who went Chaplain to a regiment in Ireland, and was buried at Halifax, September 24, 1591.

John Broadley, who, during the building of the last chapel, preached thirteen Sundays on the dial-stone in the chapel-yard, without so much as a shower of rain to disturb him. He was buried at Halifax, February 14, 1625, and called in the Register there, Pastor dignissimus.

1635, Nathaniel Rathband, M. A. also March 16, 1645.

1646, Henry Roote, also, May 8, 1662. Mr. Calamy, vol. ii. page 809, says that in 1645 (which must be soon after the death of Mr. Rathband,) he gathered a congregational church, and was Pastor to them till 1662; that he preached in his chapel for half a year after Bartholomew-day, but was, at length, dragged out of his chapel, and sent to York Castle, where he continued three months. He died October 20, 1669, aged about 80, and was buried at Sowerby. He was educated at Magdalen Coll. Camb. and was a considerable traveller in his younger days.

May 1664, Edward Wilkinson.—May 1665, Christopher Jackson.—May 6, 1668 to 1670, ... Bovile.—May 1672,

James Bowker, who was banished for criminal conversation with a daughter of Mr. Farrer, of Gatelands.—May 1676, Christopher Etherington, who died suddenly, January, 4, 1678-9, and was buried at Sowerby.—May 1679 and 1682, John Witter, who was buried at Sowerby, December 27, 1697, aged 66.—Benjamin Baron, or Berron, and son, held Sowerby and Sowerby Bridge.—The elder was afterwards Vicar of Bradford.—May 7, 1701, William Midgley, who died of a palsy, May 7, 1706, and was buried in Halifax church, aged about 30.—1708, Archibald Young, who was thrown out at York by the Inhabitants of Sowerby, and was afterwards Curate of Haslingden, in Lancashire.—1710, Richard Marsden, who left Sowerby that year. — 1711, Nicholas Jackson, who was buried at Sowerby, February 11, 1729.—May, 1730, John Sheffield, who died November 23, 1735, and was buried at Sowerby.—May 1736, Christopher Gunby, who was buried at Sowerby.—1750, John Welsh, M. A.

—::—

CURATES OF CROSTONE.

1650, ... Smethurst.—1652 and 1662, George Stott.—August 1663 and 1665, Robert Dewhurst.—August, 1670, ... Gregson.—August, 1671, John Sunderland.—August, 1682 and 1689, Richard Robinson, who died April 28, 1690. —1703, Thomas Ferrand. — September, 1706, Archibald Young. — 1708, and 1711, and 1714, and 1716, Edward Metham.— August 1728, Michael Godley.— August 1732, Joshua Brooke.—December, 1734, entered John Grimshaw. —August, 1744, Tobit Sutcliffe.—August, 1745, John Welsh. —1750, John Law, who died September 6, 1768.

—::—

EXTRACT FROM THE

SURVEY of the MANOR of WAKEFIELD,

MADE IN 1314.

AT the head of my copy of this record, is wrote, " E " libro vocato, Domisday-booke;" and then follows, " Extenta redditus et servicii liberorum sokæ de Wakefeild, "facta ad natal. Dñi. anno Dñi, 1314." What relates to Halifax parish is as follows: "Fekisbye, Will. son of Tho. de Totehill, 4s. Peter, son of William, 3s. Joworthe, relict of Robert, 3d. Hen. son of Constan. 14d. Barnard, 18d. Tho. son of Adam, 2s. Rob. son of Richard, 21d. Alan, son of Alan, 20d. John, son of Robert, 3s. Rastricke, Will. son of Annabel, 5s. 3d. Will. son of Walter, 1d. ob. Alexander de Rastricke, 2d. Staynelande, Tho. de Thorneton, 10s. Hen. de Frankyshe, 6d. foreign service from both, 2s. 9d. Brighowse, Hugh de Totehill, 3s. 3d. Tho. del Roods, 18d. Hipperholm, the tenants there, and in Priestley, 3s. Presteley, Hen. de Northend, 4s. 3d. Ric. del Rooks, 4s. 1d. ob. Tho. del Brooke, 15d. Alice de Coldeley, 15d. Tho. de Rooks, 3s. 6d. Elias del Brooke, 7d. ob. Hugh de Prestley, 6d. Hen. de Copley, 2s. Elias de Shelfe, 4d. ob. Northourome, John de Birstall, 1d. Shipden, Adam de Stancliffe, 8s. 6d. Rob. son of Christian, 13d. ob. Rob. de Rigge, 3d. John de Shipden, 8s. Margaret de Bentley, 12d. Shelffe; the men of sir John de Thornhill, for foreign service, 4s. 6d. Midgley, Dns. Adam de Everingham, for the vill of Midgley, 2s. Rastricke, John del Okes, for one tenement, and one bovate of land, 4d. Alex. del Okes, one ten. 8 acres, 1d. Richard, son of Maud, for five acres, 2s. ob. Skircoit and Norlande; the men of Tho. de Langfeld, Matthew de Bosco and John de Lepton, for foreign service, 2s. The men of Tho. de Thorneton, for the same, 10s. The men of Tho. de Langfeld, for the same, 6s. And the men of Tho. de Thornehill, 12d.—And then follow the words, "Finis terræ liberæ."

Graveship of Fekisbye and Rastricke.—Peter, son of Will. one ten. 5 acres, called bordelands, for homage, fealty, and 3s. yearly. John, son of Rob. one ten. two bovates, and three acres for homage, fealty, and 3s. Rob. son of Ric. one ten. and one bovate, for hom. fealty, and 21d. Tho. son of Adam, for hom. fealty, and 2s. Alan, son of Alan, one ten. two bovates for hom. fealty, and 20d. Bernard, one ten. one bovate for hom. fealty, and 18d. Henry, son of Constance, half a bovate for hom. fealty, and 13d. ob. Jowet, half a ten. and half a bovate, for hom. fealty, and 3d. All these were due at Michaelmas, Purification, and Pentecost; and every one who held the aforesaid eight bovates, was to give for a bovate, and take fourpence half-penny at the feast of St. Andrew. The said tenants paid yearly, for two ploughs to plough the said eight bovates, eight-pence in the time of spring, and if they had more, they paid four-pence for every plough, except Peter, son of Will. who paid nothing. And the above, **and all** other householders who kept fires in the moiety **of the vill** of Fekisby, gave each for reaping 3d. at the Assumption **of** the Virgin Mary, except the said Peter; and there **were** then five houses which had fires; if they increased, they **were to** pay more, at the will of the lord.

Lands granted from the waste of the said vill. Richard, son of Thomas, 4 acres, for 16d. Hen. son of Tho. 4 acres, for 12d. Hen. son of Will. 3 acres, for 12d. Ric. de Anneley, 4 acres and half for 18d. Tho. son of John, 5 acres for 20d. Hen. de Totehill, 2 acres, for 8d. Will. son of Stephen, 2 acres, for 8d. Tho. at the wood, 2 acres, for 8d. Eve, wife of Hugh, 3 acres, for 12d. Beatrix, daughter of Tho. 3 acres, for 12d. Tho. de Yelitherigg, half an acre, for 3d. all due at the times above-mentioned.

The nativi in Rastrick. Adam, son of Ynon, one tenement, half a **bovate,** and **ten** acres, for 6s. 4d. and repair of Wakefield **mill dam.** Roger, son of Matthew, **one** ten. half a bovate, **and** six acres, for 3s. for tak. 14d. and repair of said dam. Will. de Wodehowses, one ten. half a bovate, for 2s. for tak. 2d. and repair of said dam. The same person 12 acres, for 4s. Roger de Wodhous, one **ten.** 5 acres, for 19d. and for tak. 5d. Beatrix, wife of Alan, one ten. half **bov. 12 acr.** for 7s. and repair of said **dam.** Matthew, son of Richard, one ten. **half** bov. 10 **acres,** one rod, for 6s. 5d. for tak. 12d. and said repair. Matthew de Totehill, one ten. half bov. and 4th part of **a** bov. &c. for 9s. 11d. **and said repair.** Will. de Totehill, one **ten.** 4th part of a bov. 3 acres for 2s. Tho. del Okes, one **ten.** half bov. 12 acres and half, **16s.** 2d. and said repair. John Seele, one ten. half bov. 7 acres, for **4s.** 4d. Hen. son of Modest. one ten. 6 acres, 2s. John de Botherod, one ten. half bov. and 4th part of a bov. and 8 acres, for 6s. 8d. He was also to reap one day, **and** plow as he plowed his own land, or give 4d. for a whole plough, 2d. for half, and repair said dam. John Coward (one MS sais Crowder,) one ten. half bov. 6 acr. for 6s. shall reap to the value of a penny, and repair said dam. John, son of Alexander, one ten. half bov. 6 acr. for 5s. 5d. and said repair. Hen. son of John, one ten. half bov. and 4th part of a bov. 17 acr. for 8s. 9d. ob. qa. and said repair. Adam . . . one ten. 9 acr. 1 rod and half, for 3s. 4d. Will. son of Hen. one ten. 8 acr. for 2s. 6d. qa. and one penny reaping. Tho. de Rodes, one ten. 4th part of a bov. 6 acr. for 3s. 4d. ob. one penny reaping, and said repair. Will. son of Hugh, 4 acr. for 15d. John, son of Ric. one ten. half bov. 10 acr. and half, for 5s. 6d. one penny reaping, and said repair. Peter, son of Hen. one ten. 5 acr. and half, for 18d. and one penny reaping. Margery, d. of Ynon, one ten. half acr. 1 rod, for 4d. Hen. s. of Peter, one ten. half bov. 8 acr. for 4s. 1d. and said repair. John, s. of Ric. one ten. 4th part of bov. and acre, for 3s. 6d. and said repair. Will. s. of Adam, 3 acr. for 9d. Roger, s. of Matthew, half of 9 acr. for 1d. ob. Alex. Cissor, 2 acr. 4th part of a rod, for 9d. John, s. of Roger, 4 acr. for 13d. Hen. s. of Will. 4 acr. for 12d. ob. Alex. de Brighouse, 1 acr. and half rod, for 7d. ob. John de Shepele, 10 acr. for 3s. 4d. Rog. de Brighowse, sen. 1 acr. and half, for 16d. Peter de Sowtcliff, 4 acr. half rod, for 16d. ob. Symon de Shipden, 1 acr. for 4d.

Free tenants. John del Okes holds freely one toft, one bov. for 4d. and for plowing 4d. if he have ale or plough, if not, he shall pay nothing, and for reaping 3d. Alex. de Okes holds freely one ten. 8 acr. for 1d. and for reaping 3d. Ric. s. of Maud, holds freely 5 acr. for 2d. ob. "All the "nativi in this graveship shall make the mill dam of Wake, "and pay marchet money for the said bovates, which they "hold, and grind all their corn at the mill of Rastrick, and "pay for take 6s. 8d."

This may serve as a specimen of the whole survey. What is farther worth remarking therein so far as it relates to the parish of Halifax, I shall here set down.

Graveship of Hipperholm. One Tho. son of Tho. was to pay 8d. for the take of Hogs for one bovate; and for grinding of malt 2s. and for other lands to plow with 4 oxen or pay 2d. and reap or pay 1d. Also to assist the grave in driving cattle taken in making distress throughout the whole grave-ship, to Wakefield, as often as he should be called upon by the said grave. Several others were bound in like manner, and, in case of refusal, were to be fined. Some of the free tenants of Hipperholm were tied to give to the lord for a whole plough 4d. and for as many **beasts** as they should plough with, two oxen in one yoke, one penny, and for reaping one penny. Under the free farm of Northouram. The men of John de Eland for foreign service 3s. The men of sir John Thornhill, for the same, 4s. 6d. **The** forinseca of Stainland, **2s. 9d.** The pannage of Hipperholm, comunibus annis four pounds, and 4s. 6d. for take, and 3s. 8d. for plow work, **2s. for** grinding, 3d. for Bakstones from one Tho. del Northend, 2s. 9d. for reaping, and an **hundred** shillings for **perquisites** of **court.** The rents which sir **John** de Eland received yearly in the graveship of Hipperholme **were of** Will. de Sunderlande 19s. 1d. of John de Sunderlande, 12s. 10d. of Symon de Supeden, 3s. and of Tho. Bland, 6d.

Graveship of Sowerby. **Here the lord** has a manor in his chase. Will. de Townend for his lands bound to grind at the mill of Soland **at the** twentieth vessel, to assist in making the eldest son of the lord a knight, in marrying his eldest daughter, and shall go a hawking with the lord as often as he shall come thither, for the first day at his own charges, and **if not,** shall pay **1d.** Several others were bound to the **same** service. Each **of** the tenants in the manor of Sowerby having hogs, **to give** for **every** hog 2d. and for **an** hoggete 1d. for take, **worth** yearly **on an** average **in** Sowerbye, Warluley, and Soland, in **an** hundred hogs, **and as many** hoggets, if the sows bred **as** usual, 30s. The **hogs to** be reckoned at Michaelmass, and **the** money to be **paid at** Martinmass. There **is** in the forest an iron forge, **which may** continue for **ever, worth** 9l. 12s. yearly, viz. 4s. **in each** week, except fifteen days at Christmas, and fifteen **days at** Easter and Whitsontide. **The** lord may have in **the forest five** score cows and bulls **in three** vaccaries, and eight **score fat** beasts may be in **Baytinge, where** may be agisted, **besides** the aforesaid beasts, **an hundred great** beasts between the feasts **of** St. Helen and **St. Giles, worth** yearly 40s. The pannage **of the** whole **graveship** worth yearly about 100s. The **herbage in** Hadreschelfe **24s.** Herbage in Mankanhulls **16s.** Escape of the cattle **of Midgley** and Luddingden 10s. **Escape** at Ryburne 5s. **The mill** at Soland 46s. 8d. The **mill** of Warlulley 26s. 8d. Perquisites of court 10l. Escape of beasts out of Northland 2s. 6d. Agistments in the common pasture 36s. 8d. In Soland. John de Hole was bound in all things as Will. de Townend abovementioned, as were several others in this district. All the rents arising from seventeen tenants here amounted to 69s. 11d. ob. These paid to the lord for foreign service 2s. Rishworth paid foreign service to the same 12d. Out of which were paid to sir John Eland for his life 2d. yearly.

Warley. Here the men of Tho. de Langfeild, Matthew de Bosco, and John de Lepton; as also the men of Tho. de Thorneton, and Tho. de Thornhill, are said to pay the same foreign service money as already mentioned in this survey after Skircoit and Norlande; and the tenants are said to hold their respective lands in this township, "per servicium de Sowerbye." **In the margin is wrote** "Skircotes & Northeland."

At the foot of this survey was **wrote,** "The sum total of "**the** whole extent 375l. 16s. 11d. ob. qa." The whole of earl Warren's rents in the north parts is also there made to **am**ount to 668l. 3s. 6d. ob. qa. out of which there was paid yearly about 100l. to constables, watchmen, and gate keepers at **castles.**

—::—

ACCOUNT OF THE

EARL OF LEICESTER'S LAND

IN HALIFAX PARISH.

QUEEN **Eliz.** did, by letters patents under the seal of the **dutchy** of Lancaster, bearing date at Westminster, 9 Oct. in the **8th** year of her reign, grant to the right hon. the earl of Leicester, 522 acres one rood and half of land, and a parcel of land containing by estimation eighty yards **in** length, and forty **in** breadth, four watercourses, and two parcels of land and waste within the graveship of Sowerby. Also **221** acres, two roods and half of land, and certain pieces **of** land containing by estimation fifty yards in length, and twenty **in** breadth, with one watercourse, in the graveship of Hipperholme. Also twelve acres and half a rood of land in the graveship of Rastrick, together with certain

parcels of land (the whole being new improvement) in **the**
graveships of Holmefrith, Wakefield, Stanley, Thornes, **and**
Alverthorp, all which were parcel of the demesne lands of
the lordship of Wakefield. He **had also in the** same letters
patents, a grant **of** lands in the graveship **of** Bradford; to
hold of the **said** queen, &c. all the above **premises** in free
and **common soccage,** and not **in capite.** These lands, &c.
the **said earl did, by** indenture made **Dec. 6, 9 Eliz. grant** to
sir **Thomas** Gargrave, of Kinsley, **knt. and Henry Savile,**
of Lupset, **esq**; and their heirs for **ever, to hold the same,**
together **with the said** letters patents, **on** the **conditions** in
the **said** letters patents mentioned. The rent **for the** above
lands **to** the crown was four **pence for** every acre; and **at the**
death **of** a principal tenant **four pence,** in the name of **a** fine
or heriot; also the like fine **on every** alienation, and suit of
court.

NUMBER of INHABITANTS in the PARISH of HALIFAX, in 1763 and 1764, &c.

In Halifax division, 1764.	houses	Empty	Families.
Halifax ...	1312	40	1272
Skircoat ...	263	12	251
Warley ...	503	16	487
Midgley ...	224	7	217
Sowerby ...	618	31	587
Ovenden ...	616	19	597
Northouram	660	30	630
Shelf ...	186	6	180
Hipperholm	367	15	352
Southouram	466	18	448
	5215	194	5021

Heptonstall division, 1764.	houses	Empty	Families.
Stansfield upper third ...	129	3	126
Stansfield middle third ...	207	4	203
Stansfield lower third ...	140	5	135
Langfield ...	139	2	137
Eringden ...	183	6	177
Heptonstall ...	367	15	352
Wadsworth ...	396	8	388
	1561	43	1518

In Eland division, 1763.	houses	Empty	Families
Brighouse ...	77	3	74
Rastrick ...	186	11	175
Fixby ...	56	2	54
Eland ...	262	23	239
Greetland ...	122	6	116
Old Linley...	42	2	40
Stainland ...	201	6	195
Barkisland...	267	17	250
Soyland ...	264	9	255
Rishworth ...	131	2	129
Norland ...	195	17	178
	1803	98	1705

TOTALS.

Houses	8579
Empty	335
Families	8244
Population (?) ...	41220

The whole number of families in the above table, taken from the vicar's Easter books, is 8244, and if we allow but five to a family, the amount will be 41,220; an amazing increase, if Camden's information was any thing near the truth, which he received as he travelled through these parts, that the number of inhabitants in this parish was about twelve thousand men; in which yet I am apt to think he was not very much mistaken; for in the certificate of the archbishop of York, and others, 2 Ed. VI. concerning chantries, &c. it is said, that "in the parrysh of "Hallifaxe the nomber of houslyng people is eight thousand five hundred, and is a great wide parrysh." And during the rebellion in the north, when every protestant, who could carry arms, was zealous to shew his attachment to his religion and the queen, archbishop Gryndall sais, in a letter to queen Elizabeth, that the parish of Halifax was ready to bring three or four thousand able men into the field. But the most striking instance of the increase of inhabitants in this neighbourhood is from an old paper in my possession, which I shall here faithfully transcribe. "By this underwritten yow may "gather the great encrease of howsinge and people within "the towne of Halifax in not many yeares by paste, written "by John Waterhowse, of Shipden, and some time lorde of "the mannor of Halifax.

"Note, there is in Halifax this yeare 1566, of housholders "that keepes fires and answers Mr. vicar in his fermours of "dutyes as householders 20 and six score and noe more (as "I am crediblye enformed;) and in the time of John Water- "house, late of Halifax, deceased, who dyed at Candlemas, "26 yeares agoe, att his deathe beinge very neare 100 yeares "of age (I trow three yeares under,) and when he was but a "childe there were but in Halifax in all 13 howses. God "be praysed for his encrease."

There were but then in Halifax, about the year 1443, when Mr. Waterhouse was born, thirteen families; these in about 123 years were increased to 520, and in less than 200 years more to 1272 families, and they are at present, I think, increasing more than ever, owing to the flourishing state of their trade, which is not confined to this town, and the precincts thereof, but extends its influence to the remotest corners of the parish, planting colonies in parts which, in former times, could scarce be said to be inhabited; thus in

Fixby are 54 families, where, in 1314, were only five houses which had fires, as appears from the extent above recited.

As an addition to the above, it appears from the **register book** at Heptonstall, that **there were** baptised in the **parochial** chapel there · **for** twenty **years, beginning** at **1741, 3714** children, and **for twenty** years before that period only 2375, so that **there was an** increase of **1339.** Buried there **in** twenty years, beginning at **1741, 2220, and for** twenty years before that period, **only** 1792, so **that there** was **an** increase of 428 ; the **country must** therefore, **of course,** have many more inhabitants in **it than** formerly ; a truth which is often attested by **living witnesses.** And these improvements have been made in **some of the most** wild and mountainous parts **of** that parish, which Camden has described **to be** "solum " sterile, in quo non modo commode **vivi, sed vix vivi** possit."

—::—

BARKESEY, OR BARSEY, IN BARKISLAND.

The family which it gave name to, had considerable possessions, and perhaps were **the** first improvers of the land hereabouts, which lies in a pleasant and tolerably fruitful valley. Some **of their names** I have met with in **dated** deeds, which shew they were in being during a great part of the fourteenth century. At Oaks, in Rishworth, **is a** deed, wherein John, son of Alan de Barkesay, grants to John, son of Richard de Barkesay, certain lands, lying near the brook **called** Blakeborne, within the divisions of Stainland, Barkesland, **and** Greteland. Dated **at** Barkesay, in 1326. At the same **place is a** deed of **land,** quit-claimed here, which for its conciseness is worth preserving. "Sciant " presentes **& futuri,** quod ego Matild. **de Eues,** dedi, con- " cessi, relaxavi, **& omnino** de me & heredibus **meis** quietum " clamavi, Johanni **filio** Roberti de **Clay, &** heredibus suis, " vel suis assignatis, totam terram quam emi de Ada patre " meo in Barkesay, pro quadam summa pecuniæ mihi pro- " priis manibus data. In cujus rei testimonium sigillum " meum apposui. Hiis testibus Ric. de Schaye, Tho. Cler. " Rog. del Haye, Johē de Ponte, & aliis."

A John de Barksey entered into possession of Clogh-houses in Barkisland, (which John de Clay had held,) at the court of the prior of the hospital of St. John of Jerusalem, in England, held at Batley, 41 Edw. III, 1367.

—::—

BRISKO.

Height [in **Barkisland,**] probably **takes** its name from its situation, standing high on the side of a steep hill.   Dr. Johnson, in his MS collections for an History of Yorkshire, sais, this is a place of great antiquity.   It was, **some** years ago, the residence of the family of the Firths, **who bore** for their arms, Or, a fess between three mallets, **sable ; and** afterwards of Musgrave Brisco, esq ; whose pedegree **is as follows.**

The first lords of Byrkscaye, in **the** county of Cumberland, took their surname from the place **of** their habitation, which **has** been written Byrkscaye, Birkskeugh, Briskugh, Briskoo, Brisko, Brisco, and (as the families in Northamptonshire and Herefordshire write it,) Briscoe.   Their arms are, Arg. three greyhounds current in pale, sab.

Robert de Brisko had Allan de Brisko, **who had** Jordan **de** Brisko, **who** had Robert de Brisko, who was witness to a deed in 1292.   He married Matilda, daughter of sir John Crofton, knt. lord of Crofton, &c.   She released her dower and feoffment to her eldest son John, **in 1313.**   She had by the said Robert, another son Isold, who, as John died s. p. inherited the estate, and married Margaret, d. and h. of sir John Crofton, of Crofton, **knt.** by whom the manors of Crofton, Whinnow, and Dundraw. This Isold had Christopher Brisko, of Crofton, **who** kept fourteen soldiers in pay at Brisco Thorn upon Hesket.   He had Robert (one MS. **sais** Richard) who married **Isabel, d.** of Will. Dikes, of Warthol, in Cumberland, by whom Robert, who married Katharine, d. and h. of Clement Skelton, of Pettrelwray, by whom John, who married Jennet, d. of Tho. Salkeld, of Corkby, by whom Richard, Roger, Simon, Christopher, and three daughters.   Richard married Elizabeth, d. of John Leigh, of Frisington, by whom Robert, who married, 1st, Barbara, d. of John Coldale, of Haryngton. 2dly, Mabel, d. of Robert Carlisle, esq ; By his first wife he had John, who purchased the Leigh's part of Orton, from Wilfrid Lawson, and Maud, his wife, widow of Tho. Leigh, of Isal, to whom he had given his estate, and another third part thereof from Tho.

Blenerhasset, of Carlisle. He took for his crest, a greyhound sab. bearing an hare proper. This John married Ann, d. of Will. Musgrave, of Hayton-castle, who died before his father sir Edward. By her he had William, who married Jane, d. of William Orfeur, of High-close. He purchased the advowson of the rectory of Orton, and some remaining parts of the manor. He had John, who married Mary, d. of Tho. Braithwaite, of Burnside, in Westmoreland, esq; about 1582, by whom William, who died in 1687-8. He was member of parliament for the city of Carlisle, as several of this family had been successively before. He married, 1. Susanna, d. of sir Randolph Cranfield. 2dly. Susanna, d. of Francis Brown, merchant and citizen of London. By his first wife he had John, who died in 1690, having married Mercy, d. of Will. Johnson, of Ribblesworth, com. Durham, by whom, 1. William, who died s. p. John, a justice of peace for the county of Cumberland, who married Catharine, d. of sir Richard Musgrave, of Hayton, in Cumb. bart. by whom, 1. Richard, who married Margaret, d. and h. of Tho. Lampleugh, of Lampleugh, esq. 2. John, of Crofton, D. D. who married Catharine, d. of John Hilton, of Hilton-castle, com. Durham, esq: by whom, 1. John; 2. Richard, killed in Germany; 3. Hilton, dead s. p. 4. Horton, 5. William Musgrave, 6. James, 7. Catharina Maria, dead s. p. 8. Dorothy, who married Jacob Morland, esq: 9. Margaret. William, 3d son of John, was a clergyman, and M.A., he married Margaret Langstaff, by whom, 1. Richard, and 2. William Musgrave, also, 3. Catharine, 4. Mary Horton, and, 5. Ann. Musgrave, 4th son of John, married Mary Fletcher Dyne, d. and h. of Edw. Dyne, of Lankhurst, in Sussex, esq; by whom, 1. Richard Horton, 2. John, 3. Edward Dyne, 4. Wastel; also a daughter, named Mary Horton, who died very young. James, 5th son of John, married, and had issue. Wastel, 6th son of John, married, 1st, . . . Beckford, in Jamaica; 2dly, . . . Campbell, no issue. Ralph, 7th son of John, married Dorothy Rowland, by whom Dorothy, and Anna Maria. Thomas, 8th son of John, died an infant. The said John had also four daughters, viz. 1. Dorothy, who married, 1st, Richard Lampleugh; 2dly, . . . Ward. 2. Katharine, who died young; 3. Another Katharine, who married John Holmes, of Holme-hill, in Cumberland; and 4. Ann, who died young. The last named Katharine had John, Edward, and Katharine, who married . . . . Somner, esq; who, in 1766, was next in command to lord Clive.

COPLEY—See Savile.

—::—

CROMWELLBOTHOM—See Lacy.

—::—

PEDEGREE OF DEAN, OF EXLEY.

William Dean, of **Exley, married** Isabel, daughter **of** John Bairstow, **by whom Robert,** to whom his father **gave** Exley; **and** William, who had the Spout-house and Yeat-house in Halifax, and who married Judith Hanson, who surviving him, married, secondly, Jasper Blythman. She was buried **at** Eland, March 7, 1638. Robert **lived** part of his **time at** Exley, but removed to Priestley, **in** Hipperholme, where he was living Jan. 12, 1651. He married Ann ...... by whom Gilbert, William, and five daughters. Gilbert was a Lawyer, and belonged **to** the Six Clerks' Office; **he had** William, and a daughter married to Bishop **Lake,** which daughter was buried at Halifax, Feb. 22, 1699-700, **aged 71**; he also had other daughters, one of which married ...... Kirk, **of Oller-**thorp. The above William, as well as his father Gilbert, was a man of a melancholic temper. During their indisposition, the estate was much impaired, yet so intailed, that, for default of male issue, after the death **of William,** it came to Robert Dean, mentioned below, who enjoyed **it** several years, and at last sold it to Mr. Henry Greame, **being** at that time an hundred pounds per ann.

William, son of Robert, **above** named, **was** apprentice to a **Turkey** Merchant, and being taken prisoner by the Turks, and losing all his effects, he returned to London, and having **sold** all his estate in Yorkshire, went a second voyage, and **was** taken by the Tartars, **and confined** several months in great misery. Being redeemed **by exchange of** prisoners, he returned to London, and died soon after; he had Robert, and **a daughter. Robert** was sent down **from** London, a child of four years old, to one Mr. Savile, of Greetland, who was his father's agent, and with whom effects were left for the child's **education,** in case the **father** met with bad fortune. **This Robert** married, and had a numerous family. The daughter was **left** in London, but married, and had children.

I know not whether this family ever laid claim to any coat of arms, but the Deans, of Dean-house, in this parish, bore, Argent a fess dancy, in chief three crescents gules.

DRAKE AND SHIBDEN.

Shibden formerly gave name to a family, who on some account or other, changed their name to Drake. The following account of whom was drawn up from deeds and family papers by the late Mr. Drake, of York, author of the " Eboracum, &c." assisted by the late Dr. Burton, of York, author of the " Monasticon Eboracense."

William de Schepden, of Nether Schepden, lived temp. Edward I, as by charter dated at Schippedene in 1306, had John de Schipeden, alias Drake, and William. John had John, as by deed 36 Edw. III. He had also John Drake, of Schipeden, as by deed 2 Hen. IV. This John had likewise a son John, as by deed 9 Hen. VI. This last John had Richard, who lived, as by deed, temp. Edw. IV. He had John, as by charters dated 1443, 1476, and 1483, as also by his marriage settlement deed: he married Cecilia, daughter of John Roper, of Thornton, in Bradford-dale, by whom William, Laurence, Robert, John, Elizabeth, Alice, and Ellen. William lived temp. Hen. VII, as by deed, and married Christobella, daughter of ...... by whom John, who lived temp. Hen. VIII, as by deed. He had Thomas, of Horley-green, in the same township, as by deed temp. Phil. & Mar. (Mr. Drake sais nothing when the family sold Shibden, but it is plain that it had taken place at this time, by this Thomas being removed to Horley-green; I find also, in the Testamentary Burials at Halifax, extracted from Mr. Torr's MS. that Richard Waterhouse, of Shipden, was buried in 1538, 27 Hen. VIII; so that either this Thomas, or his father, disposed of the old family estate.) Thomas had, 1. William, commonly called William of the Lee, in Halifax parish; 2. Gilbert; 3. Humphry, of Pikeley; 4. Sibilla, or Isabella, who married Mr. Robert Bentley, (and quære if not a son called John.) William had, 1. Joseph, who married a daughter of ...... Quously, of Lightcliffe, whose father and mother lived to be each an hundred years old. 2. Nathan of Godley; 3. Jeremy; 4. Timothy, of London, merchant; 5. Susan, who married ...... Lister, of* Shibden-hall; 6.

*Qu: Did not the Estate pass by this marriage into the Lister's family? Richd. Waterhouse might be merely a Tenant.

Phœbe, who married ...... Hemingway, of Shibden-mills ; 7. Esther, who married Humphry, son of Humphry Drake ; 8. Grace.

Nathan above named, second **son of** William, was a soldier in the civil wars, and served **as** one of the garrison of Pontefract-castle, for which he lost Godley, &c. He had Samuel, D.D. Rector of Hansworth, and Vicar of Pontefract, who was expelled from his Fellowship at **St.** John's, Cambridge, and afterwards served the King at **the siege** of Newark ; **he married** ...... daughter of ...... **Abbot ;** his sisters were, **Elizabeth,** married to ...... Stables, of Pontefract ; **and** Mary, to ...... **Knowles,** of Pontefract. Jeremy **above** named had Timothy ; Abraham, a merchant **at** Newcastle ; Jonathan ; Grace, and Esther. Timothy, the eldest, **was** brought up by his uncle Timothy, who left him a good estate. He married, and had Richard, D.D. Precentor of Sarum, and the Publisher **of** Bishop Andrews's " Greek Devotions." Both **he** and his father were Benefactors to Pembroke-hall, **in** Cambridge, and their Arms are in the Catalogue in the Library.

Joseph, **who** married ...... daughter **of** Quousley, had Joseph, Thomas, **Susan,** and Esther. Thomas had William, Elizabeth, and Esther. Joseph, **last** named, had, 1. Marmaduke, 2. John, **(who** had William,) 3. William, **4.** Thomas (who had Jeremy, **Joseph,** John, William and Elizabeth,) 5. Nathan, 6. Elizabeth, **7.** Mary, **8.** Maud, and 9. Esther. Nathan, last named, **was** Rector of **Kirby** Overblows, and had Robert, Nat, Joseph, Mary, and Betty.

Gilbert, second son of Thomas Drake, of Horley-green, **above** mentioned, married Alice, daughter of Christopher **Booth, of** Booth's-town, **near** Halifax, 1 Edw. VI, by whom **John,** Sibilla, and Isabella. N.B.—This is agreeable **to** the account drawn up by Drake and Burton ; but these Gentle**men** seem to have made a mistake ; for in one of Mr. Drake's deeds, dated in 1494, **there** is mention made **of John** Drake, son, **and** heir apparent **of** this William. **The** question is, whether William, or Gilbert, married **Alice** Booth ; for I have copies **of** two other pedegrees of **this** family, which agree that John, who married Grace Bairstow, as below, was son of the said Alice. I rather think, that Alice Booth was the wife of William, not Gilbert, and that this William was father of John, who married Grace, daughter of John

Bairstow, of Northbridge, near Halifax, by whom, **1.** John, **2.** Thomas, **3.** Francis, M.A. of Christ's College, Cambridge, s. p. **4.** Samuel, **5.** Daniel, **who** married the daughter of **Holdsworth,** by whom John. John, the eldest, married Mary, daughter of John **Hoyle,** of Hoyle-house, in **Hipper-**holme, by whom Thomas, **s. p.** Thomas, second **son of** John, was Rector **of** Thornton in Craven, and married, **about** 1625, Mary, **daughter of** Christopher Foster, of Leighbourn, in the Bishopric **of** Durham, by whom William, of Barn-oldswick Cotes, **living in** 1667, **Justice** of Peace for the West-riding, **who married** Mary, daughter of John Stilling-ton, of Kelfield, **near** York, by whom William, Thomas, Francis, John, Robert, Mary, Ursula, who married Henry Gill, and Margaret. William married Abigail, daughter of ...... Yates, **a** Merchant, at Blackburn, in Lancashire, by **whom William,** Francis, Mary, Ann, and Abigail. William **died in 1758, and** left his estate about Halifax to his kins-man, Mr. Francis Drake, of York.

Humphry Drake above mentioned, son of **Thomas, and** brother to William, and Gilbert, lived at Pykeley, **and had** Humphry, who married Esther Drake, his uncle William's daughter, by whom 1. Nathaniel, s. p. who was a Fellow of a College in Oxford, and 2. John, Sub-dean of Ripon, Pre-bendary of York, and Rector of Dunnington, who married Grace Hey, relict of ...... **Foxley.** This John had, **1.** Hum-phry, **2.** Gilbert, s. p. **3.** Esther, 4. Susanna, who died unmarried, and 5. Frances, who married ...... Ridsdal, of Ripon, by whom Edward. Humphry **the** eldest, married Catharine Rigby, of Cosgrave, in Northamptonshire, by whom, **1. John,** 2. Christopher, **3.** Montague. 4. Humphry, died young; **5. Humphry,** 6. Catharine, **7.** Susan, 8. Sarah, 9. Elizabeth, **and 10.** Mary.

Samuel Drake, **D.D.** born at Pontefract, made **Vicar there** at the Restoration, and wrote the life of his tutor and friend Mr. Cleveland, married ...... daughter of Abbot, as above, had **by** her, 1. Francis, 2. Samuel, of Leeds, Clerk, who **married** ...... daughter **of** ...... Benson, but died **s. p.** 3. Nat, **who** had Thomas, Nat, Samuel, and Richard. 4. John, 5. Edmund, 6. Ann, and 7. Elizabeth, who married ...... Stapleton, D.D. Francis the eldest was M.A. and succeeded his father in the vicarage of Pontefract. He married, first, Hannah, daughter **of** ...... Paylin, of York, merchant; 2dly,

Elizabeth, daughter of John Dixon, of Pontefract, by whom Francis and Margaret. This last Francis was Fellow of the Royal Society, Author of the "History of York," the "Parliamentary History of England down to the Restoration," and of several tracts in the "Philosophical Transactions." He married Mary, daughter of John Wodyear, of Crookhill, near Doncaster, by whom 1. Francis, Vicar of Womersley, Lecturer at Pontefract, and Fellow of Magdalene College, Oxford; 2. William, first sent to be third master in Westminster school, and afterwards presented to the school of Felsted in Essex, by the right honourable the Earl of Winchelsea and Nottingham. This William married Mary, daughter of Nat Drake, of Lincoln. He had two younger brothers, John and Henry, who both died young. The above Francis, by his first wife, Hannah Paylin, had 1. John, 2. Samuel, 3. William, 4. Frances who died young; 5. Frances, who married Thomas Barnard, of Leeds, Clerk, and 6. Hannah, who married Francis Lascells, of Pontefract, Clerk. John the eldest, B.D. Prebendary of York, succeeded his father in the Vicarage of Pontefract; he had Elizabeth, who married ...... Fenton; Samuel, the second son, was D. D. Rector of Frecton and Holme, in Spaldingmore, Author of the life of Archbishop Parker, or, as another account sais, the publisher of a beautiful edition of Archbishop Parker's "Antiq. Britan. 1729." He married Elizabeth, daughter of Darcy Dalton, Clerk, by whom Samuel, Elizabeth, and Frances. His younger brother William was captain of a man of war, and married Judith, daughter of Edward Langley, of Hipperholme, near Halifax, by whom Samuel, s. p. and Edward, a Surgeon and Apothecary in York, who married Elizabeth, daughter of George Coates, of York, by whom Judith, born 1752.

The above pedegree is such as, for antiquity and authenticity, will not often, in private families, be exceeded; it begins before surnames were in use, and it is extracted from antient deeds, and other evidences, which are still preserved, and collected together. Concerning the family taking the name of Drake, there was an account of it in the writings belonging to the late Abraham Sunderland, esq; but whether those writings are now in being I cannot say, so that probably this anecdote is lost. Tradition sais, that this family came originally from Devonshire, where was lately an opulent family of the name of Sir William Drake, which had been long settled there, and of which the famous sir Francis Drake was a branch.

The arms which some of this family have **used** are, Argent, a wivern, his wings displayed and queue nowed gules, the same, except the addition of legged or, **which** an old manuscript collection of arms in **my** possession gives to a Devonshire family **of** this name, and which, viz. argent, **a** cockatrice gules, the said MS. sais **was** born by Francis Drake, of Buckland, esq; in Devon.   (**Bart.** 20 James I.) whose crest was, a rheine deer's head **erased** or, attired, and collared with a crown sable.

ELLAND.

The best account I can give of this once famous family is this :

Leisingus de Eland, as by deed **sans date, and who** gave name to Lasing-croft, in Yorkshire, **married, and had** Henry de Eland, who married the daughter and **coheir of** Whitworth, who bore, argent, a bend sable, in chief a garb gules. By her he had sir Hugh de Eland, as by deed sans **date.** He married and had sir John de Eland, who was living **30** Hen. III. and also 3 Edw. **I.** for **in** this latter year **a** riot was presented at Brighouse **Turne,** upon John Eland and John Quermby, about **a** distress which Eland had taken from Quermby, for aid **to** make his son a knight, for lands **in** Stainland.   This sir **John** married, and had sir Hugh de Eland, who married Joan, daughter and **coheir** of sir Richard Tankersley, **knt.**   This sir Hugh is said **to** have died 3 Edw. II.   He was **witness** to a deed of John earl Warren, dated at Koningsburgh, **5** Oct. 1 Edw. II. 1307, wherein the earl confirmed **to** the **free** burgesses of Wakefield and **their** heirs their privileges, viz. to each a toft **of** an acre in free burgage, **for** six-pence rent per ann. with liberty **of** free trade in all **his** lands in Yorkshire, and wood to burn; for which charter **they** gave to earl Hamelin, his countess, and son, seven pounds; and amongst the witnesses was Hugh de Elond, the grandfather of this sir Hugh.   Besides this confirmation, the said earl John, by the deed above-named, granted to the said burgesses to be toll free in all his lands for all wares and merchandize of their own manufacture, and that they should not be obliged to answer at any court but his, called

Burman-court, in Wakefield, **unless** for trespasses against himself; and that whatsoever goods should be bought of any burgess for **him** or his use, at certain rates, should be paid for within **forty** days, and pawnage for every hog 2d. and pig 1d. and **to** have commonage for all cattle but goats, in all woods, moors, &c. except **New** and Old **Park**, and the great meadow, (only not in fawning time,) and that they might inclose **and** hedge their corn ground, and fright away his deer **from** thence without horn. This Hugh also had released, **on the** Monday **next** before the Feast **of the** Apostles Peter and **Paul**, (June 30,) 1306, by the name of Hugh, son **of John de Eland, to** Thomas de Langfeld, and Elen **his wife, and others, ten** marks **of** yearly payment, which **see under** the account of **the** manor of Barkisland. Sir Hugh had, by Joan his wife, 1. sir Thomas de Eland, 2. Richard, 3. Margaret, and, 4. Wymark. **Of** these, Margaret married **to** her first husband, John Lacy, **to wh**om, and to his heirs by the said Margaret, her father gave, by deed, in 1293, all his land in Southouram, and all his tenants there, and their services, except his manor of Eland, and the service of his tenants in Eckisley, **and** the pasture in the Stony-bancke, for a rent **of** 26s. yearly, and suit to his mill. They had issue. **The** said Margaret married, to her second husband, William, the constable of Nottingham castle, when earl Mortimer was there taken prisoner. In a book, intitled " The Cronicles of Englonde, with the fruyte of tymes, im- " prynted at London by Wynkyn de Worde, in 1528," folio 114 and 115, is the following account how this William de Eland betrayed earl Mortimer : " In haste came unto kyng " Edward syr Willyam of Mountagu, that than was in the " castell, and pryvely tolde him, that he nor none **of his** " **company** sholde not take Mortimer without counseyle and " helpe **of** Wyllyam of Eland, constable of the same castell. " Now truly sayd the king, I counseyle you that ye go to the " constable, and comaunde hym in my name, that he be " your frende, and your helpe for to take Mortimer.—Than " went forth the foresayd Mountagu, and came to the con- " stable of the castell, and told him the kynge's will. And " he answered and sayd, the kynge's wyll shold be done in " as moche as he myght—and so he swore and made his " othe. Than sayd syr Willyam of Mountagu to the con- " stable—Us behoveth to werke, and do by your advyse for

"to take Mortymer, syth that ye be keper of the castell, and
"have the keys in your warde. **Syr,** sayd the constable—
"the gates of the castell ben **locked** with the lockes that
"**dame Isabell** sente hyther, and by nyght she hath **the keys**
"therof, and layeth them **under the** levesell of the bedde
"tyll on the morowe, **and so ye may not come into** the
"castell by the gates **in no maner of wyse** ; but I knowe an
"aley that stretcheth **out of the warde** under the erth into
"the foresayd **castel, that goth into the west,** whiche aley
"dame Isabell, **the quene, ne none of her men,** nor Morty-
"mer, ne none **of his** company, **knoweth it not.** And **so I**
"shall lede **you** through that aley, and so ye shall come into
"the castel without espyenge of ony men that be your
"enemyes.—And Willyam Eland—prively lad syr William
"of Mountagu and his company **by the foresayd way,** under
"the erth, tyl they **came** into the **castel,** and **went** up into
"the toure where as Mortymer **was** in.—Than toke they
"Mortymer as he armed hym at **the toure's dore.**" The
existence of the other daughter is proved from a deed in the
chartulary of Whalley Abbey, folio 234, wherein Robert de
Mitton grants **to** Gilbert de Notton, for his homage **and**
service, and 20s. of **silver,** two bovats of land in Wordelword,
and two bovats in Heleye, which Hugh de Elond, **father** of
Richard de Elond, gave with Wymark his daughter, in free
marriage **to** Jordan de Mitton, grandfather to the said
Robert, paying yearly **4s.** of silver at the feast of St. Oswald,
of which 2s. was to be yearly paid at Martinmass to Hugh
de Elond. **From hence also** I think it appears, that Richard
de Eland, by the manner of his being mentioned here, was
the **eldest son of sir** Hugh, but dying perhaps in his minority, without **issue, in** the life time **of** his father, the **said** sir
Hugh was succeeded **in** title and **estate** by his son, sir
Thomas de Eland, **who** married **and had sir** John **de** Eland,
knight of the shire for Yorkshire, with sir William Gram-
mary, 14 Edw. III. and sheriff **of** Yorkshire, 15 Edw. III. in
which year it is said, that he marched privately **in the** night,
at the head of a body of his tenants, and put to death three
neighboring gentlemen **in** their own houses, an account of
which **will** be given below. This sir John married three
wives, **1.** Alice, daughter of sir Robert Lathom, who bore,
or, on a chief dancette, az. three plates. 2dly. Ann, daughter
of ...... Rygate, **s. p.** 3dly. Olive ...... By Alice, his first

wife, he had 1. Sir John de Eland, who had a son, name unknown, and Isabel. 2. Thomas de Eland, esq; 3. Henry, 4. Margery, 5. Isabel, and, 6. Dionysia. In the account of the feodary of the honour of Pomfret, of the lands and tenements in Eland in the hands of the lord, by the minority of the heir of Thomas de Eland, is £6 18s. 2d. for the term of Whitsontide, 1350. After the death of sir John de Eland, and his son and heir, sir John Savile, of Tankersley, purchased, in 1350, the wardship of Isabel Eland, daughter of the said sir John, from the lord of the honour of Pontefract, for £200. See "Comput. seneschall. honoris de Pontfrete," p. 17. After this purchase he married her, and in her right became possessed of the estates belonging to that family.

By the above-named Olive, sir John Eland had Robert, and James, which last died s. p. Robert married Alice, daughter of Fitz-Eustace, by whom, Thomas Eland, of Carlinghow, in Batley, who is mentioned as son and heir of Robert Eland, of Carlinghow, in a fine, 1 Hen. VI. This Thomas married Alice, daughter and coheiress of ......Serfe, of Neway, by whom Robert, who married Jane, daughter of Robert Holme, of Beverley, by whom Robert Eland, of Carlinghow, who married Rosamond, daughter of Humphry Littlebury, of Kelton, in Lincolnshire, by whom, Marmaduke Eland, of Carlinghow, who married Cecily Butler, of Hertfordshire, by whom William, Giles, Marmaduke, Francis, Isabel, Ann, and Margaret.

The arms which Eland, of Eland, is said to have borne, are, Barry of six pieces, argent and gules, on the latter six martlets, or, three, two, and one; but I find several variations, particularly the charter of the manor of Brighouse (already mentioned) was sealed, 19 Edw. III. by sir John Eland, to John his son, and Alice his wife, with an escallop shell, and Eland, of Essex, bears argent, on a bend gules, three escallops, or; but the coat of Robert Eland, esq; in a MS. in the British Museum, No. 2118, is, gules, two bars argent, between eight martlets of the second, three, two, and three.

EXLEY, OR ECCLESLEY.

I have several copies of undated deeds, wherein the Ecclesleys of Ecclesley, within Southouram, are mentioned, but they were never lords of a manor here.

o

In the **31st** of Edward I. a royal pardon was granted, at Dunfermelyn, to Richard, son of Will. de Ekclesleye, for the death of William, **son** of William de ......eye (here was a flaw in the parchment,) the motive for which pardon was, **the good** service which **the** said Richard had done the king in Scotland. Another **royal pardon,** in general terms, was granted, 38 Hen. VI. to Robert Eklesley, late of Southouram, **Yoman.** One Henry de Grene de Ecclesley granted by deed, **without date, land** in the vill of **Ecclesley,** to Richard, son of **Roger** de Ecclesley. Test. John de Lascy, Hugh de Coppeley, Richard de Hipperum, William de Ecclesley.— Elen, daughter of Henry, son of Hugh de Ecclisley, grants to Richard, son of Roger de Ecclisley, lands in Ecclisley, by deed without date. Test. John de Eland, William de Astay, son of William the Steward, Adam the Brewer, of Schircotes, Henry de Astay.—Robert, brother of said Elen, grants the same. Test. John de Lascy, Hugh de Coppeley, William de Astay —William de Ecclisley grants, by deed without date, to said Richard, son of Roger, a place called Grenebawale, on the north side of a way leading from Schircotes-bridge to Southouram, and a messuage, for exchange of the Pighill, in Ecclisley. Test. John de Eland, John de Lascy, Hugh de Rastrick, Hugh de Coppeley, Richard de Hipperum, William, son of Henry de Haye, Henry, son of William the Steward, William, his brother.—Robert, son of Henry, son of Hugh de Ecclisley, grants to said Richard, son of Roger, land in Ecclisley, for a rent of one arrow yearly. Test. John de Lascy, Hugh de Rastrick, Hugh de Coppeley, John de Greteland.—He also grants to him five acres and a half in Ecclisley. Test. Hugh de Rastrick, William, son of Simon de Northland, William, son of Henry de Haye, Helias, son of Walter de Schircotes.—Henry, son of Hugh de Ecclisley, grants to said Richard, half quarter of an acre there. Test. John de Lascy, Hugh de Rastrick, William de Ecclisley, William de Astay, Adam the Brewer, of Schircotes.—William, son of William de Dewisbyri, grants to said Richard, a certain Pighill, within Ecclisley. Test. John de Eland, John de Lascy, Hugh de Rastrick, William de Astay, Alan de Fckisby, Roger de Bradeley. All these deeds without date.

Hugh de Eland, by deed, without date, grants to Hugh, son of Swain de Ecclesley, all his demain lands there, except his park, mill, and assarts, in consideration of twelve-pence yearly rent, the homage and land **of Ric.** his brother, **and** Basia, his sister, **and** receiving reasonable aid when he made his eldest son **knight, or** married **his** eldest daughter. Test. Hen. de Greetland, Henry **de Crumwell,** Richard, **son of** Hugh, Roger **de** Rastrick, and Hugh, **his son.**

Thomas Pek, Chaplain, **and** Henry **del Scolefeld,** confirm to John de Eckylslay, and heirs, lands, &c., **which they** had of the gift and feoffment of **John de Eckylslay, in the vill** and territory **of Southouram; for want of issue to said John, then to** Richard **de** Eckylslay **and** heirs, **remainder to** Thomas, son **of John de** Waterhouse, and heirs, **remainder** to right **heirs of** said John de Eckylslay, **2 Hen. IV.**—Roger, **son of Richard** de Eklisley, **grants** by deed, without date, to **Richard, son of** William, **his brother,** lands **called Le Croftys,** and another parcel lying **near** the Grene. **Test.** Thomas de Thornhyll, and **Matthew de Bosco.**—Isabel, relict of Richard Eckilslay, of Burton, **quit claims to John** Beamonte, **of** Murefeld, Gentilman, her right of dower in **a** messuage called Eckilslay, in the vill and territory of Eckilsley **and** Southourome. **Test. Richard** Beamonte, Esq; Alexander **Paslew, esq;** John Wilkinsone, Thomas Eckilslay.—John **Beamonte** regrants the same, **17 Hen. VII. to** Alexander Paslew, **of** Redilsden, John Boswell, of Gunthwait, esqrs. and John **Hall,** Chaplain. **Test.** Thomas Sotill, Richard Beamonte, **esqrs.,** John Rokes **de Rokes,** Richard Bairstow, of Brownhurst.—Henry, son and **heir of** Thomas **de Ecclisley,** grants **to Richard,** his brother, **all his land** in Ecclesley. Test. Robert **de Hulton, John de Bairstow,** Michael de Gretlond, William de Bradelee, Thomas de **Hemingway,** John de Nortcleve, **sans** date. Hugh, son **of** Robert, the clerk of Priestley, **and** Rose, his wife, daughter of William **de Ecclisley,** grant **to John, son of** William de **Ecclisley, a** sixth part of **all the** land in **Ecclisley, which** William de Ecclisley, father **of said John,** formerly held. Test. Ingolard Turbard, Vicar of Halifax, Hugh de Eland, John, his brother, Henry de Rissworth, Thomas **de Coppeley,** Richard **de Ecclisley.**

FARRER.

The following is the pedegree **of the** Farrers, who are the oldest family which **appear** to have **been** settled at Ewood.

An Henry Farrer had Henry, and John; the former of
these who wrote himself Henre Faror, was of Eawood and
Brearley, and was a Justice of Peace, as Thoresby, p. 196. in
a pedegree of the family, tells us, 32 Eliz. or 1590; but I
meet with Henry Ferrer, of Ewwod, and John his brother,
in a deed 28 H. VIII, or 1536. This Henry purchased
Clubcliffe, in Methley, of sir Edward Dymock, knt. built a
great part of that house, and also Eawood. He married
Mary, daughter of John Lacy, of Brearley; but having no
issue, his estate came to his brother, John Farrer, of
London, esq; according to Thoresby; but I find John Farrer,
of Elfabrugh-hall, brother to Henry Farrer, of Eawood, 28
Hen. VIII, as above. This John, by Isabel...... had Henry,
John, Charles, and (Thoresby sais) Humphry, a Divine.
Henry, the eldest of these, married Ann, daughter of William
Barcroft, of Barcroft, 1 & 2 Phil. and Mar. He sold Ea-
wood to his brother John, and having bought lands in
Lincolnshire, he settled there, as did his posterity. John
Farrer, of Eawood, esq; was Justice of Peace 14 Cha. I. and
Treasurer for lame soldiers in the West-riding of Yorkshire,
and is named in the corporation charter of Halifax. He
married, first, Dorothy, daughter and heiress of Mr. Nicholas
Hanson, of Eland, by whom John, Henry, s. p. and Mary,
who married Mr. John Green, of Liversedge. John married,
first, Ellen Banister, by whom, 1. Jonathan; 2. Dorothy,
who married Mr. William Foxcroft; and 3. Abigail. He
married, 2dly, Dorothy West, s. p. and, 3dly, Judith,
daughter of Mr. Edward Oldfield, by whom seven children.
John Farrer, who married Dorothy Hanson, married to his
second wife, Susan, daughter of Mr. Anthony Waterhouse,
by whom, 1. William; 2. Edward, first Fellow, and afterwards Master of University College, Oxford; 3. Susan, who
married Mynheer Isaac Van Ogarden, a Dutch man.
William Farrer, of Ewood, the eldest, was a Justice of
Peace thirty years, and died of a paralytic stroke at his
son's in law, Mr. Greenwood, of Stapleton, Oct. 8, 1684; he
married Frances, (see below) daughter of Richard James, of
Portsmouth, by whom, 1. John, 2. William, 3. James, a
soldier; 4. Henry, Rector of Hemsworth, who married
Mary Brearley, widow; 5. Richard, a Physician; 6. Mary,
who died unmarried; and, 7. Frances, who married James
Greenwood. John, the eldest, died March 22, 1722-3,

having married Elizabeth, daughter and heiress of James Creswick, of Beghall (or Beal,) near Ferrybridge, B. D. by whom James, and Lydia, who died, and was buried at Halifax, Oct. 1719, having married Mr. Samuel Shaw, of Bristol, merchant. James, who died suddenly; Dec. 18, 1718, married, August 1696, Mary, daughter of Mr. John Brearley, of Rochdale, **by whom** James, lord of the manor **of** Wortley, in 1764, **and William,** who died s. p.

Farrer, **of Eawood, bore, On** a bend ingrailed **sable, three horse shoes** argent.

The Epitaph of the above Henry Farrer, **who removed** into Lincolnshire, seems, by the time, to be that **which Le** Neve, in his Monumenta Anglicana, vol. i. p. 152. **has** given **us out of** Wisbich church, **in the** Isle of Ely, thus : " M. S. " Hic jacet Henricus Farrour, **arm.** una cum charissima " uxore Margareta, ex qua 56 annos Tori socia xvii liberos " genuit. Hæc obiit Sept. 26. A° Dom. 1670, Æt. suæ 72. " Ille vero Aug. 22, A° Dom. 1672, Ætat. suæ 82."

I have followed Thoresby in mentioning Frances, daughter of Richard James, of Portsmouth ; but in Drake's Eboracum, p. 341. is her epitaph, thus : " Here lyeth the body of Tho- " masin, **wife** to William Farrer, **of** Ewode, within the " vicarage of Hallifax, and county of York, esquire, daughter " of Richard James, of Portsmouth, esquire, who departed " this life Jan. 10, 1660."

—::—

FIXBY—See Thornhill.

—::—

GLEDHILL AND HORTON.

At Howroyd is a beautiful pedegree on vellum of this family, &c., entitled " The pedegree of John Gledhill, of " Barkisland, collected out of antient deeds and evidences, " finished, perused, and confirmed by William Seager, knt. " alias Garter, principal king of arms, in 1632." The " following is an exact copy of it. Richard de Barkisland " had Thomas and Robert. Thomas had Peter and John. " Peter had two daughters, one of which married Henry

"Gledhill, who had William, who had Adam, as by deed,
"1327, who had John, as by deed, 30 Edw. III. who had
"Thomas, as by deed, 27 Hen. VI. who had John, as by
"deed, 16 Edw. IV. who had Thomas, as by deed, 18 Hen.
"VII. who had John, as by deed, 35 Hen. VIII. This John
"was twice married, as proved by deed, 37 Eliz. By his
"first wife he had Thomas and Michael. Thomas had
"John, Thomas, Richard, Elizabeth and Judith." Wrote
"under, "This pedegree, with the armes thus marshaled, I
"doo ratifie, alowe, and conferme. Witnes my hand, this
"25th day of June, 1632. William Segar, Garter." Near
the arms, (viz. for Barkisland, parted per pale, sab. and
gules, on a bend, or, three martlets of the first; and for
Gledhill, azure, three lozenges in fess, argent,) are these
words: "This peternall and ancient coate of Gledhill was
"granted and alowed by pattine, with the hand and seale of
"sir Richard St. George, knt. Norroy kinge at arms, unto
"Thomas Gledhill, of Barkisland, in the county of Yorke,
"Dec. 24, 1612." The arms of Gledhill, in a window at
Barkisland Hall, and in other places, are, argent, three
lozenges in fess, azure; the reason of which difference I do
not understand.

John Gledhill, who, in the above pedegree, is said to have
been twice married, had by his second wife a son John, who,
I think, removed from Barkisland to Leedes; by his first
wife Cecily, daughter of John Thornhill, of Fixby, esq; he
had Thomas and Michael. Thomas bought the manor
house called Cromwelbottom, of John Lacy, for £700. 9
James I. He married Edith, daughter of John Harrison, of
Leedes, whose will is dated in 1636. By her he had John
Gledhill, of Barkisland, Thomas, s. p. sir Richard, s. p.
Elizabeth, and Judith. Of these, John married Sarah,
daughter of William Horton, by whom Sarah, s. p. and
another who died young. Sir Richard was knighted by the
marquess of Newcastle, and slain at Hesssaymoor, near
York, in 1644. He was captain of a troop of horse in the
regiment of sir Marmaduke Langdale. Elizabeth married in
1636, William Horton, esq; who became in her right possessed of this estate at Barkisland. The account of this
family of Horton is as follows:

Their original settlement seems to have been at Horton,
in Bradford-dale, in Yorkshire. It appeareth that one

Robert de Horton manumitted a bondman or villain to his manor of Horton, long before the days of Henry Lacy, last of that name, earl of Lincoln, who died in 1310, for the deed is very antient, and of a Saxon character; it is also certain that the Hortons had a manor house in Great Horton, and a mill, and certain demesne lands thereto belonging, the scite of which house is known to this day, and some of the grounds bear the name of the Hall-lands. Hugh de Horton was lord of Horton in 1292, and one **of the same** name, probably the same person, had lands in Northouram **in 1314.** I have mentioned the earl of Lincoln **here,** because about the same time that he gave the honour **of** Pontefract to king Edward I. about 1293, and took the **same** honour in tail, this earl had inclosed three acres of **the** wastes or common of Horton, **very** near unto Bradford, **for the** attachment of his mill-dam, and for **case** and liberty about his mill of Bradford; but concerning this inclosure, a dispute **arose** between him and Hugh de Horton, lord of the waste there, which was ended about 22 Edw. I. and it was agreed **by writing** indented, that **the** earl should have the three acres **to him and his heirs, and** should pay therefore to the said Hugh Horton and his heirs three shillings of rent, and that the said Hugh de Horton should warrant it against **all his tenants of** Horton. This **parcel** of land is known at present by the name of Tyrrels, and the 3s. are paid for the same to the lord of Horton. But when queen Philippa held the honour of Pontefract in dower, about 9 Edw. III. this rent was detained; whereupon Hugh Leventhorpe, then lord of Horton, petitioned the queen for receipt **of it,** who referred the cause **to** Skergell and Neigham, her stewards of the honor, who charged a jury at Bradford **to** enquire of the right. These found that Henry Lacy did **improve** three acres of land in Little Horton, of the sale of Hugh Horton, then lord of Horton, which Hugh was grandfather **to Hugh** Leventhorpe, the **petitioner.** On this verdict, **a warrant** was made to the graves of Bradford to pay the rent to the lords of Horton, according to the first **composition.** In a MS. in my possession is the following entry relating to this subject: "Etiam annualem firmam "solutam Galfrido Leventhorpe pro placea in Horton ad- "quisita de Hugone de Horton, antecessore ejusdem

" Galfridi, & cui per successionem ipse est hæres per Henri-
" cum Lacy nuper comitem de Lincoln. Reddendo annuatim
" **predicto** Hugoni & heredibus tres solidos ut in quadam
" **litera** Regis de warranto præ solutione ejusdem summæ
" **receptori** directa. Dat. apud Westm. 20 Junii, 5 Hen. V."

This lordship of Horton, which thus clearly belonged to a
family who took their **name from it,** is divided into **two**
hamlets, viz. Horton Magna and Horton Parva ; the **first**
containing twenty-seven oxgangs and an half, the latter
about eighteen oxgangs. It continued in the name of
Horton, till **the** lands belonging to that family came to the
Leventhorpes **by** marriage ; from the Leventhorpes it also
went by marriage with Alice, sister and heir of one Oswald
Leventhorpe, to John Lacy, esq ; a descendant of whom,
called also John Lacy, sold it to Joshua Horton, of Sowerby,
esq ; a younger branch of **the above** family of Horton, of
Horton, whose great great grandson, sir Watts Horton, of
Chaderton, in Lancashire, bart. now enjoys it.

I have not been able to procure, or make out an uninter-
rupted pedegree from **the** antient lords of Horton to the
present owner of that manor, but I doubt not the truth of
that descent, on account of its having been so satisfactorily
proved to the Herald's office, **as** appears by **the** following
authentic paper.

Mrs. Ann Horton, of London, having her arms challenged
by some of the officers belonging to the college of **arms,** she
produced her proofs in support of her right to the same,
which caused the following grant to be made, which was
entered in the college of arms, in a book marked Grants,
vol. vii, p. 533, 534. " To all and singular to whom these
" presents shall **come,** John Anstis, **esq** ; garter principal
" king of arms, and Peter le Neve, esq ; norroy king of arms,
" send greeting. Whereas Mrs. Ann Horton, youngest
" daughter, and **one of the** three **coheirs** of Thomas Horton,
" **of** Barkisland, in the west riding of the county of York,
" esq ; deceased, by Everilda his wife, daughter of John
" Thornhill, of Fixby, esq ; and great grandchild of William
" Horton, of Barkisland aforesaid, gentleman, by Elizabeth,
" daughter of Thomas Hanson, of Toothill, gentleman, all
" in the aforesaid county of York, hath represented unto the
" right honourable Talbot Yelverton, earl of Sussex, and
" knight of the **most** noble order of the bath, **and** deputy

" (with the royal approbation) to the most noble Thomas,
" duke of Norfolk, earl marshal, and hereditary marshal of
" England, that her ancestors having, for many generations,
" lived in the credit and reputation of gentlemen, whose
" father left her above eleven hundred pounds per annum,
" did bear for their arms, gules, a lion rampant within a
" border ingrailed, argent, charged on the shoulder with a
" boar's head, couped, azure ; and for the crest, on a wreath
" of the colors, a rose gules, seeded, barbed, and surrounded
" with two laurel branches proper, as descending from the
" family of Horton, of Horton, within the parish of Brad-
" ford, in the said west riding, who flourished there in the
" reign of Edw. I. as appears by an antient folio MS. now
" remaining in the hands of Mr. Midgley, of Scolemore, in
" the said parish of Bradford. And the said Mrs. Ann
" Horton having farther represented unto his lordship, that
" the coat arms above mentioned now remain, and are to be
" seen in the several houses of Barkisland-hall, Howroyd-
" house, and Sowerby, all within the parish of Halifax,
" either in painted glass, stone, or plaister, as the same
" doth appear by an affidavit made for that purpose, which
" said houses were and are now possessed by several of the
" Hortons, all of her family, for above four-score years ; as
" also the same coat arms in several funeral and other
" escutcheons, some whereof are much above an hundred
" years old, and agreeable to the draught in the margin
" of her memorial : But in regard that the descent of the
" family of Horton, of Barkisland, was certified in the Visit-
" ation Book of Yorkshire, made by William Dugdale, esq ;
" Norroy king of arms, ann. 1666, by Edward Hanson, on
" the behalf of Thomas Horton, (father of the said Ann
" Horton,) then a minor, aged fifteen years, through whose
" neglect no arms were then exhibited ; the said Mrs. Ann
" Horton hath therefore prayed his lordship's warrant for
" our exemplifying and confirming the same coat of arms to
" her, which, together with the crest, may be likewise law-
" fully borne by all the descendants of her great grandfather
" respectively, with their due differences, according to the
" usage and custom of arms. And forasmuch as his lord-
" ship, being well satisfied of the truth of the premises, by a
" certificate annexed to the said memorial, did, by warrant
" under his hand and seal, bearing date the 2d day of this

" instant August, order and direct us to exemplify and con-
" firm the same coat arms and crest accordingly : Now know
" ye, that we the said Garter and Norroy, in pursuance of
" the consent of the said earl of Sussex, and by virtue of the
" letters patent of our offices to each of us respectively
" granted under the great seal, have confirmed, and do each
" of us confirm, exemplify, and confirm unto the said **Mrs.**
" Ann Horton the same coat arms above expressed, **to be**
" borne and used by her, the said Ann Horton, which,
" together with **the crest** above described, shall and may **be**
" likewise lawfully borne by all the descendants of her great
" grandfather respectively, with their proper differences, **ac-**
" cording to the law and practice of **arms,** without let or
" interruption of any person **or** persons whatsoever.   In
" witness whereof, we, the said Garter and Norroy king of
" arms, have to these presents subscribed our names, and
" affixed **the** seals of our several offices, **the** tenth day **of**
" August, in the 12th year of the reign of our sovereign lord,
" George, **by** the grace of God king of Great Britain, France,
" and Ireland, defender **of the** faith, annoq. Dom. **1725.**
" Signed and sealed by **Anstis.**"

At p. 535 of the said vol. **of Grants, is** a warrant from **the**
earl of Sussex, reciting, "**That** whereas he had, by warrant
" under his hand and **seal, dated** 2 August, 1725, directed
" **John** Anstis, esq ; Garter principal king of arms, and
" **Peter le** Neve, esq ; Norroy king of arms, **to** exemplify and
" confirm to Mrs. Ann Horton the above arms and crest ;
" **and** the said Norroy did twice absolutely refuse to comply
" with **the same ; in order** to do justice **to** the family of
" Horton, he **did** thereby order and direct, that the said
" exemplification and confirmation should be as effectual
" according to **the law** of arms, as if **the** said Norroy had
" also sealed **and** signed the same." This warrant was
dated 10th Feb. 1726-7, and a memorandum is annexed
thereto, dated 24 April, 1727, signed by James Green, blue
mantle, importing, " that the reason why Norroy refused to
" execute the above was, because the same proofs had not
" been produced to him, as had been to Garter," which
could **not be done,** as he was then, and for several months
after, at **his** seat at Great Wickingham, in Norfolk, ninety
miles from **London.** Also it appeared to the said Blue
Mantle, on a due examination of the several books in the

herald's office, that the above arms belonged to the name of Horton, in Grafton's alphabet, and he did not find the said arms to be claimed or borne by 'any other family of that name, amongst the different arms and families of the said name of Horton.

To this account of the arms of the Hortons of Barkisland, Sowerby, Chaderton, and Howroyd, it may be added, that all others of the name have different coats, of which there are about seven; that I have seen the same on a seal which belonged to Joshua Horton, of Sowerby, esq; who died in 1679; that Dr. Buckley, of Pontefract, in Yorkshire, is said to have known the collateral derivation of the families from Horton, of Horton, and also knew that the above coat belonged to Horton, of Horton, and was acquainted with the reason of the addition of the boar's head. The motto used by the present heir of this family under the above arms, is "Pro Rege et Lege."

In 1603 lived William Horton, as appears by deed. He married Elizabeth, daughter of Thomas Hanson, of Toothill, in the parish of Halifax, which Elizabeth made her will July 16, 1660, and was then in her old age. By her the said William had, 1. William, 2. Joshua, (whose pedigree will be given under the article of Sowerby,) 3. Thomas, 4. Sarah, and 5. Elizabeth. These are all mentioned in the will of Thomas Hanson, dated 27th July, 1673. Of these, Sarah married John Gledhill, as already mentioned. Elizabeth had no issue. Thomas was brought up a merchant at Liverpool, and the following inscription is on a board, and fixed to a pillar under the east gallery of the parochial chapel of our Lady and St. Nicholas, at Liverpool: "Here "lieth interred the body of Thomas Horton, of Liverpoole, "merchant, sonne of William Horton, of Barkisland, in the "county of Yorke, gentleman, who married Frances, eldest "daughter of Thomas Throppe, of the citty of Chester, "alderman and justice of the peace. He dyed the 30th day "of March, 1660." Over the inscription are the arms of Horton, (as above,) with a crescent for difference, impaled with checky arg. and sab. on a fess or, three martlets of the second, which also I have seen painted on a tablet at How-royd, with a martlet's wings displayed, or, for crest. This Thomas had no known descendants.

William, eldest son of William above named, bought Howroyd, in Barkisland, where he lived, his residence before this purchase having been at Firth-house, in that neighborhood. He married Elizabeth, daughter of Thomas Gledhill, of Barkisland-hall, by whom, 1. Thomas, 2. William, 3. Elizabeth, 4. Sarah, and 5. Judith; of these, William married at Ripponden, Dec. 12, 1700, Mary, fourth daughter of sir Richard Musgrave, of Heyton-castle, in Cumberland, bart. and died Feb. 19, 1715-6, having had, by the said Mary, two sons, viz. William Horton, of Coley, esq; justice of peace, who was baptized at Ripponden-chapel, Feb. 11, 1702, and died in 1739-40. Richard, baptized at Ripponden, Nov. 11, 1706, and died at Howroyd, s. p. William, last named, married Mary Chester, by whom Mary, who died unmarried, and was buried at Eland, in June, 1769; and a son, who died young, of the small-pox, and was buried at Eland, in August, 1730. I have been well informed, that this child was a second time attacked by this disorder in the natural way, about a week after his recovery from the former, and died of it. Elizabeth, last named, married William Batt, of Oakwell, in Burstall parish, esq; by whom William, Gledhill, and Judith. Sarah, second daughter of William, married Alexander Butterworth, of Belfield, near Rochdale, esq; by whom William, Alexander, and Elizabeth. Judith, youngest daughter of William, married Joseph Finch, of Weston Hanger, in Kent, merchant. She died in child-bed, in Kent, (after her husband's decease,) Oct. 12, 1678, and the child and her were carried to London to be buried. She left six children.

Thomas, eldest son of William, by Elizabeth Gledhill, was born April 2, 1651, and died Jan. 2, 1698-9, buried at Eland. His will is dated Dec. 20, 1698. He married, in 1672, Everild, daughter of John Thornhill, of Fixby, esq; by whom, 1. Elizabeth, who married Richard Bold, of Bold, in Lancashire, esq; who lived some time at Crawstone, in Greetland, and whose descendants are now in possession of Barkisland-hall, and whose coat armor is, argent, a griffin passant, sab. but see Guillim, p. 189. 2. Susanna, who married Richard Beaumont, of Whitley, in Yorkshire, esq; a descendant of whom was married to the rev. John Watson, author of this book. 3. Gledhill, baptized at Ripponden.

Dec. 31, 1685, and died young. 4. Ann, baptized at Ripponden, Nov. 3, 1687. 5. Thomas, baptized at Ripponden, May 9, 1689, who also died young; as also did, 6. Everild and William, two other of their children. Ann was interred at Eland, April 22, 1750. Her father gave £5000. a-piece to her two sisters, and settled his estate, of £1100. per annum, on her, and her issue male, obliging her, **if** she married, to take an Horton, or one who should assume the name.

Barkisland-hall, above-mentioned, was probably **built** by John Gledhill, **who** married Sarah, daughter of William Horton, **for** he lived there in the reign of K. Cha. I. and in the window of the hall part are the painted figures of **a** man **and two** children: under the first, ætat. 36, 1641; under **one** of the children, ætat. 4, 1641; under the other, ætat. 2½, **1641.** Over the back door is cut **in** stone, "Nunc mea, mox " hujus, sed postea nescio cujus;" which may be seen in Camden's Remains, p. 125, edit. **1636.** If this was put there by the above John Gledhill, the observation was soon remarkably verified, when the **estate** passed into the name of Horton, and, after a very short possession, to that of Bold.

HORTON.

Sowerby Hall, once the seat of the eldest **branch** of the family of Horton, whose pedegree is as follows:

Joshua Horton, esq; second son of William Horton, of Barkisland, born in 1619, was Justice of the Peace in the West-riding, and purchased the manor of Horton, in Bradford-dale, Stansfield-Hall, &c. He died of the stone at Sowerby, 7 April, 1679, and **was** buried there, aged 60. **He** married Martha, daughter and coheiress of Thomas Binns, esq; **of** Rushworth, in the parish of Bingley, who died July **23,** 1694, and was buried at Sowerby. By her he had, 1. **Joshua,** who only lived three months. 2. Sarah, born June 22, 1654, and who died Sept. 4, 1670, 3. Martha, born April 30, 1656, who married John Gill, esq; of Car-house, near Rotherham, by whom two sons and one daughter; 4. Joshua; 5. Elkana, a Counsellor, born at Sowerby, Aug. 31, 1659, and buried s. p. at Sowerby, Jan. 28, 1728-9. He lived at Thornton, and left his estate to his nephew Thomas. 6. Thomas, M.D. born Nov. 26, 1660, and died in London, s. p. March 4, 1694, buried in St. Thomas's church, Southwark.

He married ...... daughter of ...... Watmough, of London, M. D. and left his estate in Halifax to his eldest brother. (N. B. Joshua, Elkana, and Thomas Horton, three brothers, were all Gentlemen Commoners of Brazen Nose College, Oxford.) 7. Elizabeth, who died young. Joshua, the eldest surviving son of Joshua, was born at Sowerby, Jan. 22, 1657, and died Dec. 15, 1708, being buried in his chapel at Oldham church. He purchased Chaderton, and lived there. Feb. 27, 1678, he married Mary, daughter of Robert Gregg, of Bradley, or Hapsford, in Cheshire, who died Dec. 27, 1708, as it is said, of grief, for the loss of her husband, and was buried in the same place with him. By her he had thirteen children, of which I can only put down the following: 1. Thomas, who died young; 2. Thomas, who succeeded to the estate; 3. William, baptized Oct. 12, 1686; 4. Sarah, baptized Jan. 6, 1687, who married Thomas Williamson, of Liverpool, Merchant. 5. Elizabeth, baptized May 28, 1689, who married William Williamson, of Liverpool, Merchant. 6. Mary, baptized Feb. 4, 1690. 7. William, baptized Sept. 27, 1692. 8. Joseph, s. p. baptized March 8, 1693. 9. James, baptized April 18, 1695, died unmarried. 10. Mary, s. p. baptized August 13, 1696. 11, Martha, who married Richard Clayton, of Adlington, in Lancashire, esq; on the 30th of Nov. 1697. 12. Jane, who married John Parr, of Liverpool, Merchant.

Thomas Horton, son of Joshua, was born at Chester, May 4, 1685, and died March 18, 1757, at Manchester, buried at Oldham. He was Justice of Peace for Lancashire, and Governor of the Isle of Man for the earl of Derby. He married Ann, daughter and coheiress of Richard Mostyn, of London, Merchant, a younger branch of sir Roger Mostyn's family, of Mostyn, in Wales. She died at Chaderton, June 17, 1725, and was buried at Oldham, in the 39th year of her age. By her the said Thomas had, 1. Mary, living and unmarried in 1774. 2. Sir William Horton, High Sheriff for Lancashire, in 1764, and before that an acting Justice of Peace for the county of Lancaster, created Baronet by patent, dated Jan. 10, 1764, died in Feb. 1774. 3. Ann, living and unmarried in 1773. 4. Jane, who died Oct. 24, and was buried at Oldham, Oct. 29, 1768. 5. Susannah, who married, March 24, 1742, George Lloyd, of Holme, near Manchester, esq; by whom several children. 6.

Joshua, of Howroyd, in Yorkshire, who married, to his first wife, Ann, daughter of George Clarke, esq; sometime Governor of New York, who died, s. p. May 25, 1764. Arms of Clarke, Azure, three escallops in pale or, two flanches ermine. To his second wife, Mary Bethia, daughter of the Rev. John Woolin, Rector of Emley, in Yorkshire, and Vicar of Blackburn, in Lancashire, by whom, 1. Thomas, 2. Joshua Sidney, and others. 7. Thomas, seventh child of Thomas, died young, at Castletown, in the Isle of Man. 8. Sarah, the youngest, is living and unmarried in 1773. Sir William above-named married Susanna, daughter and heiress of Francis Watts, of Barnes-hall, in Yorkshire, esq; by whom, 1. Sir Watts, 2. Thomas, and 3. William.

N.B. The pedegrees of Horton, of Sowerby, and Horton, of Barkisland, which were drawn up by myself, I entered in the Herald's office in London, March 1766, in a book intitled 5th D 14, p. 237. For an account of this family, see under Barkisland, as also for their arms. Sir William Horton's motto was, Pro rege et lege.

There are at Chaderton two fine heads of Martha, wife of the above Joshua Horton, esq; of Sowerby, and a portrait of her son Thomas, the Physician; also another of William, grandson of the said Martha. One of Joshua Horton, esq; of Chaderton, in 1700, and Mary his wife, same date. Likewise Thomas Horton, of Chaderton, esq; drawn in the character of Governor of the Isle of Man, sir William Horton, and his Lady, all three half lengths, by Hamlet Winstanley. Watts, son of sir William, by Henry Pickering, who also drew, at Howroyd, the portraits of Joshua Horton, of Howroyd, and both his wives.

HANSON AND RASTRICK.

At Rastrick lived a considerable family, who took their name from this vill, and whose pedegree I have added, taken from a MS. pedegree at Fixby, another in my own possession, and a third mentioned in Wright's History, p. 135, intitled, " Observationes quædam collectæ tam ex antiquis chartis, & " rotulis curiarum, & aliis scriptis, & genealogiis, quam de " progenia & familia in Rastricke, olim vocata Rastricke, ac " modo Hanson."

Roger de Rastrick lived about 1251. His name is found in many Deeds in the time of Henry III, amongst the chief men of the weapontake of Morley. He held lands in Rastrick, Skircoat, and Clayton, in Bradford-dale. I have the copy of a Deed without date, wherein Henry de Eland, father of sir John de Eland, grants to this Roger, by the name of Roger, son of William de Bingley, and his heirs, for his homage and service, two bovats of land in Rastrick, one of which, Alexander, son of Alexander, held with the said Alexander, and all his sequel: the other held by Leisingus, son of Herbert, with the said Leisingus, and all his sequel. This was confirmed by Emma, daughter of Hugh, son of Orme de Batelin, and Assulf her son and heir. He also grants to him Linlands, with other lands. It is probable that the above Roger, after this grant, removed to Rastrick, and settled there, having other estates, and the services of several villains, as appears by Deeds. He used a proper seal, with this inscription, SIGILL. **ROGERI DE** RASTRICKE. He had, 1. Hugh, 2. John, the Chaplain, to whom his father gave a toft with a garden, in the vill of Rastrick, which one Alexander formerly held, and three acres of land in the fields of Rastrick, and fifteen pence of a yearly rent, and all the service thereto belonging, out of a farm which Simon, his son, and Adam the Smith, of Huddersfield, son of the said Simon held. His third son was, 3. Simon, who occurs by the name of Simon le Faber (or Smith) de Rastrick. This Simon had Adam, and Hugh. Adam lived at the Castle in Rastrick, and had Simon. Hugh, son of Simon, had William.

Hugh de Rastrick, son of Roger, lived in the time of Hen. III. and Edw. I, and resided at Linlands. He is witness to a Deed, by the name of Hugh de Rastrick, mentioned in Burton's Monasticon, p. 313, along with Matthew de Shepley, and others, which Matthew was witness to a Deed in 1257. He gave to Leisingus, son of Orme de Rastrick, the moiety of an assart in Rastrick, called Hee Hawkeswode; confirmed to John the Chaplain, his brother, the yearly rent of fifteen pence above mentioned; gave to his brother Simon an assart in Rastrick, containing four acres (super toftum Raveri) for six-pence yearly rent; also to Adam, son of his brother Simon, the land which his father held of him, viz. the moiety of three bovats, which Leisingus, son of Herbert, held of Roger, father of the said Hugh, in Rastrick, for two shillings yearly rent. Also to Hugh, son of his brother

Simon, all the land in Rastrick, which Leisingus, son of Eve, held, with the building thereon, and a messuage and other lands in Rastrick. This Hugh married Agnes ...... by whom John de Rastrick and William de Rastrick.

John gave by Deed without date, **to Simon, son of Adam,** at the Castle of Rastric, for his homage and service, &c. two acres in the lower field of Rastric. Round the seal appendant to the Deed, in capitals, s. JOHANNIS DE RASTRIC. He also granted to John de Toothill, for his homage and service, two acres in Rastrick, by Deed without date. A MS. pedegree at Fixby sais, this John had an only daughter Helen, married to one Alan de Rastrick, who died 1 Edw. III, by whom John, who, it seems, when his mother became a widow, was called the son of Elen, or Elenson. This John married Margaret, daughter of Roger le Teyler, by whom Isabel, who married John, surnamed Scot, by whom Helen and Alice. Here the above pedegree ends, and so far I find it confirmed by evidence, that one John, son of Elen de Rastrick, was witness to a Deed 32 Edw. III. And in one of the Harleian MSS. N° 797, under the article of Rastrick, are these words: " I Alice, daughter of John Scot, of " Rastrick, and Isabel my mother, have given to Elen, " daughter of John Scot, for a certain sum of money, all " that land and meadow called Linlands, in Rastrick." They were contemporaries with one Hugh de Rastrick, for they granted by Deed without date to John de Barne de Tothill, and heirs, three roods of land, abutting on one side on the garden of the said Hugh, and on the other, on Le Ollerode: three of the witnesses to which Deed were living in the year 1287, viz. Robert de Bosco, Matthew de Fekisby, and Alexander de Fekisby. However, notwithstanding these proofs, in a beautiful pedegree of this family, belonging to Mr. Roger Hanson, of Halifax, but not authenticated by any of the Heralds at Arms, the above John de Rastrick is said to have had a son John, who had Henry de Rastrick, who had John de Rastrick, alias Hanson (a contraction of Henry's son,) and from hence the addition of de Rastrick was dropt by this branch of the family, and that of Hanson used in its room. Here the disagreements in the two pedegrees begin to disappear, for I find John, son of Henry de Rastrick, a party in a Deed dated in 1337, and one of the witnesses was John, son of Elen aforesaid. This John

P

married Alice, daughter and heiress of Henry de Woodhouse, which Henry was son of Alexander de Woodhouse, who married Beatrice, daughter and heiress of Thomas de Totehill. By the said Alice the said John had a son, John Hanson, of Woodhouse, **who married** Cecily de Windebank, by whom John Hanson, **of Woodhouse**, who married Cecily, daughter of John Ravens[l]aw, by **whom** John Hanson, of Woodhouse, who married Catharine, daughter of **John** Brooke, by whom **John** Hanson, of Woodhouse, who married Agnes, eldest **daughter of John Savile, of** Newhall, **esq ; by** whom John Hanson, **of Woodhouse ; 2. Edward** Hanson, **of** Nether-Woodhouse ; 3. Thomas **Hanson, of** Rastrick ; and 4. **Arthur Hanson.**

John, the eldest son, lived **at** Woodhouse, **in** Rastrick, and **was** buried **at** Eland **in** 1599, aged eighty-two, as appears from a grave-stone there, and which is said to be the oldest date they can shew. **He married, first,** Margaret, second daughter, and one of **the three coheiresses** of Thomas Woodhead, sometime of Howroyd, **in Barkisland ;** secondly, Margaret, daughter of Robert Wade. By **his first** wife, he had, 1. John Hanson, of Woodhouse ; 2. Thomas, 3. **Nicholas,** who had Robert and Dorothy ; and, 4. Judith, married **to** Jasper Blythman. John, the eldest, died in the seventy-third year of his age ; his will was dated August 14, 1621. He married Joan, daughter **and** heiress of William Rayner, of Liversege, by whom, 1. John, who died **an** infant ; 2. **Ag-nes,** who married Richard Lawe, of **Halifax ;** 3. Mary, **who** married Walter Stanhope, of Horsforth ; 4. Grace, who **died s. p. 5.** Margaret, who married Thomas Brooke, of **New-house ;** and, 6. Katharine, who died s. **p.** Thomas, second son of John Hanson, by Margaret Woodhead, married Margaret, daughter and coheiress of **John** Royde, of Shaw, in Soyland, by **whom,** 1. John, who died an infant ; 2. Thomas, of Brighouse, who **died s. p. 3.** Arthur, who married Sarah, daughter and coheiress of Thomas Bothomley, by whom John, Thomas, Joseph, Richard, Joshua, and Judith ; 4. Richard, **who married** Elizabeth Jenkinson ; 5. Robert, 6. Joseph, 7. Margaret, and, 8. Judith. Richard, last named, had Thomas Hanson, of Backhall, buried at Eland, Jan. 6, 1695, aged sixty-four ; and John, who married Elizabeth, daughter of Thomas Brooke, of Huddersfield, by whom John, Richard, Elizabeth and Mary. Thomas, last named, married Hester, daughter and heiress of John Farnel, by whom John, and Thomas, who married a daughter of Anthony Foxcroft, by whom Anthony. John, the elder brother, of Backhall, married a daughter of George Booth, of Snowden, by whom, 1, Thomas, 2. John, s. p. 3. Dorothy, who married Abraham Dyson, **of** Sunnybank; 4. George, of Backhall, who married Elizabeth, **daughter of** John Stott, by whom John, Roger, Nathan, Esther, Robert, Rebecca, **and** Elizabeth; 5. Mary, who married John Dawson; 6. **Esther**; 7. Rebecca, who married Thomas, son **of George** Booth, **of** Snowden; 8. Sarah, and 9. Eleanor. **Thomas,** eldest son of John, married Martha, daughter of **Nathan** Gledhill, by whom John, who died an infant, **Thomas,** Nathan, Arthur, George, Edward, Joshua, Richard, **Joseph,** Mary, Esther, and Agnes.

Edward Hanson, of Nether Woodhouse, second son of John, by Agnes Savile, was buried **at** Eland, Dec. 16, 1601, in the eighty-second year of his **age**; his will dated Nov. 30, 1601. He married, first, Joan, daughter of Edward Kaye; second and third wives unknown; **he** married, fourthly, Nov. 2, 1590, to Margaret Malinson, widow, daughter of Edward Hoile, of Hoile-house, in Lightcliffe. She died Feb. 23, 1614, and was buried the day following, ann. ætat. 87. By his first wife he had Thomas Hanson, of Tothill, buried at Eland, Aug. 3, 1623, ann. æt. 71; his will dated July 27, 1623. He married Katharine, daughter of Thomas Brooke, of Newhouse, who was buried at Eland, Feb. 4, 1621, in the 74th year of her age. By her he had 1. Edward; 2. Elizabeth, who married William Horton, of Barkisland; 3. Katharine, who married Thomas Sharp; also Abraham Beaumont; 4. Mary, who married William Mallinson; and, 5. Agnes.

Edward, the eldest, married Dorothy, daughter **of John** Gledhill, **of** Barkisland, and Cecily his wife, daughter of John Thornhill, esq. By the said Dorothy he had Edward, Dorothy, and Margaret. Edward Hanson, of Woodhouse, married Jane, daughter of Thomas Beaumont, by whom John, Edward, Dorothy, Margaret, Catharine, Mary, Jane, Elizabeth, Frances, and Cecily.

Thomas Hanson, of Rastrick, third son of John, by Agnes Savile, married Jennet, daughter of John Gledhill, of Little-Even, in Barkisland, by whom, 1. Roger, 2. Thomas, of

Rastrick, who married Martha, daughter of Edward Naylor, by whom John, and Roger. 3. John, of London, who married Frances, daughter of John Pritchard, by whom John, Thomas, and Edward. 4. Robert, of Rastrick, who married Sarah, daughter of William Thorpe; 5. Elizabeth, and 6. Judith.

Arthur, fourth and youngest son of John, by Agnes Savile, had 1. John, of Norwood Green, who had Edward, and John. 2. Edward, who had John, and Margaret, who married Richard Wilton.

The following grant was in the hands of Mr. Roger Hanson, of Halifax : " To all and singular unto whom these "presents shall come. William Ryley, esq ; Norroy King "of Armes, sendeth greeting. Whereas Edward Hanson, of "Woodhouse, in the county of Yorke, gent. hath requested "me to confirme and declare those Armes which have "formerly been born by his Ancestors. I do therefore, by "these presents, confirme and allow the said Edward Han- "son to bear the said Armes and Creast hereafter mentioned, "viz. Or, a cheveron counter componed, argent and azure, "between three martlets sable. And for his Creast, On a "helme a chapeau azure, lined argent, a martlet volant "sable, mantled gules, doubled argent. Which coate and "creast I the said Norroy do by these presents allowe and "confirme unto the said Edward Hanson, and the heires of "his body lawfully begotten, to bee born and used by them "in banners, pennans, shieldes, and seales, in warr and "peace, with theire several respected differences for ever. "In witness whereof I have hereunto affixed the seal of my "office, and subscribed my name, the 17th day of July, "1652. William Ryley, Norroy King of Armes."

The Arms of Rastrick, of Rastrick, were, Argent, a chevron between three roses gules, and, as one account adds, barbed and seeded proper.

Woodhouse, of Woodhouse, in Rastrick, according to Mr. Hanson's pedegree, bore, Azure, a chevron between three mullets or; but in Hopkinson's Collections the mullets are pierced of the field.

Windebank, (as in the above pedegree,) bore, Vert, a chevron between three hawks standing, wings displayed, or.

Ravens[l]aw (as above) bore, Sable, two fesses argent, wavy, on a chief of the second three ravens proper.

Brooke, (as above,) bore, Argent, on a bend sable, a lure, with a line and ring or. This was borne by Joshua Brooke, of Newhouse, in the township of Huddersfield, as appears by a seal appendant to a Deed dated in 1647.

Kay, (as above,) bore, Argent, two bendlets sable. .

Prichard, (as above,) bore, Gules, a fess or, between three escallops argent.

The following Certificate was granted to one Elias Rastrick, said to be a descendant from the above ancient family.

" Frater **Andreas ab Arco**, Ordinis Minorum, &c. in
" partibus Orientalibus Apostolicus Commissarius totius
" terræ sanctæ Custos, ac Sanctæ Montis Sion Servus &
Gardianus.

" Universis & singulis Christi fidelibus præsentes nostras
" inspecturis, lecturis, pariter & audituris, salutem in Dom-
" ino sempiternam. Notum sacimus & attestamus, Domin-
" um Eliam Rastricke, Anglum, ad hanc sanctam, Jeruso-
" limorum urbem provenisse, necnon terram sanctam, nempe
" gloriosissimæ resurrectionis Domini Christi sepulchrum ;
" sacratissimos montes, Calvariæ scilicet, ubi Salvator noster
" **propria** morte nos redemit in cruce ; Oliveti, ubi in cælum
" mirabiliter conscendit ad Patrem ; Sion, augustissimæ Eu-
" charistiæ sacramenti institutione, Spiritus Sanctæ missione,
" compluriumque nostræ salutis mysteriorum celebratione
" insignis ; Thabor, naturâ, & gloriosa transfiguratione,
" Patrum testimonio vetustorum, & beatitudinibus admirabili·
" ejusdem Domini sermone decorati. Præterea, sanctissimum
" nativitatis Domini Præsepe in Bethlehem Judeæ civitate
" David sacra. Item Nazareth Domum, Angeli annunti-
" atione Deiparæ, & etiam Verbi incarnatione celeberrimum ;
" Vallémque Josaphat, pluribus Dominicæ passionis misteriis,
" ac venerabilis Assumtionis Dei genetricis Mariæ monu-
" mentis exornatum ; Bethaniam quóque hospitio Domini,
" & Lazari suscitatione honestatum ; sed & montana Judeæ
" sanctissimæ Genetricis Dei visitatione, ac Præcursoris
" Nativitatis ejus Deserta, nobilitata ; Theberiadis mare
" quorundem Apostolorum vocatione, Petrique in Ecclesia
" Capitis electione clarum ; necnon Emmaus Dominica
" Apparatione illustratum. Ac demum cætera omnia sancta,
" piáque loca quæ tam in Judæa, quam in Galilæa, ac Sam-
" aria, a Fratribus, fidelibúsque Peregrinis visitari solent,
" visitasse. In quorum fidem, præsentes has manu nostra

"subscriptas, ac majori nostri officio sigillo munitas, ex-
"pediri mandavimus. Datum Jerusolymis, in Conventu
"nostro Sancti Salvatoris, die vicesimo nono mensis Octo-
"bris, anno Dom. 1639."

HAMERTON.

Langfield was **the estate of sir** Stephen Hamerton, of
Hamerton, knt. **who** being attainted of high treason **in the**
reign of Henry **VIII,** and executed at Tyburn, it came **into**
the hands of the crown. Hollinshead, in his Chronicle, p.
1569. sais, " About the latter end of this 28th year, the lord
" Darcy, Aske, sir Robert Conestable, sir John Bulmer, and
" his wife, sir Tho. Percye, brother to the earl of North-
"umberlande, sir Stephen Hamilton, (it should be Hamer-
"ton,) Nicholas Tempest, esq; William Lomley, son to the lord
" Lomley, began eftsoons to conspire, altho' every of them
" before had received their pardons ; and now were they all
" taken, and brought to the tower of London as prisoners."
Sir Stephen, therefore, had been in Aske's first rising, called
the Pilgrimage of Grace, and had been pardoned with the
other ringleaders of that conspiracy.

Of this family I find that Adam Hamerton, of Hamerton,
in Boland, married about the time of Henry V, Katharine,
daughter and coheiress of Elias de Knoll, who bore, Argent,
a bend between two bendlets, sable ; in her right he was
seized of the lordships of Wigglesworth and Hellifield Peel,
in the parish of Long Preston, in Craven. By her he had
Richard Hamerton, of Hamerton, who married......daughter
of......Underhill, **who bore,** Argent, on a chevron sable, between three trefoils gules, a leopard's head of the first. By
her he had Laurence, who married Isabel, daughter of sir
John Tempest, **of** Bracewell, in Craven, by whom sir Richard,
James, from whom the Hamertons, of Munk Rode, near
Pontefract, and others. Sir Richard Hamerton, of Hamerton,
knt. married the heiress of Langfeld, of Langfeld, and found-
ed a chantry of our Lady and St. Ann, in the parish-church
of Long Preston, valued, 37 H. VIII, at £5. 17s. 8d. Sir
Richard had sir Stephen Hamerton, of Hamerton, knt. who
had John Hamerton, of Hamerton and the Peel, who married
Elizabeth, daughter of Thomas Middleton, of Middleton, in
Westmorland, who bore, Argent, a cross ingrailed, sable.
By her he had sir Stephen, executed as above ; Thomas and

Laurence, both slain in Ireland on one day; also Richard, who had John Hamerton, of the Peel, who had Laurence Hamerton, of the Peel, who had Stephen, who had John, of the same place. It was either the above Laurence, or his father John, who being a servant in the court of king Hen. VIII, got a grant from the Crown to himself and heirs of Hellifield Peel.

Sir Stephen last named had a son Henry, who had two daughters. The arms of Hamerton, of Hamerton, in a folio collection of Pedigrees in my possession, are, Argent, three hammers sable, two and one. But another authority sais, Argent, a chevron between three hammers, sable. This last I take to have been born by Hamerton, of Munk-Rode.

LACY AND CROMWELLBOTHOM.

Cromwelbothom was long the seat of the Lacys, as appears by the following pedigree:

John Lacy, Steward of Chester, had Robert Lord Vice Chancellor of Chester, and John, of Fowton, or Falton, com. Ebor. Robert married Eleanor, daughter of sir Robert Baskerville, who bore a chevron ingrailed, gules, between three hurts, (one MS. sais Clemence Baskervile,) by whom Brian Lacy, of Chester, who married Amicia, daughter of Richard Archdeacon, who lived at Warmicham, in Cheshire. By her he had John Lacy, to whom the Office of Arms has allowed the Lacys of Cromwellbothom, and Brearley, to ascend, but no farther. This John married Ellen (some say Eleanor) daughter and heiress of Robert de Cromwelbothom, by whom John Lacy, of Cromwelbothom, who married Ann (one MS. sais Alice) daughter of John de Eland, by whom John Lacy, of Cromwelbothom, and Gilbert Lacy, of Brearley, near Halifax. John married Florence, daughter of Robert Molineux, of Lancashire, who bore, Azure, a cross sarcele, or. By her he had William Lacy, of Cromwelbothom, who married Joan, daughter of sir William Skargill, of Thorpe Stapleton, near Leeds, who bore, Ermine, a saltire, gules. By her he had Thomas Lacy, of Cromwelbothom, who married Eleanor, daughter of Robert Nevile, of Liversedge, by whom John Lacy, of Cromwelbothom, who married first, Matilda, (some say Mary,) daughter of sir Nicholas Wortley, of Wortley, by whom no issue. Secondly, Joan, (one MS. sais Alice,) daughter and heiress of ...... Leventhorp, of

Leventhorp, near Bradford, in Yorkshire, esq; in whose right he was seized of Leventhorp. By her he had John, Leonard, and Ann, married to Edward Oldfield, of Halifax. John married, first, Ann, (one MS. sais Jane,) daughter of sir Richard Tempest, of Bracewell, knt. Secondly, Mary, daughter of Alveray Gascoign, of Garforth, near Leeds, s. p. By his first wife he had, 1. Richard, 2. John, who married ... ... Hole, by whom John and Ann; 3. William, 4. Nicholas, who married Alice, daughter of Brian (Hopkinson sais Peter) Hardy, by whom Lucy, Alice, and Bridget; 5. Peter, the youngest, had no issue. The said John had also three daughters, viz. 1. Dorothy, married to John Waterhouse, of Sowerby-bridge; 2. Rosamond, to Thomas Wood; 3. Ellen, to Walter Paslew, of Ridlesden; secondly, to Thomas Lee. Richard, the eldest son of John was buried at Halifax, July, 16, 1591. He married Ellen (some say Alice) daughter of Laurence Townley, of Barnside, according to Hopkinson, but as others say, of Townley, by whom 1. John, 2. Ellen, who married Philip Waterhouse, and 3. Ann. Concerning the elder of these two sisters and her husband, there is the following inscription, in brass, on a pillar in Thornhill church, in Yorkshire: "Here lyeth the body of Philip "Waterhouse, 3 sonne of John Waterhouse, of Halifax, "esq; Maister of Artes, and sometimes Felow of University "Coll. Oxon. He dyed the 16th of Januari, 1614, the 57th "yere of his age. Hellen, daughter of Richard Lacye, of "Cromewelbotome, esq; his beloved wife, dedicated this "monument to his memori." Arms of Lacy and Cromwelbothom.

John, eldest son of Richard, sold the manor house of Cromwelbothom to Thomas Gledhill, 9 James I. Also Old Syddall-hall to John Scolfield, of Coley, Nov. 20, 32 Eliz. He married, first, Alice, daughter of Martin Birkhead, Attorney to Queen Elizabeth's Council in the North, at York, by whom Sarah, who was aged five years in 1585, and Elizabeth; secondly, ... daughter of Michael Lister, of Frerehead in Craven, by whom John, s. p.

Hopkinson's Collection of Lancashire Pedegrees makes the last mentioned John Lacy, of Cromwelbothom, to have, 1. Thomas Lacy, of Longworth, esq; com. Lanc. 2. Bridget, married to Thomas Summerscales of Gisborn in Craven; 3. another daughter, married to Richard Monke, also of

Gisborn : 4. John, s. p. and 5. Margaret, married to Robert Bladen, of Himsworth, near Pontefract. Thomas is said to have married Ann, daughter of Roger Winckley, of Winckley, in Lancashire, by whom Thomas, who married, first, Ann, daughter of Adam Hilton, of Hilton, in Lancashire ; secondly, Winifred, daughter of sir Francis Armitage, of Kirklees, bart. By the first of these wives he had Roger, **born in 1654,** Thomas, Adam, John, Ann, and Ellen.

What **I know** of the family of **Cromwelbothom is this, that** Oliver **de Cromwelbothom** married Julian, **daughter of sir** John Radcliff, of Ordfall, by whom John de Cromwelbothom, who had Robert de Cromwelbothom, who married ... ... daughter of Henry Leyburne, by whom Ellen, daughter **and** heiress, married to John Lacy, as above. I find likewise a Richard de Cromwelbothom a witness to deeds **with John de** Lacy, in 1298 and 1307.

There was also an Ann, daughter of John Cromwelbothom, knt. married to Hugh Copley ; possibly the John above-mentioned.

Arms of Cromwelbothom, Argent, six ogresses, three, **two,** one. Of **Lacy, of** Cromwelbothom, Or, a lion rampant purpure, langued **and** armed, azure. But in the " Visitation of York-shire, in 1584," the Lacy's arms are, Sable, a chevron between three bucks heads cabossed, argent, which i take to have been born by the Lacys of Dickering. They have been also allowed by the Heralds, to **the** Lacys, of Fowton, in the East-riding. It **seems** plain to me that the Lacys, of Crom-welbothom, descended from the earls **of** Lincoln of that **name,** and one proof arises from bearing the same arms ; **for** though the said earls bore sometimes Quarterly, or and gules, a bendlet sable, a label of five points of the second, yet their proper coat was, Or, a lion rampant purpure, as above.

In **the** Harleian Collection of MSS. Nº 797. it is said that John Lacy, of Cromwelbotham, and Margaret his wife, passed a fine of the manor of Cromwelbothom to **the heirs of** said John, 30 Edw. I. but I find not who this Margaret was. The said MS. **sais, from** Will. Booth's Register, **fol. 4,** that John Lacy, of Cromwelbothom, was buried in the parish church of Halifax, in 1474.

The name of Cromwelbothom continued here after the match of John Lacy with the heiress of that name ; for in the Pleas, 32 Edw. III. I **find** a claim of Richard Lacy, son and heir of John, against John, son and heir of John Cromwelbothom, and Agnes his wife, for eighteen acres of land in Southouram, removed by certiorari.

PEDEGREE OF LACY, OF BREARLEY.

Gilbert, second son of John Lacy, of Cromwelbothom, married Isabel, daughter and heiress of Gerard Soothill, of Brearley, in the township of Midgley, near Halifax, who bore, Gules, an eagle displayed argent.

By her he had Gerard Lacy, of Brearley, who married Joan, eldest daughter of Richard Symms, who bore, Gules, a fess dancetté between three crosses bottoné fitché argent. By her he had, 1. Hugh; 2. Dunstan, a Priest; 3. William, who married, and had two daughters; 4. Edward, **a** Priest; 5. Richard, who married ...... Green. Hugh, **the eldest, was** buried **at** Halifax, April 13, 1573, having married Agnes, daughter of Nicholas Savile, of New-hall, by whom, 1. John, 2. Thomas, 3. Leonard (one MS. calls him Edward, though there was a Leonard Lacy, of Southouram, gent. 29 Hen. VIII.) 4. Gilbert; 5. Alice, who married John Holdsworth; 6. Agnes, who married Christopher Deighton, cf Lincolnshire; 7. Ellen, who married John Dean, of Deanhouse, in Warley; and, 8. Isabel, who married Jasper Blythman. John, the eldest, was buried at Halifax, August 19, 1585, having married Ann, daughter of Thomas Woodrove, of Woolley, esq; who bore, Argent, a chevron between three crosses formée fitché gules. By her he had, **1. John,** witness to a deed in 1599; 2. Elizabeth, married to Francis Osborne; 3. Ellen, married to John Oldfield; **4. Isabel, to** William Savile, of Copley, esq; 5. Mary, 6. Susan, and, 7. Muriel, who married Rich. Wheatley, of Brearley, near Barnsley. John, the eldest, who sold Brearley, married Dorothy, daughter of Godfrey (one MS. sais Raph) Bosseville, of Gunthwaite, esq; who bore Argent, five fusills in fess gules, in chief three bears heads erased, sable; Guillim, p. 372, adds, muzzled or, for one of this family. By her he had, 1. John, 2. Hugh, both s. p. 3. Henry, of London; 4. Ann, s. p. 5. Dorothy, who married John Payne, Rector of Sherland, in Derbyshire; 6. Jane, who married Edward Revell, of Ogson, in Derbyshire; and, 7. Elizabeth, who married Arthur Dakin, of Stubbin Edge, in Derbyshire. Henry, third son, had William, a merchant in London; and Jane, who married Richard Halliwell, of Mansfield, in 1641.

A black's head, full faced and bearded, with a cap azure turned up or, on a wreath of his colors argent and sable, was granted for crest to Seth Lacy, of London, son and heir to Leonard Lacy, second son of Richard Lacy, of Bryerley, gent. by Robert Cooke, esq; Clarencieux.

LISTER.

The next owners of Shibden-hall [after the Waterhouses and Hemingways] were the Listers, whose pedigree is as follows:

Samuel Lister, of Shibden-hall, died in 1632, leaving, 1. **Thomas**, 2. John, 3. Joseph, who died Dec. 27, 1644, leaving **two** sons, who died **s. p.** and **Mary**, who married **Moses** Jenkins.

Thomas married, first, Sibyl, daughter of Robert **Hemmingway**, of Upper Brea, by whom Samuel, John, Thomas, and Mary. Samuel married Hester **Oats**, who died in bed by her husband, **Jan.** 26, 1692-3, **aged** sixty, leaving **1.** Thomas, **who died s. p.** and was buried April 5, 1690, aged thirty-four; **2.** John, who died s. p. and was buried Aug. 9, 1691; 3. Samuel, who died about 1702, having married, May 16, 1695, Dorothy Priestley, who married at Coley, Nov. 16, 1703, to her second husband, Richard Sterne, esq; of Woodhouse; 4. Mary, and 5. Elizabeth. Thomas Lister above named married a second wife, by whom Joseph, who had, 1. Joseph, who married a daughter of sir John Jordan; 2. Catharine, 3. Elizabeth, and 4. Martha, who married **William** Walsham, esq; of London. None of these four **had** any issue. Thomas above named died in 1677, as appears from the following entry in Oliver Heywood's Diary: "Jan. "30, 1677, went to the funeral of Mr. Tho. Lister, of "Shipden-hall, at Halifax. Heard Dr. Hooke's commend "ation of him, and censures of us."

John, second son of Samuel first named in the above pedigree, married Phœbe, daughter of Robert Hemmingway, of Upperbrea, by whom Samuel, John, s. p. and Jeremy. Samuel married Mary Holdsworth, by whom, 1. John, who married Dorothy Hanson, by whom one child, which **died** young; 2. James, 3. Jeremy, 4. Thomas, 5. Susan, 6. Phœbe, 7. Mary, 8. **Martha**, 9. Elizabeth, **and** 10. Hester. James the second son was living in 1719, having married the daughter of William Issot, of Horbury, by whom, 1. Samuel, s. p. 2. John, 3. James, 4. Samuel, 5. Thomas, married in Virginia; 6. William, married in Virginia; 7. Jeremy, who married Ann Hall, of Butterworth-end, in Norland, by whom John, James, Joseph, Jeremy, Mary, and Phœbe. 8. Joseph, s. p. 9. Japhet, who married Elizabeth Wainhouse, of Broadgates, by whom, Edward, Samuel, John, and Elizabeth. 10. Martha, who married William Fawcet, of Halifax, by whom James, William, and Barbara. 11. Mary, married George Rose, of Hamstead, s. p. and Phœbe, who married William Wilkinson, of Hull, s. p.

Arms of Lister, of Shibden-hall, Ermine, on a fess sable, three mullets or, a canton gules.

—::—

MARION—See Stansfeld.

—::—

PRIESTLEY.

Adjoining to White-Windows, is a large modern house, built by Mr. John Priestley, whose pedegree, collected as well as I could from family papers, is as follows:

Henry Priestley, in 1608, married Helen ...... who was a widow in 1623. He had by her Robert and Henry, which last was living in 1649. Robert had, 1. Jonathan, of Sowerby, whose will was dated in 1662; 2. Henry, 3. Francis, 4. Grace, and, 5. Robert. Of these, Henry had, 1. Jonathan, of Priestley-green, living in 1689, 2. Thomas, 3. Francis, and, 4. Mary, who married Matthew Nicholson.

Henry, second son of the first Henry, had, 1. John, a Merchant in London, who had Joseph, living in 1649; 2. Joseph, of Goodgreave, a Clothier, who died in 1689; 3. Thomas, of Quickstavers, who died about 1689, having had Thomas, s. p. and Joseph, slain at the battle of the Boyne; 4. Jonathan, of Winteredge, in Northouram, who married Mary ..... by whom, Jonathan, s. p. Nathaniel, of Ovenden, and John, of Westercroft, in Northouram. Of these, Nathaniel had Jonathan, of Winteredge, who had Jonathan, of Leeds, and John.

Joseph, of Goodgreave, above-named, married Hester......
by whom, 1. John, of York, born Oct. 14, 1645, and who
died May 9, 1697, having four children, viz. Jaques, Israel,
Grace, s. p. and Sarah, s. p. 2. Hannah, born Nov. 21,
1647, and who died Oct. 25, 1655. 3. Joseph, of White-
Windows, born June 23, 1650. 4. Sarah, born June 29,
1655, and who died May 19, 1656. 5. Israel, born June 8,
1657. 6. Timothy, born January, 1660. Joseph, of White-
Windows, above-named, had lived at Wat-ing, in Norland;
he married Mary Morvel, Feb. 1, 1674-5. She was born at
Beckfoot, near Bingley, July 3, 1653. By her he had, 1.
Hannah, born Sept. 23, 1676. 2. John, born Aug. 18, 1678.
3. William, born Dec. 6, 1681. 4. Sarah, born Jan. 22,
1683-4. 5. Joseph, born June 18, 1686, and who died of the
small-pox, June 6, 1695. 6. Timothy, born May 30, 1688.
7. Mary, born Nov. 25, 1690. 8. Grace, born July 2, 1693,
and who died Feb. 6, 1694-5.

John, last-named, married Mary, daughter of Israel Wilde,
of Ball-green, in Sowerby, by whom John, of White-windows,
who built the new house there in 1767 and 1768. He
married Susanna, daughter of Benjamin Holroyd, of Wood-
lane, in Sowerby, Oct. 24, 1749, by whom, Joseph, John,
and Mary, which last died young. Arms of Holroyd, Azure,
five roses in saltire argent.

Arms used by Priestley, of White-windows, Gules, on a
chevron argent, three grapling irons sable, between as many
towers argent, issuing out of each a demi lion rampant or.

—::—

RASTRICK—See Hanson.

—::—

ROOKES, OF ROOKES.

Here lived a considerable family of the name of Rookes,
some of which resided at Rodes-hall, in Bradford parish;
their coat armor was, Argent, a fess between three rooks,
sable, and their pedigree is as follows, copied from Mr.
Hopkinson. William married Dorothy, daughter of John
Pecke, of Wakefield and West Ardsley, esq; by whom
Richard, esq; who lived in the time of Henry VII. and

married Mary, daughter of John Ramsden, of Rawden, by whom Richard, esq; who lived in the time of Hen. VIII. and married Elizabeth, daughter of Robert Waterhouse, of Halifax, esq; by whom John, esq; who married Jennet, daughter and coheiress of Richard Watson, of Lofthouse, by whom William, esq; who married Elizabeth, daughter of Richard Wilkinson, of Bradford, by whom, twelve children, **viz.** William, esq; Jonas, Fellow of University College, Oxford; Richard, Robert, Tempest, Maximilian, John; Bridget, married to Mark Hoppey, of Esholt; Barbara, to Richard Pearson; Grace, to Richard Rawlinson; Susan, to Michael Holdsworth; and Prudence, to John Ramsden. William, the eldest son, lived 20 Charles I, married, first, Jane, daughter of John Thornhill, of Fixby, esq; by whom William and Jane, **who** both died young; **to** his second wife, Susan, **daughter of** Mr. Rosethorn, widow of …… Radcliffe, com. Lanc. **by whom** William, esq; who married Mary, daughter of George Hopkinson, of Lofthouse, by whom, 1. William, **who** died a student in University College, in Oxford, in 1667; 2. George, who married Jane, daughter of Captain Henry Crossland, of Helmsley, in the North-riding, by whom Catharine, who died young; 3. John, esq; third son of William, inherited the estate as heir male to his brothers. The daughters were, Jane, who married Robert, second son of Edward Parker, of Browsholme, esq; and Mary, who died young. John, the third son of William, as above, died suddenly, May 31, 1713; he married, first, May 27, 1684, **his own cousin, Ann,** daughter and **heiress** of George Hopkinson, **of** Lofthouse, by whom **William** and George. William, **esq**; married, Jan. 27, 1712, Mary, daughter of William **Rodes,** of Great Houghton, **esq;** by whom, 1. Edward, **esq; born March 23, 1714, who** married, in 1740, the daughter **and heiress of** …… **Leedes,** of Milforth, esq; and took the name of Leedes; 2. William, who died in 1732, **and his** widow in 1734; 3. John, who died young; **4.** Mary; 5. Jane; 6. Ann, died young, and Elizabeth. John above named, third son of William, married to his second wife, Dec. 8, 1687, Elizabeth, daughter of Marmaduke Cook, D.D. Vicar of Leeds and Prebendary of York, by whom Elizabeth, Mary, John, who died young; and another John.

This estate called Rookes did once give name to a family, of which we meet with Richard de Rokes in 1313, and John del Rokis in 1362. Also John Rokes, de Rokes, in 1502.

PEDEGREE of the Family of SALTONSTALL.

Gilbert Saltonstall, of Halifax, 8 Eliz. as by deed at Coley, purchased Rookes, and other lands, in Hipperholme, and accordingly is mentioned as of Rookes, by deed 37 Eliz. He had Samuel and Sir Richard. Samuel, of Rookes and Huntwick, married Ann, daughter of John Ramsden, of **Longley**, esq ; by whom Sir Richard and Gilbert, which last died young. Sir Richard, knt. Justice of Peace, 1 Ch. I. married, first, Grace, daughter of Robert Kay, of Woodsom, **esq** ; by whom Richard, esq ; born at Woodsom, 1610, and **other** children. After his wife's death this Sir Richard sold his lands, and went, with his children, into New England ; from whence he returned, and resided in London, marrying 2dly, a daughter of Lord Delaware ; and, 3dly, one Wilford.

Sir Richard, son of Gilbert, was Sheriff of London with Hugh Offley, in 1588, and Lord Mayor in 1597, when, as usual, he was knighted. He died in 1601, having married Susanna, daughter of Thomas Poyntz, of North Okyngdon, esq ; by whom sixteen children. From him are descended the Saltonstalls of Hertfordshire. This family was originally, in all probability, of Saltonstall, in Halifax parish ; for the wife of Ric. Saltonstall, of Hye Saltonstall, was buried at Halyfax, 20 Febr. 1582.

Samuel Saltonstall above named, married, 2dly, Elizabeth, daughter of Thomas Ogden, by whom Samuel, John, Thomas, Ann, Elizabeth, Mary, Margaret, and Barbara. To **his** third wife, Elizabeth Armine, of Hull, by whom **no issue.** It is a question whether he was not knighted, because I **find that** sir **Samuel Saltonstall**, of London, held **lands** in **Hipperholm in** 1607. Also at a court held at **Wakefield**, 11 Jan. **8 James** I. Samuel Saltonstall, of London, knt. and Elizabeth **his** wife, surrendered lands in Hipperholm.

Who was the father of Gilbert, first above named, is uncertain ; but a John Saltonstall, of Halifax, was buried there, Mar. 30, 1557, and a Robert Saltonstall, of Halifax, also buried there, 18 Oct. 1561, as had, the February preceding, sir William Saltonstall, curate of Halifax.

In a large MS. Collection of Arms, in my possession, sir Richard Saltonstall, skinner, Lord Mayor of London in 1597, is said to have born, Or, a bend between two eaglets displayed, sable; but in Thoresby, p. 236, they are, Argent, a bend gules, between two eaglets displayed, sable.

It appears from various accounts, that several of the name of Saltonstall were officers of earl Warren for Saltonstall, and to them were divers parts thereof granted.

In 1343, 17 Edw. III, John de Brownhirste surrendered in court two parts of a sixth part of Saltonstall, with the reversion of a third part of the said sixth part, which Isabel, mother of said John, held as dower; the moiety of which was granted to John, son of Thomas de Saltonstall, another moiety to Richard, son of Thomas de Saltonstall, and William de Saltonstall, and heirs.

At Halifax, in 1376, John Cape surrendered a sixth part of Saltonstall to the use of Richard Saltonstall, and heirs.

As the last earl of Warren and Surry died June 30, 1347, 21 Edw. III. it is plain, from the first of the two instances above, that the vaccary of Saltonstall was demised by copy before the lordship of Wakefield came to the crown.

6 Hen. IV. Ric. Saltonstall surrendered two sixth parts of Saltonstall, and half a sixth part, lying between Blakebrook, Depeclough, the water of Luddingden, and Hoore Stones, in Sowerby, to the use of Richard Saltonstall and heirs. 15 Edw. IV. this Richard surrendered the same to Gilbert Saltonstall his son, which Gilbert, 23 Hen. VII. surrendered the same to Richard Saltonstall, his son; after the death of which Richard, son of Gilbert, Richard Saltonstall, son and heir of the same Richard, 30 Hen. VIII. made fine of heriot for the said lands. This last Richard had issue Gilbert, who died before his father, leaving a son Samuel, who, after the death of Richard his grandfather, made fine of heriot, 40 Eliz. for the same lands.

SAVILE AND COPLEY.

Copley-Hall is famous for giving name to an antient respectable family, the first of which was Adam de Copley, slain when William the Conqueror laid siege to York, in the year 1070. He married Ann, daughter of Thomas Rishworth, of Rishworth, near Halifax, according to a pedigree in Thoresby, p. 9, taken from Hopkinson's MSS. but of

Richard, as in an old MS. pedegree in my own possession. By the said Ann he had Hugh de Copley, who married Margaret, daughter of Richard Liversedge, by whom, 1. Rafe, 2. Richard, (as by the MS. notes to a copy of Thoresby, in the hands of **Mr.** Charles Barnard, of Leedes,) **3.** Adam, called by Thoresby, Vicar of Halifax, but he should have said Rector, for that living was a rectory **till** the year 1273, and **two hundred years** could hardly have passed between the above **first** mentioned Adam, and his grandson. **Lastly,** Margaret, **married to** William Lockwood. **Rafe, the el**dest, **married** Jane, daughter of John Stansfeld, of Stansfeld, esq; **by whom** Thomas, who married Margaret, daughter of Hugh **Eland, of** Eland, esq; **by** whom Adam, Robert, and Ann, **who** married John Exley. Adam married Ann, daughter of **John** Leventhorpe, of Leventhorpe, esq; by whom Thomas Copley, of Copley, (not Batley, **as in** Thoresby,) who married Winifred, daughter of Thomas Mirfield, esq; (as in Thoresby, but my MS. sais Robert,) by whom, 1. Hugh, 2. Ralph, who had **a** place at court, and by his wife Mary, daughter and heiress of **sir** Richard Walsingham, of Suffolk, knt. had John, **s.** p. and Robert, commonly called Grosthead, or Greathead, **the** famous bishop of Lincoln. Lastly, Cicely, who married William Quarmby, of Quarmby. Hugh, the eldest, witness to **a deed** in 1324, married Ann, daughter of sir Robert Cromwelbothome, knt. (my MS. sais John,) by whom Thomas and Raphe, which last married, first, Ellen, daughter of John Rookes, of Rookes, esq; by whom Raphe and John, both s. p. 2dly,......daughter of Adam de Batley, from whom the Copleys, of Batley. Thomas, the **eldest,** married, and had a daughter, Helen, who married Henry, second son of John Savile, by Margery, youngest daughter, **and** coheiress of Henry Rishworth, of Rishworth; and from **this** time this branch of the Saviles settled at Copley, which **I take to** have been about the year 1485, as in a will **of** that date at Howroyd, are mentioned Henry Savile, **of** Copley, and **John, son** of Henry Savile. The issues **from** this match are as follow:

Henry Savile, above named, by the said Helen (or Ellen,) had John Savile, of Copley. Thomas, from whom the Saviles of Hollinedge, and Nicholas, from whom the Saviles of Bank, alias Blaidroid, in Southouram. John, the eldest, married Maud, daughter of Thomas Trafford, com. Lanc. by whom Thomas, who married Margaret, daughter of Henry Rushworth, of Coley-hall, by whom, 1. Henry, 2. Thomas, 3. Edward, parson of Adley, in Suffolk, 4. Humphry, chaplain to lord De la Ware, 5. Leonard, s. p. 6. John, s. p. 7. **Jane**, unmarried, and 8. Margaret, married to William Milner. **Henry, the eldest,** married Sibill, daughter of Lionel Copley, **of Batley,** by whom Thomas, who married **Alice,** daughter of Richard Beaumont, of Whitley, buried at Halifax, Dec. 8, 1552. By her he had, 1. Henry, 2. Thomas, s. p. 3. Robert, 4. Gilbert, and 5. Humphry, which **three** last died **young.** Also five daughters, **viz.** Elizabeth, Ann, and Alice, who all died unmarried; **Ellen, who** married Thomas Savile, **of Bank; and** Grace, **who married** Hugh Savile. There was an Henry Savile, of Skircoat, buried at Halifax, March 4, 1554, probably the **last named.** This Henry married Alice, daughter of Thomas **Midhope,** of Morehall, **by** whom Thomas, **buried at** Halifax, **Feb. 3, 1569. 2. Nicholas,** who married Alice, **daughter of ......** **Birkhead, by** whom Brian, Martin, Henry, Agnes, **and** Isabel. Also, 3. John, who had three sons. 4. William, **parson** of Cranhurst, in Sussex; 5. Edward, who died young, **and,** 6. Henry, who married Ann, daughter of ...... Parkinson, **of** Richmondshire. **The** above Thomas married **Ann,** daughter of Thomas Danby, second son of sir James Danby, knt. This Ann, as I take it, was buried at Halifax, **Dec. 2,** 1588. By her the said Thomas had, 1. Robert, 2. Anthony, **who** married Sibil, daughter of Robert **Oates,** of Halifax: 3. **Joseph,** 4. Thomas, who married Ursula, daughter of ...... **Brett, of Wales,** in Yorkshire; 5. John, 6. George; and **ten** daughters, **viz. 1.** Esther, 2. Ruth, **3.** Dorothy, who married Henry Briggs, 4. Elizabeth, who married John Platts, 5. Ann, 6. **Sarah,** buried at Halifax, April 19, 1579, 7. Esther, 8. Agatha, 9. Jane, and 10. Grace. **Robert,** the eldest, was buried at Halifax, June 11, 1588, having **married, 1.** Jane, daughter of Roger Ellis, of Riddal, by whom no **issue;** 2dly, **Alice,** daughter of William Moor, of Austhorpe, **near** Leedes, **widow** of William Hopey, by **whom** William; **Mary,** who married John Bentley, of Shipden; and Bridget, who married Robert Crowder, of Sowerby. William, the eldest, was living in 1592, having an infant buried that year at Halifax. He married Isabel, daughter of John Lacy, of Brearley, near Halifax, by whom, 1. Henry; 2. Francis, s. **p.** buried at

Halifax, Feb. 11, 1585; 3. Thomas, of York; 4. John, an attorney, who married Isabel Law, by whom Robert. The above William had also three daughters, viz. 1, Jane, who died young, and was buried at Halifax, August 9, 1585; 2. Joan, and 3. Elizabeth. Henry, the eldest, was seven years old in 1585. He married Ann, daughter of Michael Darcy, and sister and heiress to John, lord Darcy, by whom, 1. Thomas; 2. Henry, s. p. buried at Halifax, Jan. 16, 1642; 3. Michael, s. p. 4. John, 5. Anthony, and 6. Henry. Thomas, the eldest, married, 1. Frances Preyn, of London, s. p. 2. Frances, daughter of George Dawson, of Azetly, near Rippon, by whom William and Mary, both s. p. John, the fourth son, married Elizabeth, daughter of sir George Palmes, of Naburne, near York, by whom sir John Savile, of Copley, created a baronet by K. Cha. II. July 24, 1662, and William, who married two wives, and had several children. Sir John married Mary, daughter of Clement Paston, of Barningham, in Norfolk, esq; She died in August 1710. By her he had a daughter, Elizabeth-Maria, who married lord Thomas Howard, brother to Henry, duke of Norfolk, who being sent ambassador to Rome, died at sea, either on the 8th or 9th of December, 1689. They had Thomas, duke of Norfolk. (See the Peerage.)

The above pedigree was compared with a number of painted pannels in an old wainscotted room in Copley-hall, down to William, who married Isabel Lacy, and they agree, except that after Thomas, who married Alice Beaumont, there is one Robert Savile, with the date 1575.

With regard to the arms of the above two families, I have seen in Methley church, in Yorkshire, on a monument, the arms of Savile, viz. Argent, on a bend sable, three owls of the field, with a mullet for difference, and seven other bearings; amongst which, for Copley, of Copley, Argent, a cross moline, sable. In the center, the bloody hand. For crest, On a wreath of his colors, an helmet, above all, an owl proper. Motto, " Paciencia y. Basta." Another motto under the like eight coats, but without the bloody hand, " Je veille." Three figures on the tomb, and two children on the side.

The crest of Adam Copley first above named, is said to have been a cup covered, sable.

SAVILE :—LORD HALIFAX.

The following is a Genealogical Account of this part of the Family of Savile. Some think that the family of Savile came into England with **the Conqueror,** and that they are inserted in the roll of Battle **Abbey, by** the name of Shevile; **but** others suppose them **to have come** with Geoffry Plantaginet, **because** there **are two towns of** this name on the frontiers **of Anjou, both which were annexed** to the crown of England, **when the said Geoffry married** Maud, daughter and heiress **of Henry I.**   It is looked upon to be a family of **very** great antiquity, being **even supposed** to be descended **from** the Sabelli, **or** Savelli, **of** Rome, which Richardson, in his Account of some of the Statues, &c. in Italy, printed in **1722, sais, was** the most **antient family in Rome.   It** was, it seems, extinct there a few years ago.   The prince Savelli **was, in 1747,** guardian **of the conclave of cardinals at** Rome. Some **of his** ancestors were **consuls at Rome before** our Savior's time.   The family **is even said to have** existed three **thousand** years.   The first **I met with of** this family in England, **is** sir John Savile, **of** Savile-hall, in Dodworth, near Barnsley, in Yorkshire, **who** married a daughter **of** sir Symon **de** Rockley, who bore lozengy, argent **and** gules, a **fess,** sable, Thoresby, p. 25.   I **have also** met **with** argent, **seven** fusils, gules, three, three, and one, oppressed with **a** fess, sable.   By her he had sir Walter de Savile, and John de Savile.   Sir Walter married a daughter **of Adam Everingham,** of Stainbrough, by whom, **an** only daughter, **Elizabeth, married** to sir John Everingham, knt.   John Savile, **brother of sir** Walter, **married** about 1240, Agnes, daughter and heiress of sir Roger Aldwark, knt. who bore gules, a fess between six fusils, or.   By **her** he had Henry Savile, who married Agnes, daughter **and** heir of John Golcar, esq ; by whom, Thomas, who married ...... daughter and coheiress of sir Richard Tankersley, of Tankersley, knt. by whom, sir John Savile, of Tankersley, knt. (Some pedegrees make this Henry marry to Ellen de Copley.) Henry, s. p. **and** Alice, wife to ...... Lockwood. Sir John married Agnes, daughter and coheiress of ...... Rochdale, esq ; who bore sable, an escutcheon, within eight martlets in orle, argent ; this I take to be the true coat of the father of this Agnes, because **it was** formerly put up in Eland chapel, as such: but I **have** seen another belonging to the family, **viz.** argent, a fleur **de** lis between eight martlets, sable. By Agnes, his wife, sir John had John Savile, of Tankersley, esq; Elizabeth, married to Thomas **Kay, and** Margery, married to **John** Thornton. John **Savile, esq;** married Isabel, daughter and coheiress of sir Robert Latham, knt. who bore **or, on a** chief, azure, **indented, three plates;** by her he had **sir John Savile,** and Jane, married to ...... Ashton, in Lancashire. Sir John married **Jane, daughter** of **Matthew de Bosco** (or Wood) by **whom, John, and Margaret, Prioress of** Kirkless, **32** Edw. III. John married **Margery,** daughter **and** coheiress of Henry **Rushworth, of Rushworth,** in Halifax parish, **esq; who bore argent, a bend sable, an** eagle displayed, **vert, and a** cross **crosslet of the second, according to one MS. but I** find **to the name of** Alexander Rushworth, **in sir William Fairfax's "Book of Arms** for Yorkshire," **in the British Museum, argent, a** cross **crosslet, sable;** also argent, **a cross** botoné **fitché,** sable; **by her he had** sir John **Savile, of Tankersley, knt.** and Henry, **who married** Ellen, **daughter** and **heiress of** Thomas **Copley, of** Copley, in **the parish of** Halifax, **esq;** Sir **John was** high sheriff **of** Yorkshire **3d and** 11th **of Rich. II.** and knight of the shire for the said **county, 7th and** 8th of **the** said king; he married Isabel, **daughter and** heiress of sir John de Eland, knt. (some pedegrees **have it** sir Thomas,) by whom, sir **John** Eland, knt. **and Henry, who** married Elizabeth, daughter and heiress **of Simon** Thornhill, **of** Thornhill, esq; **who bore** gules, **two bars** gemells, **and a chief,** argent. **Also a** daughter **Jane,** married **to John Wortley,** esq; Sir John last **named married** Isabel, **daughter of** Robert de Radcliffe, **of the Tower,** by whom, **sir John Savile, knt.** who **married Isabel,** daughter **of sir William Fitzwilliams, knt. and a** daughter Isabel, **who married Thomas Darcy,** second son **to the lord Darcy; both these** died s. p.

Henry Savile above named had **sir Thomas** Savile, **knt.** in the **time of Hen. VI.** and a daughter Jennet, who married William **Leeds,** of Leeds, **esq;** s. p. Sir Thomas married Margaret, **daughter of sir Thomas Pilkington, by whom, sir** John Savile, **of Thornhill,** Eland, **and Tankersley, who** married Alice, daughter of sir William Gascoigne, of **Gaw-**thorp, knt. com. Ebor. **and three** daughters, **viz.** Margaret, married to John Hopton, **of** Swillington, esq; Alice, to sir John Harrington, of Brearley, knt. and Elizabeth, to Edmund **Aske**, of Aston, esq; Sir John had three sons, viz. sir John, **who** married **Jane**, daughter of sir Thomas Harrington, **of** Brearley, knt. **William**, who died s. p. and Thomas **Savile**, of Lupset, esq; Sir John, the eldest, had sir John, who married first, Alice, daughter of **Henry Vernon**, esq; by whom no issue. Secondly, Elizabeth, daughter and coheiress (one account sais sister) **of sir William Paston**, of Woodnoth, by whom sir Henry, and three daughters, viz. 1. Ann, who married, first, sir Henry **Thwaites**; secondly, **William Thwaites**. 2. Elizabeth, who **married, first, sir** Thomas **Conyers**, of Sackborn, knt. secondly, **to** Thomas Soothill. **3.** Margaret, **who** married, **first**, Richard **Corbet**; secondly, **Thomas** Wortley, **of** Wortley, esq; **Sir Henry, created knight of the** Bath, **25 Hen. VIII.** married **Elizabeth**, daughter and **heir** of Thomas Soothill, of **Soothill, esq;** by whom, **1. Edward, who** married Mary, daughter **of** sir Richard Lee, **of St. Alban's, com.** Hertf. from whom he was divorced "frigiditatis **causa."** 2. John, **the second son**, died young; and 3, Dorothy, **was married to** John Kay, **of** Woodsam, **esq;**

Thomas Savile, of Lupset, above named, married Margaret, **daughter of Thomas** Balforth, esq; **(or as one** pedegree sais, Basford,) by whom, 1. John Savile, of Lupset. **2.** Thomas **Savile, of** Wakefield, who married Catharine, daughter and **heiress of John Chaloner, of** Stanley, **alias** Midgley-hall, **near Wakefield, from whom** the Saviles of Stanley and **Wakefield, now extinct.** 3. George, of Cotham, in Nottinghamshire, **and of** Grantham, in Lincolnshire, who married according to **one pedegree, a** daughter and coheiress of ...... Rooke, of Hipperholme, **near** Halifax; but according **to** another, **the** daughter **and** heiress of Henry, son of Henry Shyrley, of Lumley, from whom **the** Saviles **of** Grantham and Homeby, in Lincolnshire.

John Savile, of Lupset, esq; above named, married, 12 Hen. VIII. Ann, daughter **of** William Wiatt, and widow of John Spilman, esq; by whom Henry Savile, of Lupset and Barrowby, com. Linc. who married Joan, daughter and heiress of William Vernon, of Barrowby aforesaid, by whom 1. sir George Savile, the first baronet. **2.** Francis, who married Catharine, daughter and coheiress **of William, lord**

Conyers. 3. Cordell Savile, who married Mary, daughter and heiress of William Welbeck, of Sutton, com. Nott. esq; 4. Bridget, married to Henry Nevile, of Grove. 5. Friswolde. Sir George abovenamed, created a baronet, 9 James I. married, first, Mary, daughter **of** George Talbot, earl of Shrewsbury; secondly, Elizabeth, daughter of sir Edward Ascough, of South Kelsey, in Lincolnshire; by his first lady he had **sir** George Savile, of Rufford, who, Dugdale, in his Baronage, Vol. II. p. 463. has omitted, but who married, first, Sarah, daughter **and** coheir of John Rede, **of Cotesbrook, in** Northamptonshire, s. p. Secondly, Ann, daughter of sir William Wentworth, of Woodhouse, sister to **the** earl of Strafford; by **her** he had sir George, who died unmarried; **and** sir William, who married Ann, daughter of Thomas, **lord** Coventry, by whom, amongst others, George, earl of Halifax, as abovementioned, whose marriages and descendants the printed accounts will shew.

Hullenedge, near Elland, perhaps from Hollin-hedge, was the seat of a branch of the Saviles, the first of whom **was** Thomas Savile, of Hullenedge, second son of Henry Savile, of Copley; he married Ann, daughter of John Stansfeld, of Stansfeld, by whom John, Thomas, who married lady Elizabeth Waterton, s. p. Henry, a yeoman of the guards, and Nicholas, from whom the Saviles of Newhall. John, the eldest, married Alice, daughter of Ralph Lister, of Halifax, by whom John, Robert, William, Gilbert, and Leonard. Of these, John, the eldest, married Ann, daughter of John Hopton, of Armley, esq; by whom Leonard, who **died** an infant. Robert and John. Robert married Elen, daughter of Robert Fulverley, of Fulverley, com. Linc. esq; by whom Thomas, **who** married, 1st, Elen, daughter of Arthur Pilkington, esq; 2dly, Sarah, daughter **of** ...... Thornton, s. p. By said Elen he had Thomas, who **married** a daughter of Charles Radcliffe, of Todmorden, by whom **Isabel,** and Jane. Robert, 2d son of John Savile, by Alice Lister, **married** Jane Chaworth, of Warton, by whom Thomas, Leonard, D.D. and parson of Lewis, in Sussex, and three daughters, 1. Sibyl, married to Robert Waterhouse. 2. Isabel, **to John** Deighton; and 3. Grace, to Richard Briggs, of Warley. Thomas, the eldest, was seized of the rectory of Mirfield, and some lands there, as appears by a livery sued out by Cuthbert, his son, after his death, dated

July 1, 1 Edw. VI. He married Elizabeth, daughter of James Shaw, by whom Cuthbert and Elizabeth; Cuthbert married Margaret, daughter of John Hardy, of Halifax, by whom Thomas, who married Mercy, daughter of George Kay, of Whitley, and two daughters, Sibyl and Dorothy.

William Savile, of Wakefield, third son of John, by **Alice Lister,** married Phœbe Rishworth, by whom William, **John,** Gilbert, and Agnes. William married Agnes, daughter **of** James Simpson, by whom William, Michael, Gabril, Grace, **and Ann.** William, **the eldest,** was an attorney at law at Wakefield, **and lived at the** parsonage house there; he married Jennet, daughter of John Fawcet, by whom William, Martin, Henry, a traveller, who died at Grand Cairo, Samuel, and **others. William,** the eldest, married Margaret, daughter of Thomas Harris, of Huntington, by whom William, **s. p.** and Gabriel, a captain of foot under king Charles I. who married the daughter **and** coheir of captain Ralph Rokeby, of Skiers, near Rotherham, by whom no issue.

Newhall was the seat of a branch **of the Saviles of Hullenedge, whose** pedegree is this: Nicholas **Savile,** fourth son **of Thomas** Savile, of Hullenedge, married Margery, **daughter of William** Wilkinson, **by whom John,** Thomas of Welborne, Henry, Edward, Nicholas, **Alice,** married to Arthur Pilking**ton, of** Bradley, Agnes **to Hugh** Lacy, Isabel to Richard Waterhouse, of Hollings, **and** Jennet to John Thornhill, of Fixby, esq. John, the eldest son, married Margery, daughter of John Gledhill, by whom Nicholas, John, Henry Savile, **of** Bradley, **Thomas,** from whom the Saviles **of** Watergate. Agnes, **married** to John Hanson, of Woodhouse, Alice to Richard Holt, of Stubley, Jane to Thomas Gledhill, of Barkisland, **and** Elizabeth to John Blythe, of Quarmby. Nicholas, the eldest, married Jennet, daughter of Thomas Foxcroft, **by** whom Thomas, who married **a** daughter of Trygot, of South-Kirkby, esq; **by** whom Nicholas, who married Jane, daughter of Thomas Burdet, by whom John, **s. p.** John, second son of Thomas, died at Newhall, having married Frances, daughter of Godfrey Bosseville, of Gunthwaite, **esq;** by whom four daughters. The third son of Thomas was Thomas, who married a daughter of Thomas Burdet, by whom Thomas and Francis. The above Thomas had also two daughters, Frances and Elizabeth.

Bradley-Hall, the present owner of which is Savile, earl of Mexborough. It once was the seat of the Saviles, whose pedigree I have subjoined, and in all probability was a very considerable building; but only a small part of it now remains, sufficient for a farmer, but the ground about it shews, by its inequality, and by a number of stones lodged near the surface, that it has been more extensive. **Over** the gate are the figures 1577, and the letters I. S. John **Savile.** On the kitchen wall is 1598. The chapel, being re-edified, **serves** the tenant **for a** barn; most of the tower also remains, **and** the whole has the appearance of a church to such as are travelling between Eland and Ripponden. The bells are said **to** have been removed from hence to Methley church, near which this branch of the Savile family have a **seat.** The chapel here, as Dr. Johnson sais, in his MS. Collections, was pulled down in the time of **the** civil wars, but the hall was burned down in 1629. There **is** a tradition in this neighbourhood about this fire, and **it** is likewise said, that it caused the family to remove to Methley.

Henry Savile married Ellen, daughter and heiress of Thomas Copley, of Copley, by whom, 1. John, who married Maud, daughter of Thomas Trafford, of Trafford, com. Lanc. esq; from whom the Saviles of Copley; **2.** Thomas; 3. Nicholas, who married Jennet Lacy. Thomas, second son, married Ann, daughter of John Stansfield, by whom, 1. John, from whom the Saviles of Hullenedge; 2. Thomas, who married Elizabeth Lady Waterton; 3. Henry, Yeoman **of the** Guards; and 4. Nicholas, of Newhall, who married Margaret, daughter of William Wilkinson, by whom, amongst others, John, of Newhall, his eldest son, who married Margery, daughter of John Gledhill, of Barkisland, by whom amongst others, Henry of Bradley, his third son, living 8 Eliz. who married Ellen, daughter of Robert Ramsden, by whom, 1. sir John Savile, of Medley, Baron of **the** Exchequer; 2. sir Henry Savile, Warden of Merton College, Oxford; 3. Thomas, and five daughters. Sir Henry married Margery, (Biogr. Brit. p. 3600. sais Elizabeth.) daughter of George Dacres, of Cheshunt, in Hertfordshire, esq; by whom Henry, who **died s.** p. and Elizabeth, **who** married sir John Sedley, bart. of Alisford, in Kent, or, as the author of Anglorum Speculum, p. 902, sais, sir William.

Inquisition 19 Edw. IV. of Wasts committed in the lordship of Wakefield, Tho. Sayvell, knt. held lands and tenements in Stainland, Berksland, and Northland, by **soccage,** paying yearly 13s. 2d.

Henry Savile, knt. and bart. died seized of a messuage called Over Bradley Hall, in Stainland, as by inquisition post mort. at Shirburn com. Ebor. 6 Sept. 8 Charles, 1632.

Sir John Savile, of Methley, Baron of the Exchequer, **son of** Henry by **Ellen** Ramsden, **and** who died in 1606, married, **first,** Jane, daughter of Richard Garth, of Morden, in Surry, by **whom,** 1. sir Henry Savile, of Methley, created a baronet in 1611; Elizabeth, who married sir John Jackson; and Jane, who married sir Henry Goodrick, of Ribston, knt. Sir Henry Savile above named died in 1632, having married Mary, daughter and coheiress of John Dent, of London, esq; by whom, according to one epitaph in Methley **church,** he had no issue; but according to another **in** the same church he had John, (who died **on** his travels in France, in 1631, aged twenty-one, as by epitaph **in** Methley church;) Henry, and others, who all died s. p. Sir John Savile, above named, married, secondly, Elizabeth, daughter of Thomas Wentworth, of North Empsall, esq; relict of **Richard** Tempest, esq; 3dly, Dorothy, daughter of Lord Wentworth, and relict of sir W. Widmerpool and sir Martin **Forbisher,** knights, by whom no issue. By his second wife, **Elizabeth,** he had John Savile, of Methley, esq; sheriff of **York 24 Cha. I.** who married, first, Mary, daughter of John **Robinson, of** Rither, esq; by whom several children, who died s. p. 2dly, Margaret, daughter **of sir** Hen. Gareway, of **London, knt. by** whom John Savile, **of** Methley, and six daughters. **John** married Sarah, daughter of ...... Tryon, esq; **by whom John,** Charles, James, **s. p.** Samuel, and four daughters. John Savile, esq; died in **1711,** having married Mary, daughter of sir John Banks, knt. by whom John, **Henry,** and Elizabeth. Charles, above named, married Aletheia, daughter and coheiress of Gilbert Millington, of **Felley** Abbey, in the county of Nottingham, esq; by whom John, created, first, Lord Pollington, afterwards Earl of Mexborough.

There is in Methley church a marble monument to the memory of this Charles, the inscription on which sais, thro' mistake, that he **was** the fifth **in a** lineal descent from sir

John, who was Baron of the Exchequer. This Charles died June 5, 1741, aged sixty-five. On the monument is his figure in a reclining posture, and his wife weeping over him. She died about Midsummer 1759.

In Methley church, on the south side of a monument, is a long Latin inscription to Baron Savile above named, intimating, amongst **other** things, that he died Feb. 2, 1606, aged sixty-one, **that his** body was buried in the church of St. Dunstan **in the** west, London, and his heart **at** Methley, amongst **his ancestors.**

On the **north side of** the said monument is another Latin **inscription to sir Henry** Savile, son of the Baron; but **not relating** immediately **to Halifax parish** men, I omit them all.

Arms of Savile, Argent, on a bend sable, three owls proper. **These** Thoresby, **p.** 110, has put down as the general arms **of** the family; but in my MS. Alphabet are the following entries: "Ebor. Savile, of Howley, Baron Savile in England, "and Viscount Castle Barre in Ireland, per K. Ch. Argent, "on a bend sable, three owls proper. His Crest, an owl "argent."

Savile, **of Newhall,** Argent, on **a bend** ingrailed between two cotises sable, **three** owls argent.

Savile, **sir** George, **of** Thornhill, **bart. 9 K. James,** Argent, on a bend ingrailed sable, three owls proper. His Crest, a demi maid, full faced, proper, crowned or, adorned with pea**cock** feathers stuck in the crown, proper, garments gules, **hair** disheveled, or.

Savile, sir Henry, of Methley, bart. 9 K. James, Argent, **on a** bend sable, three owls proper, a crescent sable for difference. His Crest, On **an owl** argent, a crescent sable.

To **a** Deed in 1601, the seal of Edward Savile, esq; **son** and heir of sir Henry Savile, knt. deceased, was an owl on a **fess.**

BLAITHROYD was the seat of a branch of the family of Savile, whose pedigree here follows, taken chiefly from a MS. in the Harleian Collection, No 1034, called Visitation of Yorkshire, by Glover, in 1585. Henry Savile, who married Ellen, daughter and heiress of Thomas Copley, of Copley, had John, of Copley; Thomas, of Hullenedge, and Nicholas, of Bank, who married Joan, daughter of John Lacy, of Cromwelbothom, by whom, 1. John, who died young; 2. Thomas, who married Euphemia, daughter of ... ... Soothill, of Soothill, (one copy

sais Jennet, daughter of Thomas Soothill, of Brearley, near
Halifax ;) 3. Joan, who married Thomas Whitley, of Whitley ;
4. Elizabeth, who married ... ... Nettleton, of Thornton Lees ;
5. Helena, who married Robert Gibson, a Lawyer ; 6. Alice,
who married Thomas **Firth**, of Dewsbury ; and 7. Agnes,
who married Richard Sandal, of Sandal. Thomas, last
named, had 1. Thomas, of the Bank ; 2. John, of Rothwell,
who married Ann, daughter of George Cawthorn, of Carleton,
near Skipton in Craven, by whom fifteen children ; 3. **Miles**,
a Priest ; 4. Henry, 5. Brian, 6. Isabel, who married Edward
Saltonstall ; 7. Johanna, who married William Holme ;
8. **Jane**, who married John Smith ; and 9. **Alice**, who married
William Cliffe.

Thomas, of the Bank, was buried at **Halifax**, Sept. 22,
1570 ; he married Alice, daughter of Thomas Savile, of
Copley, by whom Henry, of Blaidroyd, living in 1585, and
Thomas, who died young. Henry married Frances, daughter
of Adam Moyser, of Farlington, widow of Edmund Greenbury,
of York, by whom Henry, aged seventeen in 1585 ; and quere
if not a daughter Bridget ?

—::—

SHIBDEN.—See Drake.

—::—

SIMPSON.

The following pedegree of Simpson, of Hipperholme, I
drew up **from** family deeds and papers. Thomas Sympson
as by deed **1409.** John Sympson, as by deed 1465. John
Sympson as by deed from Robert Killyngbek, Abbat of Kirk-
stall, to him, dated Oct. 27, 16 Hen. VII. (1500.) Henry
Sympson, as by his will, dated in 1601, had William Symp-
son, de Rawden, who married Alice ... ... His will dated
Aug. 8, 12 James I. He had John Sympson, of Rawden,
Mary, and Mercy. John's will was dated Febr. 26, 1667.
He married Mary ...... by whom Joseph, Joshua, Mary, and
Martha. Joseph was of Woodhouse, in Leedes parish.
His will is dated May 29, 1706. He married, first, Hannah
Ingram ; 2dly, Ann Marshal ; by the latter he had Hannah,
Susanna, and Ann ; by the former, John, Joseph, and Mary.

John was of Hipperholme, his will dated July 12, 1721. He married Mary ...... who died in childbed of her first child, John. This John was of Hipperholme, and married, first, (March 4, 1726-7,) Dorothy, daughter of the Rev. Mr. Nathan Sharp; 2dly, Grace, daughter of John Brogden, of North-Bierley, by whom William and Richard, who both died young; also Sarah, Susan, and Grace. By his first wife, Dorothy, he had John, Ann, who died unmarried, Mary, Joseph, Elizabeth, and Dorothy, which three last died young. John Sympson, of Hipperholme, married Mary, daughter of ...... Scholfield, of Rochdale, by whom John, who died young, and others.

STANSFELD.

Stansfield-Hall. Here lived a family of considerable repute, who took their name from their situation. The original of them was one Wyan Marions, probably of Norman extraction, and in all likelihood a follower of earl Warren, on whom this Lordship was bestowed; he had Jordan de Stansfield, who married a daughter of John Townley, of Townley, knt. by whom, 1. John de Stansfield, 2. Thomas, 3. Robert, and 4. Oliver, Constable of Pontefract-castle. John married Elizabeth, daughter of Thomas Entwisle, by whom Richard Stansfield, of Stansfield; and Jane, married to Raphe Copley. Richard married Alice, daughter of sir Thomas Tunstall, knt. of Thurland-castle, in Lancashire, by whom, 1. Edmund Stansfield, of Stansfield, 2. Robert, 3. Hugh, and 4. Roger. Edmund married a daughter of Tho. de Midgley, by whom Ralph, Bryan, and Gilbert. Ralph married Jane, daughter of Tho. Copley, of Copley, by whom, 1. Henry, (Thoresby, pag. 115, calls him, through mistake, William,) 2. Raphe, 3. John, and 4. William. Henry married Dionis, daughter of Brian Thornhill, of Thornhill, esq; by whom William, Richard, Mary, Jane, and Elizabeth. William married Joan, daughter of sir John Burton, of Kinsley, in Yorkshire, knt. by whom Thomas, (about the beginning of Henry VII,) Mabil, Jane, and Meryon. Thomas married Barbara, daughter of John de Lascels, of Lascel-hall, near Almondbury, com. Ebor. esq; by whom John, Robert, Anthony, and William. John married Mary, daughter of John Fleming, of Wath, com.

Ebor. by whom Thomas, Henry, Ann, who married Thomas
Savile, Isabel, Jane, Elizabeth, and Mary. Thomas married
Alice, daughter of John **Savile**, esq; by whom William,
Robert, Richard, Henry, Julian, and Mary. William married
Elizabeth, daughter of **John** Duckenfield, of Duckenfield,
esq; by whom James Stansfield, who removed to Hartshead,
com. Ebor. in **1536, and** married **a** daughter of ...... Holden,
in Lancashire, by **whom** Ashton Stansfield, Barrister at Law,
who lived at Wakefield, and married a daughter of Philemon
Speight, of **Earls Heaton**, near Dewsbury, by whom several
children, **who all died young.**

The **Arms** of **Stansfeld, of Stansfeld, were, Sable, three
goats trippant, argent, and were so** painted in the chapel
window at Heptonstall; but in Eland chapel they were
collared and belled or.

STERNE.

Woodhouse was purchased for £1800. **by Simon Sterne,
third son** of Dr. Richard Sterne, Archbishop **of** York. **This
Simon, who** was Justice of Peace, was buried at Halifax,
April **17, 1703, and was** resident here, as **was his** son
Richard, both whom are mentioned in a short pedegree **of**
the family, in Thoresby, p. 215. Arms **of** Sterne are, in
Thoresby, p. 214, and Guillim, p. 77. Or, a chevron between
three crosses flory, **sable.** Their crest is, **On** a wreath **of**
his colors, a starling proper.

It may here be pardonable to remind the reader, that the
Rev. **Mr. Sterne, author of** Tristram Shandy, &c. was of
this family; **and that the above crest** furnished him with the
hint for that fine **story of the** Starling, in the second **volume**
of Yorick's **Sentimental** Journey through France and Italy.

The arms which I have noted to have **been** born **by** any
inhabitants of this township, are, **1.** Greame of **Heath,** viz.
Or, on a chief sable, three escallops of the first. **This name,
no** doubt, has been altered from Graham; for Guillim, **p.**
243, has attributed this very coat to sir Richard Graham, **of
Netherby,** in Cumberland. **2.** Laycock, **of** Shaw-hill, Sable,
a gauntlet, argent. **3. Lees, of** Willow-hall, Argent, **a**
chevron between three leopards heads, sable. **4.** Rossendale,
Gyrony of six, argent and gules, six roses counterchanged.

SUNDERLAND.

High Sunderland, **gave** name **to a family** of which the following is the pedegree.

Richard Sunderland, of **High Sunderland**, had Richard, who married Agnes, daughter of Rushworth, of Coley, by whom 1. Richard Sunderland, esq; Justice of Peace, and Treasurer **for lame soldiers** in the West Riding, buried at Halifax, **June 25, 1634.** 2. Abraham, of the Middle Temple, unmarried. 3. Jennet, married **to Robert Hemingway,** and Agnes, to Robert Dean. Richard last named married Susan, daughter of sir Richard Saltonstall, Lord Mayor of London in 1597, by whom 1. Abraham Sunderland, **esq; of High Sunderland, Barrister at Law, and Justice of Peace** in the West-riding. 2. Samuel, born in 1600, who **died s. p.** in **1676,** having married Ann, daughter of Edward Waterhouse, 3. Richard, 4. Robert, both died **young.** 5. Peter, who **died s. p.** December 24, 1677, 6. Susan, who married William Beilby, and Mary, **who married** Edward Parker, of Browsholme.

Abraham **the eldest** married Elizabeth, daughter **of Peter** Langdale, **of Santon,** in Yorkshire, by whom Langdale, **and** Ann, who **died** unmarried. Langdale Sunderland, esq; sold High Sunderland, **and** purchased Aketon, **near** Pontefract, **to** which he removed. He **was** captain **of a** troop of horse for king Charles **I.** and was **at** Marston-moor fight. He gave, in Oliver's time, £878 composition money for his estate. He died in 1698, and lies buried in Fetherstone church; his wife was Elizabeth, daughter of Thomas Thornhill, **of Fixby,** esq; by whom **1. Richard, and 2. Marmaduke,** who both **died young; 3.** Brian, **of Aketon, and** 4. Abraham. Brian married Ann, daughter of ...... Appleyard, **by whom 1.** Peter, 2. John, **3. Mary, 4.** Elizabeth, **and 5. Susanna.** Peter sold Aketon to Edmund Winn, esq; in 1714, having **married** Ann, daughter of George Thornhill, of Fixby, **by** whom Richard, Peter, **who** died young, Ann, **who married** ....Wordsworth, and Elizabeth, who **married John Wormald,** of Batley.

There **is a** pedegree in Dr. Johnson's MS. Collections, which sais, that Abraham Sunderland, of High Sunderland, married Judith, daughter of Thomas Oldfield, of High Oldfield, in Luddenden Dean, by **whom** Richard, Edward, and Bryan. Richard married, first, Mary, daughter of Robert Moor, of Midgley, by whom Abraham, and three daughters. Abraham married Susan, daughter of Ralph Waterhouse, by whom a son, who died young, therefore the estate descended to Richard Sunderland, of Coley. The above Richard, son of Abraham, married, secondly, Ann, daughter of John Rishworth, of Ridlesden, by whom Richard, of Coley, who married Mary, daughter of Alderman Saltonstall, of London, by whom Abraham, who had Langdale, who had Abraham and Bryan. Utrum horum mavis, accipe.

At the end of the third volume of Halifax Register is this Mem. "That I Henry Ramsden, Vicar of Halifax, did this "15th day of March, A.D. 1632, give unto Richard Sunder"land, of Coley, esq; in regard of his present weakness, "and indisposition of body, a licence to eat flesh during the "time of his sickness, as the laws of the land have in that "case provided." Signed Hen. Ramsden. The same licence was given to Abraham Sunderland, of High Sunderland, esq; March 18, 1632, and five other licences, to others.

Arms belonging to the above pedigree, for Sunderland, Parted per pale, or and azure, three lioncells passant counterchanged: Thus it is in a window at High Sunderland; but the coat is generally depicted with the lioncells guardant. For Langdale, Sable, a chevron between three estoils argent. For Saltonstall, Or, a bend between two eaglets displayed, sable. Thus it is at High Sunderland, and thus I saw it born in 1766, by Samuel Saltonstall, esq; Alderman of Pontefract; but Thoresby, p. 236, has given us a coat of this family in which the bend is gules.

THORNHILL AND FIXBY.

It has been said, that the chief habitation in Fixby gave name to a family which had a good estate here, till William de Toothill married the daughter and heiress of Thomas Fixby, of Fixby. How considerable this family was I cannot say, as I have met with no pedigree of them, nor coat of arms, nor title of knight belonging to any of them. I have copies of many deeds wherein the name occurs, between the years 1255, and 1312, as also deeds without date, but in the extent of all the lands within the soke of Wakefield, already said to have been made in 1314, there is no mention of this family at all, notwithstanding, two years before, John, son of Henry de Fekisby, had conveyed some lands here to Thomas, son of Robert de Fekisby, and amongst the witnesses was William, son of Roger de Fekisby. The deed was dated at Fekisby, in 1312. It is far from clear that all who are said in the above deeds to be de Fekisby were of the same family; it seems more probable that in some of them nothing more was meant than to distinguish the parties from others of the same name, by putting down the township where they lived; for this might be necessary to prevent their being confounded with those of neighboring towns, who might attend when deeds were read over at public meetings, in order to be sealed before a competent number of witnesses. This is certain, that there are so many of the same date, that the persons said therein to be de Fekisby, could not live together at one particular house, or family seat, and therefore the whole township must sometimes be meant, and consequently such as had no relationship to one another. At all events it is wrong, with Mr. Thoresby, and others, to call them by the name of Fixby of Fixby, for this never occurs in any deed, the reason of which may be, because the family became extinct before surnames were fully settled.

THORNHILL.

Pedegree of Thornhill, of Thornhill and Fixby. **1.** Askolf de Thornhill had, according to Thoresby, **p. 115**, **John**, who lived about 1165, and left no issue. 2. Jordan, who succeeded to the estate. 3. Thomas. He had also 4. Helie, to whom as at p. 87 of this book, this **Jordan**, son of Askolf, granted the fourth part of his inheritance in Sowerbyshire, and other lands in that neighbourhood, which fourth part the said Helie, and his heirs, were to hold of the said Jordan, and his heirs, as of the first begotten; it may therefore be questioned whether Thoresby (and **Hopkinson, from** whose collections Thoresby copied this account,) did not mistake in making John the elder brother of **Jordan.** It seems most likely that this estate in Sowerbyshire was divided equally amongst the four brothers, and that the three younger were to hold under the eldest, or first begotten.

R

(2.) Jordan de Thornhill, son of Askolf, is said, in Collins's Baronetage, vol. i. p. 157, to have had great possessions in Ovenden, Skircoat, Rishworth, Norland, Barkisland, &c. as by evidence, sans date, and that Hameline Plantaginet, earl Warren, owner of the manor of Wakefield, confirmed to him his inheritance in Sowerbyshire about 1169. This Jordan had

(3.) Jordan de Thornhill, who lived about 1189, and was father of

(4.) Sir John Thornhill, of Thornhill, knt. who (as I take it) was witness to a deed of Jordan de Scorchys, printed in the appendix to Stevens's Monasticon, p. 258, and dated 1248. He is also mentioned in a deed at Kirklees in 1240. He married Olive de la Maie, by whom, sir Richard Thornhill, of Thornhill, knt. and John Thornhill, who married Marion, daughter of Mr. Richard Heton, of Mirfield. This sir John (as already mentioned, p. 87) seems to be the person who granted to William earl Warren, that the said earl and his heirs should keep their wild beasts, deer and fowls, in the ground of the said John, in Sowerbyshire, for the consideration (inter alia) of five stags of grease, and five hinds in winter. A John de Thornhill occurs in 1275, and 1287, as by deeds of those dates. The above sir John had, by the said Olive,

(5.) Sir Richard, who lived in 1279, and is mentioned in Burton's Monasticon, p. 303. He married Maud, daughter of ...... by whom, sir John and Thomas, who had Richard.

(6.) Sir John was witness to a deed, along with his brother Thomas, in 1313; and the year following (8 Edw. II.) he granted to the prior and convent of Lewes, in Sussex, and their successors, licence to attach their mill-dam of Heptonstall on his soil in Wadsworth, over the water called Hebden, where it should please the said prior and his successors. He married Beatrice, daughter of ...... by whom sir Bryan, John, and Thomas, which last married Agnes, daughter of Henry Smith, by whom, Margery. Between this sir John and Simon de Thornhill are three sir Bryans in a pedigree at Fixby, the last of which lived 34 Edw. III. but I think it is of little authority.

(7.) Sir Bryan was one of the knights of the shire for Yorkshire, 29 and 31 Edw. III. He married, according to

Thoresby, Joan, but Collins, in the supplement to his Peerage, page 238, calls her Isabel, daughter of sir John Fitz Williams, knt. by whom, Simon, Thomas, Elizabeth, who married Henry Masters, of Kirklington, and another daughter, who married sir Henry Staunton, of Staunton, in Nottinghamshire. This sir Bryan, who stiled himself de Thornhill, knt. gave leave, by deed dated at Batley, in 1334, to Adam de Oxenhoppe, to assign over to William de Carlinghou, the chaplain, one messuage, two bovates of land, and thirty shillings rent, which the said Adam held of the said Bryan as parcel of the manor of Batley; and in consequence of this licence, and with the leave of the king, and William Melton, archbishop of York, the said Adam de Oxenhoppe founded a chantry in Batley church, for his soul, and the soul of Margery his wife, and for the souls of Robert his father, and Maud his mother, William de Copley, John, William, and Thomas, his brothers, and the souls of sir John de Thornhill, and Bryan his son, Thomas de Thornton, and Elen his wife, and John de Maningham, for all whose goods he had ill-gotten, and for all the faithful departed. He also founded a chantry in Bedal church, in Yorkshire, as appears from the following, taken out of a MS. in the herald's office. "Bedale p. canter: in ecclesia S. Gregorii "ibid. 6 mess. 36 acr. ter. & dim. 4 acr. prati & 3s. red. in "Gilling iuxta Richmond concedend. p. Brian de Thornhill "2 pars pat. 16 Edw. III. m. 34." This sir Bryan was knighted on or before the 15th of Edw. III. 1341, for in that year he granted by deed to Henry, son of William Soothill, and his heirs, two acres of waste ground in the township of Wadsworth, to be holden of him and his heirs, by the title of sir Bryan Thornhill.

(8.) Simon, eldest son of sir Bryan, married, according to **Thoresby, p.** 115, and also Burton, in his Monasticon, p. 436, Mary, daughter (and coheiress) of Edward Babthorp, of Bapthorp, esq; but in the British Museum is a MS. N°· 797, wherein is the following entry under the title of Ovenden : " 43 Edw. III. Simon de Thornhill, who held of the "lord in Stansfeld, Skircoat, Ovenden and Wadsworth, "certain tenements, and lands in soccage, died, and Eliza-"beth, daughter and heir, of the age of two years, and in "the custody of Elizabeth her mother, comes, and gives for "relief ten shillings." Which words are repeated under the title of Wadsworth, in the said MS. but without any date prefixed. Also under Skircoat with the above date, but without any name of the mother. She is called, however, by the name of Elizabeth, in some manuscript additions to Magna Britannia, by the late Mr. Lucas, of Leeds. By this Elizabeth, or Mary, **Simon** de Thornhill, esq; (called sir Simon in a MS. **pedegree at** Fixby, but query,) had Elizabeth, as above, **though in** the pedegree **at** Babthorpe, in Burton's Monasticon, it is said, through mistake, that Mary, wife of **Simon Thornhill**, esq; died without issue.

(9.) Elizabeth, married Henry Savile, esq; and in right **of** this match, the Saviles lived at Thornhill till the time of king Charles I. **when,** during the civil wars, Sir William Savile **having** fortified his house there, and made it a garrison **for the** king, **it** was **taken** and burnt, on which account the family thought proper **to remove to** Rufford, in Nottinghamshire.

Here was **an end of** the eldest branch **of** the Thornhills, **but the family** was continued by

(1.) Thomas Thornhill, **son of sir** Bryan above-named. **He was** living in 1374, **and married** Margaret, daughter of ...... Lacy, of Cromwelbothom, by whom,

(2.) Richard, who married Margaret, daughter and heiress **of** William Toothill, of Toothill, by Sibil, (or, as some say, **Maud,)** daughter and **heiress** of Thomas **de** Fekisby, in **whose** right he **was** seized **of** Fekisby and Toothill. She survived her husband, for by inquisition **at a** court held at Wakefield, **on** Friday next after the Feast of All Saints, 4 Hen. **IV.** it appeared, that Margaret, late wife of Richard Thornhill, **held** in **demesne,** the day she died, lands, &c. in Fekisby, **Rastrike,** Hipperholm, Linley, and Northowrom, with moor, **turbary,** and wood **of** Old Linley, with wards, marriages, reliefs, **and** escheats; after whose death, William Thornhill, son and heir of said Margaret, entered &c. This Margaret, according to Thoresby, married to her second husband, Richard de Liley, **but a** MS. pedegree at Fixby calls him Riley, by whom, Catharine, who married John Leventhorp, of Leventhorp, esq; by whom William, as by deed **in** 1439. The above Richard Thornhill had, by Margaret his wife, William, John, and Robert. John is called rector of Thornhill, in a deed, dated 1398, and rector of Thorsbye in another, dated 1411.

(3.) William Thornhill, of Fixby and Toothill, esq; seems to have been at age in 1393, for Margaret, formerly wife of Richard de Thornhill, in her pure widowhood, and William de Thornhill, her son, joined in a deed for exchange of lands, dated at Fekisby, on Monday next after the Feast of St. Martin in winter, 17 Ric. II. I find him also in a deed, dated 1438, called William Thornhill de Fixby, esq; about which time it is probable that he removed to Toothill; for in the year following, William Leventhorp, son of John, and Katharine his wife, of Sabrige, in Hertfordshire, quit-claimed to him their right in the manor of Toothill, by the name, &c. of William Thornhill, late of Fixby, esq; He married Barbara, daughter of William Hopton, of Swilling-ton, by whom, Brian Thornhill, of Fixby and Toothill, esq; Robert, Richard, John, Laurence, Isabel, and Joan.

(4.) Brian, married ...... daughter of ...... alderman of York, with whom he had lands at Akeham, near York. By her he had John, and a daughter named Dionis, who married William, or (according to a pedegree of the Stansfeld's in the British Museum, N° 2118, fol. 144,) Henry Stansfeld, of Stansfeld, esq;

(5.) John de Thornhill married Elizabeth, daughter of Robert Mirfield, esq; by whom, William. In an heraldical MS. in the British Museum, N° 1052, fol. 80, this John is said to have descended of a third brother of the house of Thornhill; but this is overthrown by the inquisition men-tioned below. Mr. Thoresby has made a greater mistake in copying Mr. Hopkinson too closely, for he has entirely left him out of the pedegree, making William to be the son of Brian, and to marry Elizabeth Mirfield; but against this I have met with the following authorities: 1st, In the British Museum is a MS. N° 803, containing (inter alia) the sub-stance of an inquisition taken at York, 2 Rich. III. (it is there said through mistake, 2 Rich. II.) in these words: " The jurors say that Brian de Thornhill died this year, and " William de Thornhill his cousin and next heir, viz. son of " John, son of the foresaid Brian, sixteen years of age, had " lands in Fekisby, gave the manor of Fekisby to certain " feoffees, 18 Edw. IV." 2dly, In a MS. pedegree of the family at Fixby is the following entry: " Yt appeareth by " covenants of marriage, that the eldest sonne of Brian was " called John, for John maryed Elizabeth, daughter of Ro.

" Mirfeyld."   3dly, To put the matter out of all dispute, I
have the copy of a deed, dated in 1459, wherein Brian
Thornhill. of Fixby, esq: and others, feoffees to the use of
the said Brian, give and confirm certain estates in Rastrick
to this John, in these words: " Johanni Thornhill, filio et
" heredi ipsius Briani, et Elizabethe uxori sue, filie Roberti
" Mirfeilde."   That John died in the life-time of his father,
appears from a deed dated in 1477, wherein Elizabeth
Thornhill, wife of John Thornhill, late of Fixby, deceased,
makes a grant of land with the consent of Brian Thornhill.

(6.) William Thornhill was sixteen years of age when his
grandfather Brian died. He married according to a MS.
pedegree at Fixby, Jen. daughter of John Ditton, esq; but
this must either be a mistake, or he had two wives, for in
the south quire of the parochial chapel of Eland was formerly a Latin inscription to this purpose, " Pray ye for the
" prosperity of William Thornhill, and Elizabeth his wife,
" and of John Thornhill, their son and heir, &c." which
suits no other part of the pedegree but this. By the said
Jen. or Elizabeth, the said William had

(7.) John Thornhill, of Fixby and Toothill, esq; who
married Jennet, daughter of Mr. Nicholas Savile, of Newhall, near Eland, by whom, John Thornhill, of Fixby and
Toothill, esq; Thomas, Richard, Brian, Alice, and Elen.
Alice married William Priestley, of Stainland. Elen married
Jo. Holdworth, of Selby, by whom, Isabel, who married
George Helliwell, of Stainland, and Agnes, who married
Thomas Clayton, of Clayton. In the register office for wills
at York, in the time of T. Woolsey, it appears, that the will
of one John Thornhill, of Fixby, was proved May 2, 1529,
which, by the date, must be this. He ordered his body to
be buried within the chapel of our Blessed Lady St. Mary of
Eland, in St. Nicholas quire, or in the chancel thereto
adjoining.

(8.) John, son of John, was collector of the tenths and
fifteenths, 37 Hen. VIII. in the wapontake of Staincliffe and
Ewcross, as appears by his quietus out of the Exchequer.
He married Elizabeth, daughter of Thomas Grice, of Sandal,
near Wakefield, esq; by whom, 1. Brian Thornhill, of Fixby,
esq; 2. John, 3. Nicholas, 4. Richard, 5. William, a clergyman, M. A. installed a prebendary of Worcester, in the
eighth stall, May 4, 1584, and died in 1626. For William

Thornhill, prebendary of Worcester, see Casley's Catalogue of Mss. in the King's Library, p. 38, where, after the mention of "Prophetæ xii minores & liber Job, cum Glossis," it is said, "In fine manu recenti scribitur ; Liber Ecclesiæ beatæ "Mariæ Wigorne, teste scriptore **Guil.** Thornhill, Eboracensi "ejusdem Ecclesiæ prebendario **octavo.** **Idem reperias** scriptum **in fine** codicis 2 F I, & 3 A VIII, & in aliis." 6. Katharine; 7. Elizabeth, who **married Roger** Reyne, of Smerley; 8. Cecily, who married **John Gledhill,** of Barkisland ; **and 9. Ann. See a** MS. in the **British Museum,** Nᵒ· 1052, fol. 80. **Mr.** Thoresby sais also, that **one of the daughters of John married** Richard Watkin; **another Jo.** Priestley, and **another ...... Longdale.**

(9.) Brian, **the eldest, married Jane,** daughter **of John** Kay, of Woodsome, esq ; **but died in** 1598, without issue, and was succeeded in the estate **by his** next brother, John.

(10.) John Thornhill, of Fixby and Toothill, esq ; (not Thornhill, as in Thoresby,) married Jennet, daughter of Mr. Edmund Marsh, by whom, John Thornhill, esq ; Thomas, and Jane, who married Mr. William Rookes, (not Rodes, as in Thoresby,) of Rhodes-hall, near Bradford.

(11.) John, eldest son of John, **was a justice of** peace in the time **of James I. and** dying without issue, was succeeded in the estate **by**

(12.) Thomas, **his** brother, who was also justice of peace 2 Charles I. and treasurer for lame soldiers, with sir Thomas Wentworth, of North Emsal. He married Ann, daughter **and heiress of** Thomas Triggot, esq ; of South Kirby, by **whom,** John Thornhill, of Fixby, esq ; Brian, who died **unmarried;** Elizabeth, who married Langdale Sunderland, **of** High Sunderland, esq ; and Margaret, who married **sir John** Armitage, of Kirklees, bart.

(13.) John, son of Thomas, was justice of peace in the West Riding, and major of the **foot** regiment for **Agbrig and Morley.** He married **to** his first wife Dorothy, daughter and heiress of George Collenbell, of Derbyshire, esq ; by whom, a daughter Ann, who died in her second year. To his second wife, Everild, eldest daughter and coheiress of sir George Wentworth, of Wooley, knt. to whom he was married Sept. 7, 1650 ; by her he had Everild, who married Thomas Horton, of Barkisland, **esq ;** Elizabeth, John, who both died young. George, who **succeeded** to the estate. Frances, who printed a Catechism; Thomas, and another married to one Grantham. It appears from the register at Hartshead, that the above Everild, daughter of John, was baptized Sept. 11, 1651. Elizabeth, John, and George, are also registered there. This John was buried in 1669.

(14.) George **Thornhill**, of Fixby, esq; who was baptized August 16, 1655, and died suddenly August 19, 1687, married Mary, daughter and heiress of Thomas Wyvill, of Constable Burton, in the North Riding of Yorkshire, esq; by whom Brian Thornhill, of Fixby, esq; Thomas, John, George, William, Michael, Marmaduke, Askolf, (these four last died young;) Everild, who married sir Arthur Caley, bart. Mary and Ann, who both died unmarried. Of these, George, the father, was a justice of peace, and died in the 32d year of his age, being buried at Eland. Brian died July 26, 1701, aged twenty-four. Thomas died May 18, 1751, aged seventy-one. John died Feb. 25, 1756, aged seventy-seven. George died Dec. 30, 1754, aged seventy-three.

(15.) Brian, eldest son of George, married 29 August, 1699, Frances, daughter and heiress of Joshua Wilson, esq; by whom one daughter, who died young. She survived, and married to her second husband, sir Francis Leicester, bart.

(16.) Thomas Thornhill, of Fixby, esq; second son of George, and brother of Brian, was high sheriff of Yorkshire in 1745, and died unmarried. At his death the estate came to his brother.

(17.) John Thornhill, esq; of Gray's-inn, barrister at law, who also died unmarried, leaving the estate to his brother,

(18.) George Thornhill, who lived at Diddington, in Huntingtonshire, and married Sarah, daughter of John Barne, esq; of Kirkby, in Lincolnshire, by whom, Mary, who married Miles Barne, esq; of Sotterley, in Suffolk. Thomas, the present owner of Fixby, who is unmarried. John, who died young. George, of Diddington aforesaid, now living, and unmarried. Sarah, who married sir John Blois, of Cockfield-hall, in Suffolk, bart. and Miles, who died young. Arms of Thornhill, of Fixby, gules, two bars gemells, and a chief, argent; but in sir William Fairfax's Book of Arms of Yorkshire, p. 347, in the British Museum, Brian Thornhill · is said to have borne gules, two bars, ermine.

TOOTHILL.

Near this hill lived a flourishing family who took the surname of Toothill, the first of whom was Richard de Toothill, who had Thomas, Matthew, and Richard. Matthew had lands in the graveship of Hipperholm, in 1314, and was witness to a deed in 1337. He had John, who lived at Silkeley, and who had Hugh, (a witness to deeds in 1438) and John de Toothill, which Hugh had Thomas.

Thomas, **eldest son of the** first Richard, **married Modesta ...... and is said in a** manuscript pedegree **belonging to Thomas Thornhill, esq.,** of Fixby, to have had **the lands of** Isabel, relict **of** John Scot, and her daughters. Now **it appears** from several deeds without date, but which, as the **witnesses** shew were wrote about 1287, that this Isabel and **her** daughters granted to one **John** de Toothill, certain lands **in** Rastrick, called Linlands ; **this** John, therefore is omitted in the above pedegree ; and it is **no** farther certain who he was, than that Thomas was his heir, and that he occurs in deeds before, and after the year 1300. Thomas, above named, had by Modesta, William, **Hugh,** John, and three daughters, the **eldest** of whom married......Sanesmer, (or Sansmer,) the **next** ...... de Hyle, and the youngest ...... de Fleming, of Bradley. Most of these descents from Thomas, are proved from deeds belonging to the above Mr. Thornhill, **in** which William, son of Anabil de Rastrick, and Elen, his **wife,** daughter of John Scot, with Alice **her** sister, grant **lands to** Thomas de Toothill, for his life, and after his **decease,** to William, son of the said Thomas ; and if William **died** without issue, to John, **son of** the said Thomas ; and **for default** of issue in the **said** John, to all his sisters. As **Hugh is** not mentioned here, he probably was dead. but his existence is proved from the copy of a deed in 1331, **wherein** Thomas de Tothill, grants to William de Tothill, **and** his heirs, remainder to John, brother of said William, remainder to Hugh, brother of said John, remainder **to the** sisters of said Hugh.

William de Toothill, son of Thomas, married Sibil, daughter and heiress of Thomas de Fekisby. Thoresby, p. 115, calls her Maud, but in a MS. in the British Museum, Nᵒ· 803, John de Schepley is said to have released to Sibil, late wife of William de Totehill, and her heirs, the claim he had in the lands which lately were Thomas de Totehill's, in Fekisby, dated 1340. By this Sibil, he had Margaret, his daughter and heiress, who being in her minority at the time of her father's death, was in the custody, or wardship, of earl Warren. This Margaret married Richard de Thornhill, in the time of Edward III. and carried all her father's estates into that family, where they still continue.

Arms of Toothill, of Toothill, were, Or, on a chevron sable, three crescents argent; though, as I remember, the field is argent, on a monument in Eland church.

TILLOTSON.

Haugh-End is for ever rendered famous, on account of that excellent Prelate Archbishop Tillotson, who drew his first breath here, and whose pedegree is as follows:

Nicholas de Tilston, Lord of Tilston, in Cheshire, had John de Tilston, who had Nicholas de Tilston, 9 Edward III. who had John Tilston, of Tilston, who married Johanna, third daughter of Thomas Danyers, of Bradley, in Cheshire, by whom Robert Tilston, of Tilston, who had Roger Tilston, of Tilston, esq; in the time of Henry V. who married Catharine, second daughter of sir John Leigh, of Baguly, in Cheshire, knt. by whom Thomas Tilston, of Tilston, esq; who married Elizabeth, daughter and heiress of Hugh Heath, of Huxley, in Cheshire, by whom, 1. Hugh Tilston, of Huxley, esq; (or, as one authority calls him, John,) and 2. Richard Tilston. This Richard married Maud, daughter of Richard Bostock, by whom, 1. Thomas, who had issue; 2. Richard, and others. This Richard Tilston was of Newport, in Shropshire, and, by an unaccountable mistake, Dr. Birch, in his Life of the Archbishop, calls him first Roger, and then Ralph. He married Elizabeth, second daughter of William Leighton, second son of sir Thomas Leighton, of Watlesborough, in Shropshire, knt. by whom, 1. Ralph Tilston, of Goldeston, 2. Tristram Tilston, 3. Thomas Tilston, of Woolliff, in the parish of Carlton, in Craven, 4. William. This Thomas changed his name from Tilston to Tillotson, as I was informed by the late Rev. Mr. Tillotson, of St. Paul's school, who heard his father say that the name was altered as above. The said Mr. Tillotson's father was told so by his grandfather, who was father to the Archbishop, and who might remember his grandfather Thomas, who altered it. This Thomas Tilston, alias Tillotson, had George Tillotson, who married Eleanor, daughter of Ellis Nutter, of Pendle-forest, in Lancashire, by whom Robert Tillotson, of Sowerby, who **was** buried at Sowerby, Feb. 22, 1682-3, aged ninety-one, having married Mary, daughter of Thomas Dobson, of the Stones, in Sowerby, by whom, 1. **Robert**, 2. **John**, the Archbishop, 3. Joshua, of London, and 4. Israel. John, the Archbishop, married Elizabeth, daughter of **Peter** French, D.D. Canon of Christ-church, Oxford, **by whom Mary, who** married James Chadwick, esq; **Joshua, the** younger **brother of** the Archbishop, had John, **who died in** the East-Indies, Elizabeth, who died in the East-Indies, **and** Robert, who was **M.A.** Fellow **of** Clare-hall, afterwards Rector of Elme cum Emneath, and who died s. **p. at** Cambridge, Nov. 12, 1738, aged sixty-two. Israel, the youngest, married Mary, daughter of Samuel Mawd, by whom Joshua and John. Joshua was of Sowerby, and died in 1747, having married Martha, daughter of James Stansfeld, of Sowerby, by whom, 1. John, 2. Joshua, M.A. Sur-master of St. Paul's school, **who** died in August, 1763. 3. Mary, 4. Elizabeth, 5. Hannah, and 6. Martha. John, second son **of** Israel, had Mary and Elizabeth; Mary married Richard Windsor, of London, by whom one son, and two daughters.

The arms of Tilston, or Tillotson, are now, or lately were, on the walls of Wookliff-chapel, viz. Azure, a bend cotised, **between** two garbs, or. Crest, a bear's head issuing out of a mural crown. Motto, Jactor, non mergor. These are the **arms of** Tilston, of Tilston, in Cheshire, **and** were also confirmed **by** William Flower, Norroy, Aug. 28, 1580, 22 Eliz. to Ralph Tilson, (or Tilston,) of Huxley, in Cheshire. **Seo** Guillim, p. 125.—Haugh-end belongs at present to **a Mr.** Lea, who has built a new house **near it.** He bears, Argent, a chevron ingrailed between two leopards heads sable. **For** crest, a bull's head cabossed, couped at the neck, **or.**

WADE.

But what makes this King Cross the most remarkable, is, that a little below it is an house where for some time resided the family of Wade, of which take the following account:

Camden sais, p. 907, that the Wades derive their pedigree from Wada, a Saxon duke, who gave battle to king Ardulph, at Whalley, in Lancashire, and died in 798, but of this I

have seen no proof, any more than I have that Armigel
Wade, esq; who was clerk of the council to Hen. VIII. and
Edw. VI. (as his son, sir William, was to queen Elizabeth,)
and one of the first discoverers of America, was, as Thoresby,
p. 155, has hinted, one of their ancestors. This Armigel
Wade died in 1568, and was buried at Hampstead, in
Middlesex, in the chancel belonging to which church, his
son, sir William, erected a stately monument for him; **his
arms thereon are, Azure, a saltire between four escallops,
or, which are entirely** different from those of Wade, of King
Cross, as will appear below.

John Wade, of the city of Coventry, **married, and had**
Henry Wade, of King Cross, who married Elizabeth,
daughter of ...... Ramsden, by whom, 1. Anthony Wade, of
King Cross. 2. William, of Ball-green, in Sowerby, near
Halifax. 3. Judith, who married Robert Dene, of Exley.
4. **Mary,** who **married** ... ... Longbothom, of Longbothom.
Anthony, the eldest, died about 1620, having married Judith
daughter of Thomas Foxcroft, of New Grange; married at
Leedes, Nov. 3, 1590: By her he had 1. Benjamin, 2. John,
3. **Elizabeth, who married** Cotton Horne, of Wakefield; 4.
Sarah, who married John Hargreave, of Leedes; 5. Judith,
who married, first, **Henry** Power, Clerk; secondly, Joseph
Stock; 6. Priscilla, who married William Favour, citizen of
London; 7. Susan, who married Dr. Jennison, of Newcastle
upon Tyne. Benjamin, esq; the eldest, was of New **Grange,**
married **Edith,** daughter **of John Shanne, of Leedes,** but died
s. p. in 1671, in the eighty-first year **of** his age. **John,
second son, lived at** King Cross, and died about 1645, having
married Mary, daughter of Anthony Waterhouse, of Woodhouse, **by** whom, 1. Benjamin, s. p. 2. Anthony; 3. John,
who married Hannah, daughter of John Milner, by whom,
Benjamin, of Leedes and Burley, 1712, who married Dorothy,
sister of William Jackson, by **whom,** Mary and Ann. 4.
Judith, daughter of John, by **Mary** Waterhouse, died un-
married. Anthony Wade, esq; **was** Mayor **of** Leedes 1676,
and died 14 Dec. 1683, in the forty-ninth year of his age,
having married Mary, daughter of John More, of Greenhead,
gent. by whom Benjamin Wade, of New Grange, in 1712,
Justice **of** Peace for the West-riding, who was buried May
19, 1716. He married Ann, eldest daughter of Walter
Calverley, of Calverley, esq; and sister to sir Walter Calverley,

of said place, bart. by whom, 1. Calverley, born Feb. 3, 1684, who died before his father, in 1710. 2. Benjamin, s. p. 3. Thompson, a captain, died s. p. at Brussels, Nov. 21, 1709. 4. Henry, **s. p.** 5. Walter; 6. Mary, who married ... ... Morehouse; 7. Ann, who married Thomas Grosvenor; and 8. Frances, who married Croft Preston, of Leedes, merchant. Walter, fifth son of Benjamin, was Mayor of Leedes in 1757, he married Beatrix, daughter of Benjamin Killingbeck, of Moor **Grange, alias Allerton Grange,** by whom Benjamin, **who died young, and Walter, of New Grange, who married Ann, daughter of Robert** Allenson, of Royd, **in Halifax parish, by whom** Walter, **who died** young, Robert, **who died young, Ann,** Benjamin, William, and Thompson.

The above pedegree was taken chiefly from one **drawn up by Mr.** Segar, who stiles him, " Si. Segar fil. filii. **a filio Gul.** " Segar Mil. Garterii Regis Armor." and by him extracted out **of the** last Visitation of **Yorkshire,** p. 174, and by him continued to the year **1715. The rest I have** added by information from the **family.** The original **is** lodged at New Grange.

For the arms of Wade, viz. Azure, within a bordure, argent on a bend or, two gillyflowers gules, slipt vert, we are refered in the **above transcript to** Guifts of arms among Vincent's (Rouge Croix) books **in** the College of Arms, No 76. p. **137.** Also to Hawley's Grants, H. 5. fol. **37 B,** in the said Office; the crest being granted then, viz. Jan. **16,** 34 Hen. VIII. unto John Wayd, (so the name was spelt,) of Coventry, by Thomas Hawley, Clarenceux King of Arms.

The arms belonging **to** the above pedegree are thus marshalled : Quarterly of six, first and last, Wade, (as above.) **2.** Argent, a chevron sable frette of the first, in chief a scythe blade azure, by the name of Thickness, of the **county of Stafford.** 3. Gules, a chevron between three foxes **heads erased,** or, by the name of Foxcroft. 4. Or, a pile ingrailed sable, by the name of Waterhouse, both of the county of **York.** 5. Sable, a swan rising, argent, **bequed and** membered, within a bordure ingrailed, or, by the name of More, com. Lanc. The whole atchievement mantled, gules, doubled argent. And for Crest, Over an helmet proper, on a wreath, or and azure, a griffin's head erased, quarterly of the same, charged with four goutes counterchanged, holding in his beque a gillyflower of **the** field. Motto, " Rien sans travail."

In Thoresby's Topography, p. 151, are the epitaphs of Benjamin Wade, and his son Anthony, both of New Grange, who were interred in Hedingley chapel, where, on a monument, as that writer informs us, are the arms of Moore, (or Mowre,) viz. Argent, a chevron sable, fretted of the first, in chief a scythe azure, which I apprehend to have been a mistake in the person who ordered it to be thus put up; for the arms of this family of Moore (as I take it) were, sable, a swan, &c. as above.

WATERHOUSE.

The most considerable family which hath been resident in the town of Halifax, I take to be that of Waterhouse, whose pedigree is thus put down in a MS. in the Harleian Collection in the British Museum, called the Visitation of Yorkshire, by Robert Glover, Somerset herald, in 1584. Nº. 1394.

Richard had John, who married Agnes, daughter of John Rishworth, of Coley-hall, by whom, Robert, who married Sibyl, daughter and coheiress of Richard Wilkinson, of Bradford, by whom, 1. John, of Halifax and Shipden. 2. George, of Hearthill, who married, and had issue. 3. Gregory, of Syddal, who married, and had issue. John, the eldest, married Jane, daughter and heiress of Thomas Bosseville, of Conysburge, by whom, 1. Robert, of Halifax, living in 1585, who married Jane, daughter of Thomas Waterton, of Walton-hall, by whom, Edmund. The second son of John was, 2. Thomas, of Braithwell, who married Dorothy, daughter and heir of Thomas Vincent, of Braithwell, by whom several children. The other children of John were, 3. Philip, M.A. and fellow of University college, Oxford. 4. Stephen, M.A. 5. John. 6. David. 7. Samuel. 8. Sarah. 9. Grace. 10. Susan. And 11. Mary. More of this family may be seen in the account of the Waterhouses, of Shipden, in Southouram.

After the Drakes, Shibden-hall became, by purchase, as I conceive, the property of the Waterhouses, of which family there is the following pedigree in a MS. late lord Oxford's, called "The Visitation of Yorkshire," by Robert Glover, Somerset Herald, as Marshal to Norroy king of arms in 1584 and 1585, No. 1394, p. 247.

Richard Waterhouse, had John, who married Agnes, daughter of John Rishworth, of Coley-hall, by whom Robert, who married Sibil, daughter and coheiress of Richard Wilkinson, of Bradford, by whom John, of Halifax and Shibden, George Harthill, and Gregory of Siddal. John the eldest married Jane, daughter and heiress of Thomas Bosseville, of Conysburgh, by whom, 1. Robert, of Halifax, living in 1585, who married Jane, daughter of Thomas Waterton, of Walton-hall, by whom Edmund. 2. Thomas, of Braithwell, who married Dorothy, daughter and heiress of Thomas Vincent, of Braithwell, by whom Vincent, Thomas, Mary, Penelope, and Edward. (Vincent, of Braithwell, bore, Argent, two bars and a canton gules, charged with a trefoil slipt, or.) 3. Philip, M.A. and Fellow of University College, Oxford; 4. Stephen, M.A., 5. John, 6. David, 7. Samuel, 8. Sarah, 9. Grace, 10. Susan, and 11. Mary.

George, of Harthill, married Euphemia, daughter of Richard Wilkinson, of Bradford, by whom Robert, John, Francis, Ann, Prudence, Isabel, and Elizabeth.

Gregory, of Syddal, married Margaret, daughter of Nicholas Tempest, of Bracewell, by whom Nicholas, Robert, Jonas, Lewis, Richard, Jeremy, Toby, Susan, Sibill, and Ann.

No arms are annexed to the above, but the coat which the family bore was, Or, a pile ingrailed, sable. "This (sais Guillim, p. 47.) "was the paternal coat armor of Dr. Edward "Waterhouse, a great lover of Antiquities and Heraldry. "This was the Gentleman that wrote the octavo, entitled, "The defence of Arms and Armory, and he that was "supposed to have a chief hand in Morgan's Sphere of "Gentry." At p. 430, he also tells us, that the same was born by Edward Waterhouse, of Greenford, in Middlesex, esq. Their crest, according to my old Folio MS. Collection of Arms, was, An eagle's leg standing, couped close by the body, and upon the top a dexter wing adjoining displayed sable. These are over the Workhouse door at Halifax, built by Nathaniel Waterhouse.

I cannot but observe, that I have the copy of a pedegree of this family of Waterhouse, which makes a Robert Waterhouse, of Shipden, to marry Sybil, daughter of Robert Savile, of Hullenedge, agreeable to what is said in the pedegree of Savile, of Hullenedge, already mentioned. Another calls him Robert, son of John, and makes him marry Sibil, daughter and heiress of Robert Savile, of Shipden, which, if true, would account for the manner in which the Waterhouses **came** by this estate. And so far is certain, that the arms of Waterhouse and Savile were repeatedly quartered on the old tomb belonging to the Waterhouses in Rokesby's chapel, in Halifax church, which shews a match between them, though the above pedegree takes no notice of it.

The Epitaph of **Jane**, wife of John Waterhouse above **named**, is in "Drake's Eboracum" thus: "Here lyeth **Jane**, "wife to **John Waterhouse**, of Shibden, **in** the county **of** "Yorke, esquier, who dyed the first day of May, 1592." She was buried **at** St. Michael's Belfrays, **York.**

Another Epitaph belonging to this family is cut in brass on a pillar in the chancel at Thornhill." "Here lyeth the " body of Phillip Waterhous, **3d sonne** of **John** Waterhouse, " **of** Halifax, esq; Maister of Artes, and sometimes Felow of " **University** Coll. Oxon. **He dyed** the 16th **of** Januari, "1614, the 57th yere **of his age.** Hellen, daughter of " Richard Lacye, of Cromewelbotome, esq; his beloved wife, " dedicated this monument to his memori." Arms of Water- **house** on this plate, Or, a pile engrailed, sable; motto, Veritas liberabit; alluding, perhaps, to John viii. 32. There are also the arms of Lacy and Cromwelbothom.

—::—

CHAUNTRIES.

In the Certificate **of** Robert, Archbishop of York, and others, authorized by commission to survey all chauntries, hospitals, colleges, free chapels, fraternities, brotherhoods, gilds, and salaries of stipendiary priests having perpetual salaries, &c. with the goods and ornaments to the same belonging, within the county of York, city of York, and Kingston upon Hull, with the yearly deductions going out of **the same,** it appears **(from an** old copy in my possession) that **in** Halifax Church were, 1. The Chauntry of the Trinity, founded by John Willoughby, yearly value four pounds. 2. Hunter's Chauntry, yearly value four pounds thirteen shillings. 3. The perpetual stipend or service at the rood altar there, yearly value three pounds eighteen shillings. 4. Brigg's Chauntry, yearly value four pounds, thirteen shillings, and four-pence. 5. Firth's Chauntry, yearly value three pounds, six shillings, and eight-pence. To which Stevens, in his Supplement, vol. i. p. 68, adds, " The service of the Morrow Mass in the said Church, yearly value fifty-one shillings and ten-pence ; " differing in nothing else from the above, except making the yearly value of Brigge's Chauntry four-pence less, and that of Firth's eight-pence. As to the first of these, I find that Thomas Willeby founded a Chauntry on the south side of Halifax Church, and to endow it, feoffed Sir John Nevil, Knt. Thomas Nevil, Esq; his son and heir, Thomas Willeby, his kinsman, and others, in lands in Priestley, in Hipperholm, to the yearly value of six marks, in June, 9 Henry VII. In Halifax Register is the following entry : " Dom. Thomas Gleydehyll Cantarist. " in Cantar. voc. Wylbe Chantre, ac quondam Vicarius de " Cunnesburghe, sepult. 12 Maii, 1541." The lands belonging to this Chauntry were granted by Edward VI. in the third year of his reign, to Thomas Gargrave, Knt. and William Adam, jun. In Willis's History of Mitred Abbies, vol. ii. p. 292. in a list of pensions paid in 1553, to incumbents of Chauntries, under Wylby's, one Richard Northend was then in possession thereof, but his annuity, on some account or other, is only put down at three pounds twelve shillings, which gives room to suspect that the rest are undervalued.

The following is the original institution of this Chauntry, taken from an old Manuscript in my possession, transcribed verbatim, though it appears to be a little incorrect :

" In nomine Patris, et Filii, et Spiritus Sancti, Amen. Universis sancte matris ecclesie filiis presentibus et futuris ad quorum notitiam hoc presens scriptum indentatum et tripertitum pervenerit, Johannes Willebye, parochie de Halifax, Salutem in Domino sempiternam, et rei geste memoriam perpetuam. Cum inter cetera reperationis humane remedia, Missarum solemnia precipua tutissimaq ; ab omnibus Christi cultoribus, condecet reputari, in quibus a malis retrahimur et confortamur in bono, ac ad virtutum et gratiarum proficimus incrementum ; ut igitur per frequentem missarum celebrationem presentium in ecclesia parochiali S. Johannis Baptiste de Halifax, in com. Ebor. divinus cultus augmentetur, et eo celebrior habeatur, quodq ; in eadem ecclesia, sive cemeterio ejusdem, corpus meum Deo

s

disponente recipiet sepulturam. Hinc est quod ego prefatus Johannes Willebye, per cartam meam indentatam et tripertitam, concessi, tradidi, feoffavi, et liberavi Johanni Nevil, Militi, Tho. Nevil, filio et heredi apparenti ipsius Johannis, Magistro Ricardo Symmes, Vicario Ecclesie parochialis de Halifax, Willo. Symmes, filio et heredi Willi. Symmes, Johanni Lacy, filio **et** heredi apparenti Tho. Lacye, Armigeri, Magistro Tho. Savile, Vicario de Brayvell, Willo. Rookes, Johanni Stanclif, Law. Bairstowe, Tho. Smith, Tho. Willeby, Robo. Otes, et Tho. Oldfeld, omnia messuagia, **terras, tenementa,** redditus, servicia, et reversiones mea, **cum pert. in Hipperh**ome, in parochia de Halifax predict. una cum omnibus aliis terris et tenementis **meis** in eadem parochia. Et similiter sursum reddidi in **manus** tenentium Manerii **de** Hipperhom, omnia **terras et tenementa** mea, **cum pert. in** Hipperhom **et alibi, in** parochia de Halifax predict. tent. **per** rotulam Curie, secundum consuetudinem ejusdem **manerii, ad** opus predictorum Johannis Nevil, etc. et heredum suorum, prout per predictam cartam indentatam, et similiter in predicta sursum redditione plenius liquet. Cujus quidem carte et similiter copie sursum redditionis predict. cum una parte hujus scripti indentati, una pars remanet cum predictis feoffatis meis, alia vero pars ejusdem Carte, cum copia predicta, et alia parte hujus scripti indentati, remanet cum Tho. Gledhill, primo Capellano per me prefatum Johannem Willeby ordinato administrandum in celebratione Missarum ad **altare S.** Trenitatis, in Ecclesia parochiali **de** Halifax, **ex parte australi** ejusdem Ecclesie, et successoribus suis, imperpetuum. Tertia vero pars ejusdem carte, simul cum copia **predicta,** et tertia parte hujus scripti indentati, remanet penes presatum Tho. Willeby, et heredes suos, imperpetuum. **Que** quidem omnia et singula predicta messuagia, terre, tenementa, redditus, servicia, **et** reversiones, cum suis pert. sunt annui valoris sex marcarum ultra reprisas. Hab. et ten. omnia et singula predicta terre, tenemente, redditus, servicia, et reversiones, **cum** suis pert. prefatis Johanni Nevil, &c. her. et assig. **suis** imperpetuum, modo et forma conditionibus subsequentibus, viz. quod iidem Johēs, &c. et assignati sui, et eorum quilibet, permittent Tho. Willobye, consanguineum meum, et heredes suos, tenere et occupare omnia et singula predicta messuagia, terras, et tenementa, cum suis pert. imperpetuum, in forma sequente, viz. iidem

Tho. et heredes sui annuatim reddendo et solvendo de eisdem tenementis Tho. Gleedhill, primo Capellano, per me prefatum Johēm Willebye ordinandum ad ministrandum et celebrandum cotidie Missas, et alia **divina** servitia, in dicta ecclesia parochiali S. Johis, Baptiste **de Halifax**, ad **altare** S. Trinitatis, **in** parte australi ejusdem Ecclesie, sex marcas, exeuntes de omnibus messuagiis, terris, et tenementis **supradictis, ad** duos anni terminos, viz. ad festum Pentecostes, **et S. Martini** in hyeme, **per** equales porciones **annuatim solvendas. Et si contingat** predictum redditum sex **marcarum aretro fore in parte,** vel in toto, per aliquod festum **quo** solvi debeat, per spacium dimidii unius anni, prefato **Tho.** Gleedhill, primo Capellano, vel successoribus suis, non solutum, ex tunc volo et ordino, quod predicti Johannes **Nevile,** etc. feoffati mei, intrabunt in omnia et **singula** predicta messuagia, terras, **et tenementa, cum** pert. imperpetuum, et predictum Thomam, **et** heredes suos, expellent **et** amovent, **et** dimittent eadem **tenementa** alicui alie persone, **sive** aliquibus personis, ad placitum et voluntatem suam, **ad** usum et magis proficuum predicti Capellani, et **successorum** suorum : Ita semper, quod permittent Capellanum Cantarie predicte, et successores suos, annuatim percipere **exitus et** proficua omnium et singulorum messuagiorum, terrarum, et tenementorum predictorum, ad sustentationem suam, circa Missas **et** alia divina obsequia et servitia supradicta ministrand. **et** celebrand. Proviso **semper,** quod si contingat Johannam, uxorem mei prefati **Johis** Willebye, **me** eundem Johēm supervisere, quod **tunc predicti** feoffati mei permittant eandem Johannam habere **et tenere** tertiam **partem omnium** terrarum et tenementorum predictorum, durante **vita** sua, pro et nomine dotis sue, vel quod permitterent ipsam percipere et recipere exitus **et** proficua de **tertia parte** omnium et singulorum eorundem messuagiorum, **terrarum, et** tenementorum predict. cum **pert.** durante **vita sua, et post** mortem suam, tunc predictus Capellanus, et **successores sui,** precipiant et habeant predictas sex marcas **de exitibus et** proficuis terrarum **et** tenementorum in forma predicta. Item **volo et ordino,** quod cum predicta Cantaria vacaverit, post mortem mei predicti Johis Willebye, quod predicti feoffati mei permittent unum idoneum Capellanum, **per predictum** Tho. Willebye, **seu** per heredes **ipsius**

Tho. juxta formam subscriptam ad dictum officium observandum, post quamlibet vacationem per imperpetuum nominandum, recipere sibi et successoribus suis imperpetuum, sex marcas, exeuntes de omnibus messuagiis, terris, **et** tenementis supradictis, ad duos anni terminos superius limitatos. Et ulterius ego prefatus Johēs Willebye **volo** et ordino, quod predictus Capellanus modernus, et omnes alii Capellani **per** prefatum Tho. **Willebye, et** heredes suos, **ac** omnes **alii** Capellani, quacunq; **forma** ad dictum officium temporibus futuris ordinand. **et** nominand. sint personaliter residentes infra dictam **ecclesiam** singulis diebus dicendo matutinas, horas canonicas, vesperas, et completorias, **ac** missam, quotidie ad altare prenominatum .... **in** honorem et laudem S. **Trinitatis,** et gloriosissime **Virginis** Marie, Matris **Domini** nostri Jesu Christi, **et beati Petri Apostoli,** et **omnium** Sanctorum, et quod **oret pro anima mei** prefati Johannis Willebye, **cum** ab hac **luce migravero, ac** pro animabus **uxorum** et omnium **liberorum meorum, necnon** parentum **et** omnium benefactorum meorum, **et omnium** fidelium defunctorum. **Et quod** idem Capellanus, **et omnes** alii poste **se,** qualibet **die lune** celebrent Missam de **requic** pro anima mei predicti Johannis, et animabus **supradictis.** Item volo **et** ordino, quod idem Capellanus modernus, et omnes alii Capellani post ipsum, ad missam suam quotidie ad primum lavatorium suum oret pro me in forma sequente : " Ye shall **praye** for the soule of John Willebye, founder of " this Chauntrye and Service, and for the soules of his two " wives, **his** children, his fader, his moder soules, and all his elders **soules ;"** et instanter ibidem **dicat** De profundis usq; ad **finem. Et quod dictus** Capellanus modernus, nec aliquis Capellanus **post** ipsum, non **se** absentent a dicto servicio et **ecclesia ultra** spatium unius mensis ad unum tempus, aut vicibus interpolatis numerandis singulis annis ad majus, quin sit cum licentia predicti **Tho.** vel heredum suorum, sub pœna amotionis ab officio suo, revocationis, et adnullationis concessionis **suo** ejusdem officii per presens **factum.** Item volo et ordino, quod predictus Tho. Gledhill, **Capellanus** modernus, et omnes alii Capellani, post mortem, sessionem, **seu** amotionem ejusdem Tho. Gledhill, temporibus futuris nominandi, singulis diebus dominicis et festivis personaliter sint presentes in choro ejusdem Ecclesie temporibus matutinarum missarum et vesperarum, suis suppeliciis induti, ut legant et psallent, prout Vicario ejusdem Ecclesie pro tempore existenti decenter et congrue videbitur expedire, ut in constitutionibus Ecclesie Metropolitane proinde constitutis plenius liquet. Et predictus Capellanus modernus, et omnes alii Capellani, post mortem, sessionem, seu remotionem dicti Capellani ab officio suo, temporibus futuris nominandi, singulis annis facient anniversaria predicti Johis Willebye, illa die qua contingat eundem Johannem obire. Item volo et ordino, quod predictus Capellanus modernus, **et omnes** alii Capellani post ipsum, ad predictum officium **aliquo** modo ordinandi et nominandi, omnia res, libros, jocalia, **et** ornamenta dicto officio pertinentia, non alienabunt, **impignorabunt**, nec elongabunt. Preterea volo et ordino, quod predictus Tho. Gledhill, Capellanus modernus, aut aliquis alius Capellanus post ipsum, ad dictum officium temporibus futuris quoquomodo nominandus, aliqua bona, res, jocalia **ad** officium predictum pertinentes, consumpserit, delapidaverit, non sufficienter reparaverit, et conservaverit, seu si de incontinentia, furto, rapina, perjurio, seu aliquo alio notabili et famoso crimine convictus fuerit, vel si suspensionem, vel irregularitatem, **seu** alicujus membri mutelationem, quibus ab executione ordinis Sacerdotalis, et missarum celebrationem per imperpetuum impediatur, ex reatu suo proprio incurrat aut quod officio predicto deservire, seu ibidem moram trahere non poterit, extunc a dicto officio tanquam inhabilis per ipsum prefatum Tho. Willebye, aut **per** heredes suos, seu alios ad hoc deputatos, amotus sit penitus **et** privatus. Et ulterius volo et ordino, quod quoties contingat predictum Tho. Willebye, et heredes suos, **seu** aliorum aliquem in hujusmodi nominationis et ordinationis negotio, cum officium ministrationis in celebratione missarum ad altare predictum, **in** forma predicta, sessaverit, nec legentes, seu remissos existere. ita quod infra quadraginta dies tempore sessionis officii predicti continue numerandos nullum idoneum Capellanum ad officium predictum exercendum, ut permittitur per literas suas patentes sigillatos, ordinet seu nominent, si notitiam inde habuerunt, totiens incontinenter vigore presentis ordinationis et voluntatis mee, absq; aliquo hujusmodi .... aut ministerio jure nominand. et ordinand. ea vice sicut al. consimiles casus defectus, vel negligentia predicti Tho. Willebye, et heredum suorum a se obtulerit, et non aliter ad Vicariam

Ecclesie parochialis de Halifax, qui pro tempore suerit, hoc pacto et hac lege devolvatur, ut ipse Vicarius infra quadraginta dies post habitam ei notitiam de defectu, sive necligentia hujusmodi predicti Tho. Willeby, aut heredum suorum, aut alicujus eorundem consimiliter numerandos, habilem et idoneum Capellanum ad dictum officium ordinet **et nominet, in forma** predicta. Quod **si** contingat negligentem vel remissum in hac parte fore, **et** nequaquam infra quadraginta dies unum habilem et idoneum Capellanum **ad** officium predictum **nominare** et ordinare, extunc transacto **quadraginta dierum** spatio jus plene providendi, ordinandi, **et nominandi habilem et idoneum** Capellanum **ad** officium predictum, ad predictos feoffatos, seu ad **majorem** partem **eorundem, si inde** inter eos plane concordare nequiverint, **devolvet et pertineat** ut ipsi secundum Deum et **sanam conscientiam** suam de idoneo Capellano **ad predictum** officium frequentandum in forma superius **ordinata** provideant. Et insuper ego prefatus Johannes Willebye volo et ordino, quod quotiens contingat predict. Johēm Nevile, **etc.** feoffatos meos, in messuagiis, **terris, et tenementis** supradictis, **ab** hac luce migrare et obire, ita quod sint nisi quatuor persone viventes ad minus, totiens illi qui socios suos superavixerint, facient statum duobus senioribus et discretis Presbyteris in **parochia de** Halifax, vel prope eandem parochiam residenti**bus,** in omnibus messuagiis, &c. cum pert. ita quod iidem Presbyteri instanter et incontinenter post dictum statum eis factum refeoffabunt predictis quatuor feoffatis superviventi**bus, una cum novem** aliis personis de nobilioribus, valencioribus, dignioribus, et discretioribus residentibus infra totam parochiam **de** Halifax predict. ita quod **sint** in toto **ad** numerum tredecem personarum, ad intentionem **et** effectum ut hec mea voluntas robur perpetue firmitatis obtineat et perquireat. **Ita volo et** ordino, **quod** predictus Capellanus modernus, et omnes alii Capellani, **ad** dictum officium imposterum nominandi **et** ordinandi, **in** primo introitu suo ad dictum officium, antequam aliqua proficua dictarum sex **marcarum** recipient, Sacramentum prestabunt corporale coram **Vicario** Ecclesie de Halifax antedict. qui pro tempore fuerit, quod ipsi omnia et singula premissa eisdem Capellanis et successoribus suis qualitercunq; incumbentia bene et inviolabiliter observabunt, custodiant, et perimplebunt. Ei vero qui premissa inviolata illabefactaq; servaverit, pax sit perpetua, salus eterna, scelerum venia, et in bonis actibus perseverantia diuturna. Et qui eadem infringere presumpserit, sit anathema Christi, excommunicatio omnium Sanctorum, et dies ejus sint pauci, nisi citius duxeret penitentiam. In quorum omnium et singulorum testimonium omnibus et singulis partibus predictis, ego prefatus Johannes Willeby, Sigillum apposui. Datum, &c. per me Johannem Willeby, decimo die Junii, anno Henrici septimi nono."

As for Hunter's Chauntry, I know nothing more about it, than that in a list of the compositions for tythes paid in Halifax parish is the following entry: " John Paslew, " Chaunter of the Chauntry called Hunter's, for five closes " in Halifax and Skircoat, near Shasike, to the said Chauntry " belonging, 18d." The burial of this John Paslew is thus entered in the parish register at Halifax: " Doms. Johēs Paslew, Cant. apud Halifax sepult. March 9th, 1538."

The perpetual stipend, or service, at the rood altar, is thus described in the Certificate of the Archbishop of York and others, dated 14 Feb. in the secounde yeare of his Grace's reygne, (Edw. VI.) Hallifaxe Parrysh. "The Rode Obite, or perpetual stypend of a Preyst in the parish church there—John Waterhouse, incombent, 47 yeares of age, hath nothing else to live upon but the profitts of the said Chauntry. Goods, ornaments, and plate belonging to the said service, as appyth by the inventorye. Goods, £2. Plate, £2. The yerely value of the freehold land belonging to the said service, as particularlie appyth by the rentall, 5s. Coppiehold by yeare, 77s. whereof resolutes, viz. of the freehold by yeare, 4s. resolutes of the coppiehold by yeare, 4s. So remains clere of the coppiehold yearly, 73s. and to the King's Majestie clere of freehold yerely, 12d."

This, I apprehend, was founded to celebrate the death of Christ, as rode, or rood, signifies a Cross, and obit the time when any one died.

In the Harleian Manuscripts in the British Museum, Nᵒ. 797, under Halifax, it is said, that in 1532, (24 Hen. VIII.) William Brigg founded a Chantry in the north part of Halifax church, adjoining to Rokeby's chapel, which is all I know relating to this foundation.

I have seen mention made of the Chaplain who celebrated or said divine service at the altar of St. George, in the parish

church of St. John Baptist, of Halifax, but which of the
above Chantries it belonged to I cannot say.

—::—

ACCOUNT OF LANDS, &c., IN HALIFAX PARISH,
BELONGING TO RELIGIOUS HOUSES.

THERE never was either abbey, monastery, or nunnery
in the whole parish of Halifax, but lands in different
parts thereof belonged to religious houses in other places, as
appears from the following.

FOUNTAINS ABBEY.

Burton, in his Monasticon Eboracence, p. 148, sais, "That
" Abulay-grange, in the chapelry of Eland, in Halifax parish,
" belonged to the Abbey of Fountains; and that on July 12,
" 1478, 18 Edward IV. Thomas de Swinton, the abbot
" thereof, granted it to John Nesfield, prior of Nostel, for
" life." This Abulay I take to be what is now called
Aneley, contracted from Avenley; and in the Ledger Book
of Fountains, under the title of Yeland, it was said, "That
" by an indenture, 14 Edward IV. the Grange of Ainley, in
" the chapelry of Eland, was divided equally between John
" Savile, of Hullenedge, esq; and William, son of Robert
" Wilkinson, by Sir John Savile, knt. and Thomas Savile,
" esq; his son." This, I apprehend, is mentioned again by
Burton, at p. 152, under the name of Awndelay, when he
sais, "Roger de Thornhill gave all his land and wood in this
" town, he also gave eight acres, called, Eleis juxta aquam,
" with lands in Kildeker and Pihel, and common pasture in
" Eland, with necessary wood for their own burning and
" building; which were confirmed to them by Gilbert de
" Whetelay, and Alicia his wife, relict of Roger de Thornton.
" —William de Horbury gave what he had here, except the
" chapel.—Thomas, son of William de Horbury, confirmed
" what Roger de Thornton gave, granting also a free passage
" through his fee every where." At p. 163, the same author

informs us, " That Hugh de Eland gave pasture (to Fountains-
" abbey) for two hundred sheep in Eccleslay and in Uncrum,
" and also gave Godwin Pighil."   And under Eland, " That
" Henry de Heland confirmed all that Gamel, son of Ulchel,
" gave—that Thomas, son of William de Horbury, gave his
" land there, lying in Sumerode, with another acre of land
" —that Hugh de Eland gave ten **acres** here **in** Blacklaa,
" lying between Haghebrock and Horsecroft, **in Amen**delay-
" flat—that Henry **de** Horbiri gave one oxgang here in
" Braiothik—that Lete, prioress of Kirkless, gave firmagium
" **of their** pool, upon her ground, for the mill upon Kelder—
" **that** John de Fekesby gave fourteen acres of land here."
And at p. 164, " That Hugh de Eland gave all his land, viz.
" **five** acres and one half here, which Yvo Talvaz held of him,
" lying between the essart **of** Henry de Prikestrike, and
" Marfaldecloh, and between **Gilder** and Sidgate ; also that
" John de Fekesby, son of Ivo Talvaz de Fekesby, gave one
" oxgang, ten acres, and two **essarts of** land in Fixby, for
" the use of those who came to the **Gates,** which was confirmed
" by Ivo Talvaz ; **and** Roger, son of Jordan de Stanley, con-
" firmed **what** they held of his fee in Fixby."

This, **I** apprehend, **is** all which has yet been made public
concerning the possessions of the monks of Fountains-abbey,
within the parish of Halifax.   I have farther observed, with
regard to the gift of Roger de Thornton, that in one of the
Harleian MSS. N° 797, under the title of Eland, it is said,
" **That in** Hilary term, 32 Edward I. it **was** commanded by
the Sheriff that he should cause the abbot of Fountains to
acknowledge by what services he held **his** tenements **of**
Thomas de Thornton, in Eland, which **services** the **said**
Thomas **had** granted to Hugh de Eland, by fine, &c.   **And**
the said abbot said, **that he held one** carucate of **land, and**
twenty acres of wood, **with the appurtenances, in the** aforesaid village **of** Eland, by **fealty, and the service** of twelve-
pence by the year **for** all service, **by a certain charter** of one
Roger de Thornton, ancestor of **the foresaid** Thomas."   This
charter I have not seen, **but** the following **is in** Hopkinson,
vol. i. **fol. 80,** and in a **very** old M.S. in **my own** possession,
fol. 330.

" Omnibus sancte matris Ecclesie filiis, presentibus et
futuris, Alicia, quondam uxor Rogeri de Thornton, salutem.
Sciatis me in viduitate **et** ligittima potestate mea concessisse,

relaxasse, et presenti carta mea quietum clamasse, de me et heredibus meis imperpetuum, Deo et Monachis Ecclesie sancte Marie de Fontibus, totum jus et clameum quod unquam habui, aut habere potui, nomine dotis, jure hereditario, aut aliquo modo alio, in omnibus terris, possessionibus, redditibus, et rebus aliis, que **fuerunt** quondam Rogeri de Thorneton, **viri** mei, in villa et territorio de Eland. Tenend. et habend. **dictis** Monachis **in** perpetuam eleemosinam, soluta, **libera,** et quieta, **sicut carta** predicti Rogeri, viri mei, quam **dicti** Monachi haben**t, inde** confecta testatur.—Ita quod ego, **vel** heredes mei, vel **aliquis** alius per nos **clameum** vel calumpniam versus **predictos** Monachos de predictis omnibus movere **non** poterimus imperpetuum. In huius **rei** testimonium presenti scripto Sigillum meum apposui. **Dat.** apud Ebor. die Mercurii proxime post festum Sancte Trenitatis, Itinerantibus Justiciariis Domini Regis, Domino **Abbate de** Burgo Sancti Petri, Rogero de Thurkelby, Petro de Percye, **Nicholao** de Handelon, Johanne de Wywill, **A°** R. R. Henr. **quadrag**essimo primo. Hiis testibus Johanne de Eland, **Matheo de** Shepley, Ada de Whitewodd, Johanne de Lascy, **Johanne** Clerico, Fratre ejus, Michaele Talvas Willielmo de Alnaldlay, Roberto de Povel, et aliis."

In Hopkinson's MSS. vol. I. fol. 15, is the following entry:

" Donatio et confirmatio Monasterio de Fontibus, a Willielmo **de** Horbury, per cartam suam **factam** Abbati et Monachis, de omnibus edificiis et **curt.** et gardin. que fuerunt Henrici **de Eland ad** Awnleiam, in puram et perpet. Eleemos. Etiam donatio, et concessio, et confirmatio Tho. de **Horbury, per cartam** suam factam eisdem Abbati et Monachis, **de omni** quod habuit in Swinrode, **in** terra de Eland, **in pur. et** perpet. Eleemos. Donatio etiam et confirm. **Thome** fil. Will. de **Horbury,** per cart. **suam** fact. predict. **Abb.** et **Mon.** de tota **terra** et de **bosco que** ad ipsum, vel **heredes** suos pertinebant, in Aunley, **in** pur. et perpet. Eleemos. Donatio etiam que idem Tho. per **cart.** suam fecit eisdem **Abb.** et Mon. de omni quod ad ipsum pertinebat in Kildercar, **et in** Pighill, cum toto prato quod iidem Abbas et Monachi **prius** habuerunt de Patre suo in **Eland, et de** comuni pastura **totius** Ville **de** Eland, **nec non** de **libero** transitu per feodum suum ubiq ; extra bladum et pratum **ad** ipsos, et ad omnes res suas, et de omnibus necessariis in boscis ejusd. Ville ardend. et edificand. in

predict. ter. de Annundeley, in pur. et perpet. Eleemos.
Donatio insuper que idem Tho. per cartam suam fecit predict. Abbat. et Mon. de octo acris terre in territoria de
Eland, in loco vocato Eleys, cum om. pert. suis in puram
et perpet. Eleemos."

In Hopkinson's MSS. vol. I. fol. 79, and in the old MS. in
my own possession, fol. 330, are the following:

"Omnibus sancte Ecclesie filiis, presentibus et futuris,
Thomas, filius Willielmi de Horbery, salutem. Sciatis me
dedisse, concessisse, et presenti carta mea confirmasse, Deo
et Monachis Ecclesie Sancte Marie de Fontibus, homagium
et totum servicium Helye, filii Richardi de Wlfrunwell, et
heredum suorum, que idem Helias, et heredes sui, mihi et
heredibus meis facere debebant, pro tota terra de Wlfrunwell,
[now called Wormald] quam Johannes, filius Ivonis de
Fekisbye, eisdem Monachis contulit in Eleemosinam. Tenend. et habend. in perpetuam eleemosinam, solutam, liberam
et quietam ab omni servitio, cum omnibus libertatibus et
easiamentis ad predictam terram, infra villam de Rishword
et extra pertinentibus. Et idem Monachi solvent mihi et
her. meis xviii denarios ad festum Sancti Oswaldi annuatim,
pro omni servitio et omni re ad eandem terram pertinente.
Dedi etiam eisdem Monachis et confirmavi totum essartum
de Prikescirckerode, cum pert. suis, quod est in divisis de
Eland, quod jacet inter Biscopegate et Gildeker: Reddendo
inde mihi et her. meis annuatim duodecim denarios, ad idem
festum Sancti Oswaldi, pro omni servicio. Et ego et heredes
mei omnia prenominata, cum omnibus pert. suis, eisdem
Monachis contra omnes warrantizabimus, acquietabimus, et
defendemus imperpetuum. Hiis testibus, Johanne de Playz,
tunc Seneschallo Comitis Warren, Hugone de Eland, Johanne
de Heton, Johanne de Thornhill, Hen. de Dicton, Hugone
de Rastrych, Johanne de Wittelay, Rico de Dicton, et aliis.

"Omnibus Sancte Ecclesie filiis, presentibus et futuris,
Thomas de Horbyre salutem. Sciatis me dedisse, et quietum
clamasse, de me et heredibus meis, Deo et Monachis Ecclesie
Sancte Marie de Fontibus, redditum trium solidorum, scilicet
decem et octo denarios quos solebam annuatim recipere de
Elia de Rissewarde, pro tenemento quod idem Elias de me
tenuit, scilicet Wulrumwell; et decem et octo denarios quos
predicti Monachi mihi annuatim reddere solebant, scilicet
sex denarios pro terra Ade Purcell, et duodecim denarios pro

Prickstrickroode. Preterea dedi eisdem Monachis redditum
duodecim denariorum in parte mea Molendini de Eland, re-
cipiendum annuatim a Preposito meo, et heredum nostrorum,
vel ab aliis quibuscunq ; modo assignavimus partem predicti
Molendini. Tenend. et habend. in puram et perpetuam
Eleemosinam, solutam, liberam, et quietam ab omni seculari
servicio et exactione, sine aliquo retinemento mei, vel heredum meorum. Et ego et heredes mei predictum redditum
quatuor solidorum prefatis Monachis warrantizabimus et
defendemus contra omnes imperpetuum. Hiis testibus
Johanne Flandrensi, Johanne Thornill, Johanne de Heton,
Johanne Sotyl, Jo. de Eland, Hen. de Dickton, Hugone de
Rastrick, Radulpho Tagium, et aliis."

In my old MS. above-mentioned, p. 331, is also the
following :

"Sciant omnes, tam presentes quam futuri, quod ego
Henricus de Helanda dedi et concessi, et hac presenti carta
confirmavi, Deo et Sancte Marie et Monachis de Fontibus,
pro salute anime mee et uxoris mee, heredum, et omnium,
antecessorum meorum, imperpetuum, totam terram et pasturam, cum omnibus aisiamentis, q. tenui de Gamielo filio
Ulchel, et her. suis, per divisas et metas que continentur in
carta quam habui de predicto Gamello. Tenend. de me et
her. meis in puram et perpetuam eleemosinam, liberam et
quietam ab omni terreno servicio et seculari exactione. Et
ego et her. mei warrantizabimus et acquietabimus et defendemus predictam terram prenominatis Monachis. Hiis testibus, Gilberto, Capellano de Almonburye, Rob. Parsona de
Sandala, Rado de Winnvilla, Hen. filio Roberti de Liversege."

At p. 330 of my old MS. is the following deed, and also in
Hopkinson :

"Omnibus sancte Ecclesie filiis, presentibus et futuris,
Johannes de Fekisbyc salutem. Sciatis me dedisse, concessisse, et presenti carta mea confirmasse, Deo et Monachis
Ecclesie sancte Marie de Fontibus, in liberam eleemosinam,
tresdecem acras terre in territorio de Eland, que jacent inter
essartum Henrici Prykscirc et Maresaldecloh, et inter Gilde-
kier et Siddegate, Tenend. et habend. cum omnibus pert.
libertatibus, et aisiamentis suis, infra prefatam villam de
Eland et extra, libere, quiete, et pacifice. Reddendo inde
annuatim Hugoni de Eland, et her. suis, tres solidos argenti

ad festum S. Oswaldi, pro omni servicio et exactione. Et ego et her. mei totam prefatam terram, cum pert. et aisiamentis suis, prefatis Monachis contra omnes warrantizabimus imperpet. Hiis testibus Tho. de Horberye, Johe de Heton, Hen. de Hyperum, Hen. de Vuerum, Hen. de Digton, et aliis."

At folio **331 is this,** and also in Hopkinson :

" Sciant **omnes** presentes et futuri, quod **ego Hugo de** Eland dedi, concessi, et presenti carta mea **confirmavi, Deo** et Monachis **Ecclesie sancte** Marie de Fontibus, **in puram et** **perpetuam Eleemosinam,** pasturam ad **ducentas oves in** **territorio de Vuerum et de** Eccleslay ubiq ; **extra pratum et** bladum. Dedi etiam eis totam terram quam **habui in God-** **win**pighill, sicut sepe includitur, sine retenemento, **ad** Berchariam inde faciendam, **et** sufficientem **materiam ad** eandem Berchariam edificandam, **et** quociens **necesse fuerit** reparandam de Bosco de Vuerum **et** de Eccleslay. **Et pre-** terea totum pratum quod ipsi quon**dam** habuerunt de me ad terminum, aut aliqualiter habere poterunt, apud Eland, de Asseranto meo, in Gildekar (Bosco quem Monachi inde essartari **fecerint mihi** et her. meis remanente.) Pro **hac** autem libera **mea** donatione, dicti Monachi **concesserunt** mihi, et her. meis, **fimum** provenientem **ex ovibus, sive** cum jacuerint in Bercharia, **sive extra; et nos** [so in original] inveniens eis singulis annis decem carectas littorie. Ita, **viz.** quod Monachi eandam littoriam facient falcari **et attorizari,** et **nos** illam ad prenominatam Berchariam Monachorum **per** carectas **nostras,** vel **hominum** nostrorum **[so in original]** faciens carriari. Inveniens etiam eisdem **Monachis suf-** ficientem materiam ad **faldas** faciend. dictis **ducentis ovibus.** —Sciendum etiam, **quod si** prenominati Monachi **numerum** **dictarum** ducentarum **ovium** aliquando **excesserint, nihil a** **me, vel her.** meis, inde [so in original] **causabuntur, si eas** que superfuerunt **ad** summonitionem **nostram** amoverint. Similiter etiam **non** causabunter **si aliquo tempore** predictum numerum **in** dicta pastura **non habuerint. Et** ego et her. mei omnia prænominata **prefatis Monachis** sustinebimus, warrantizabimus, **et defendemus contra** omnes imperpetuum. Hiis **testibus** Johanne Flandrensi, **Jo.** Tilly, Rogero de Thorneton, **Jo.** de Heton, Roberto de Flaynesburgh, Henrico **de Sayvill, et aliis."**

In a deed at Fixby, dated in 1255, being an Agreement between John, son of Hen. de Fekisby, and Hugh, son of Thomas, of the same place, concerning Hannerode, in Rastrick, this is said to lie, "inter fossam Abbatis de Fontibus ex parte aquilonis, et terram Elene et Ysabele ex parte australi." And in another Deed, at the same place, without date, is mention made of the " Boscus Fratrum de Fontibus in Rastrick." This Wood is also mentioned in another Deed at Fixby, dated 5 Edw. III. by the name of " Boscus Monachorum."

St. JOHN of JERUSALEM in ENGLAND.

In the MS. collections which I purchased of the executors of the late Mr. Bayliffe, of Leeds, I found the following:

" Curia Prioris Hospitalis S. Joh. de Jerusalem in Anglia, tent. apud Batley, die Jovis prox. ante fest. Ascens. A° Regis Edw. tertii 41°. Joh. de Barksey venit hic in Curiam, et ingressus est in omnibus terris et tenementis que vocantur Cloghhouses, cum pert. in Barkisland, que Joh. de Clay quondam tenuit. Tenend. sibi et her. suis secundum consuetudinem Manerii, reddend, annuatim duodecim denarios, et duos adventus [attendance twice a year] ad Curiam de Batley. Finis Domino pro ingressu 6s. 8d." Called Cloughhouse to this day.

In the old MS. in my own possession, fol. 332, is this:

" Hec Indentura testatur, quod cum Henricus Milner, de parochia de Halifax, teneat de religiosis viris, Fratre Johanne Radington, Priore, et fratribus Hospitalis Sancti Johannis Jerusalem, unum messuagium et decem acras terre, prati et bosci, cum pert. suis, jacent. in Shepiden, in villa de Northouram, per certum redditum sex denariorum, reddendo annuatim Preceptori de Newland, qui pro tempore fuerit, incessu suo vel decessu, et cujuslibet heredum suorum, nomine obitus, sex solidos et octo denarios tantum. Ad cujus summe solutionem incessu et decessu, dictus Henricus, et cujuslibet heredum suorum, fideliter, ut predicitur, faciendum ; idem Henricus obligat se, heredes et executores suos, ac tenementa predicta, omnia bona sua et catalla districtioni dictorum Prioris et Fratrum, et successorum suorum, per presentes. In cujus rei testimonium, Sigillum dictorum Prioris et Fratrum commune, et Sigillum dicti Henrici, hiis Indentatis alternatim sunt appensa. Dat. apud Clerkonwell,

in celebracione Capituli dictorum Prioris et Fratrum, die
Martis prox. ante festum Sancti Barnabe Apostoli, A° R. R.
Ricardi secundi post conquestum undecimo."

In the same **MS. fol.** 837, is the following :

" Sciant omnes presentes et futuri, quod ego Johannes,
filius Henrici de Barkesland, dedı et concessi, et hac presenti
carta mea confirmavi, Domino et Beate Marie et Fratribus
Milit. Templi **Salomonis** de Jerusalem, in liberam, puram,
et perpetuam elimosinam, totam donationem Johannis filii
Gilberti **de eadem, viz.** de tota terra sua quam tenuit **de me,**
et de **feodo** meo, infra divisas de Barkeslande et **de Bothem-
laye,** cum omnibus pert. et libertatibus predicte **terre pertinentibus,** sine retenemento, adeo liberam et solutam **et quietam,** melius, liberius, et quietius, prout aliqua Eleemosina
aliquibus viris religiosis **potest** confirmari. Predictus **vero**
Johannes, et heredes **sui, totam donationem dicti Johannis
filii** Gilberti predictis **Fratribus contra Thomam de** Horburye,
et Rogerum de Thornton, **et** heredes **suos,** per tres solidos
argenti, **sibi et** heredibus suis annuatim persolvendos, pro
omni **servicio et** exactione seculari, warrantizabunt, et contra **omnes homines** et feminas defendent et acquietabunt
imperpetuum, **viz. pro** omnibus serviciis que tenuit in eodem
feodo, **scilicet pro servicio** Walteri filii Gilberti 10d. et Ade
ejus fratris **10d. et 8d.** pro servicio **Ilic. fil.** Ric. **et 9d.** de
servitio Rogeri filii Assolfi, et **4d. de** servitio Roberti filii
Gilberti de Bothumlay, **et** 3d. de servitio Willielmi **de Helis-
tannes,** et 2d. de servitio Ricardi filii Roberti ad fontem de
Hippham. Et ut hec **mea** confirmatio et warrantizacio rata
et inconcussa permaneat, presens scriptum Sigilli **mei im-
pressione** corroboravi. Hiis testibus Domino Johanne **de
Thornhill,** Dom. **Johē de Heland,** Rob. de **Flamburge,**
Michaele Talface, Johē Clerico **de** Crumbholbothem, **Petro
Clerico de Birstall, et multis aliis.**"

In the same **MS.** fol. 344, is likewise **this :**

" **Sciant,** etc. quod ego Johannes, filius **Henrice** de Barkisland, **dedi, concessi,** et hac presenti **carta mea** confirmavi,
Deo et Beate **Marie,** et Sancte domui Hospital. Jerusalem,
et Fratribus ejusdem Domus Deo servientibus, duo asserta
in territorio de Barkisland, illud scilicet assertum quod Arn-
oldus quondam tenuit, et dicitur Arnoldrode, et illud assert-
um quod vocatur Williamrode, quorum capita extendunt

versus orientem super aquam que vocatur Blacborne, et
versus occidentem super quoddam rivulum sicut continetur
in latitudine inter Northclough et Barcolclef, cum bosco,
sine aliquo retenemento, infra predictas divisas, pro salute
anime mee, et omnium antecessorum meorum, in liberam,
et puram, et perpetuam eleemosinam, cum libera com-
munione, et cum omnibus liberis aysiamentis ad predictam
villam de Barkisland predict. in bosco, plano, pasturis,
molendinis, aquis, **et** in omnibus aliis aysiamentis. **Hanc**
autem donationem et confirmationem ego Johannes filius
Henrici, **et heredes mei, warrantizabimus predict.** Domui
et predict. **Fratribus** contra omnes homines imperpetuum.''

At Howroyd, in Barkisland, is the following rental of all
the sums paid to St. John of Jerusalem in England, within
the parish of Halifax, in 1533.

'' Johannes Rushworth de **Coley, pro certis terris et tenementis in Coley,** 5s. Richardus **Sunderland, pro certis
terris et tenementis in** Shibden, **7½d.** Henricus Batt, **pro
certis terris et tenementis** vocat. Hayley Hill, **6d.** Richardus
Saltonstall, pro certis terris **et tenementis in Shibden vocat.
Godley, 2d.** Johannes Northend, **pro** terris et **ten. in Shibden, 1d. ob.** Edwardus Kent, pro certis terris **et ten. in
Whetley, infra** Villat. **de Ovenden,** 1d. Robertus Northend,
pro certis ter. et ten. in Shibden vocat. Horner's, **2½d.
Edw. Kent** supradict. **pro** Shelve-park, **4d.** Rob. Deane,
pro Ekersley Hall, juxta **Eland,** 6d. Summa totalis 7s. 6½d.''

PRIORY of LEWIS, in SUSSEX.

The principal **church** in **this parish** belonged to **this**
Priory, but I shall defer the account **of this till** I **come to**
speak of the places **of worship** within **the parish, and** therefore shall only **here take** notice, **that at Oaks** (commonly
called Slithero) **in** Rishworth, **is a deed without** date, of
Adam de Eland, to John, **son** of **William de** Gretland, of an
acre of land in Eland West Field, **to hold of** the Prior and
Convent of Lewis, paying yearly to the said Prior and
Convent **two** pence at Pentecost, and **St.** Martin in winter,
for all services and demands. This land was conveyed by
another deed without date (lodged with the above) by John,
son of **John,** son of William de Gretland, **to** John del Clay,
to hold of the Prior of Lewis, by services due and accustomed.

And again, (as by another deed at the same place,) John del Clay made a grant thereof to John his son, 18 Edw. III. to hold as above.

KIRKLEES.

In the Monasticon, vol. I. p. 488, is an imperfect copy (like most of the rest in that Collection) of a confirmation charter of King Hen. III. of several gifts to the Nuns of Kirklees. The original deed is now at Kirklees, where, by the favor of sir George Armitage, I took a copy of it, and that part of it which relates to Halifax parish runs thus :—
" Ex dono Johannis filio Aumundi quasdam partes terre in Shelf, scil. unam terram que vocatur Wetecroft, et aliam que vocatur Hallecroft, et culturam que vocatur Northcroft, et communam pasture que ad prefatam villam pertinet ad quadringentas oves per magnum centum, cum tot agnis, et ad decem vaccas cum tot vitulis, et ad octo boves, et ad unum equum." Part of the royal Seal remains at this deed.

Besides the lands, &c. in Halifax parish which belonged to religious houses, the clergy of a few churches in other parts had some small claims within the limits thereof. Thus I find in a list of the tythes paid in the vicarage of Halifax, in the reign of King Henry VIII. that one John Lum, of Sowerby, paid 4d. yearly for lands there belonging to a chauntry in the church of Prestwich, in Lancashire. Also at Fixby is a deed of one John de Wridlesford to Michael Brertwisel, concerning the manor of Fekisby, in which is the following clause : " Reddend. inde annuatim Capelle S. Helene de Farnel unam libram cero ad unam ceream faciendam coram crucifixo ardendam, et ad sustinendam unam lampidem coram altar. beate Virginis Marie in eadem Capella singulis annis ardend. ad missas et ad matitinas pro omnibus serviciis, etc."

CHANTRY PRIESTS AT EALAND.

Names.	Time of Institution.	Patrons.	Vacant by
Dom. Johannes de Brough-ton, Preb.	April 13, 1402	Isabel, relict of Sir John Sayvell, Kt.	
Dom. Radulphus Pillay	- -	- - - - -	Resignation
Dom. Tho. Bogher, or Bower, Preb.	Feb. 5, 1418	Tho. Sayvell, Lord of Thornhill	Death
Dom Johannes Littestre, (Lister), Capel.	July 18, 1450	Assign of John Saywell, Esq;	Death
Dom. Rich. Stoke Capell.	May 4, 1483	Sir John Sayvell, Kt.	Resignation
Dom. Rob. Gledhill	Sept. 20, 1489	The same	Death
Dom. Johannes Halywell Capell	Nov. 10, 1520	Assigns of Henry Sayvell, Esq;	

The above is from Mr. Torr's MS. at York, to which should be added, John Syssons, or Seysson, as will appear below.

I do not find that there was more than one Chantry at
Ealand, the history of which is this. By an inquisition
taken at Pontefract, 19 Ric. II. the Jurors say, that it is not
to the damage of the Lord the King, if the King grant to
John Neele, Parson of Tankersley, John Wath, Vicar of the
church of Huddresfeld, John de Dishford, Chaplain, and
Will. de Heton, that they may of new make, establish, and
found, a certain Chantry of one Chaplain in the chapel of
Elande, annexed to the parish church of Halifax; and may
give and assign to a Chaplain of the Chantry aforesaid, one
messuage with appurtenances in Elande, and a certain yearly
rent of eight marks, to be perceived out of the manor of
Wyke, near Okenshaw, and of one messuage, 200 acres of
land, 20 acres of meadow, and six acres of wood, with the
appurtenances, in Himsworth. In consequence of this, the
above-named persons founded the said Chantry for one
Chaplain, presentable by Sir John Savill, Knt. and Isabel
his wife, and their heirs, within fifteen days from the time
of any vacation, for the said Chaplain to celebrate therein,
at the altar of St. John Baptist, for the good estate of John
Duke of Acquitain and Lancaster, of John Sayvill, Knt. and
Isabel his wife, and the children of the said John and Isabel,
and for the souls of the said Duke, and said John and Isabel,
and the souls of their children after death; and for the souls
of Henry late Earl of Lancaster, John Sayvill, and Margery
his wife, parents of said John Sayvill, Knt. also of Thomas
de Eland, and Joan his wife, parents of the said Isabel, of
John Rylay, Thomas Cross, Chaplain, and Richard Schepard,
of Eland, and the friends and benefactors of said John
Sayvill, Knt. and Isabel, and for the souls of all the faithful
deceased.

It does not appear who was first appointed to this office,
as the first person in the above table is one Broughton,
nominated by Isabel, relict of Sir John Sayvill, between five
and six years after the foundation of the Chantry. This
Broughton is said to have resigned to one Ralph Pillay, but
at what time is uncertain. I have copies of two deeds,
dated Feb. 16, 1411, in both which he is called "Radulphus
de Pillay, Capellanus Cantorie de Elande;" and the same
stile is given in another deed, dated 37 Hen. VI. 1459, to
John Lister.

The manner of the institution to this Chantry may be seen in Woolsey's Register at York, fol. 51. from which I took the following:

"Decimo die mensis Novembris, Anno Dom. 1520, Johannes Halywell, Capellanus ad Cantariam perpetuam S. Johannis Baptiste, in Capella de Eland, Ebor. Dioces. per mortem Dom¹. Rob. Gledehill, ultimi Capellani eiusdem vacantem, ad presentationem Tho. Sayvill, Gen. dicte Cantarie hac vice patroni ratione cuiusdam donationis, sive concessionis, advocationis, sive iuris patronatus dicte Cantarie, sibi et Robᵒ. Waterhous, cum clausula illa coniunctim et divisim per Hen. Sayvill, Arm. **verum** ipsius Cantarie patronum fact. admissus fuit, et **canonice** institutus in eadem, etc. et prestito obedientie iuramento mandatum erat directum Archidiacono Ebor. aut eius Officiali, ad inducendum eundem Dominum Johannem Halywell, aut eius Procuratorem, quemcuncq; nomine **suo** in corporalem possessionem dicte Cantarie, etc."

In the Certificate of the Archbishop of York, and others, concerning Colleges, Chantries, &c. in the order and survey of the King's court of the augmentations, and revenue of the crown, dated Feb. 14, in the 2d year (as I take it) of Edw. the VIth, this Chantry is thus described:

"The Chūntrie in the Chapell of Heland, in the Pōch of
" Hallifaxe. John Sysson, incumbent **of the** foundacōn of
" **John** Savyle, Knt. to the entent to pray for the sowle of
" **the** Founder, and **all** Xpēn sowles, **and** to do dyvyne
" **service in the** said chapell, and to mynystre Sacrements
" in **the same,** havynge thereunto belonginge 1800 people."
(N.B.   **This 1800 is wrote** in a later hand, and something
put **out where it stands, in the attested** copy on stampt
paper, **from whence this is taken.**)

"The same is in the Pōch abovesaid, **distunte from the**
" Pōch Church **two myles.** The necītie is to have divyne
" **service** and sacrements **and** sacrementalls **done** and myn-
" **ystred ther.** Ther is **no land** alienate **or sold** sithence the
" **4th day of** Februarye, **Anno** R. R. Hen. 8ᵗ. 28ᵒ."

" Goods, ornaments and plate perteynynge to the same,
" as apperyth **by the** inventorye, viz. Goodes valued at 13s.
" 8d. Plate **at 52s.** First, **the** Mancōn-house of the said
" Incumbent, **rented at 2s. 6d.** and **one annuall** rente, **goynge**

" furth of the lands of Sir Henrie Savell, Knt. lienge in
" Wyke, of 106s. 8d. Sum of the said Chuntrie 109s. 2d.
" wherof payable to the King's Matie. for the tenths 10s.11d.
" And so remanyth £4 18s. 8d." In the list of pensions and
annuities paid in 1553, to Incumbents of Chantries, published
in Willis's History of Abbies, **v. ii. p. 291.** the pension to
John Scisson, at Eland, is only called £5, but, from other
authorities, I judge this to be a mistake.

It is worth remarking, that from what has been said it
evidently appears, that Eland chapel was not erected purely
as a chantry chapel, since it was more than a century after
its being first built that we hear of a chantry Priest there.
The argument, therefore, made use of, to exclude the Vicar
of Halifax from presenting to this, because it has been a
chantry chapel, and privately endowed, is ill founded, both
because it was set up merely as a chapel of ease to Halifax;
and supposing it had been otherwise, yet we find, that the
Priory of Lewis first granted it to the Vicar of Halifax, and
afterwards the King himself did the same, when, after the
dissolution, he was impowered by statute to present to this
living.

There was a Light kept up here in former times, as I find
by deed, but when founded I cannot say. The original
deed I saw at Okes, in Rishworth, importing that Walter
de Frith granted to John his son a moyety of his land in
Arnaldelyes, and a moyety of the land which he bought of
Tho. de Thornton, lying within Boynley (Bottomley) and
Barkeslond, and a moyety of the land which he bought of
Hugh, son of Julian, and others, paying yearly to Hugh de
Eland a farthing and half farthing (quadrant. et dim. quadrant.) to Tho. Thornton two pence of silver and one halfpenny, to John de Barkislond one arrow feathered with a
goose feather; and also paying yearly to the said Walter
three-pence and one halfpenny of silver at Martinmass, and
after the death of the said Walter the same to go to the
Light of the Blessed Virgin Mary of the church of Eland
(debent reverti ad Lumen beate Marie Virginis ecclesie de
Eland.) There is no date to this deed, but amongst the
witnesses are Hugh de Eland, Hen. de Risseworth, and
Tho. de Coppeley, all whom I find about the year 1287.

HEPTONSTALL.

The chantries which were founded therein were these, as inserted in the Archbishop's certificate mentioned under Ealand : 1. A chantry there (no Founder's name mentioned) worth yearly five pounds. 2. The service of our Lady there, worth four pounds yearly. From this there is a variation in Willis's History of Abbies, v. ii. p. 292 ; for under the title of Heptonstall is this : " Virgin Mary's Chantry. To Richard Michell, Incumbent, £8 12s." But I have an old MS. wherein the sums to both agree with the Archbishop's certificate, as does Steven's Supplement to the Monasticon, vol. i. p. 68. In the list of the tythes paid in the vicarage of Halifax, in the reign of Hen. VIII. is the following entry : " For the lands in Stansfeld belonging to the Chauntry of " the blessed Virgin Mary in the church of Heptonstall, 12d."

—::—

LONGEVITY.

In Halifax Register is this entry, Roger Brook, of Halifax, sepult. 11th day of October, 1568, of the age of 6 score and 13 years. One John Roberts, of Hipperholm, also died Nov. 10, 1721, in the 114th year of his age. There was one Littleton, in Rishworth, in 1700, aged 100. Nathan Wood, near Baitings, in Soyland, was buried Dec. 25, 1704, aged 108. Dec. 3, 1708, died Peter Ambler, of Shelf, aged about 108. In the year 1757, there were seven sons and daughters of one John Firth, of Sowerby, then living and well, the eldest of which was 87 years old, and the youngest 69.

GIBBET LAW.

The following is a list, carefully collected from the Register Books at Halifax, of such persons as have been beheaded there, since entries were made of such transactions.

"Ricūs Beverley [Bentley*] de Sowerby decollat. 20 die Martii, 1541.—Quidam Extraneus capitalem subiit sententiam 1° die Jan. 1542.—Johēs Brygg, Capellanie de Heptonstal, capitalem subiit sententiam 16° Septembris, 1544.—Johēs Ecoppe, de Eland, capitalem subiit sententiam ultimo die Martii, 1545. —Thomas Waite, de Halifax, capitalem subiit sententiam, & suit sepultus 5° die Decemb. 1545.—Richard Sharpe, de North^m, John Learoyd, de North^m, beheaded the 5th day of March, 1568, for a robbery done in Lancashire. —William Cokekere was headed the 9th day of Oct. 1572.—John Atkinson, Nicholas Frear, Richard Garnet were headed at Halifax, the 9th day of January, 1572. —Richard Stopforthe was headed the 19th of May, 1574.—James Smyth, de Sowerby, was headed at Halyfax, the 12th of Febr. 1574.—Henry Hunt was headed at Halyfax the 3d of Novemb. 1576.—Robert Bayrstall, alias Fernesyde, was headed the 6th of February, 1576.—John Dicconsone, de Bradford, was headed the 6th of January, 1578.—John Waters was headed at Halifax, March 16, 1578.—Bryan Cassone was headed at Halyfax, the 15th of October, 1580. —John Appleyard, de Halyfax, was headed the 19th of Febr. 1581.—John Sladen was headed at Halyfax, the 7th of Febr. 1582.—Arthur Firthe was headed the 17th of Jan. 1585.—John Duckworthe was headed at Halifax, the 4th of Oct. 1586.—Nicholas Hewett, de North^m, Thomas Masone, vagans, were headed the 27th of May, 1587.—Ux. Thom. Robarts, de Halifax, was beheaded the 13th of July, 1588.— Robert Wilson, de Halifax, was headed the 5th of April, 1589.—Decollatus Petrus Crabtrye, Sorby, 21 Decemb. 1591. —Decollatus Barnard Sutcliffe, North^m, 6th of January, 1591.—Abraham Stancliffe, Hal. capite truncatus, Sept. 23,

* This has always been recorded as *Bentley*, but there is not the slightest doubt that it is *Ben-ley*, i. e. *Beverley*. There is an earlier entry in Halifax Register which was discovered by the late Mr. E. J. Walker: "Carolus Hawworth capitalem subiit sentenciam X^{mo} die [January, 1539.] We should no doubt have had many other instances if the Registers had been commenced earlier.

1602.—Ux. Peter Harison, Brad. decoll. Feb. 22, 1602.—
Christopher Cosin decollatus Dec. 29, 1610.—Thomas Briggs
decollatus, April 10, 1611.—George Fairbanke, preditissimus
nebulo, vulgo vocatus Skoggin, **ob** nequitiam. **Anna,
ejusdem Georgii** Filia spuria, ambo meritissimè ob furtum
manifestum decollati, Dec. 23, 1623.—John Lacy, perditi-
ssimus nebulo & latro, decollatus Jan. 29, 1623.—Edmund
Ogden decollatus **April 8, 1624.**—Richard Midgley, of Midgley, **decollatus April 13, 1624.**—Ux. Johan. Wilson decollata
July 5, 1627.—Sara Lume, Hal. decollata Dec. 8, 1627.—
John **Sutcliffe, Sk.** [Skircoat,] decollatus 14 May, 1629.—
Richard **Hoile,** Hept. decollatus Oct. 20, 1629.— Henry
Hudson. Ux. Samuel. Ettal **ob** plurima furta decollati,
Aug. 28, 1630.—Jeremy Bowcock, de Warley, decollatus
April **14, 1632.**—**John** Crabtree, **de** Sourby, decollatus Sept.
22, 1632.—Abraham Clegg, **Norland,** decollatus May 21,
1636.—Isaac Illingworth, Ovenden, decollatus Oct. **7, 1641.**
—John Wilkinson, Anthony Mitchell, Sowerby, decollati
April 30, 1650. In all forty-nine; of which five were
executed in the six last years of king Henry VIII, twenty-
five in the reign of queen Elizabeth, seven in that of king
James I, ten in that of k. Charles I, and two during the
inter-regnum.

—::—

BENEFACTIONS: CONCLUDED.

EXTRACT FROM THE

WILL OF ISAAC BOWCOCK,

OF TONGUE, [TONG.]

Dated Feb. 11*th*, 1669.

—" I GIVE so much money as will buy so much land for the
preferring or putting forth of five poor men's sons to
trades yearly, as are not to be put forth town prentices, or
for the relief of such as **are in** necessity, and not through
wastfull expences, nor such as have relief from the parish,
or for setting in trade or stocking such young persons as **are**
hopefull to make good **use of** it, **at** the discretion of my
Feoffees hereafter named.—**Item, I give** to the townships of

Halifax and Ovenden my lands in Ossett, that the rents may be yearly bestowed after the same manner (alluding to the clause above) by my Feoffees chosen for that end, and that six pounds thereof be given to Ovenden.—For Halifax and Ovenden I chuse and ordain Mr. Fournes, John Illingworth, William Illingworth, John Hodgson, James Hodgson, his brother, Daniel Greenwood, and John Brearcliffe, Feoffees for both towns jointly; and my mind is, that if any of these die, the rest shall meet together and choose another before anything be acted; and I give power to my said Feoffees to buy lands, to make out what I leave not in lands already purchased, to make leases, receive rents, give acquitances, and every such matter as may be necessary for the performance of my Will herein."

In the Manuscript, from whence the above was taken, was wrote under: "A true copy, taken 8th of March, 1670, by me John Brearcliffe."

This is one of the charities which Mr. Wright, p. 131, sais, he could procure no particular account of; he has told us, however, that the farm lies at Osset-yate.

The last choice for this charity, which I know of, was by Deed, dated Dec. 22, 1710, and the Trustees then chosen neglected to convey, as the Will requires, for the late Mr. John Caygil was the only surviving Trustee, and whether he took care to fill up the trust before his death is uncertain. The farm, as I am informed, lets for eighteen pounds per annum, and is capable of being raised. It is also said that there are coals in it.

Samuel Sunderland, Esq; of Harden, in the parish of Bingley, but of the family of the Sunderlands, of High Sunderland, near Halifax, gave, but whether by Will or Deed I have not seen, the sum of two hundred pounds, to purchase therewith ten pounds a year, for the use of the Vicars of Halifax Church for ever. With this money a purchase was made of a field adjoining to Southgate, in Halifax, and another in Southouram, called *Hawkingroid*. See more of this Gentleman's benefactions, in the township of Hipperholme. He was buried Feb. 4, 1676.

EXTRACT FROM THE

WILL OF ALICE CROWTHER, Widow,

Dated Oct. 12, 1722.

—" I HEREBY give and devise all that cottage, and an outhouse to the same belonging, scituate in the Dean Clough, now in my own occupation, and also all those four other cottages, or tenements, scituate and being in the Dean Clough aforesaid, (then follow the names of the occupants,) with all and singular the appurtenances whatsoever unto the said cottages, or any of them belonging, or in any wise appertaining, unto Joshua Marcer, of Halifax, Hardwareman, and Timothy Scholfield, of Halifax aforesaid, Hempheckler, and their heirs and assigns, and the survivor of them, and his heirs and assigns for ever, as my Feoffees or Trustees, in trust to the several uses hereafter mentioned (that is to say) that they the said Feoffees or Trustees, and the survivor of them, and his heirs and assigns shall for ever hereafter, after my decease, after paying of all my just debts, funeral expences, and probate of this my Will, legacies, and other incident charges, distribute and pay out of the rents, issues, and profits of all my said cottages, unto and amongst such poor, indigent and poor housekeepers, and other poor people, within the town and township of Halifax, as have not any allowance from the town and township of Halifax, the same to be given and distributed by my said Trustees, by such sums of money, and to such person and persons, as they in their judgment shall think necessary and fit, and to be paid to the said poor people at Christmass yearly for ever." From an attested copy.

N.B. A memorial of the above was registered at Wakefield, July 5, 1723, in Book S. p. 466, No. 634.

The Trustees of this Charity, about thirty years ago, assigned over their power to the Churchwardens and Overseers of the Poor of Halifax, who still execute the same.

EXTRACT FROM THE
WILL OF WILLIAM CHAMBERLAIN.

Dated Sept. 22, 1728.

"I GIVE, devise, and bequeath the sum of twenty shillings per annum of lawfull money of Great Britain, yearly, from and after my decease, to be paid to the person that reads prayers twice every day in Halifax, and for want of such usage or reading prayers twice every day, then I hereby give, devise, and bequeath the said sum of twenty shillings yearly unto the Lecturer, or Afternoon Preacher in Halifax Church for ever. And I do hereby charge the same shall be paid forth out of the housing in Mr. James Ingham's occupation."

This is all I was allowed to take out of the above Will, and it is sufficient to prove, that Mr. Wright, p. 129, was mistaken in supposing, that the Testator had limited the times of reading prayers, as above, to eleven o'clock and two. Probably that Author (any more than myself) had never a copy of this Will in his own possession; for I am credibly informed, (though he is silent about it,) that Mr. Chamberlain left also six shillings yearly, for which the twelve widows in the alms-houses are to have each a dinner and a pint of ale every Christmas-day; likewise twenty shillings yearly for ever, payable out of the whole estate given to his daughter Mary, for teaching the Blue-coat children in Mr. Waterhouse's Hospital to write, at the discretion of the said Mr. Waterhouse's Feoffees.

This Benefactor died May 15, 1729.

—::—

EXTRACT FROM THE
WILL OF ELIZABETH BINGLEY,

Dated May 12, 1729.

"I GIVE and devise all those my two cottages in or near the lane leading to Mount Pellon, at the upper end of Halifax town, with their and every of their appurtenances, now in the several tenures or occupations of me the said Elizabeth Bingley, and John Morris, the rents, issues and profits thereof to go and be to and for the Reader of **Prayers** twice every day in Halifax Church for ever; and if **prayers** reading twice **every** day shall cease **from** being **read, then to** the Lecturer or Afternoon man in Halifax Church **for** the time being, for ever."

Her Executor **was** John Holt, of Halifax. This Benefactress was born in 1684, died May 14, 1729, and was **buried** on the 16th following. These premises being copyhold, were **conveyed** by Lord Irwin, by Deed, to Trustees, **for the** uses mentioned in the Will.

Mary Drake, **of** Halifax, widow, who was buried, as Mr. **Wright sais,** in June, 1729, left twenty shillings yearly for **ever, to the Lecturer** at Halifax, and his successors, for **preaching a Sermon every** second Wednesday in June for **ever.**

John Tenant, of Halifax, Grocer, left the interest of ten pounds yearly for ever, for reading prayers twice every day in the parish Church of Halifax. He died, as Mr. Wright sais, about the year 1729. A messuage or dwelling-house in Bury-lane is the security for this.

—::—

EXTRACT FROM THE

WILL OF JOHN SMYTH, of Heath, Esq;

—" WHEREAS I built a school at Halifax, I do devise and give the same unto those persons called Governors of Mr. Waterhouse's charity there, and to their successors for ever, for them from time to time to elect such a School-master as shall be approved of by my son, John Smyth, and his heirs, or such persons as shall hereafter for the time being for ever be owner or owners of my estate at Halifax, to be upon every vacancy nominated and put into the said school by him or them, to teach six poor boys or girls, whose parents pay no assessments therein, to read, and not elsewhere. And I give and bequeath to the said Governors, and to their successors for ever, all that my* house in Halifax aforesaid, let to John or Thomas Bairstow for eleven years, under the yearly rent of four pounds, and

* This house is in Northgate.

the window money, in trust only for them and their successors, to let, set, and dispose thereof as will be most advantageous for that purpose, to **any person** or persons, other than the School-master there, **and his** successors for the time being, and **to** receive the **rents**, issues **and** profits thereof for ever, and to pay the **same over**, by half yearly payments, **to** such Master and Masters for ever, teaching six poor boys **or girls as** aforesaid, there to be placed **by the** said Governors, or **the** major part of them, for **ever**, with the advice **and assistance** of the Churchwardens **and** Overseers **of the Poor there, if** desired. And I do **revoke** and abrogate this my **last** request to the Governors **of Mr. Water**house's charity, in case they or any of **them**, or any **of** their successors, shall ever suffer the said School-master **or** any **of** his successors, to live in the said Bairstow's house **or** School-house, for **so** long time as they shall permit him **or** them to inhabit in either of the said houses. Item, I give, devise and bequeath to my said **son** John Smyth, his Executors and Administrators, the farm **in** Reavey, in the parish of Bradford, and county **of** York, **I** hold by lease under **William** Rookes, Esq; wherein there is yet above eighty **years to** come, and will so long subsist, and is of the clear **yearly value** of fifteen pounds **per** annum, and in the **present** tenures **or** occupations of George Kellet and Thomas **Dewhirst,** he **and they** yearly paying out **of the** issues, rents, **and profits** thereof, **four** pounds of lawful money, by four **quarterly** payments in every year, to Abigail Marshall, now **of Halifax,** an old widow, during her natural life only, and **also in** trust for the several charitable uses, intents and purposes **herein after** mentioned **and** appointed, **that is to** say, upon trust and confidence **that** my **son** John Smyth, his heirs and assigns, **shall and do pay, or cause to be paid,** given and disbursed, **out of the rents and profits of** my said farm at Reavey, during the **continuance of the said** lease, the several gifts and disbursements, **and to and for** such uses, intents and purposes, and upon **such terms,** provisoes **and** conditions, subject to such limitations, devises, order **and** appointments as are herein after directed, devised, bequeathed, ordered and appointed, viz. the sum of forty shillings per **annum to** the Vicar of Halifax, and his successor or **successors, upon** every twenty-ninth day of September and **twenty-fifth day of** March, by equal portions, in every

year during the said term, for preaching, or procuring to
be preached, two charity sermons, in Halifax Church, in
the afternoons of one Sunday in every month of June,
and of one Sunday in every month of December yearly, during the said term, the first sermon to be preached
in June next after my decease; and catechize or cause to be
catechized all the poor boys or girls that shall from time to
time be taught in the said school in the summer seasons
every year; and in default of any and every such catechiz-
ing or preaching, it is my will and mind that nothing be
paid or liable to be paid by my said son John, or his heirs
or assigns, to the said Vicar or his successors that year, and
every year any such default or neglect shall happen in; and
I give that year, and every such years, payment of forty
shillings a year as aforesaid, wherein every or any such
default shall happen, to my said son John, his Heirs, Executors, and Administrators. And I desire the Churchwardens of the said town of Halifax for the time being, to
go about the Church when every such sermon is preached,
there to collect the charity of well-disposed persons, for the
benefit of such poor children as shall from time to time be
taught in the said school, in the manner now used at Wakefield and Leeds. Also that my said son shall yearly pay
unto the said Governors and their successors, on every
twenty-fifth day of March, five shillings and six-pence, to
be laid out as follows, (viz.) three shillings and six-pence for
a good and well bound Bible, with the Common Prayers and
Singing Psalms in it, and eighteen-pence for the Whole
Duty of Man, and six-pence for putting these letters following, *I. S. of Heath, Esq:* with the year of our Lord
when so given on the back, and give the same so marked to
one of the said six poor boys or girls, that shall yearly be
put apprentice out of the said school (if any such there be,)
if not, then to any other of the poor boys or girls aforesaid,
to be yearly put out as herein mentioned. And I desire the
Governors and their successors to take the trouble of executing this last request, and the Churchwardens and Overseers to see it done, or else no money to be paid. And also
it is my desire, that the said Governors or Feoffees, and the
Churchwardens and Overseers for the poor of Halifax aforesaid, will meet every first Monday in June in every year, at
some convenient place in Halifax aforesaid, to enquire into

the said trust, and regulate and settle the same as they shall
see occasion ; and that my said son John Smyth, his Heirs,
Executors, Administrators, and Assigns, shall, out of the
rents and profits of my said estate at Reavey, spend ten
shillings at every such meeting or meetings."

Mr. Smyth was living in the year 1730, but how long after
I cannot tell. On the south end of this school is the following inscription. "Hoc ædificium de fundo extruxit pro-
"priis suis sumptibus JOHANNES SMYTH, de Heath, in hoc
"comitatu, armiger, quo pauperiorum pueribonis moribus
"honestentur, idem ut exemplo fuo alios ad hujusmodi opera
"excitarat, annuam quandam stipem Ludi-Magistro in per-
"petuum de suo solvendum addixit anno Salutis 1726."
Importing, that Mr. Smyth erected that edifice at his own
charge, for the education of poor men's children ; and that
he might excite others by his example to the like good
works, he had settled an annual stipend for ever on the
School-master, in the year 1726.

JONATHAN TURNER, of Halifax, Butcher, left by Will (but
at what particular time I have not learned) forty shillings
yearly to the poor prisoners in Halifax Jail, to be given
them in bread. This annuity is charged on some housing
in Cheapside, in Halifax, or the street leading from the
north end of Southgate to Bull Green.

These are all the perpetual Charities in the township of
Halifax which I know of ; except three pounds a year to be
lent to three poor Tradesmen of Halifax, from year to year,
by the Churchwardens, given by WILLIAM WHITAKER ; but of
this I can give no farther account, than that it is thus
entered in the second volume of the Register-books belonging to Halifax Church.

HEPTONSTALL.

JOHN GREENWOOD, of Cottingley, gave (as appeared by the
copy of a Deed, dated Feb. 20, 1598, produced to the Inquirers after Charities at Halifax, Dec. 22, 1651) the sum of
forty pounds, to be lent from year to year, for ever, to the
Poor of Heptonstall parish, by the discretion of the Churchwardens for the time being of the said parish.

The above is mentioned both in Mr. Brearcliffe's manuscript, and in Halifax Register, vol. ii.

For Paul Greenwood's legacy to the Preacher at Hepton-stall, see under Wadsworth.

—::—

EXTRACT FROM THE

WILL OF RICHARD NAYLOR,

OF BURNT ACRES, IN ERINGDEN.

Dated May 29, 1609.

—" WHEREAS I by one Indenture or Deed, bearing date the tenth day of February, which was in the year of our Lord 1604, have given, granted, and con-firmed unto George Halstead, Anthony Naylor, of High Hurst, in Wadsworth, Richard Naylor, of Heptonbrigg, Henry Naylor, of Eringden, and Robert Halstead, one my annuity or yearly rent of three pounds five shillings yearly issuing forth of certain lands and tenements, with their appurtenances, in Ovenden, to have, hold, receive and take the same unto them the said George Halstead, Anthony Naylor, Richard Naylor, Henry Naylor, and Robert Halstead, their heirs and assigns, for ever, upon confidence and trust, and to the intent only that they should, within the space of six months next after my decease, lawfully convey and as-sure the said annuity or yearly rent of three pounds five shillings unto such person and persons as I shall, by my last Will, name and appoint, as in and by the same Deed more plainly may appear. My will and mind is, that they the said George Halstead, Anthony Naylor, Richard Naylor, Henry Naylor, and Robert Halstead, and their heirs, and the survivors or survivor of them, and his or their heirs, shall yearly and every year, from and after my decease, for ever, faithfully disburse the said annuity or yearly rent of three pounds five shillings to the uses hereafter following, and in such sort as is hereafter declared, viz. thirty-two shillings and six-pence, the one half hereof, for and towards the keeping and maintaining of a Preacher at Heptonstall for the time, so as he be a Master of Arts, yearly, from and after my decease for ever, to be paid at the Feast of St. John Baptist, for all the year. Item, I give and bequeath the other thirty-two shillings and six-pence, together also with the other thirty-two shillings and six-pence, if it shall at any time fortune that there be no Preacher at Heptonstall for the time so being, shall yearly and every year after my decease for ever, be bestowed and employed at the discretion of them the said George Halstead, Anthony Naylor, Richard Naylor, Henry Naylor, and Robert Halstead, upon and towards the maintaining of the poor children of and within the parish of Heptonstall."

Taken from Heptonstall Register.

By Deed, dated June 2, 1747, George Halstead, of Hougham, in Eringden, eldest son and heir of George Halstead, formerly of Hougham aforesaid, which last George was brother and heir of Robert Halstead, late of Burnt Acres, in Eringden aforesaid, which Robert was eldest son and heir of Robert Halstead, of Height, in Eringden aforesaid, and which last named Robert was the surviving Trustee of the Annuity left by the above Richard Naylor, conveyed the same to Henry Cockcroft the younger, of Burlees, in Wadsworth, Jonathan Greenwood, of Hanging Royd, in Heptonstall, Luke Crosley, of Great House, in Stansfield, and John Sutcliffe, of Hoo-Hoyle, in Eringden aforesaid, in trust for the purposes contained in the grant of the said Richard Naylor; in which Deed of Conveyance it is declared, that the above annuity is issuing or payable out of three closes of land, meadow, and pasture, called the Gould Pit, the Great Hay, and the south end of the Crag in Mixenden, within the township of Ovenden, containing, by estimation, seven acres. Also that, upon the death of two of the said Trustees, the survivors should elect two good, able, honest, and sufficient men, inhabitants of the parish of Heptonstall aforesaid, in their room; and this rule and order to be for ever hereafter observed, to perpetuate, as much as possible, the charitable donation of Richard Naylor, the Testator, as aforesaid.

U

EXTRACT FROM THE

WILL OF ABRAHAM WALL.

Dated Sept. 12, 1638.

—" I GIVE and bequeath unto the Churchwardens, for the time being, of the Church or Chapel of Heptonstall, in the parish of Halifax, in the county of York, where I was born, twenty shillings a year for ever, for to buy three Bibles, for the use of poor men's children, where most need shall be, they being capable to read in them. And I give unto the said Church or Chapel of Heptonstall, for ever, four pounds, upon condition that they, the said Churchwardens, and other Antients of the same place, provide some one honest man to instruct or bring up poor honest men's children in learning. And I give unto the same Church or Chapel of Heptonstall, for ever, three pounds yearly, for the sending and placing of one of the same scholars up to London, to be apprentice, whom the Churchwardens of the time being shall think fittest, with the consent of a Vestry; and if this my yearly gift to the said poor children of Heptonstall be not duly performed, then I wholly give it to the town of Halifax, to the same use, for so many poor children as the Churchwardens, and other of the Antients there, can get to be taught and brought up in learning, and the twenty shillings yearly for Bibles, and the three pounds yearly for the preferment of poor men's children to prentice."

From the Register at Heptonstall. N.B. One copy of the above Will is dated Sept. 20, 1638, but is probably a mistake, as he only died on that day.

—::—

EXTRACT FROM THE

WILL OF CHARLES GREENWOOD, Clerk,

RECTOR OF THORNHILL.

Dated July 14, 1642.

—" NOW for and touching the messuage and tenement, with appurtenances, in Heptonstall, situate near the Church-yard there—which I have now made into a

School-house, and the two messuages, tenements, and farms, and all the lands, closes, and grounds therewith, now or commonly demised, used, or occupied, with appurtenances in Colden aforesaid, forasmuch as it hath pleased God to put me in **mind to** build a Free Grammar school within the township of Heptonstall aforesaid, and to make provision for some small maintenance of the annual rent or value of twenty **pounds** ten shillings **for a** School-**master,** who shall teach **school** of the children **and** inhabitants **of the** town **and** parish **of** Heptonstall aforesaid; therefore, **in the** first **place,** my will and mind is, and I hereby devise, that the **said** John Greenwood, son **of** Robert Greenwood, John Greenwood, **of** Elfaburgh-hall, William Mitchell, Thomas Greenwood, of Learings, and Richard Robertshaw, and their heirs, and the survivors and survivor **of** them, and his and their heirs, shall, by force and **virtue of** these presents, and **of the** Deed of Feoffment, stand and **be** Feoffees, and seised of **the** said **messuage or** tenement, **with** appurtenances, in Heptonstall **aforesaid,** now made **into a** School-house; and my will and **mind is,** that the same shall remain **and** continue for **a School-**house to succeeding ages for ever, unto which **said John** Greenwood, son **of** Robert, and other his co-feoffees, **and** their heirs, and **the survivors** and survivor of them, **and** his heirs, I hereby give, devise, and bequeath the same accordingly to the only use aforesaid: And also my will and mind is, and I do hereby devise, that the said John Greenwood, son of Robert, and other his co-feoffees, **and** their heirs, and survivors and survivor of them, and his **and** their heirs, shall, by force and virtue of these presents, **and** of the said Deed of Feoffment, stand and be Feoffees, **and** seised of the said two **messuages,** tenements, and farms, **and** all the lands **therewith** occupied, with appurten-**ances in** Colden aforesaid, **to the** use and **for** the main-tenance **of a** sufficient School-**master,** which hath well profited **in learning,** for **teaching of children** and inhabit-ants **of the town** and parish **of** Heptonstall aforesaid, within **the said** School-house **to** succeeding ages for ever, unto which **said** John Greenwood, son of **Robert,** and other his co-feoffees, **and** their heirs, and the survivors and sur-vivor of them, **and** his heirs, I hereby give, devise, and bequeath the same lands and tenements in Colden above-said, **to** the Feoffees abovesaid, **and** their heirs, for the only use and maintenance of such a School-master as aforesaid, to hold of the chief Lords of the fee thereof by the services therefore due and of right accustomed."

The Testator also left **rents** for the founding two Fellowships and two Scholarships in **University** College, in Oxford, of which he had **been** Fellow, appointing Anthony Foxcroft, of Halifax, and **Thomas** Radcliffe, his Executors, the latter of whom obtained a **Decree** in Chancery against the former, who, **for nonperformance of the** said Charles Greenwood's Will was **imprisoned in the** Fleet, **and during** the time of his imprisonment, **the said** Radcliffe got a Sequestration of the said Foxcroft's **estate in that Court, yet** nothing **was obtained so** as **to put the Testator's intentions in** execution, **so that the** College **was wronged of this benefaction, as** also, (according to Groome, **in his Dignity and Honor of** the **Clergy, p. 253,) it was of** fifteen **hundred** pounds **more, given by** the said **Mr. Greenwood towards** building **a new quadrangle** there.

—::—

EXTRACT FROM THE
WILL OF CALEB COCKCROFT,
OF LONDON.

Dated Nov. 2, 1643.

—"**I** GIVE twenty pounds **to** the parish of Heptonstall, whereof **ten** pounds of it for Wadsworth, **and** ten pounds for Heptonstall **and** Eringden, which money shall be lent to twenty poor **men, to buy** them **bread** corn, from two years to two years, and with one **sufficient** surety, and **to** be lent **by the advice of** the Minister, Churchwardens, **and** Overseers **of the Poor, and to** be lent **where** they see most need **to lend, and to be lent to such men** who have no relief from **the parish** at all, **and** this **in the least not to be** any hindrance to the **charity of those townships, but** a **help to** poor men to buy corn **at best hand, and cheapest.**"

The original of this Will **is in the** Prerogative Court of **Canterbury; the** above **was** copied **from Heptonstall** Register. By an Inquisition at Halifax, **Feb. 16,** 1651, **it** appeared, that, in 1647, the Minister **and** Churchwardens distributed the money according to the donor's Will, but it was not found that they made any account thereof to their **successors or others.**

EXTRACT FROM THE

WILL OF JOHN GREENWOOD,

OF LEARINGS, IN HEPTONSTALL.

Dated Feb. 10, 1687.

—" I GIVE, grant, and bequeath unto the owner or inheritor of Learings, in Heptonstall, and to the Churchwardens and Overseer of the same for the time being, and to their heirs and successors for ever, one annuity, or yearly rent, of forty shillings a year, issuing out or forth of one messuage and tenement, with appurtenances, in Stansfield, commonly called Dovescout, with my full power to distrain for non-payment thereof, in trust and confidence, and of intent and purpose that the said owner of Learings, Churchwardens and Overseer of Heptonstall, and their heirs and successors, shall yearly pay the one moiety or half part thereof unto Daniel Town, Curate at Heptonstall, for preaching every year a Sermon upon the first Wednesday in June yearly, at Heptonstall, during his natural life, if he be able in body, and can be admitted; and after his decease, it is my will and mind that the owner of Learings, Churchwardens and Overseer, and their heirs and successors, shall pay the same to the Curate of Heptonstall for the time being, he performing as aforesaid for ever. And of intent and purpose also, that the said owner of Learings, Churchwardens and Overseer of the Poor, for the time being, and their heirs and successors, shall every two or three years, at their discretion, for ever, pay and distribute the other moiety, or half part of the said annuity, with a poor man's child, male or female, of the township of Heptonstall, where most need is, to place them apprentices to some trade or occupation to get their living without begging."

From Heptonstall Register.

EXTRACT FROM THE

WILL OF JOHN GREENWOOD,

OF HIPPINGS, IN STANSFIELD,

Dated Dec. 13, 1705.

—"I WILL that he who shall be lawfully admitted as Parson or Minister of Heptonstall, to officiate there, shall preach a Sermon upon the first Wednesday in August yearly, for ever, in lieu of which Sermon, and his yearly wages for Hippingsland, I give him and his successors twenty shillings yearly, for ever. Also I give unto the poor of Stansfield twenty shillings yearly for ever, to be bestowed on canvas cloth, by the Churchwardens of the same town, and their successors yearly, for ever, and to be by them distributed unto such poor persons as they, for the time being, shall think fit objects of charity, or have no relief; both which said two legacies I do hereby authorize both the same Minister and Churchwardens to have, perceive, and receive, and take out and forth of one messuage and tenement in Wadsworth, called Crimsworth, now in the possession of Joshua Dawson, or his Assigns.—And if it shall happen that the said sum of forty shillings shall be behind, and unpaid, on the said first Wednesday of August, as is said yearly .... for ever, that then it shall and may be lawful for the same Minister, and his assigns, and also the same Churchwardens, and their assigns, successively, for ever, to enter into the same messuages, and tenements, and premisses, and make distress according to law."

From the Register at Heptonstall.

—::—

EXTRACT FROM THE

WILL OF THOMAS SUNDERLAND,

OF HATHERSHELF, IN SOWERBY.

Dated Nov. 13, 1721.

—"I GIVE and devise unto Henry Cockcroft and Abraham Farrer, and their heirs, one annuity or yearly rent of twenty shillings, to be issuing and payable out and forth of one messuage and lands thereunto belonging, called New House, in Turvin, and all my estate, right, interest, title, claim, and demand, into or out **of** the same messuage or lands, or any part **thereof,** provided he or they, pay yearly to such orthodox Curate, or Parson, of Heptonstall Church or Chapel, **in** this county, for the time being, as **shall** be conformable to the present Established Church of England, both in **doctrine** and discipline, and shall, on the second Wednesday in the month of March, for ever, preach one Commemoration Sermon, for, or on account of, my only son and child, Thomas Sunderland, whom **it** pleased Almighty God, **in that** month, to take to himself."

From the Register at Heptonstall.

—::—

HEPTONSTAL CHAPEL.

The parochial Chapel of Heptonstall was, in 1747, augmented by lot, with two hundred **pounds,** part of Queen Ann's **Bounty;** in consequence **of which,** a purchase was made **of a** messuage and lands **thereto** belonging, called *West-croft-head,* in the parish of Bradford, Chapelry of Haworth, and Township of Oxnop, yielding the clear yearly rent of eight pounds ten shillings. In 1736 its clear yearly value was returned to have been ten pounds ten shillings, 3d of Queen Anne.

—::—

HIPPERHOLME cum BRIGHOUSE.

Original ENDOWMENT of LIGHTCLIFFE CHAPEL.

RICHARD ROOKES gave by Indenture, dated **1** March, 20 Henry VIII. one parcel of ground in the **end** of a close wherein the Chapel of Lightcliffe standeth, and also 13s. 4d. a-year for ever, out of the rest of the said close, towards the maintenance of a Priest there. The following yearly rents were also given to the said Chapel:

	s.	d.
By John Smith, out of his chief messuage called Royd House,	6	8
—Richard Waterhouse, out of his lands within the hamlet of Priestley,	6	8

—Edmund Fairbank, out of his two messuages, and all his lands at Lidyate, in Lightcliffe, -	3	4
—James Waterhouse, out of his lands and tenements in Northwood, - - -	3	4
—John and Thomas Thorpe, out of three chief messuages and lands in Lightcliffe, -	3	4
—Richard Cliffe, out of Cliffe house, and lands thereto belonging, in Lightcliffe, - -	3	4
—Edward Hoyle, out of Hoyle House, and all the lands, &c., thereto belonging in Lightcliffe,	3	4
—John Scolfield, out of his messuage and lands in Lightcliffe, - - - -	1	4
—Gilbert Saltonstall, out of his messuage and lands in Lightcliffe, - - -	1	0
—Richard Scolefield, out of Gibhouse, and lands thereto belonging, - - -	1	0
—William Whiteley, out of his New House, and two acres of land called Eastfield Knowle, in Lightcliffe. - - - -	1	0

—::—

ORIGINAL ENDOWMENT OF COLEY-CHAPEL.

JOHN RYSSHWORTH, of Coley, Esq; and his son JOHN RYSSHWORTH, of Collyn, conveyed a parcel of land in Coley, within the vill of Hipperholm, held of the capital house or hospital of St. John of Jerusalem, in England, as it lay between Edwardrode on the east, the King's common, or waste ground, on the west, Coolay Slakke on the north, and a certain inclosure called Wynters, on the south, and a yearly rent of twenty shillings, payable out of a messuage, with lands, in Shelf. At the same time also, Matthew Oglethorp, of Thornton, conveyed a yearly rent of three shillings and four-pence out of all his lands and tenements in Hipperholm; Richard Rookes, of Rodeshall, a yearly rent of three shillings and four-pence, out of a messuage, with lands, in Shelf; Thomas Fournes, of Bothes, a yearly rent of three shillings and four-pence, out of a capital messuage, with lands, in Shelf; Richard Haldeworth, of Hipperholm, a yearly rent of three shillings and four-pence, out of his capital messuage and lands lying on the north side of Hipperholm; Henry Batte, of Haylay, a yearly rent of three shillings and four-pence, out of a messuage and lands in Northouram; William Cowper, of Kighley, a yearly rent of three shillings and four-pence, **out of** a messuage, with lands, called Deynehouse, in Shelf; John Boy, of Northouram, a yearly rent of three shillings and four-pence, out of lands and tenements in Shelf; Thomas Northend, of Hipperholm, a yearly rent of twenty-pence, **out of all his** free lands **and** tenements in Hipperholm; and William **Saltonstall**, of Shelf, a yearly rent of twenty-pence, **out of** a messuage and lands in Shelf, to certain Trustees named in a Deed, dated the 15th of November, 21 Hen. VIII. in trust, as appears by another Deed, dated the 14th of February, 21 **Hen.** VIII. for the use of a chapel and cemitery, to be made, founded, and built on the parcel of land above named; the aforesaid yearly rents or annuities to be received **yearly** at Pentecost and St. Martin in winter, by equal **portions**, amongst other things **to the use and** sustentation **of Richard** Northend, Capellane in the **said** chapel, and his successors, saying, singing, and celebrating Divine Offices therein **for** ever.

This **account is** taken from two original Deeds belonging to the late **Mrs. Horton**, of Coley.

William Thorpe gave, **as** appears by a Deed of Feoffment, dated the 9th of February, 28 Hen. VIII. the yearly sum of six shillings and eight pence, payable out of his messuages, lands, tenements, &c. in the town and fields of Shelf, to be for **ever** bestowed at the discretion of certain Feoffees therein named, to and for the amending and repairing of highways, or helping of poor maidens towards marriage, or other things necessary; and after the death of Isabel his wife, the whole rent of the above messuages, &c. to the use of **a** Priest, to sing within the township of Hipperholm, and there **to pray** for the soul of the said William Thorpe, and others.

The above Deed of Feoffment in Latin, with an English **one** of the same date, to declare the uses thereof, were in possession of the above Mrs. Horton, of Coley.

Robert Hemingway, of Upperbrea, gave by Will, dated March 3, 1613, forty pounds, towards the maintenance of a Preacher at Coley Chapel, to be bestowed at the discretion of his Executors; they were also given for the same purpose, by Isabel Maud, of Halifax, widow, twenty pounds; by

Agnes Royde, of Northouram, five pounds; by Matthew Whiteley five pounds, by their several Wills; eight pounds were likewise given to the same use, by Henry Northend and Joseph Wood; with which sums, Richard Sunderland, of Coley-hall, Esq; and seven others, as Trustees, did purchase of one William Kershaw, of Wike, a messuage or tenement in Wike, in the parish of Burstal, with a close of land and meadow called Mappleynge, divided into two parts, in one of which the said messuage standeth; and also a house or cottage in Wike aforesaid, and a close of land called Far-hinging Royds, divided into three closes. This purchase was made with the approbation of all the inhabitants within the Chapelry of Coley; and for the better explaining the true intent and meaning of the conveyance and assurance made of the premises to the said Richard Sunderland, and others, by the said William Kershaw, and to the end the rents, &c. might for ever afterwards be employed for the use aforesaid, it was covenanted and granted in an Indenture, bearing date Oct. 11, 17 James I. made between the said Richard Sunderland and others, of the one part; and Abraham Sunderland, of the Middle Temple, Esq; Joseph Midgley, of Overbrea, M.A. and others, of the other part, that the said Richard Sunderland, &c. should pay yearly the said rent, by equal portions, at Martinmass and Pentecost, to the preaching Minister at Coley aforesaid, for the time being, towards his maintenance, and in no other manner, nor to or for any other use. When only three Trustees survive, they were to convey to others in three months.

I have seen no Trust Deed relating to the above, of a later date than Jan. 3, 1658, which, with another made in the year 1637, were in the hands of Mr. Simpson, of Hipperholm.

RICHARD SUNDERLAND, Esq., of Coley-hall, gave by Will thirty shillings a-year, for ever, out of a tenement in Shelf, to the preaching Minister at Coley Chapel. His Executors were his three sons, Abraham, Samuel and Peter Sunderland. He was buried June 25, 1634. This estate was afterwards sold by his grandson, Langdale Sunderland, Esq., to John Lum, of Westercroft, in Northouram. He also gave tythe-rents within Hipperholme cum Brighouse, amounting to twenty two shillings and sixpence yearly, to the Chapel at . Coley, which rents, as I take it, had been parcel of the Rectory of Dewsbury.

WILLIAM BIRKHEAD, of Brookfoot, in Southouram, gave by Will, dated Dec. 29, 1638, the sum of five pounds, to Samuel Hoyle, of Hoyle-house, in Lightcliff, and Robert Hargreaves, of Hipperholme, in trust, and to the intent, that they should bestow the same on some parcel of land, or yearly rent of inheritance, the one half of the yearly profit whereof should be paid yearly to the Curate or Preacher of God's Word at Lightcliffe, and the other half to the poor people of Lightcliffe and Hipperholme, from time to time, to succeeding ages for ever. His Executor was his brother, John Birkhead, of Gomersal. In 1651, as appears from some minutes of an Inquisition taken in that year at Halifax, the above five pounds remained in the hands of Samuel, son of the above Samuel Hoyle, who paid the benefit thereof as directed.

For William Birkhead's benefaction to the poor of Brighouse, see under Rastrick.

—::—

EXTRACT FROM THE

WILL OF MATTHEW BROADLEY,

OF LONDON,

Dated Oct, 15, 1647.

—" I GIVE to my brother Isaac Broadley, of Halifax, my tenements, with all the appurtenances, situate in the township of Hipperholme, to him and his heirs for ever, provided he pay out of the same yearly, the sum of five pounds per annum towards the maintenance of a Free School, to be erected near Hipperholme aforesaid, where my Executor shall appoint. Item, I give towards the erecting of the said Free School the sum of forty pounds. Also I do give unto Matthew Broadley, (he was sole Executor, and son of Samuel Broadley,) the sum of one thousand pounds, for which Sir William Waters, and Sir Thomas Chamberlain, Knt. and Richard Spencer, Esq; stand bound, provided that upon receipt thereof he bestow five hundred pounds thereof, partly upon settling a convenient yearly means for the aforesaid Free School, and partly in providing fifty-two shillings in bread yearly to be given by twelve-pence each Sunday, at Coley Chapel, to the poor of Hipperholme town and the Lane-Ends."

Mr. Brearcliffe's manuscript, called Halifax Inquiries, sais, that the estate left to Isaac Broadley, was called Lane-Ends, in Hipperholme; also that Matthew Broadley's Will was dated Sep. 6, 1648; in the first Settlement Deed of Hipperholme school, described below, this **Will** is likewise said to **have** been dated August **31**, 1648. These variations I mention, **to make the** discovery of the original more certain, though **the first** has the most authorities.

May 22, 1661, an Indenture tripartite was made between Samuel Sunderland, **of Harden, Esq; of the** first part; Matthew Broadley, of London, Gent. Executor of Matthew Broadley, late of London, Esq; deceased, **of the** second part **; and** William Farrer, of Midgley, Esq; John Lake, of Southouram, Clerk, Abraham Mitchel, of Halifax, Stephen Ellis, Richard Langley, Nathan Whiteley, Joshua Whitley, Joseph **Hargreaves**, Henry Brighouse, Joshua Scolfield, and Joseph **Lister, all of** Hipperholme, **of the third part,** reciting, that **whereas Matthew** Broadley, party **to** these presents, had **received one** thousand pounds, **and** being willing to perform the will and good intention of Matthew Broadley, deceased, he had, with the advice **and** consent **of** some of **the** principal inhabitants of Hipperholme **and** Halifax, agreed with **the above** Samuel Sunderland **for the** purchase of certain **lands and tenements,** with the **sum of** five hundred pounds, **agreeable to the Will** of the above Testator: This Indenture therefore witnesseth, that the said Samuel Sunderland, for **the** said consideration, hath sold, **&c.** to the said Matthew Broadley, William Farrer, &c. their heirs and assigns, **for ever, two** messuages or tenements, **two** barns, **two stables, two gardens, two** folds, and all outhouses, orchards, **lands, and all other** appurtenances thereto belonging, **in** Hipperholme **aforesaid;** and one close of land in Lightcliffe, within the **said township of** Hipperholme, called **Brookroyd,** lately divided **into three** closes; one other close **of land,** called Highroyd **Ing, and** one other close of land, in Lightcliffe aforesaid, **called the** Heyroyd **Ing;** and also one annuity or yearly **rent charge** of eleven pounds, issuing out of a messuage or tenement, with lands, at Brookfoot, in Southouram, and also out of a water corn mill, called Brookfoot mill, at Brookfoot aforesaid; and also **one** other annuity, or yearly rent charge of thirty shillings, issuing **out** of certain messuages **and lands in** Shelf, to have and to hold the said messuages, lands, rent charges, &c. to the said Matthew Broadley, William Farrer, &c. their heirs and assigns, for ever, in trust, to receive and apply the issues and profits thereof yearly, for ever, as well for the yearly payment of the said annual sum of fifty-two shillings at the Chapel of Coley aforesaid, by twelve pence to be laid out in bread every Sabbath-day, for the better maintenance and relief of the most poor, aged, maimed, needy, and impotent people of Hipperholme, and the Lane Ends of Hipperholme aforesaid, or to such, or so many of the said poor people of Hipperholme, and the Lane Ends of Hipperholme, and in such manner as the said Matthew Broadley, &c. and the survivor and survivors of them, their heirs and assigns, shall from time to time, find most necessitous and indigent, and in their discretion shall think most meet to be relieved therewith, so as at no one time there be under the number of four poor persons to share and have the said charitable allowance. And also for the support, and keeping in repair of the School-house for the said Free School, to be erected in or near the town of Hipperholme aforesaid, from time to time, for ever hereafter, as often as need shall require ; and to take and employ all the residue of the said yearly rents, profits, improvements, and advantages made, or to be made, of the said premises, (which they might let to the best yearly value and advantage, so as no lease or leases thereof exceeded the term of twenty-one years, and to be made in possession, or at least not above two years before the expiration of the old lease, or leases thereof, the old accustomed rents of the premises, or more, being reserved,) together with the said annual rent of five pounds, for the maintenance, stipend, &c. of one learned, able, and sufficient person, being a Graduate of the Degree of Bachelor of Arts at the least, of and within one of the Universities of Cambridge or Oxford, to be School-master of the said Free School, to educate and instruct in Grammar, and other literature and learning, the scholars and children of the township and constablery of Hipperholme cum Brighouse only, gratis, and without any other reward, and allowance ; and the rents and profits of the said premises (such deductions as aforesaid being made) to be paid to the said School-master half yearly by equal portions. If the rents became

raised to a greater yearly value, such increase and augmentation was to be employed and disposed of, for the better
maintenance of the said School-master for the time being,
and to no other use, intent, or purpose; except that any
suits in law or equity, or other trouble or incumbrance
concerning the said premises, or any part thereof, should
happen; in which case, the Trustees were impowered to
deduct the expences attending the same, out of the yearly
profits of the said premises, and pay the overplus to the said
School-master. When the place or room of the said School-
master shall happen to become void by death, resignation,
deprivation, or otherwise, that then, and so often the Trustees for the time being, or the greater number of them, were
impowered, within one month next after such avoidance, by
writing under their hands and seals, to nominate and
appoint one other learned and fit person, qualified as
aforesaid, to be School-master of the said Free School:
And if no School-master is by them within two months
chosen as aforesaid, it shall and may be lawful to and
for the Vicar of the Vicarage of Halifax aforesaid, for
the time being, by writing under his hand and seal,
to nominate and appoint a meet and fit person, qualified,
and at the least of the Degree aforesaid, to be School-master
of the said Free-school; the said School-master to be allowed,
ordered, directed, and placed, or displaced, by the Trustees,
or the greater number of them, for the time being, according
to such rules, orders, and allowances as shall be made by
them, or the greater number of them, in writing under their
hands and seals, for the rule, government, and well ordering
of the said Free-school, School-master and poor people, and
as to them, and the greater part of them shall seem meet and
convenient; which rules and orders were agreed to be con-
clusive, and binding to the said School-master, poor people,
and all others concerned therein, to all intents and purposes
the same not being repugnant to the Laws and Statutes of
this kingdom, nor contrary to any Ecclesiastical Canons or
Constitutions of the Church of England which shall be then
in force. And for the better ordering and government of
the said Free-school, the Trustees for the time being were to
have full power and authority for ever, to visit, order, place,
or displace the said School-master for the time being, and

to reform and redress all and **every the** disorders, misdemeanors, offences, and abuses **in the** said Free-school,
School-master, or in any of the **said** poor people, or in, and
touching their allowances, government, order, and disposing
thereof, and for any lewdness, drunkenness, common swearing, profaneness, breaking the orders made **for the** regulating
and government **of** the said Free-school, **or for any** other
just **cause** whatsoever, **as shall be,** by **the said Trustees** for
the **time** being, or the greater number **of them, declared** in
writing, under their hands and seals, to **be a sufficient cause**
of suspension, deprivation, and displacing, **and by the** same
writing to deprive, suspend, **turn out,** and displace **the** said
School-master, **and** to elect **and place** another **qualified** as
above, in his room, to be intitled **to** the same **benefits** and
advantages as the School-master **so** deprived, **&c.** When
only three Trustees shall be living **or** resident **within** the
township of Hipperholme, or vicarage **of** Halifax, **they** shall,
together with the non-residentiaries, convey and assure **the**
above premises, with the profits thereof, **to** nine **other**
sufficient persons inhabiting in Hipperholme, **or** the vicarage
of Halifax, **so** always that there be at least six of the said
Trustees inhabitants in Hipperholme aforesaid.

It ought to be observed, that there are several **defects** in
Matthew Broadley's Will, such as, **no** person appointed to
build the School, **nor,** being built, by whom **or** how it should
be kept in repair, **nor** who should **put in or** displace the
School-master, nor **what** children **(boys or girls)** or of what
towns **or** places they were to be, **nor** in **what art or** science
they should be instructed, nor whether **the yearly** means **to**
be settled for the School should **be by the revenue** of land
to be purchased with the **money, or with** the **interest of the**
money, or by some **employment of the** stock **of money, or**
otherwise; **nor was** any **one appointed to distribute** the
bread to the poor, **nor** any **number of poor mentioned** to
whom it was to be distributed: **To remedy which** defects,
the above-mentioned Indenture **tripartite was** made; yet,
notwithstanding **the** agreements **therein** contained seem to
be good and necessary, yet, in the **eye of** the law, they are
no other than arbitrary proceedings amongst other parties
than the Testator himself appointed, and because not
warrantable by the Will, perhaps **not** altogether safe to those
who put the same in execution. **If** also any breach **of** trust

was to happen, or of the above agreements supposing them valid, no provision of remedy was directed for it, nor who should complain thereof if the Executor should die, or be absent out of the kingdom. Besides, the Testator's gift to his brother and his heirs, of his land in Hipperholme, provided his said brother paid five pounds per annum to the School, was, in construction of law, void; for as Isaac Broadley was brother and next heir to Matthew the Devisor, the law would say, that the said Isaac took the land by descent, and not by the Will. The same was also void in law, because there was no person extant who could, by taking advantage of the condition, compel the payment of the money; for Isaac Broadley, who was to pay it, being also heir at law, none but himself could enter to the land for non-payment thereof, according to the provisoe. For these reasons, the said Isaac refused to pay the said annuity till the arrears amounted to sixty pounds, and the Trustees had no remedy till about the year 1661, when laying their grievances before Council, they were told, that notwithstanding the above gift of five pounds per annum could not be recovered by law, yet, as it was made to a charitable use, such as a Free-school, which is a gift within the Statute 43 Eliz. c. 4, of Charitable Uses, it might be made good by that Statute, on a Commission to be pursued out of the Chancery by virtue of that Statute, and an Inquisition thereupon to be found and taken, and a Decree to be made by the Commissioners, with a Decree of Confirmation in Court for payment, (viz.) as well of the arrearages since the Testator's death, as of the growing rent; and though part of the land was copyhold, which cannot by law be devised or charged by a Will, yet that it might be so charged to a charitable use; however, that the Free-school might be so charged, and so the annuity decreed to be paid out of the whole.

On this account, and for the greater security of the Trustees named in the above Indenture tripartite, application was made to a Commission for Pious Uses at Halifax, August 29, 1662, on which the Commissioners, after reciting the Will of Matthew Broadley, and that it was by Inquisition found that the said Will had been fulfilled according to the intentions of the Testator, except that Isaac Broadley had not paid the sum of five pounds per annum as directed, or any part thereof, in respect the Free-school was not erected and finished till Michaelmas last past before the date of the said Inquisition, did order, adjudge, and decree, that the several sums of forty pounds and five hundred pounds, received and disposed of according to the Will of the donor, should for ever stand firm and stable, for and towards the maintenance of a School-master to teach the said Free-school within and for the township of Hipperholme, whereof fifty-two shillings to be first taken out of the **same,** to be laid out and bestowed in bread, **to** be given by twelve-pence each Sunday, at Coley Chapel, to the poor people of Hipperholme and the Lane Ends: And that the **five** pounds per annum, given by the said Matthew Broadley, should stand and be kept up for ever; and the said Isaac Broadley, his heirs and assigns, were adjudged to pay to William Farrer, Esq; John Lake, D.D. Abraham Mitchel, Stephen Ellis, Richard Langley, Nathan Whiteley, Joshua Whiteley, John Scolfield, Henry Brighouse, Joseph Hargreaves, and Joseph Lister, Feoffees for the use of the said Free-school, nominated and approved of by the said Commissioners, the said sum of five pounds yearly for ever, towards the maintenance of the said Free-school erected in Hipperholme, to be paid out of the rents, issues, and profits of the lands and tenements in Hipperholme aforesaid, at one entire payment at or upon the Feast of St. Michael the Archangel.

One Trust Deed relating to the above was Dated April 30, 1697, another July 30, 1714.

SAMUEL SUNDERLAND, Esq; of Harden, in Bingley parish, (already mentioned under Halifax) gave, by indenture, made June 30, 1671, to Richard Hooke, D.D. and Vicar of Halifax, Stephen Ellis, of Hipperholme; Richard Langley, of Priestley-green; Nathan Whitley, of Rookes; Joshua Whitley, his brother; William Brooke, of Ethercliffe; and Joseph Lister, of Thornhill-briggs, and their heirs, all that messuage or tenement (part whereof had been converted into a School-house) and the lands, buildings, &c. thereto belonging in Hipperholme. And also all that other messuage or tenement, with lands, buildings, &c. thereto belonging, at Norwood-green, within the township of Hipperholme cum Brighouse, in trust, after the decease of the said Samuel Sunderland, to the use of the School-master for the time being of the Free Grammar School, for and in respect of the

v

township of Hipperholme cum Brighouse aforesaid, the same School-master being thereunto lawfully licensed, and being of a degree of Bachelor of Arts at least, upon condition that the same School-master, and his successors for the time being, shall well and truly satisfy and pay, or cause to be paid, forth of the rents and profits of the lands and tenements first mentioned, the yearly rent or sum of six pounds to an Usher Master of the same school, at the Feasts of Pentecost, and St. Martin the Bishop in winter, or St. Martin and Pentecost, as the same shall happen to fall next after the decease of the said Samuel Sunderland, by equal portions, for ever, the same Usher Master to be from time to time nominated and elected by the above Feoffees and their successors, or the major part of them, and to be lawfully licensed and admitted thereunto, with power of distress on the said premises to the said Usher Master, in case of non payment of the said yearly rent, or any part thereof, for twenty days after the same becomes due. And upon farther trust, that the yearly rents and profits of the other messuage or tenement, with its appurtenances, at Norwood-green, be paid to the most indigent and necessitous poor people of and within the township of Hipperholme cum Brighouse aforesaid, for ever, on the Feast-days of St. Thomas the Apostle, and the Nativity of St. John Baptist, or St. John Baptist, and St. Thomas Days, or Feasts, as the same shall happen to fall next after the decease of the said Samuel Sunderland, by equal portions, in or at the aforesaid School-house, by the Ministers, Churchwardens, and Overseers for the poor within the Chapelries of Coley and Lightcliffe, from time to time. When the seven Feoffees above-named became decreased by death to the number of two of them and no more, the survivors were, within three months, to elect and appoint the Vicar of Halifax for the time being, (in case he was not one of the surviving Feoffees,) and six of the most able and discreet Inhabitants of the township of Hipperholme cum Brighouse, or seven, if the said Vicar be one of the two surviving Feoffees, the conveyance of the premises to be made at the reasonable request and costs of the said Master and Churchwardens, and this order, way, and course to be observed, and kept for ever. The Feoffees were also to take effectual care that the said buildings upon the Lands, granted by this Deed, and the fences thereof, be from time to time kept in sufficient repair, **that** the charity might not be impaired.

The Testator (**as** already observed) was buried Feb. 4, 1676. Mr. Wright, p. 127, sais, **that** this Mr. Sunderland gave, amongst other benefactions, seventeen **pounds a year** for **ever to** the Free-school of Hipperholme; **to the use of** the poor **of** Hipperholme eight pounds a year **for ever**; and to the successive Curates of the Chapel of **Coley five** pounds **a year for ever**; all **which** Mr. Robert Parker, **of** Bingley, **his Executor, saw** rightly and truly performed; **but** Mr. Thoresby's account, in his Topography of **Léedes, p.** 583, differs from this, for according to this Author **he left** yearly **to** the poor of Norwood-green eight pounds, to Hipperholme school eighteen pounds, and to Coley Chapel twenty shillings.

On the School porch at Hipperholme is this inscription: "Libera Schola Grammaticalis Hipperholmiæ a MATTHEO "BROADLEY, armigero, primitus fundata, post a SAMUELE "SUNDERLAND aucta, qui ambo patriæ chari, **et** pauperibus "benefici, hoc **legatum famæ suæ** monumentum posteris "reliquere, **1661.**" Over the gateway leading to the School-master's house, " S^L SUNDERLAND, Arm^r dedit, 1671." **On** the inside of the same, " Sumptu N. SHARPE, 1729."

THOMAS WHITLEY, of Sinder-hills, gave by Will (**but of what date** I know not) forty pounds, to be kept up as a stock, and **the** interest thereof to be distributed yearly amongst **the poor** people of Hipperholme, by his executors, with the assistance of the Churchwardens and Overseers of the said **town,** according to their several necessities. The Executors were James Oates, John Whitley, **of** Wheatley, Michael Whitley, of Shelf, **and** John Whitley, **of** Rookes, who **seem** not to have **put** this **part of** the **Will** in execution; **for at a** commission of **pious** uses it was **decreed, August 29,** 1662, that Joseph Furness, and Phebe his wife, **Executors of** the above James Oates; Judith Whitley, Richard Law, and Hester his wife, Executors **or** Administrators of the above Michael Whitley; Grace Whitley, **and** Joshua Whitley her son, Executors **or** Administrators **of the above** John Whitley, of Rookes; and Thomas Lister, Executor **of** Sibil Whitley, who was Executrix of the above John Whitley, of Wheatley, should pay **to the** poor of Hipperholme the said sum of forty pounds, **with** three years interest, and twenty shillings for the charges of prosecuting the Inquisition and Decree; which monies not being paid as decreed, a subpœna in the nature of a Scire-Facias was awarded out of the Court of Chancery, against the parties concerned.

JOSHUA OATES entered into a bond of one hundred pounds, in his life-time, to secure forty shillings a-year to the Preacher at Coley Chapel for ever, out of a parcel of land in Shelf, to be paid at Martinmass and Pentecost, by equal portions, which bond was found, in 1651, (as appears from Mr. Brearcliffe's Manuscript,) to be in the hands of one Robert Birkhead, of Shelf.

SUSANNA DANSON was a benefactress to Coley Chapel, as appears from the following inscription on a stone erected on the right hand side of the way leading from Huddersfield to Bradford, at a place called Cockhill-clough : " Mrs. Susanna " Danson gave the two adjoining Closes to Coley Chapel for " ever, and they came into possession Oct. 1730." One account sais, she left fifty shillings yearly in lands within Shelf, for a Sermon on Good-Friday.

BOUNTIES to LIGHTCLIFFE CHAPEL.

This Chapel had Queen Anne's Bounty by lot, in 1749; the purchase was at Sheard-green, in Lightcliffe; also by benefaction in 1759, when a farm called Barley Croft was bought, at Blackshaw head, in Stansfield; lastly, in 1763, by benefaction, in consequence of which, a contract was made in 1764, for a farm in Northouram, called Oatsroyd. In 1786, the clear yearly value of this Chapel was returned to have been, 8d of Queen Anne, ten pounds eleven shillings and six-pence; and that of Coley, thirteen pounds twelve shillings and two-pence.

MIDGLEY.

RICHARD DEYNE, of Deynehouse, son and heir of John Deyne, of Myggelay, gave to John Myggelay, son of Robert Myggelay, Richard Sladen, of Myggelay, the younger, Richard Patchett, of the same, William Ferroure, son and heir apparent of Henry Ferroure, Robert Shawe, son of James Shawe, and Robert Thomas, of Myggelay aforesaid, one yearly rent of thirteen shillings and four-pence, issuing out of a messuage with lands and tenements, called Herrebothlegh, in Luddyngden, within Myggelay aforesaid, to the use of John Robynson, Capel-lane, in the Chapel of St. Mary, of Luddyngden aforesaid, and his successors in the same Chapel, for the time being, for ever, and payable at the Feasts of Pentecost and St. Martin in winter, by equal portions, or within forty days after each of the said Feasts, with power of distress to the above Trustees, and their heirs, if the said yearly rent is unpaid for forty days after it becomes due as aforesaid.

This extract I took from the original Deed, in Latin, lent by the late Curate of Luddenden. It was dated at Myggelay, March 6, 17 Hen. VIII. and is in the form of a charter.

It is said that Richard Deyne left the above, because he had killed in a duel one Brooksbank, of Bankhouse, in Warley.

JOHN CROSSLEY, of Kershawhouse, in Midgley, gave (as appears from a table in Luddenden Chapel) two pounds two shillings yearly, to the Curate of Luddenden, for preaching a Sermon every first Wednesday after the sixth day of March. One account makes this only forty shillings.

—::—

EXTRACT FROM THE
WILL OF JOHN MIDGLEY,
OF MIDGLEY.

—"I GIVE to the Curate of the Chapel of Luddenden, for the time being, and his survivors, Curates there, for ever, one fulling mill, or paper-mill, with one holme or croft thereto belonging, to preach a Sermon yearly, and every year, for ever, upon every sixteenth day of February from and after my decease ; and also one loft in the said Chapel which was erected therein, (and is now standing,) by my deceased brother William Midgley, to and for the use and benefit of the said Curate for ever."

In Luddenden Chapel is kept a Faculty obtained by the above William Midgley, for erecting the loft here mentioned, dated in 1703.

The money arising from this benefaction, is said, in a table in Luddenden Chapel, to be two pounds ten shillings yearly ; but it now makes three pounds yearly, besides the loft, which raises about ten shillings more.

Edward Watkinson, Clerk, (Rector of Little Chart, in Kent, and D.D. but formerly Curate of Luddenden,) conveyed by Deed, dated June 2, 1732, to John Dearden, of Warley, Esq; and Stephen Atkinson, of Midgley, Yeoman, a messuage, dwelling house, or tenement, with the appurtenances, in Leeds, in a place there called the Vicar-lane, of the clear yearly rent of four pounds, with two cottages or tenements, with the appurtenances belonging to the said messuage, and standing in the fold or back-side adjoining, of the clear yearly rent of one pound six shillings; and also two cottages or tenements, with the appurtenances, at Hunslet, in the parish of Leeds aforesaid, of the clear yearly rent of one pound ten shillings; to hold to the said John Dearden and Stephen Atkinson, their heirs and assigns, for ever, in trust that they shall, with the rents and profits of the said premisses, purchase two shillings' worth of bread, viz. twelve two-penny loaves weekly, and every week, for the benefit of twelve poor widows, viz. six within the township of Midgley aforesaid, and six within the township of Warley aforesaid; and in default of such number of widows there, then for the benefit of the most necessitous persons in the said townships, to be distributed to them by the Chapel Wardens of the Chapel of Luddenden, for the time being, upon every Sunday in the year, soon after Morning Service; four of the said widows to be chose out of the said township of Midgley, by the Chapel Warden of that township for the time being, and other four of the said widows to be chose out of the said township of Warley, by the Chapel Warden of that township for the time being; and the remaining four widows by the said John Dearden and Stephen Atkinson, viz. two out of each township; and for want of such widows, and to supply their places, other necessitous persons to be chose by them in like manner, out of the said townships, so as always to make up the number of twelve; and after the death of the said John Dearden and Stephen Atkinson, the said twelve poor widows, or necessitous persons, in their stead, shall be chose by the said Chapel Wardens for the time being, for ever, viz. by the Chapel Warden of Midgley, six out of the said township of Midgley, and by the Chapel Warden of Warley, six out of the said township of Warley; the said twelve poor widows, or necessitous persons, to be

personally present at the distribution of the said bread, unless prevented by sickness, or some bodily infirmity; the
said Chapel Wardens, immediately after such distribution,
to enter into the books, which were given them by the said
Edward Watkinson for that purpose, the names of the said
twelve poor widows, or necessitous persons, and the day of
the month and year when the said bread was so distributed;
and in the absence of the said Chapel Wardens, that the
said John Dearden and Stephen Atkinson shall distribute,
or cause to be distributed, for so long as they shall live, the
said loaves, and make choice of the said twelve poor widows,
or necessitous persons, viz. six out of each township. Provided nevertheless, that whenever it shall happen that the
rents and profits of the said premises shall fall short to
purchase so much bread, the Chapel Wardens for the time
being shall only buy so much as the clear rents or profits
thereof will admit of, and make distribution thereof proportion-
ably amongst such poor persons as aforesaid: But as at the
time of this donation the rents of the said premises would purchase more, therefore so long as the same should so continue
it was the desire of the said Edward Watkinson, that each
such poor person should have, upon every Trinity Sunday,
sixpence in money, and upon every Sunday next before
Christmas Day, twelve-pence in money, and upon every
Easter Sunday sixpence in money, over and besides the
said bread, the remaining clear yearly rent to go and be detained by the person who shall take the trouble to collect
the rents, and look after the said premises; and if the rents
shall fall short, the distribution thereof, both in bread and
money, shall be proportioned thereto, so as the person who
shall take the trouble of looking after the premises, and
collecting the rents, and paying the same over to the said
Chapel Wardens, shall have yearly five shillings for his or
their trouble therein.

N.B. The Deed signed by Edward Watkinson is to remain
in the hands of the Vicar of Halifax, for the time being;
and that signed by the Trustees with the said Edward
Watkinson, his heirs and assigns; and a Memorial of the
former was registered at Wakefield, August 18, 1732, in
Book EE. p. 183, and number 269.

The bread was first given on Trinity Sunday, 1732; and
the Doctor gave two register books, one signed Midgley, and

the other Warley, to enter the names of the widows in, and the time when they had bread given.

Luddenden Chapel obtained Queen Anne's Bounty by lot, in 1732, with which, and with other contributions made in the Chapelry, a farm was bought in Midgley, called New-earthhead, of the yearly rent of eight pounds, as appears from a table in the said Chapel. Its clear yearly value in 1786, was returned to have been, 3d of Queen Anne, three pounds thirteen shillings and four-pence.

—::—

NORTHOURAM.

EXTRACT FROM THE

WILL OF ROBERT HEMINGWAY,

OF OVERBREA, IN NORTHOURAM,

Dated March 3, 1613.

— " I GIVE the sum of ten pounds, to be lent, from time to time, to certain of the most religious and honest poor, or decayed tradesmen, of the township of Northouram, at the discretions of my Executors and Overseer, and after their decease at the discretion of the Vicar of the parish church of Halifax, and the Churchwarden of the town of Northouram for the time being, with the assistance of one honest and sufficient man of the said town, whom I request to take, from time to time, sufficient security for the continuance thereof."

In this Will he also gave ten pounds to the Free Grammar School near Halifax.

—::—

EXTRACT FROM THE

WILL OF JEREMIAH HALL,

OF DUBLIN, DOCTOR OF PHYSIC,

Dated March 1, 1687.

— " I GIVE and bequeath the sum of fifty pounds sterling, to purchase as much ground in Booth-town as will be sufficient to build thereon an house for two old men and two old women, natives of Booth-town aforesaid, to live in, as also a little school-house; and for the building of the said houses I also give fifty pounds more; and in case a convenient house can be found already built, then the said sums to go for the purchase of such an house; this said hundred pounds to be paid out of the money in my cousin Jonathan Hall's hands. Item, I give and bequeath also out of the money in my cousin Jonathan Hall's hands, the sum of one hundred pounds sterling, together with the interest of a mortgage I have for two hundred and thirty pounds sterling, upon Mr. Thomas Hodkinson's estate, in and near the town of Wentworth, of which I am in possession—both which sums are towards the maintenance of the poor people, and the sum of five pounds per annum to those that shall teach in the school gratis ten poor boys and girls, those that are natives of Booth-town, or near it."

Of this part of the abovementioned Will, Jonathan, Abraham, and Joseph Hall were Trustees and Overseers; of these, Jonathan died in the life time of the Testator, and Abraham and Joseph, pursuant to the Will, purchased with the said sum of one hundred pounds, by surrender, three copyhold cottages, or dwelling houses, in Booth's-town aforesaid, with the appurtenances, to the use of themselves, their heirs and assigns, for ever, in trust, to be disposed of by them, and their heirs, according to the trust reposed in them, by the said Will; they also repaired, altered, and converted the said cottage houses into four dwellings and a school-house. After this the said Abraham died, and Joseph Hall, the surviving Trustee, by lease, release, and surrender dated May 1, 1695, conveyed all his interest in the estate at Wentworth, to the use of himself, and Joseph Wilkinson, James Oates, Nathaniel Priestley, John Longbottom, Thomas Hall, and William Bradley, and their heirs, in trust, that they and their heirs, and the survivors and survivor of them, and their and his heirs, should be Feoffees, and be seized of the said estate at Wentworth, and also of the said school-house and four cottages, and an annuity of twelve pounds ten shillings, to the uses mentioned in the above Will, with this additional clause, amongst others, that the Trustees, or the major part of them, might place or displace the said School-master, and four poor people, when they thought proper ; and that when only three of the said Trustees were living, they should convey to four others sufficient, and so in like manner conveyances to be ever made on the like trust and confidence.

The above mortgage money being paid in, the Trustees last named purchased therewith, and with the annuity above-mentioned, an estate in Ovenden, called Brock-holes ; the purchase deed of which is dated the 9th day of September, 1707 ; and also one other estate at a place called Moorfalls, in Northouram, with five closes of land adjoining upon one another, and some or one of them adjoining to the messuage and buildings there, (excepting one coal-pit and pit-hill in the south-east corner of one of the said closes,) and one other close of land to the said messuage belonging, lying on the east side of the highway, leading from Halifax to Bradford (except the coals which can be gotten from under the same without digging or breaking any of the soil or ground thereof) the purchase deed of which is dated the 18th day of February, 1709.

Of the above Trustees, all (except John Longbottom) died without transferring their trust to others, and the said John, about the year 1730, conveyed to Thomas Burton, Edmund Briggs, Jonathan Longbottom, John Bargh, Benjamin Wilkinson, Joseph Hall, and Robert Wood, on the same trust as in the former Deed, and under the same covenants. Of these also the said Joseph Hall became the surviving Trustee, who, in the year 1759, conveyed to George Legh, LL.D. Vicar of Halifax, John Lister, of Shibden-hall, Clerk, Cyril Jackson, of Halifax, Doctor of Physic, Jonathan Nicholl, and John Crabtree, both of Booth-town, Jeremy Lister, of Northouram, Samuel Waterhouse, of the same place, Jonathan Hall, of Eland, Benjamin Wilkinson, of Northouram aforesaid, John Watkinson, the younger, of Ovenden, John Mitchell, of Holdworth, and James Carr, of Halifax, with a particular clause in the Deed, that when these shall, by death, or otherwise, be reduced to three in number, the survivors shall, in like manner, convey to - - others on the like trusts in those presents declared.

EXTRACT FROM THE

WILL OF JOSEPH CROWTHER,

OF WHITHILL, IN NORTHOURAM,

Dated Oct. 30, 1711.

—"**B**Y virtue of one surrender of the same date with this my Will thereby impowering me, I do hereby give, devise, and bequeath all that copyhold messuage, or tenement, with the appurtenances, situate and being in Northouram, and all barns, buildings, closes, lands, commons, easements, and hereditaments whatsoever to the same belonging, now in the tenure or occupation of Widow Bothomley, or her assigns, unto Joseph Wood, of Northouram aforesaid, Yeoman, his heirs and assigns, in trust only, that the said messuage and premises, and the rents and profits thereof, may at all times, for ever hereafter, be enjoyed and received by a School-master, duly chosen and lawfully licenced, who shall, from time to time, yearly for ever, teach twelve of the poorest children, natives of Northouram, in the new erected school on Northouram-green, whose parents are least able to pay for them there."

From an attested copy.

—::—

NORLAND.

EXTRACT FROM THE

WILL OF EDWARD WAINHOUSE,

Dated September 18, 1686.

—"**I** GIVE and bequeath to the old people and poor persons of this town of Norland, two parts of the yearly rents and profits (the whole being divided into three) which shall arise and issue out of that messuage or tenement called Butterise, in Norland aforesaid, during the natural life of my said wife, and the third part also after her death, reserved to her before out of the same, to have and to hold the said messuage or tenement to the said poor people, and their successors, for ever, as aforesaid, and the rents of the aforesaid messuage or tenement to be paid at Midsummer and Christmas, by equal portions, to the Overseers of the poor of this town, for the time being, yearly, and the Overseers to take one or two of the Heads of the town to the distribution of the said rents, and but a little thereof to those persons which have allowances, or nothing at all of it. And I do hereby authorize the Overseers of the poor, with one or two of the Heads of the said town, to sett and lett, or to farm lett, the said messuage or tenement, as often as need shall require."

In a Terrier belonging to Sowerby-bridge Chapel, wrote in 1727, it is said that Edward Wainhouse left yearly to the poor three pounds five shillings.

—::—

OVENDEN.

Original ENDOWMENT of ILLINGWORTH CHAPEL.

HENRY SAVILE, Lord of Ovenden, gave one acre of land out of the waste thereof, by a Deed bearing date January 26, 17 Hen. VIII. to James Bawmeforth, and others, as Feoffees, in trust, that they should stand seized thereof to the use of a Chapel there, to be built to the honor of the Virgin Mary, paying therefore to the said Lord one red rose yearly.

For this see the Register at Halifax, vol. ii. also the Old Church Book at Halifax. In Brearcliffe's manuscript, called Halifax Inquiries, &c. dated Dec. 22, 1651, are also these words : " Item, we find by divers other Deeds, bearing date in the time of King Henry VIII. made from the said Henry Savile, Lord of Ovenden, that he gave divers parcels of lands in Ovenden to certain Feoffees and their heirs, and in the said Deeds mentioned no use ; but after we find by a Deed, made by the said several Feoffees, in the 3d year of Queen Elizabeth, with a schedule thereunto annexed, that he gave out of the said lands certain small rents to the Chapel of Illingworth ; but the townsmen do think that the whole lands were given to the said use, and not the rents only."

An Inquisition taken at Halifax, Feb. 16, 1651, runs thus: " We find that one acre of land, long ago taken in from the wastes of Ovenden, in part whereof the Chapel of Illingworth is built, and one house, called Chapel-house, and a barn thereunto belonging, are builded. And also one other acre of land, late taken from the wastes of Ovenden, and heretofore bought by one John Best, of George, late Earl of Shrewsbury, and others;—And also one annuity of seven shillings yearly, issuing out of three acres and a half of land in Bradshaw, in Ovenden;—And one other annuity of five shillings yearly, issuing out of three acres of land, with the appurtenance, in Bradshaw;—One other yearly rent of six shillings, yearly issuing (as we conceive) out of certain lands and tenements, with their appurtenances, in Ovenden;—One other yearly rent of four shillings, yearly issuing out of one rood of land in Ovenden;—One other yearly rent of two shillings, yearly issuing out of **one acre of land in Bradshaw, in** Ovenden;— **And** one other **annuity** of fifteen shillings, yearly issuing **out of one** house or tenement, **and** the buildings thereupon **built,** and three **roods** of land, meadow, and pasture, by **estimation,** called Sawre Parke, in Ovenden, **were** by **deed** indented, bearing date Dec. 25, 1640, granted and conveyed by Joseph Wood, of Old Laughton, in Ovenden, and Luke Crowther, the elder, **of** Holdsworth, **in** Ovenden, unto John Doughty, **of** the University of Oxford, and others, and **their** heirs for ever, as Feoffees in trust, **to the use** and **behoof of,** and for the maintenance **of, the** Preacher of God's Word for the time being, at the Chapel called Illingworth Chapel, and of such other person or persons after him as shall preach the Word of God at the said Chapel, and officiate the **cure** there successively from time to time to succeeding generations for ever; and for want of such Preacher at the said Chapel, then for and during such time of vacancy of a Preacher only, to the use and behoof of the poor people inhabiting within Ovenden aforesaid; or of the Supervisors **of** the highways in Ovenden, for repairing and amending the highways there, **at** the discretion of the said John Doughty, and the rest of the said Co-feoffees, and their heirs. And we find, that the same hath been duly performed hitherto.

" Also we find, that one house body in Ovenden, called Scausby, was leased by Mr. John Bairstow, and other Feoffees, for the Chapel of Illingworth, Oct. 11, 1647, to Isaac Walton, for 21 years, for one shilling and six-pence yearly, to be paid towards the maintenance of the Minister of the same Chapel."

For the Benefactions of Richard Somerscales, and Isaac Bowcock, in Ovenden, see under Halifax.

ILLINGWORTH CHAPEL had only twelve pounds sixteen shillings yearly of a certain endowment, 3d of Queen Anne; it was augmented Dec. 29, 1718, with the Queen's bounty by benefaction, through the contribution of Mr. John Wilkinson, and others. The purchase deeds are dated Jan. 1, 1721. The estates bought with the four hundred pounds are all in Ovenden. One is called Lower Scawsby, to which belong thirty-five days work of land; another Upper Scawsby, to which belong thirteen acres of land; and a third Ainsworth-house, with some cottages, and closes of land, but no particular quantity mentioned in the deed.

—::—

RASTRICK.

EXTRACT FROM THE
WILL OF JOHN HANSON,

OF WOODHOUSE,

Dated August 14, 1621.

—"I FREELY give, devise, and bequeath unto Walter Stanhope, of Horsfirth, Thomas Brooke, of Newhouse, my sons in law, and to Richard Law, son and heir of Richard Law, late of Halifax, deceased, John Stanhope, and Thomas Brooke, and to Thomas Hanson, son and heir apparent of my brother Thomas Hanson, to Edward Hanson, of Netherwoodhouse, Thomas Hanson and Robert Hanson, of Rastrick, my cousins, one close of land and meadow in Rastrick, called the Little Southedge, which I late bought of John Goodheir, and so much of one other close, called the Wellclose, as is freehold land; and I intend to surrender the residue of the same close to the said persons, to the uses hereafter declared; To have and to hold, to them the said Walter Stanhope, &c. and to their heirs for ever, in trust and confidence, nevertheless, that they shall stand and be seized of the said two closes, to pay yearly forth of the same a rent-charge of twenty shillings towards the maintenance of Divine Service in the chapel of Rastrick, and for teaching of a school there. And whereas the trade of making of cloth is a great help to many poor persons, and would be much more if men would be advised in the fear of God to make true cloth, my meaning is, that sixteen pounds of my goods shall remain as a stock in the township of Rastrick, to set poor and honest workmen in labour, but the property of the said goods shall remain and be unto Alexander Stock, Clerk, Parson of Heaton, and Edward Sunderland, Clerk, Preacher of the Word of God at Eland, and with their successors, Parsons of Heaton, and Preachers of the Word of God at Eland, from time to time, to succeeding generations for ever. Also I devise to them, the said Alexander Stock and Edward Sunderland, and their said successors, four pounds more, by them to be employed, with the said sixteen pounds, to the use of the poor aforesaid, according to such note of direction as I have left under mine own hand for the same, so there be no employment thereof made to any Clothier that useth either to flock or strain their cloth deceitfully."

Transcribed from an old manuscript in my own possession, formerly belonging to Edward Hanson, of Woodhouse.

WILLIAM BIRKHEAD, of Brookfoot, in Southouram, as appears from an Inquisition taken at Halifax, Feb. 16, 1651, and which belonged to the late Mr. Stead, of Nottingham, gave by Will, dated Dec. 29, 1638, out of his last third part of his personal estate, commonly called the *Death's part, unto Edward Hanson, of Netherwoodhouse, in Rastrick, and Richard Law, of Shelf, the sum of five pounds, in trust, that they should bestow the same on some parcel of land, or yearly rent of inheritance, to be yearly paid to the poor people of Rastrick and Brighouse, from time to time, to succeeding generations for ever.

This money was not come to the hands of the said Trustees at the time of taking the above Inquisition.

-----

* For the meaning of this expression, see Burn's Ecclesiastical Law, vol. ii, p. 782.

EXTRACT FROM THE

WILL OF MARY LAW, of Ealand,

Dated Feb. 4, 1701.

—" I GIVE and bequeath all those lands, tenements, and premises, with their appurtenances, (at Lower Woodhouse, and in Rastrick,) which are in the tenure and occupation of John Bottomley, Jonas Preston, and John Malinson, unto Thomas Hanson, of Bothroyd, in Rastrick, and to his heirs and assigns, and to the Minister of Rastrick, and his successors for the time being, to the uses, purposes, and intents hereafter limited **and** expressed, and to none other use, intent and purpose whatsoever; that is to say, **all** that messuage and tenement at Lower Woodhouse aforesaid, in the tenure of the said John Bottomley, (being **of** the yearly value of six pounds or upwards) to the use **and** towards the maintenance of four poor widows, to be **chosen within the town** and township **of** Rastrick, at the discretion of the said Thomas Hanson, and his heirs, and the said Minister of Rastrick, and his successors for the time being, for ever. And all those messuages, lands, tenements, and premises in Rastrick aforesaid, in possession of Jonas Preston and John Mallinson aforesaid, to the use and behoof **of** endowing a School in Rastrick aforesaid, for the teaching and instructing twenty poor children to read and write, to be chosen within the town of Rastrick and Brighouse, **at** the discretion as abovementioned."

The widows have each thirty shillings clear, and **the** School-master eleven pounds yearly.

RASTRICK CHAPEL received Queen Anne's bounty in 1720, by means of **Sir John** Armitage, and John Bedford, Esq; before which the returned certainty was five pounds per **annum.** I **have** the copy of a Deed, dated June 11, 1605, **reciting,** that whereas John Thornhill, and **others,** had petitioned Sir John Fortescue, Chancellor of the Duchy of Lancaster, shewing, that there had time immemorial been an antient Chapel within the township of Rastrick, called St. Matthew's Chapel, within which divine service had been celebrated, and also a school for the education of youth above fifty years ago, which Chapel, for want of due maintenance for keeping a Curate there, had for the greatest part of fifty years last past been profaned, and converted to other uses, till it was reformed by the statute temp. Eliz. for reviving of things given to charitable uses; since which time the said John Thornhill, and others, had bestowed great sums of money in repairing and enlarging the same, and maintaining divine service therein for a year last past; and that every Sunday and holiday a great number of people did resort thereto, and were likely so to do if divine service were continued, for that a great part of the inhabitants of the said township were two miles distant from their Parish Church of Eland, the ways foul in winter, and the causeways decayed for want of repairing; by reason whereof many who were willing to be present at divine service at Eland twice a day, were inforced in the afternoons to be absent; and many of the younger sort had taken occasion thereby to occupy themselves on Sundays and holidays in the afternoons at unlawful games; which abuses had been greatly reformed the last year, and were likely to continue so, if divine service might be provided for. And for that the said township of Rastrick was very small, consisting of not above twenty-four families, and the greatest part thereof poor cottagers, and the whole township not containing above twelve oxgangs of land, and therefore unable to bear the charges of celebrating divine service, or instructing youth in the said Chapel, and therefore humbly intreated his Honour to grant licence to the said Petitioners, &c. to inclose and improve from the waste and commons within the said township, some few acres of ground, as might be least hurtful to the inhabitants there, and to convert the same to the use and benefit of those who should celebrate divine service, and keep a School in the said Chapel; for which grounds they were willing to pay yearly to his Majesty four-pence of new rent for every acre. On perusal of which petition, and conference had with Sir John Savile, one of the Barons of the Court of Exchequer, who lived within two miles of the said Chapel, and affirmed the contents of the said Petition to be true, and that by means thereof the inhabitants of the manor of Brighouse, which are more remote from the Church than the inhabitants of Rastrick, may likewise resort to the said Chapel; also that none had right of common in the said inclosures to be made, except the said Petitioners, and

w

others the inhabitants of Rastrick aforesaid: It is, therefore, this 11th day of June, 3d James, ordered and decreed
by the said Chancellor, that the Steward of the Manor of
Wakefield should grant, by Copy of Court-roll, ten **acres** of
said wastes **and** commons **to** said **Petitioners** and their heirs
according **to** the custom **of** said manor, **to be** inclosed and
improved, **for** the maintenance of some **honest** person, from
time **to** time, who shall say divine service in the said Chapel
as aforesaid, the said Petitioners paying yearly four-pence
for every acre **so** inclosed, at **the** Feast of St. Michael, **to**
the Grave of the **said** township **of** Rastrick.

—::—

RISHWORTH.

EXTRACT FROM THE

WILL OF JOHN WHEELWRIGHT,

OF NORTH SHIELDS,

Dated October 14, 1724.

—"I GIVE, **devise and** bequeath all and singular my
messuages, houses, lands, tenements, and hereditaments whatsoever, situate and being in the county of
York and elsewhere, unto John Wheelwright, of Norland,
in the county of York, Miller; Ely Dyson, of Clay-house,
in the county of York, Merchant; and Abraham Thomas,
of Dewsbury, in the said county of York, Clothier; upon
trust, for the building a School at Dewsbury: And upon this
farther trust also, that the said John Wheelwright, Ely
Dyson, and Abraham Thomas, do and shall, with all convenient speed after my decease, out of my personal estate
herein after devised to them, pay and apply the sum of one
hundred and fifty pounds for the building of a School at
Rushworth, in the said county of York, and that my said
Trustees for the time being do and shall also out of my real
estate pay the yearly sum of ten pounds to a School-master
for ever, at four equal quarterly payments, to wit, at Candlemass, May-day, Lammas, and Martinmass, in every year,
for the teaching and instructing of twenty boys and girls, to
be chosen by my said Trustees, from time to time, out of

the poorest tenants children, **living** on any of my estates; and so many of the boys and girls as shall not be elected out of my said tenants children, shall be chosen by my Trustees, for the time being, out of the poor of the parish where the said School **stands, the said** Master to teach them to read and to write, and to prepare as many boys for the Latin tongue as **my** said Trustees shall judge to have capacity to learn the same : And I do hereby order **that** the said twenty children do always consist of more **boys** than girls. And my will further is, that my said Trustees do and shall, out of my said estate, pay, at four equal quarterly payments, to wit, Candlemas, May-day, Lammas, and Martinmass, in every year, the clear yearly sum of forty pounds to a School-master for ever, sufficiently instructed and skilled in the Latin and Greek languages, and of sound principles, according to the doctrine of the Church of England by law established, who shall teach and instruct as many of the aforesaid poor boys as shall from **to** time to time become fit to learn the Latin and Greek tongues; and that the said number of twenty boys and girls to be taught by the said two Masters as aforesaid, be from time to time kept up, and still to consist of a majority of boys. And I give full power to my said Trustees for the time being, or any two of them, to choose such School-master and Schoolmasters, and from time to time to place, and for any misdemeanour, neglect, or other just cause, to displace them, or **any of** them, according to their discretion. And my will further is, and I do hereby order, direct, and appoint, that **my** dwelling-house, commonly called by the name of **Goat**-house, in Rushworth aforesaid, be fitted up and made con**venient,** and so continued by my said Trustees, for the lodging of **the** said two Masters, and also for the lodging, boarding, and entertaining of the twenty boys and girls beforementioned, for ever. And I also order, will, and direct, that my said Trustees, and **such** other person and persons as shall be duly elected in their or any of their steads and places, after their, any, or every of their deaths and deceases, do, and shall yearly, **for ever,** pay and apply out of my said estate, the sum of five pounds for the maintenance of each of the said twenty boys and girls at the said Goat-house, the same to be paid at equal payments, to such person and persons as shall from time to time have the care and management of the said boys and girls, at the end of every week: And also that my said Trustees do, and shall yearly for ever, pay to a sober, discreet, and careful woman, to be employed in the dressing of victuals, washing, bed-making, and other the necessary looking after the twenty boys and girls aforesaid, **the sum of** ten pounds, **at four** equal quarterly payments, (to wit,) at Candlemass, May-day, Lammas, **and** Martinmass, in every year, such woman to be chosen and displaced, from time to time, **by my said Trustees, as** they shall see **cause.** And my will also is, that the said Goat-house shall **be** sufficiently furnished, **and kept** furnished, by my said **Trustees,** with beds, bedding, **and all** other necessary furniture, **for the entertainment and** intent aforesaid, out of my **said estate.** And I do also **hereby will, order, and** direct, **that each and** every of the said **boys shall, at his age of** sixteen years, **or** thereabouts, have **the sum of** five pounds paid or applied by my said Trustees, out of my said estate, for and towards the fitting him for, or putting him an apprentice to some **trade,** occupation, or business, such trade or **occupation to be in the choice** of the boy and his parents, **or relations,** except only one of the said boys, that shall be best **capable of** University education, which I do hereby order **shall, at the** age of eighteen years, or so soon **as** he shall have **school** learning sufficient, be **sent** to Cambridge or Oxford, **and** shall be there maintained by **my** said Trustees, **out of my said** estate, **at the rate of** forty pounds per annum **for four years, and no longer; after the** expiration of which **four years,** another **boy shall be sent** upon the same footing **as the former, and so** to be continued one after another for ever; **all and every such boy and** boys to be from time to time **chosen and elected by the** said Trustees, **or** the majority of them, **with advice of the Head** School-master for the time **being.** Item, **I give all my** houshold **goods** whatsoever, with **all my** books **that** belong **to me, either at** North Shields, or **any where** in Yorkshire, towards the furnishing the aforesaid Goat-house, the said **books to be** catalogued, and carefully placed in **some fit room, towards the** foundation of a library, for **the use of the** twenty boys **and** girls aforesaid, and the said two **School-masters.** Item, my will is, and I do hereby direct, that **in** case the said John Wheelwright shall die without heir male, that then it shall be in the power of my **other** two Trustees, or their successors, to elect and appoint another person of the sir-name of Wheelwright, who shall be invested with, and entitled unto, the same powers, profits, and privileges, as the said John Wheelwright is by this Will, in all respects whatsoever. And I do also order, that upon the deaths of the other two Trustees, Ely Dyson and Abraham Thomas, the survivor of them, and the said John Wheelwright, or his heir male, or such other person of the name of Wheelwright as shall be appointed as aforesaid, do and shall elect and appoint other Trustees, whom I desire may be honest, able, and faithful persons, living in the tenements wherein the said Ely Dyson and Abraham Thomas now dwell, in case there be any such, and for default of such, the two surviving Trustees to choose such other person and persons as they shall think fit to be Trustees from time to time, as often as occasion shall require. Item, I hereby order, will, and declare, that in case of any neglect or defaults happening by my said Trustees, or their successors, to be elected as aforesaid, in not making of such elections of Trustees as aforesaid, or in the not duly performing the several trusts hereby in them reposed, or the non-payment of any of the bequests and charges hereby made by me upon my said estates, or any misapplication thereof, contrary to the true intent and meaning of this my Will, that then, and upon any such complaint made, and not otherwise, I do hereby authorise and impower the Archbishop of York, for the time being, to enquire into, and rectify all and every such abuse or default, and to put the same again upon the footing hereby intended, but without further power to intermeddle therein. Item, I do hereby will, order, and appoint, that the clear yearly sum of one hundred pounds per annum shall be, from time to time, paid out of my said estate, to such person and persons who shall more immediately be concerned in the managing and looking after the several trusts aforesaid, the said sum to be paid at four equal quarterly payments in every year. And I do hereby appoint the said John Wheelwright, during his natural life, to manage and look after the same; and after the death of the said John Wheelwright, it is my mind that the said other Trustees shall choose the son of the said John Wheelwright to manage the several trusts aforesaid, and after his decease, shall choose of the issue male of the body of the said John Wheelwright, and for default of such issue, shall choose and elect another person of the sirname of Wheelwright, to manage and look after the trust aforesaid. And my will is, that all my estate, both real and personal, shall be chargeable with, and subject to, the several uses, trusts, legacies, devices, and charges, herein before mentioned; and whatsoever surplus may arise out of and from my said **real** and personal estate, over and above the discharge of the several trusts, legacies, orders, directions, and devices aforesaid, the same shall go and **be** applied by my said Trustees to the purchasing of lands. And it is my will, that the profits thereof shall always be applied to and for the better maintenance and support of the said twenty children, **or** to the enlarging of the number of scholars there, **or for** the sending of more of them to the University, **as the** said augmentation may allow of, in such manner **as** my said Trustees shall think fit. And I also hereby will and desire, that constant prayers may be read in the said Schools every morning and evening, by the Masters **thereof,** and that the said children be religiously and virtuously brought **up** and educated, according to **the** Doctrine of the Church **of** England as by Law established. Item, I will, and hereby order, **that** my said Executor and Trustees, or any of them, shall not demise or grant any part of my several estates, for any term or terms exceeding twenty-one years, **nor** shall they, or any of them, receive any greater or other rents upon any such lease or demise, than the same are now actually rented at, or let for."

John Wheelwright, above-named, **was** appointed sole Executor of this Will.

The above **extract** was made from a copy of the Will, lent by one of the **Trustees.**

—::—

STANSFIELD.

For John Greenwood's Benefaction to the poor of Stansfield, see under Heptonstall.

—·:+:+:+·—

EXTRACT FROM THE

WILL OF MARY HUTTON, of Pudsay,

Dated July 26, 1720.

— " I GIVE and devise to Robert Milnes, of Wakefield, William Lupton, of the same place, Robert Holdsworth, of Fetherston parish, Jonathan Priestley, of Winteredge, in Hipperholm, Richard Northorp, of Kirkheaton parish, Anthony Rhodes, of Barnsley, and Joseph Armitage, of Heckmondwike, and their heirs and assigns, all and singular my tenements situate at Horton, Bowling, or either of them, in the tenures or occupations of William Booth and John Thornton, or their respective assigns, but upon special trust and confidence nevertheless, that my said Trustees shall, at all times after my decease, receive and take the rents, issues, and profits of the same so to them devised premises, and having thereout first deducted such sums of money as they, or any of them, shall have respectively disbursed in or about the reparation or improvement of the said to them devised premises, or otherwise touching the same, or in or about the execution or defence of the trusts thereby to them reposed, or any of such trusts, or the title of the said to them devised premises, or any part thereof, shall yearly, and every year, pay over the clear remainder of such rents and profits, after such deductions as aforesaid, to such Preaching Protestant Dissenting Ministers as are herein above described, (i. e.) of the Presbyterian or Congregational Persuasion,) who shall be respectively the settled Preachers or Teachers at the several and respective Chapels or Meeting-houses now used, and duly recorded, at the General or Quarter Sessions, as places of Religious Worship hereinafter mentioned, (then follows the names, &c. of seven Chapels, amongst which is Eastwood Chapel, in the township of Stansfield, and parish of Halifax,) and their respective successors, who shall respectively reside every of them within the parish in which such Chapel or Meeting-house, at which he shall so officiate as Preacher or Teacher, is situate, to and for the benefit, better maintenance and support of such Preachers or Teachers, and their respective successors as aforesaid, and equally to be divided amongst them, share and share alike. Provided always,

and my will and mind is, that in case the said seven Chapels
or Meeting-houses last mentioned, or any of them, shall
cease to be made use of as places of Religious Worship by
Protestant Dissenters from the Church of England, having
such Teachers and Preachers as aforesaid, by the space of
four years, either through the restraint and prohibition of
the Civil Government, or otherwise, that then, from and immediately after such discontinuance of Religious Worship
there, my said Trustees, their heirs and assigns, upon
request, and at the proper costs of such person and persons
as, at the time of such discontinuance of Religious Worship
there, shall be or shall have last been Teacher or Teachers,
or Preacher or Preachers, at such of the said seven Chapels
or Meeting-houses last mentioned as aforesaid, where such
discontinuance of Religious Worship shall be, or of the respective heirs of such Preacher or Preachers, Teacher or
Teachers, in case such discontinuance of Religious Worship
as aforesaid, shall be at the same seven Chapels or Meeting-
houses, shall convey over all the same tenements, so to my
said Trustees devised, to the use and behoof of such seven
Preachers or Teachers last mentioned, and their heirs,
equally to be divided amongst them as tenants in common
and not as joint tenants ; and in case such discontinuance
of Religious Service as aforesaid shall have been only at
some or one of such Chapels or Meeting-houses last mentioned, then that my said Trustees shall so convey over one
undivided seventh part of the same tenements so to them
devised as aforesaid, to every such Preachers or Teachers of
such of the said Chapels or Meeting-houses last mentioned,
where such discontinuance of Religious Worship shall have
so been, and his heirs, and to his and their use and uses,
and to every of such Preachers or Teachers last mentioned,
his Executors, or Administrators, my said Trustees shall
pay over one full seventh part of the whole in seven equal
parts to be divided, of the clear rents and profits of the said
tenements last mentioned, which shall be or have been by
my said Trustees received and raised from and after such
discontinuance of Religious Worship at the said Chapels or
Meeting-houses last mentioned."—

On the decease of four Trustees, the survivors are, within
three calender months, to choose four honest able persons,

Protestant Dissenters from the Church of England as now by law established, and so on from time to time.

—::—

CROSTONE CHAPEL.

There is 10s. paid annually to the Curate of this Chapel, for preaching a Sermon yearly in the said Chapel, on Whit-sunday, from a farm in Harley-wood, in Stansfield, called the Jumps.

The inhabitants of Stansfield and Langfield, as it is said, did at the first building of this Chapel, charge their estates therein with the annual payment of twenty pounds to the Curate, which, as appears from an old Chapel rental, was paid in 1572, and is continued to this day.

—::—

SKIRCOAT.

The first School-master here was one Richard Wilkinson, whose presentation, (as preserved in the Register Book at Halifax Church, vol. ii.) was in the following words:

"Reverendissimo in Christo Patri ac Domino, Domino Mattheo, Archiepiscopo Eborum, Anglie Primati et Metropolitano, vestri humiles filii, Gubernatores possessionum, revenconum, et bonorum, Libere Grammaticalis Schole Domine Regine Elizabethe, in parochia et vicariatu de Halifax, in Com. Ebor. vestreque Ebor. dieces. salutem in Domino sempiternam. Ad Scholam Grammaticalem predictam, jam vacantem, Richardum Wilkinson, in Artibus Baccalaureum, per nos electum ad officium Magistri informatoris ejusdem Schole, Dominationi vestri presentamus, humiliter rogantes, ut predictum Richardum in Magistrum informatorem Schole predicte admittatis, ceteraque omnia et singula perficere et perimplere que vestro in hac parte incumbunt officio pastorali velitis cum favore. Datum apud Bradley, in vicariatu predicto, vicesimo nono die Augusti, anno predicte Domine nostre Elizabethe, Dei gratia, Anglie, Francie, et Hibernie Regine, Fidei Defensoris, quadragesimo secundo. In cujus rei testimonium, Sigillum nostrum commune apposuimus, die et anno supradictis."

The second Master was Robert Birron, who was buried April 28, 1629. The third, (though omitted by Mr. Wright,) ——Marsh. This Gentleman, as appears from the book belonging to Mr. Waterhouse's Trustees, was Master in 1649, &c. The fourth was Paul Greenwood, afterwards Vicar of Dewsbury, who was Master from 1652 to 1664, when he resigned. The fifth was John Doughty, who continued Master from 1664 till his death, which happened in October, 1688. The sixth was Thomas Lister, Batchelor in Physic, of Jesus College, Cambridge, who died about 1727. The seventh was Christopher Jackson, A.B. who resigned in 1731. The eighth was Edward Topham, A.B. afterwards A.M. and Fellow of Trinity College, Cambridge; he resigned in 1733. The ninth was John Holdsworth, A.M. The tenth, Samuel Ogden, D.D. who resigned, and was succeeded by Thomas West, who resigned to ......

The following inscription (wrote probably by Dr. Favour) is cut in stone over the School-house door:

In favorem Reipublicæ.

Terra mala, et sterilis, dumetis obsita, saxis
Horrida, quæ nullis inventa est frugibus apta:
Sed bona gens, populus **sanctus**, pietatis et ardens,
Religionis opus tantum produxit, ut inde
Terra bona, et possit bona gens bene dicier: **ecce**
Sic domini terram, dominos non terra beavit!
ELIZABETHA diu vivat quæ talia nobis
Indulsit monumenta: Deus, sic, summe, **secundes**
Hoc opus, ut vigeat, **perque** omnia secula duret:
Sic nos, Christe, tuo sic nostra dicamus **honori**.

Jacta sunt Fundam. 8 Junii, Anno Dom. 1598. ELIZAB. Reginæ, 40.

Also on a pillar within the School,

"In memory of the Reverend Mr. SAMUEL STANCLIFF, "descended from the antient family of Stancliff, in the "parish of Halifax, in the west riding of this county of "York, sometime of St. John's College, in Cambridge, and "Minister of Stanmore Magna, in the county of Middlesex, "who departed this life the 12th day of December, Anno D'ni, 1705, aged 75 years."

This benefactor gave an hundred pounds towards the adorning and improving of this School.

In the 2d vol. of Halifax Register is a list of the Contributions towards the building of this School, much more compleat than that in Wright, p. 20.   And in vol. iii. is an account of money collected in 1634, towards purchasing lands for the same.

—::—

EXTRACT FROM THE
WILL OF BRIAN CROWTHER,
OF HALIFAX,

Dated Sept. 9, 1606.

—" MY will and mind is, and I do, by this my present Will and Testament, give, devise, and bequeath to the Governors of the Free Grammar School of Queen Elizabeth, within the vicarage of Halifax, and to their successors, for ever, to the use and behoof of the said Free Grammar School, one annuity or yearly rent of twenty pounds of lawful English money, yearly issuing, and to be received of, in, and forth of all and singular my messuages, lands, tenenements, rents, reversions, possessions, and hereditaments, with their appurtenances, lying and being within the manor, lordship, town, or territories of Armyn, in the county of York, in the Feast of St. Martin, the Bishop, in winter, and Pentecost, yearly, for ever, by even portions, or contrariwise, in the same Feasts, as it shall happen by and after the death of me, the said Brian Crowther.—With power of distress to the said Governors, if the above rent is unpaid, in part, or in all, by the space of twenty days after it becomes due as aforesaid." See the Register at Halifax Church, vol. ii.

THOMAS MILNER, Clerk, formerly Fellow of St. Mary Magdalen College, in Cambridge, by Will and Codicil, bearing date 1722, made over to the said College, a reversionary grant, of one thousand pounds, for the maintenance of three Scholars, to be chosen from the Schools of Haversham, Halifax and Leedes. And in the year 1736, Mrs Mary Milner, sister to the said Mr. Milner, added two hundred pounds to the above-mentioned benefaction, to be applied by the College to the same uses.

SOWERBY.

JOHN FOURNESS, as appeared to the Inquirers after Charities at Halifax, in 1651, did, by Roll of Court, dated Oct. 9, 13 James I, assure to George Holgate, William Greenwood, George Fourness, and Richard Brigg, and their heirs, two cottages in Sowerby, to the use of three poor men of the said town, for ever.

Also the said **John Fourness** did surrender, as appeared by a Copy of the Roll, one messuage, one garden, and four closes of land, in Sowerby, to the use and behoof of John Broadley, Clerk, and Master of Arts, for term of his life, and after to the use and behoof of George Holgate, and others, and their heirs, for ever, as Feoffees, to the use of such persons as shall be Masters of Arts, and a Preacher at the Chapel of Sowerby, for and during their times, and for want of a Master of Arts being a Preacher there, then to the use and behoof of Richard Brigg and his heirs.

The above from Mr. Brearcliffe's manuscript.

GEORGE FOXCROFT (as appears from the above manuscript) gave by Will, dated May 20, 17 James I. ten pounds to the poor of the Chapelry of Sowerby, to be lent from year to year, by the Minister, Churchwarden, and Swornmen of the said Chapel for the time being, to the poor of Sowerby Quarter, Westfield Quarter, and Blackwood Quarter, taking security for the same, and nothing to be paid for the same.

EXTRACT FROM THE
WILL OF THOMAS MITCHELL,

OF SOWERBY,

Dated April 1, 1621.

_" I DO hereby give and bequeath the sum of twenty pounds to mine Executor hereafter named, to be disposed of and bestowed as followeth, viz. It is my will and mind, that the said sum of twenty pounds shall remain in the hands of my Executor hereafter named, for, during, and until my said Executor, together with the advice, assent, and consent of Mr. Broadley, now Preacher at Sowerby aforesaid, and if George Holgate and Edward

Banister can conveniently, and as speedily as may be, at after my death, bestow the sum upon one annuity or yearly rent of as great a value as possibly can be therewith purchased. And it is my will and mind, that the said annuity or yearly rent so therewith shall be purchased and yearly paid unto the said Mr. Broadley, immediately from and after the purchasing thereof, for during the term of his natural life; and from and after the death and decease of the said Mr. Broadley, then it is my will and mind, that the said annuity or yearly rent shall remain to the Churchwardens, Overseers, and Swornmen of Sowerby, for the time being, and to my Executor hereafter named, to be by them yearly bestowed for ever upon a Preacher at Sowerby aforesaid for the time being hereafter, so that he be a Master of Arts; for it is my will and mind, that if at any time or times hereafter there happen to be a Preacher at Sowerby aforesaid, which shall not be a Master of Arts, lawfully allowed and proved, that then or so often as it shall so happen such a Preacher or Preachers not being Master of Arts, shall have no benefit by this my present gift, but that the said annuity or yearly rent, for want of a Preacher being Master of Arts, shall remain to the said Churchwardens, and Overseers, and Swornmen of Sowerby aforesaid for the time being, and to my Executor hereafter named, to be by them bestowed (and at their discretions) upon and amongst the poor people inhabiting within the township of Sowerby aforesaid, yearly, for and until a Preacher, being a Master of Arts, shall serve and preach at Sowerby aforesaid. Item, it is my will and mind, and I do hereby give and bequeath the sum of ten pounds, to be disposed and bestowed by the Minister, Churchwarden, Overseer, and Swornmen of Sowerby aforesaid, and by mine Executor hereafter named during his life, as followeth, that is to say, it is my will and mind, that they, the said Minister, Churchwarden, Overseer, and Swornmen for the time being, shall bestow and lend the same sum of ten pounds, gratis and freely, to such three poor handycraftsmen inhabiting within Blackwood Quarter, as they shall, in their discretions, think most convenient and meet, and do most stand in need of the same; that is to say, every man to have the sum of three pounds six shillings and eight-pence a-piece lent to him, upon good surety by them, and by their costs and charges to be made, that they will well and truly pay the same back again to the Minister, Churchwarden, Overseer, and Swornmen for the time being, and that they may lend the said sum of ten pounds to some other three poor handycraftsmen, inhabiting within Blackwood Quarter as aforesaid, as they shall think most meet. And it is my full will and mind, that no poor handycraftsmen shall have any benefit by this my present gift, except they do inhabit and dwell within Blackwood Quarter; and that the said sum of ten pounds shall not be distributed or lent to no more persons but only to three in any one year, equally inhabiting within the circuit aforesaid."

N.B. The inaccuracies in the above were in the copy from whence this was taken. One account makes the above Will to be dated in 1618. The twenty pounds left to the Minister were laid out on some copyhold land, lying beneath Sowerby, bought of one James Dobson.

EXTRACT FROM THE

WILL OF HENRY HAIGH, of Sowerby,

Dated July 13, 1634.

—"WHEREAS I have, by surrender, dated with these presents, surrendered, according to the custom of the manor of Wakefield, one messuage or tenement, and five closes, clausures, or parcels of land, meadow and pasture, to the said messuage or tenement belonging—called by the several names of the Great Ing, Narr Croft, Little Croft on the Backside, and two townfields, parcel of ten acres of land, meadow and pasture, by estimation to the said messuage or tenement belonging—And two other closes of land lying together—of the yearly rent to the King's Majesty of five shillings two-pence, and for which composition is made for certainty of the fine thereof: And also one other messuage or tenement—and three closes, now made into two closes of land and pasture, with one house or cottage thereupon, with appurtenances, (all which above demised premises are in the Will said to be in the Graveship of Sowerby, but are not otherwise described than by the names of the then occupants) which said last mentioned premises and cottages,

with appurtenances, are of the yearly rent to the King's
Majesty of five shillings two-pence, and for which Composition is also made with the Lord, for certainty of the fine
thereof; all which **premises** contain, by estimation, thirty
acres and **an** half; and **all** rents and yearly profits reserved
upon all, or any surrender, demise, or lease, heretofore made
of the premises, or of any **part** thereof; and all other my
customary messuages, cottages, lands, tenements, and hereditaments, with appurtenances, in the Graveship of Sowerby
abovesaid, **in whose** tenures soever the same be, to the use
and behoof of my dear and right trusty friends, Robert
Priestley and Richard Brigge, of Sowerby abovesaid, Yeo-
men, their heirs and assigns, for ever, by service, according
to the custom of the said manor, therein to stand seized, as
**Feoffees in trust, to such uses, intents, purposes, limitations,
and provisoes, as I by my last Will and Testament should
mention,** limit, and declare, with **a proviso for revocation, and**
making void the said surrender, by **payment or tender of twelve**
pence, to such persons, and in such **sort, as in the said surrender**
is specified, **as further** by **the tenure thereof (reference being**
thereunto made) more plainly may appear: Now therefore
I, the said Henry Haigh, do hereby mention, limit, and **de-**
clare, that it is my full will and mind, that they the said
Robert Priestley and Richard Brigge, and their heirs, and
the survivor of them, and his heirs, shall be, and stand
Feoffees, and courted and admitted tenants of all the said
premises surrendered **as** aforesaid, **to** all the uses, intents,
limitations, purposes, **and** provisoes herein hereafter expressed, limited and declared thereupon, **(that is to** say,) of
intent and purpose that the Preacher of God's Word, for the
time being, at the Chapel of Sowerby aforesaid, being a
Master of Arts, and preaching one Sermon upon every second
Wednesday in these four months of the year, for ever, (viz.
May, June, July, **and August) shall have and** receive, and take
for his pains, twenty-six shillings **eight-pence** yearly, (viz.) six
shillings eight-pence **for** each Sermon, **to be** paid monthly
upon the same day wherein such **Sermon** shall be so made
as aforesaid, forth of the rents, issues, and profits of the said
two closes—in the occupation of John Bates, &c. Provided
always, and it is my will and mind, that during so long time
as the Minister or Preacher of God's Word at Sowerby
Chapel abovesaid, shall either not be a Master of Arts, or

not preach as aforesaid, the said monthly payment of six
shillings eight-pence shall be paid to my loving sister Sibill,
wife of John Hide, and her heirs and assigns. If unpaid for
ten days, the persons to whom the rents belong may make
distress."

At Chaderton is an attested copy of this Will, from whence
the above was taken ; also a copy of the above-named surrender, and others of later dates ; the estate which has gone
by the name of Haigh's Farm, is the property of Sir Watts
Horton, of Chaderton, Bart.

This money was once withheld for three years, on which
Mr. Nathaniel Rathband, Curate of Sowerby, and M.A. petitioned Lord Keeper Littleton. Mr. Brearcliffe's MS. sais,
that it was detained in 1651, by Samuel Foxcroft.

—::—

EXTRACT FROM THE
WILL OF JOHN BENTLEY,
OF SOWERBY.

— " I GIVE and bequeath unto the township of Sowerby
twenty pounds, to be employed for ever in manner
and form following, (viz.) to be lent unto four poor inhabitants of the said town, for four years, by equal portions or
parts, that is to say, to each of the said four inhabitants
five pounds (gratis, or without paying of any loan or other
consideration for the same) the said inhabitants putting in
sufficient sureties to the Supervisors hereafter named for the
repaying of the same at the end of the said four years ; and
after those four years, to four other poor inhabitants of the
said town for four years more, in the same manner ; and so
from four years to four years, to several men, for ever ; provided always that the said money, nor any part thereof, be
not lent to any Clothier, Indico-seller, or any that belongs
to Clothing.   And I do desire, nominate, and appoint,
Thomas Dobson, of the Stones, and Henry Priestley, of
Baytings, and their heirs, and the Ministers or Priests of
Sowerby and Ripponden, for the time being, my Supervisors
in trust, to see that the same twenty pounds be imployed in
manner and form aforesaid. And if the same shall not be
imployed as is aforesaid, then mine Executor and Overseers

of this my last Will and Testament shall **recover and** receive
the same of the said Supervisors, and **shall divide the** same
amongst those **unto whom** I have given legacies, **and their**
children."

This Trust **is at** present managed by Mr. **John Priestley,**
of White-windows, in Sowerby, and the Ministers of **Sowerby**
and Ripponden, no heir **to** the above Thomas Dobson **being**
to be found. The date of this Will I have not **seen, but it**
is older than 1651, **as it is** mentioned in Mr. Brearcliffe's
MS. of that date.

—::—

EXTRACT FROM THE

WILL OF DANIEL GREENWOOD, D.D.

Dated March 11, 1675.

—" I GIVE **to my** dear brother, John Greenwood, **and to**
his heirs and assigns, all my lands in Crowellshaws,
in the county of York, upon trust, that he do yearly pay **to**
the Minister **of** Sowerby Chapel, **who** hath officiated **there**
by the space **of** one whole year, the sum **of** forty **shillings,**
and to the poor of Sowerby chapelry forty shillings, **and**
these payments **to** continue for ever, and to be paid on **the**
first day of June, **and** first day **of** December, **or** within
twenty days after **each** day, by equal portions ; **but if my**
said brother, or his heirs **and** assigns, shall neglect **or**
refuse **to** pay **the** said **payments, or** either of **them,**
then I give and bequeath **my** said **lands in** Crowellshaws
aforesaid, to Edmond Tattersall **and** Timothy Bentley, **and**
to their heirs, for ever, **upon trust, to pay the said several**
yearly payments for ever ; **and my will is, that the first pay-**
ments be **made** on such **of the said days as shall first happen**
within twelve months after my **decease.**"

Taken from an attested copy at Whitewindows, in Sowerby.

Edward Wainhouse, of Butterisse, in Norland, gave, by
Will, dated Sept. 18, 1686, to the old people and poor
persons of **the** town of Sowerby, such as **did not receive**
allowance from the town, two parts of the yearly rents **and**
profits of an house **in** Sowerby-dean, during the life of **his**
wife, and after her decease, the whole for ever to the said
poor people, for the time being, and ordered that the rent

x

should be paid at Christmas, by one entire payment, to the Overseers of the poor of Sowerby, for the time being; and that the Overseers should take one or two of the Heads of Sowerby, to see the distribution of the rents; and also impowered the Overseers, and one or two of the Heads of the town, to let the said house to farm, for the use of the said poor persons, so oft as there should be occasion; but the Executor, Josiah Stansfield, never made the inhabitants of the town of Sowerby acquainted with the said charitable bequest, letting the house to whom, and for what he pleased, and receiving the rents thereof to his own use, for about twenty years; on which the Overseers of the poor for the town of Sowerby petitioned the Justices of Peace at the Quarter Sessions, in 1708, but what relief was obtained I have not seen.

—::—

EXTRACT FROM THE

WILL OF PAUL BAIRSTOW, Clerk,

OF ROCHESTER,

Dated March 31, 1711.

—"AFTER leaving a messuage, or tenement, with lands, in the parish of Meopham, in Kent, to his sister-in-law, Mary Goodwin, of Trottescliffe, for life, and after her decease, to John Tillotson, of London, James Stansfeld, of Bowood, and Henry Barrell, of Rochester, their heirs and assigns for ever, in trust, after the death of his said sister-in-law, to sell the same, and with the money arising from the sale thereof, to purchase a freehold or copyhold estate of inheritance, in or near the parish of Halifax, the Will proceeds thus; "In trust, that they, my said Trustees, shall and do, by and out of the rents and profits of the said premises, so to be purchased in or near Halifax aforesaid, pay unto the School-master, for the time being, of the School of Sowerby, in the parish of Halifax, &c. the yearly sum of sixteen pounds, for and in consideration of his teaching twelve poor children, living within the chapelry of Sowerby, whose parents, at the time of such childrens being elected to the said School, are not worth in real or personal estate above fifty pounds, and to be nominated and chosen

by the Minister and Churchwardens, or Chapelwardens, of
the said parish or chapelry, for the time being; and also in
trust that they, my said Trustees, shall and do, out of the
residue of the said rents and profits, from time to time,
repair the tomb of my father, Michael Bairstow, and Ann,
his wife, in Sowerby Church or Chapel yard, and pay the
yearly sum of twenty shillings to the Minister of Sowerby,
for the time being, for preaching a Sermon upon every Feast
day of St. Michael the Archangel; and shall distribute the
remainder of the said rents and profits, if any be, to and
amongst such poor persons of the said parish or chapelry of
Sowerby, who do not receive alms of the said parish or
chapelry, in such manner as the said Minister and Churchwardens or Chapelwardens shall direct; and that my said
Trustees shall take care to transmit the estate and premises,
so to be purchased in or near Halifax aforesaid, to posterity,
subject to the trusts aforesaid, in such legal and proper
manner as they shall be advised by Counsel; and that my
said Trustees shall be paid all such reasonable and necessary
charges out of the said estates as they shall be at in the due
execution of this their trust: And in case a purchase cannot
be had and made by my said Trustees of an estate in or near
Halifax, for the purposes aforesaid, in a short time after the
sale of my farm and lands in Meopham aforesaid, then my
mind and will is, that all interest that shall or can be made
by my said Trustees of the principal moneys arising by the
sale of my said farm and lands in Meopham aforesaid, shall
be added to the said principal moneys, and be all laid out
and invested in the purchase of an estate in or near Halifax
aforesaid, for the uses, intents, and purposes aforesaid, as
soon as a purchase can be had."

After the death of the above Mary Goodwin, Henry
Barrell, the only surviving Trustee, sold the estate in Meopham for six hundred and thirty pounds, which he soon after
laid out, together with fifteen pounds fifteen shillings more,
in the purchase of six hundred pounds South Sea Annuity
Stock, till a purchase of an estate in or near Halifax could
be met with; after which, he bought, for the use of the
above Charity, an estate in Thornton, in Bradford parish,
called Nether Headley, or Heathley, for which he paid six
hundred and sixty pounds. The purchase deeds were registered at Wakefield, May 5, 1735, in Book G.G. page 554.

No. 779. The present overplus, after paying the School-master sixteen pounds, is thirteen pounds per annum.

—::—

Bounty to Sowerby Chapel.

It appears by an Indenture at Chaderton, in Lancashire, dated March 9, 1722, that Elkana Horton, of Gray's Inn, Esq; in consideration of two hundred pounds from the Governors of Queen Anne's Bounty, and one hundred pounds left by Edward Colston, of Mortlack, in Surry, Esq; sold to Nicholas Jackson, Clerk, Curate of Sowerby, and his successors, for ever, Lower Langley, alias Nether Langley, in Norland, containing eighteen acres, or thereabouts, of the yearly rent of seven pounds ten shillings ; also a farm, called Birch Farm, in Sowerby, of the yearly rent of seven pounds ; likewise the Lane Ends. The bounty was obtained in 1719.

N.B. Edward Colston left a large sum for the augmentation of small livings, and his Executors, at the request of the said Elkana Horton, allowed an hundred pounds to Sowerby Chapel, and Mr. Horton himself allowed another hundred pounds in the purchase. The certainty at this Chapel, 3d of Queen Anne, was seven pounds yearly, according to the return already mentioned ; but in Ecton's Thesaurus, twelve pounds two shillings and eight-pence.

—::—

EXTRACT FROM THE

WILL OF ELKANA HORTON,

OF THORNTON, IN BRADFORD PARISH,

Dated Sept. 19, 1728.

—"HAVING observed that the worst case of the poor is a sordid habitation, I have erected six apartments at Sowerby, in the parish of Halifax, and county of York, for the habitation of three men, and three women, all born in the chapelry of Sowerby aforesaid, and inclosed some ground before the same, to be divided into six gardens, for their several uses ; also a middle room, or Oratory, for their daily assembling in for prayers, all which I give to the

six men and women I have already put into the said apart-
ment, and successors, for ever, as shall be chosen by my
said Trustees, **and such** others as their learned Counsel shall
advise. **I will that all** the said three men and **three women**
be of the **age of sixty, and** unmarried, and remain so during
their **continuing in their** apartments, **or** be removed, or
changed that condition, for **this reason** only, because the
said apartments are not **sufficient for** more than one. I give
unto each of the said **six,** two **shillings** and six pence a
month, to be paid them **at** the **end of each calendar month ;**
I will that one of the **six (1)** men **be capable of reading distinctly,** and **that twice every** day, **at nine o'clock in the fore-
noon, and three in the afternoon, (excepting Sundays in the
afternoon, on which day at the hour of five in the afternoon,)**
he assemble the other five persons, by ringing a **bell, and at
those hours** he read a chapter out of the New Testament,
and a proper Prayer out of Bishop Parker's Book of Devotions, or some other, to which Reader **I** give five shillings
quarterly for doing it ; **and I** require **that** all decently and
punctually be present thereat, and that such Reader take an
account of absenters, and mark them down as often as they
are so, **and** shew the same to such Trustees as shall be appointed to pay them their allowances, to the end they shall
deduct a halfpenny a time for every omission, and give the
same to the Reader, excepting a reasonable cause of absence
be given ; I will that regard be had to the virtue and good
nature of the persons chosen in, and they be such as have
kept off the parish by their own industry, which I expect
they continue to make out my allowance a competency,
which will be better for their health and virtue, than a pro-
vision that would have kept them in entire idleness, my
design being to reward past, and encourage future industry,
that others observing the regard I pay thereto, may qualify
them to be successors in the said apartments upon vacancies
therein ; **and I** hope I may well expect that if any of the six
persons shall, **in a** more advanced age, become incapable to
work, and thereby my allowance become insufficient for
their maintenance, that such addition be made by the parish
as will do it, but in case of refusal, they cannot but expect
such refused be turned out to their entire care, and accordingly it shall be done, and others chose to succeed. I will,

(1) So in the original.

that so much of my real estate, or as much other estate be
purchased, as will raise yearly sufficiently for paying the said
allowances clear, and also keep the buildings in good repair
for ever, and if more be set out than will do it, the overplus
to be divided equally amongst the said six, and be settled in
trust as Councel shall advise."

From an attested copy at Chaderton, in Lancashire.

ROBERT BROOKE left an house, at Hunslet, near Leedes,
to the poor of Sowerby, the rents to be paid yearly. This
house was sold about thirty years ago, for ten pounds, and
the money put out to interest.

—::—

SOYLAND.

At Chaderton, in Lancashire, is an original indenture
tripartite, made Nov. 7, 35 Eliz. witnessing that one Thomas
Priestley had surrendered at the same time into the hands
of the Lord of the Manor, one parcel of ground, the east side
thereof containing in length twenty-one yards and half, the
west nineteen yards and half, the north nineteen yards, and
the south thirteen yards and half, as the same abutted on
the lands of the said Thomas Priestley on the west and north
parts, and on the highway leading from Ripponden to Soyland on the east part, and the highway leading from Ripponden to the Baitings on the south part, as the same lay
inclosed, with the buildings, &c. thereon, in the occupation
of Henry Sharrock, Clerk, Minister of Ripponden, to the use
and behoof of certain Feoffees therein named, their heirs
and assigns, for ever; paying therefore yearly to the said
Thomas Priestley, his heirs and assigns, for ever, the rent
of six shillings and eight-pence on every first day of May,
with penalty of twenty shillings if the said rent be unpaid
for a year, and lawfully demanded, as by the said surrender
more at large will appear. This indenture also farther
witnesseth, that the said surrender was to the use and behoof
of the Preacher or Minister of the said Chapel of Ripponden,
for the time being, and his successors, or such as shall do and
celebrate Divine Service in the said Chapel; the Feoffees
and their heirs to receive the profits arising from the premises,
and to apply the same only for the public use and behoof of
the whole Chapelry of Ripponden, for the maintenance of

Divine Service there for ever, as is aforesaid. When only four of the said Feoffees remained, the surviving four Feoffees were to assure, surrender, and convey the said premises to the use and behoof of them the said four survivors, and their heirs, and to the use and behoof of the heirs of the said Feoffees that then shall be deceased, and their heirs, for ever, to the uses, intents, and purposes aforesaid, and no other; and this course, in re-assuring and surrendering, to be observed for ever, as often as the interest and estate of the premises shall be in the hands of four Feoffees only. And lastly, all the parties to this indenture, and all the inhabitants of the Chapelry of Ripponden, prayed the Lord President of the Council then established in the North, and, in his absence or default, the Chancellor of the Dutchy of Lancaster, the Lord Chancellor of England, Lord Keeper for the time being, that in case of any suit or controversy concerning the premises, they would vouchsafe to see the true intent and meaning of those presents executed, and performed.

The copy of the Surrender, said to be of the same date with the above presents, is by mistake dated Nov. 7, 30 Elizabeth; the dimensions also of the ground are mistaken in the said surrender, which is at Chaderton, and which ought to be corrected by the deed above quoted.

The Feoffees named in the above indenture were, Sir George Savile, Knt. John Savile, of Bradley, Esq; Thomas Gledhill, son of John Gledhill, of Barkisland, George Firth, of Firth-house, John Ramsden, of Bowers, Ellis Wormall, of Hill-house, Thomas Bothomley, of Bothomley, Michael Foxcroft, of Kebroide, Henry Priestley, of Baitings, Thomas Foxcroft, of Soyland, Nathan Hole, of Lighthasels, Michael Hole, of Blackshayclough, Richard Royde, of Beestonhirste, John Crosley, of Smalees, John Firth, of Royde, John Crosley, of Moor, younger, Richard Hole, of Burntmoor, Michael Godley, of Godley, John Firth, of Gootehouse, John Holroyd, of Scolecar, William Holroyd, of Cowcrofte, and Gilbert Holroyd, of the same, Yeomen; but who were the four survivors of these, or whether they conveyed as directed, is uncertain.

The Curates of Ripponden have generally, since this time, lived in the above house; but in the year 1754, when I took possession of this Curacy, the building was so ruinous and inconvenient, that it was found necessary to rebuild it, which I did at my own expence, to the amount of more than four hundred pounds, the inhabitants not giving the least assistance; and the present Curate, Mr. Thomas West, obliged me farther to allow him the sum of ten pounds, to repair the barn there, which was not to his liking. Such, it seems, is the law relating to Dilapidations!

JOHN RILEY, of Brigroyd, in Soyland, (as appears by the copy of a court-roll in my possession, dated at Wakefield, at the Court Baron of William Craven, Knt. and Edwin Wiatt, Esq; Lords of the Manor of Wakefield, in trust, for the use of Elizabeth Clapham, widow, held there Feb. 24, 34 Car. II.) surrendered, on the 25th of January, 34 Car. II. into the hands of the Lords of the Manor, the reversion, (after the death of the said John,) of a messuage or tenement called Field-end, in Soyland, with appurtenan- ances, and also of a mansion-house at Farrow-height, with two inclosures lately taken from Soyland-moor, containing, by estimation, six acres and half, to the use of John Gawk- roger, of Flathead, in Soyland, and Jeremy Riley, of War- ley, and their heirs, in trust, for the use of Martha Riley, of Brigroyd, and her lawful heirs; and for want of such, in trust, to pay the rents and profits thereof to the Overseer of the poor of Soyland, for the use of the poor of the said town, for ever: to be paid and distributed to the said poor, at the discretion of the said John Gawkroger and Jeremy Ryley, and their heirs, and the Overseer of the said poor, for the time being, for ever.

This Charity is withheld, and has been so for some time, I cannot even find that ever it was paid. A complaint was lodged at the last Commission for Pious Uses in the West Riding, but was offered too late to have proper notice taken of it.

—::—

EXTRACT FROM THE

WILL OF ELKANA HOYLE, of Soyland,

Dated March 28, 1718.

— " I GIVE and devise unto the Curate of Ripponden for the time being, for ever, one annuity or yearly sum of three pounds, of lawful money of Great Britain, to be for ever issuing, going forth, and yearly paid out of my messuage, farm, or tenement, lands, tenements, hereditaments, and premises, with appurtenances, at or near Lighthazels, called Lower Hoyle Heads, in the possession of Abraham Platts or his assigns, to be yearly paid to such Curate as aforesaid for ever, on the Ascension-day of our Lord and Saviour Jesus Christ, commonly called Holy Thursday, provided such Curate preach a Sermon on that day in Ripponden Chapel aforesaid, and provided such Curate be a sound orthodox Preacher and Divine, according to the usage of the present Church of England as by law established, and shall have had University education, and come to be Curate there with the consent and good liking of the Owners of Upper Swift Place; or else, in default of such Sermon to be preached, or for want of such Curate so qualified, or good liking and consent as aforesaid, I do give the said three pounds per annum to the poor people of Soyland aforesaid, for the time of such neglect, disqualification, or dissent."

The above was taken from an attested copy of the Will. The money has generally, if not always, been paid to the Curate of Ripponden for the time being, except from the year 1755 to the year 1761 inclusive, when it was given to the poor people of Soyland, my principles not corresponding with those of the Owner of Upper Swift Place.

—::—

EXTRACT FROM THE

WILL OF JAMES RILEY, of Kirklees, Clerk,

Dated May 6, 1723.

—" AFTER giving to his brother, Joseph Riley, an estate in trust, to pay out of the same five pounds yearly to several persons and purposes, amongst other bequests is the following:—" Item, I will that one pound, further part of the said five pounds, be paid by the said Joseph Riley, and his heirs, yearly, and every year for ever, upon the second day of February, to the Overseer or Overseers of the poor of the township of Soyland for the time being, and to their successors, Overseers of the poor of the same township, for the use of, and to be distributed to **seven** poor widowers or widows, and for want of such, to the most necessitous persons of the said town of Soyland, **at** the **discretion** of the Master or Owner of Kirkcliffe, and **of** the Overseers, and one or **more** of the chief inhabitants of Soyland aforesaid.

This charity is regularly distributed. **See** another part **of** this Will under Barkisland.

—::—

SOUTHOURAM.

Original ENDOWMENT OF ST. ANNE'S CHAPEL.

In Mr. Brearcliffe's MS. and also in the 2d volume of the Register belonging to Halifax **Church, is** the following entry. "We find, that by a Deed, bearing date the 21st day of February, 21 Hen. VIII. JOHN LACY, **of** Cromwellbothom, Esq; doth give to Thomas Savile, of Exley, with others, as Feoffees in trust, four closes of land in Southouram, (in one **of the which** a Chapel of St. Anne, by him the said **John** Lacy, with his neighbours, is built,) of intent that they the said Feoffees shall be seized thereof to the use of the said **John** Lacy and his heirs for ever, paying out of the same thirteen shillings and four-pence yearly for ever, to him that **shall celebrate** Divine Service in the **said** Chapel; and if it **happen** there be **no Chaplain there by the** space of forty days, then for **all that time of** the vacation the **said** rents **shall** be paid **to the** Chaplain that celebrateth or saith Divine Service **at the** Altar of St. George, in the Parish **Church of St. John Baptist, of Halifax."**

St. ANNE'S CHAPEL **had but a** certain endowment of **three** pounds per annum, before **the** Rev. Mr. Thomas Burton, Vicar of Halifax, Thomas Holdsworth, and John Smith, Gent. raised, **in 1720, two hundred** pounds, in order to obtain the Queen's Bounty. It **had** also a lot in 1756, and **the** whole six **hundred** pounds were laid out, in 1762, in the purchase of **an estate in** Sutcliffe Wood, of the clear yearly value of twenty-**four pounds.**

WARLEY.

BENEFACTIONS TO SOWERBY BRIDGE CHAPEL.

In a terrier, belonging to Sowerby Bridge Chapel, wrote in 1727, are the following particulars. One Chapel-house worth one pound eight shillings per annum. One cottage-house, given to the Chapel by Mr. Samuel King, eighteen shillings per annum. The title-deeds belonging to the Queen's Bounty are dated Nov. 2, 1724. The estates bought with this money are, the Lower Brig Bottom Farm, containing nineteen days work of land, then let for twelve pounds ten shillings a year; a farm called Earoyd, containing thirteen days work, rent seven pounds eight shillings a year; and a Farm called Gate Head, containing nine days work, rent four pounds a year; but these rents are considerably raised since that time.

The Certainty, 2d and 3d of Queen Anne, was six pounds a year. A MS. in my possession sais, the Bounty was obtained for this Chapel Dec. 1, 1719, by Mr. Joseph Taylor, and others.

WADSWORTH.

EXTRACT FROM THE
WILL OF PAUL GREENWOOD,

OF OLD TOWN, IN WADSWORTH,

Dated April 4, 1609.

— " I GIVE unto my brother, John Greenwood, and his heirs for ever, all that my tenement called Raw-holme, which my will is, that my said brother and his heirs shall demise for the rent of forty shillings only, and shall for ever pay twenty shillings thereof yearly unto the poor people of Wadsworth, and the other twenty shillings yearly for ever towards the maintenance of a Preacher, being a Master of Arts at Heptonstall."

COPLEY.

[I cannot find that this Parish has given to the Church of ENGLAND any more than four Bishops, yet all men of real worth and primitive piety. The first of these to be mentioned in the order of time is Robert Copley, *vulgo* GROSTHEAD, sprung from the old family of Copley's, of COPLEY, whose pedigree Mr. Thoresby runs as high as the Norman Advent. He was first Arch-Deacon of LEICESTER, and was consecrated Bishop of LINCOLN in 1235, at Reading : A very severe man in his Visitations of the Clergy, and had several quarrels with the Pope, which occasioned his suspension in 1252, as Isaackson tells us in his Chronological Tables. He was, (says Mr. Cambden in his Britan, p. 352, LOND. Edit. 1587), considering the age he liv'd in, incredibly learned both in Letters and Languages ; a terrible Reprover of the Pope ; an Adviser of his King, and a Lover of Truth. He died in 1253.   *Wright's Halifax, p.* 139.]

PRINCIPAL FAMILIES AND PERSONS, VOL. I.

Thomas Harrison, Printer, Bookbinder, &c., Queen Street Mill, Bingley.

www.ingramcontent.com/pod-product-compliance
Lightning Source LLC
Chambersburg PA
CBHW032147110726
47902CB00003B/720